NAN DARRELL;

OR,

THE HIGHWAYMAN'S DAUGHTER.

AN HISTORICAL ROMANCE.

"Hurrah! o'er Hounslow Heath to roam,
   Hurrah! for the stilly hour,
When the moon looks down from her starry dome
   Like a maid from embattled tower.
Sparks of fire, from my courser's feet,
   Flash forth at every goad,
As the distant sound of wheels I greet.
   Hurrah! hurrah! for the road."

BEAUTIFULLY ILLUSTRATED.

LONDON:
HENRY LEA, 112, FLEET STREET, E.C.

NAN DARRELL;

OR,

THE HIGHWAYMAN'S DAUGHTER.

["MONEY OR YOUR LIFE!"]

CHAPTER I.

DEATH.

It was a dull, misty morning, on the thirteenth day of February, in the year of grace 1718. The old city of London was enveloped in a thick haze—the streets were thronged with an eager and expectant multitude —a dense crowd had collected in front of Newgate— many of these had taken up their stations before midnight—some had provided themselves with links, that they might be better able to seek out a good position; for they had all come to see three wretched criminals taken in a cart from the city prison, and conveyed from thence to Tyburn, where they were doomed to suffer for their respective crimes.

Strange the love of man for all that pertains to death!

Ribald jokes had beguiled the tedium of the night. Hot pies, potatoes, coffee, cakes, and fruit had been served to the mob during the small hours of the morning.

The hours passed. The sun had risen murky and red.

At the end of the street, at the farther extremity of the prison, there was a yard, surrounded by a high stone wall, surmounted by iron spikes. The door of this yard was open; lights trembled in its mysterious depths; a group of men and women stood near it. A constable stood at each side of the door.

The stone hall of the prison was crowded by inmates of the gaol, together with those officers who were fortunate enough to obtain permission to witness the ceremony of the prisoners' irons being struck off. The man who was appointed to this office stood, with a hammer in one hand and a punch in the other, near to a great stone block, ready to fulfil his duty. Close to him stood the figure of the executioner.

The cart which was to convey the unhappy wretches to their destination had to pass through one of the most public thoroughfares in the metropolis, and consequently there was ample opportunity, along the road to Tyburn, for the mob to gratify their procreant curiosity by gazing upon the unhappy creatures who were chief actors in the day's proceedings. There was an impatient and restless swaying to and fro of the mob when they heard the bell of the city prison begin to toll, which was answered immediately by the bell of St. Sepulchre. They yelled at the prison, which stood before them dark and gloomy; they demanded their victims with fierce shouts.

They even indulged in jocularities frightful at such a moment.

"Bring them out!" shouted several voices. "It's hot-roll time; bring them out to breakfast!"

"It's a cold morning," yelled the brutes, "and there's a drop of something short waiting for them."

Then suddenly, as if by presentiment, these men ceased their jests, and the vendors their cries. It was one of those mysterious intervals of silence which sometimes fall upon great crowds.

By-and-bye the tramp of horses' feet were heard slowly ascending Snow-hill, and presently a troop of Grenadier Guards rode into the area facing Newgate. These were presently joined by a regiment of foot. A large body of the constables from Westminster next made their appearance, the chief part of whom entered the lodge, where they were speedily joined by the civic authorities.

While the process of pinioning had been going on in the press-room, every preparation had been made outside the prison. At the end of the long line of Foot Guards stood the fatal cart, with a powerful black horse harnessed thereto.

The prison door opened slowly. One of the gaolers stood in the portal.

There was a cry, as of one voice, of "Hats off!" and a thousand heads were bared—a thousand faces upturned. One would have believed that it was the performance at a theatre, or that some glorious sight was about to take place—some joyous pageant, instead of three fellow-creatures being led to an ignominious death. The crowds which had at this time collected seemed to be almost countless. Every housetop, every window, every projection had its inhabitants. The concourse extended along Giltspur-street as far as Smithfield.

No one was allowed to pass Newgate-street, which was barricaded, and protected by a strong constabulary force.

The first person who made his appearance through the doorway was the hangman. He emerged from the prison and took his seat upon one of the coffins. He was a withered, gray-headed man—not the usual one who officiated at London executions. A murmur of surprise proceeded from many of the crowd at the strange appearance of the man.

He was at first saluted with violent hisses from the crowd, and after this with jeers and derisive laughter.

He wore *white favours*, as if for a bridal!

Strange unison of marriage and death!

What could it portend?

After this there was a deep silence, broken only by the tolling of bells. The mighty sea of humanity became hushed.

Suddenly there was a cry from some thousands of throats, as they exclaimed—

"They are coming! They are in sight!"

The multitude swayed backwards and forwards; a trembling ran through the crowd, which resembled the waves of the sea beneath the first blast of the north wind. This was followed by a murmur like that of the waves when the wind lashes them into wrath.

The first of the malefactors proved to be a woman, old in years and sin. She was led to the cart by two officers. There was little beyond her sex to enlist the sympathies of those who had come to see her die, for she was ill-favoured enough. Nevertheless, there was something like a murmur of pity as she took her place in the cart.

After her followed a highwayman, who assumed for the nonce a jaunty air of reckless bravado. The crowd applauded him.

The last that came appeared to be a mere youth, apparently not more than eighteen or nineteen. The features of the latter were cast in an aristocratic mould. He had a high, broad forehead, a delicately-chiselled nose, and eyes that beamed intelligence. There was a dignity and grace in his actions, and he showed no signs of fear or trepidation as he made his appearance before the gaping faces which were looking so curiously and earnestly into his own.

"Poor fellow!" ejaculated several of the women. "It's hard to die so young."

"And so handsome, too," exclaimed another.

"Handsome is as handsome does, missus," said an itinerant purveyor of hot potatoes. "It ain't always them as has the prettiest face as does the thing that's right."

This colloquy was cut short by the appearance of the ordinary, with a book in his hand. Another and louder murmur of surprise was sent forth by the crowd.

He also wore favours.

"This gets over me," said the baked-potato man. "I'm queered! Why, hang me if the parson and the hangman are not both decked out as though they were going to a wedding!"

"Maybe they are," said a burly butcher.

"It's a strange bridal party, methinks," returned the potatoe-man.

"Don't you know," said a small man, with a cracked voice, "that people are married sometimes at the front of the gallows? Who knows but some tender-hearted virgin may take pity on that handsome youth?"

This suggestion of the man with a cracked voice soon spread through the crowd, and obtained general credence—for the vulgar are ever prone to give ear to the marvellous.

The cavalcade was now put in motion. It travelled at a slow pace at first, as the horse-soldiers wheeled round and cleared a path. The ordinary had seated himself between the youth and the woman. The highwayman was behind, waving his hand to those in the crowd whose features he recognised.

A number of javelin-men were walking three abreast, and a long line of constables accompanied the procession. Slowly descending Snow-hill, the train passed on its way, attended by the same noisy cheers and yells which had accompanied it on its starting from Newgate.

The guards had some difficulty in preserving a clear passage without resorting to severe measures, for the tide pressed from behind, around, and in front. The houses in Snow-hill were thronged, like those in the Old Bailey: every window, from the ground-floor to the garret, had its line of occupants, and the roofs were crowded with spectators.

In this way Holborn Bridge was reached, which, at the time we are describing, was a bridge in reality.

The highwayman had been recognised by some of his friends, who endeavoured to force their way to the side of the cart, for the purpose of taking a last farewell of him. Some confusion was occasioned by this. The javelin-men who walked on either side of the vehicle had some difficulty in preserving order.

"Whose bridal is this?" screamed out several voices.

"It's the bridal of death, you fools!" exclaimed a speaker, with stentorian lungs.

"Ha, ha, my brave lads! The bridal of King Death!" shouted out the same sonorous voice.

"How handsome he is!" said a woman, looking, with eyes of pity and admiration upon the fair-faced youth with the dark eyes who sat in the cart—"how very handsome! and how young! What a pity it is that he should have come to this!"

"Handsome! Even Old Nick himself was handsome when he was young," said a man beside the woman. "He's done wickedness enough, I dare say, young as he is."

"D'ye see that red handkerchief in his hand? That's to show he dies without telling any of the secrets of his friends. He's a brave lad, I dare be sworn," said another of the crowd.

"Oh! and did ye see how his face changed just now? He looked like an angel from heaven then. Maybe he saw his sweetheart in the crowd. Poor girl! she'll soon have nought but a cold corpse to love."

As the procession reached Holborn Bridge, the passage was so narrow, that there was only sufficient room for the cart to pass with a single line of soldiers on one side, as the walls of the bridge were crowded with spectators, and it was not deemed prudent to cross it till these persons had been dislodged.

The entrance of Shoe-lane, and the whole line of the wall of St. Andrew's Church—the bell of which was tolling—were covered with spectators. Upon the steps leading to the church a number of the highwayman's friends were stationed. They shouted out to him as the cart made its appearance

"Keep up your spirits, Jack! Die game, old boy!"

Such were the encouraging words with which they chose to favour him. He nodded and smiled his thanks.

"Why, who have you got to tuck you up?" several of them exclaimed, as they caught sight of the hangman's deputy. "I wouldn't be scragged by such a miserable old fool as that!"

"Hear, hear!" screamed out numbers of the crowd. "It's a cheat and a sell!"

Several missiles were hurled at the hangman, who began to be alarmed. It was the first time he had fulfilled his odious duties in the metropolis. His alarm increased as he found himself struck in the face by a dead cat, which had been hurled by one of the crowd. This nearly knocked him off his seat.

A roar of exultation was sent forth by those who had caught sight of his discomfiture.

Some doubts seemed to cross the minds of the officers that a rescue was about to be attempted. The cart was surrounded by a lawless set of ruffians, who seemed bent upon mischief. Many of these had been drinking freely during the night.

The officers surrounding the cart, seeing the state of affairs, drew their swords, and struck several of the rioters with the blunt edges of them, and eventually succeeded in driving them back. This was only for a time, however, for, shortly afterwards, a still more clamorous party of malcontents made a rush at the cart, apparently with the intention of upsetting it. The soldiers, upon this, dealt blows right and left with their swords, and even inflicted several severe wounds upon the most pugnacious of the party. The ringleaders were driven back, and the soldiers managed to gain a clear passage.

A dawn of hope had, for a moment, passed through the minds of the unhappy culprits, and perhaps they had entertained some thoughts of an escape from the miserable doom that awaited them. This hope was soon dispelled, as they observed the crowd give way, and the cart once more proceed on its journey.

The procession now wound its way without farther interruption along Holborn. Like a river, swollen by many currents, it gathered force from the various avenues that poured their streams into it. Fetter-lane on the left, and Gray's Inn on the right, added their supplies. Some there were amongst the heterogenous throng who were moved to compassion.

The gaily-dressed highwayman, the miserable, cringing old woman convicted of burglary, and the fair-faced youth, formed the centre of attraction—the last-named more especially. The highwayman at this time stood up in the cart, and bowed to a bevy of ladies who were collected on one of the balconies. The old woman rocked herself to and fro, muttering responses to the prayers of the ordinary. The youth sat, with folded arms, a mute spectator of the strange sight presented to his gaze; he had been convicted of forgery, and had obstinately refused to betray his accomplices. Of course, this in itself was enough to enlist the sympathies of the crowd.

There was no preconcerted plan of action on the part of those who were disposed to befriend the culprits. Nevertheless there were numbers among the crowd who were disposed to try and effect a rescue. The attempt which had been made was checked by the soldiers, and the passage of the cart was no longer impeded. In a short time after this it reached St. Giles's.

According to the custom of these times, criminals who were taken to execution were permitted to halt at a tavern called "The Crown," and take a draught from St. Giles's Bowl, as the last refreshment on earth.

These are good old days of which we are writing, when hanging was in fashion for a number of other offences besides murder. Such little incidents as these were marvellously pleasing to the public.

The whole cavalcade halted at the door of the tavern in question, which was situated not more than a hundred yards' distance from the church, the bell of which began to toll as soon as the procession came in sight.

Every window of "The Crown" was filled with guests, and, as is the case with St. Andrews, the churchyard wall of St. Giles's was lined with spectators. The landlord of "The Crown" drove a thriving trade on the days appointed for executions. There was a wooden balcony on the opposite side thronged with fashionably-dressed ladies, all of whom appeared to take a lively interest in the scene—so fashionable was villany at this time.

The highwayman rose up, and, looking towards the balcony, he saluted the ladies. He would have taken off his hat had not his arms been pinioned. He contented himself, therefore, with smiling graciously, and bowing to the galaxy of beauty before him. He pointed significantly to the withered old man and the ordinary, both of whom were decorated with wedding favours. Those in the balcony, like the rest of the multitude, could not understand the meaning of this strange sight.

The procession, which hitherto had attempted to assume a grave and serious character, now suddenly changed. It became festive. Many of the soldiers dismounted, and called for drink; they even condescended to crack jokes with some of the crowd. All of a sudden, it would appear as though everyone had become parched with thirst. There was an endless filling of glasses and emptying of foaming tankards. A flagon of wine was brought out by the waiter at "The Crown," and its contents handed round to some of those present.

As they drank off their glasses, a toast was given by the landlord. It was—

"Health to Jonathan Wild."

The old man who was about to officiate as hangman picked himself up a little, and pledged the renowned thief-taker in a foaming goblet. Shortly after this he pulled from his pocket a short pipe, and commenced smoking contentedly enough.

Such were the scenes on the days of public executions in the early part and middle of the last century.

The ordinary was engaged reading the prayers to those who were about to suffer. Neither the highwayman nor the dark-eyed youth appeared to take much notice of the words he gave utterance to. Several of the former's friends now got near the cart, and exchanged civilities with the knight of the road.

"You'll die like a hero, Jack," said one of these; "I know that. There never was a morsel of the white feather about you. You've been a good-'un in your time, but the game's up now. The last leap, and all will be over."

The highwayman smiled a sickly sort of smile, and nodded significantly to the party who addressed him.

"Who's t'other chap?" said the same speaker—"him with the dark hair and white forehead."

"Don't know him," returned the highwayman, sententiously. "He's a young 'un."

The landlord of "The Crown" now made his appearance. He was a jovial, contented, sleek-looking individual, with a shining, red face, a bald head, and a clean white apron. He bore in his hands a wooden bowl, filled with ale. He offered this to the prisoners in the cart.

The highwayman was the first to drain off a good draught of its contents. It was offered to the old woman: she refused to drink; but the younger of the three just put it to his lips, and passed it on to one of the javelin-men.

Orders were now given for the cavalcade to be put in motion. It passed St. Giles's Church, the bell of which continued to toll at the time; then it passed the pound, and entered the Oxford-road. It was quite open country when past Wardour-street.

The crowd now dispersed amongst the open fields, and thousands of persons were hurrying towards Tyburn as fast as their legs would carry them. They rushed on like yelping hounds at the tail of a fox, and jumped over hedges and ditches like mad things. They were anxious to be in at the death. Strange infatuation!

Meanwhile the cart, with those who accompanied it, had passed Marylebone-lane. Tyburn was in sight; a black, dismal object was visible—it was the gallows. Then, as if by presentiment, those who had been jesting suddenly ceased. A bell tolled solemnly—it was the knell of those who were condemned to die.

The ordinary began to read the burial service.

The crowd clung closer together, and looked over each other's shoulders at the black object in the distance.

The woman in the cart began to moan piteously. A slight shudder passed through the frame of the youth; it was but momentary, however, for he shook himself as though ashamed of it, and bore himself afterwards with wondrous firmness.

Pitying exclamations escaped from the crowd. A murmur of sympathy for him who was to die so young escaped from numbers of the more tender-hearted. One or two women fainted.

The procession neared the fatal spot. The executioner was dressed in black from head to foot, with the exception of his white neckcloth. He wore a skull-cap on his head, which, at such an hour and on such an occasion, gave him an appearance that was almost weird-like. He put down his pipe, as though he was about to prepare for business.

Then all voices seemed to be hushed; there was a calm deep and profound.

The cart now approached its destination.

The guards and constables had formed a wide circle round the gallows, to keep off the mob.

The trees in the park were crowded with spectators; so was the roof of a tavern hard by, standing at the end of the Edgware-road; so were the walls of Hyde Park.

Three groans were uttered by the mob as the hangman proceeded to perform his horrible duties.

The highwayman was hung first.

As the mob witnessed his dying agonies, they shuddered and clung closer together, as if for protection from this death, which many of them had seen, perhaps, for the first time.

The youth remained still calm and unmoved. Rising himself to his full height, he looked searchingly around him.

Suddenly his face brightened with inexpressable tenderness and love. His eyes beamed towards some one who was standing upon the steps of the house at the corner of the Edgware-road. A hand was seen pointing towards the sky.

How the people pitied him!

The young man examined the faces beneath him, as if there was some one he wished to find. He withdrew his eyes almost reluctantly, and turned them upon the officers in attendance.

The woman was to suffer next. When her turn came, the executioner found that he had forgotten to provide himself with a rope to tie round her clothes, which for the sake of decency was usually done. Groans escaped from the mob. The hangman became nervous: he gazed from one to the other in a state of stupefaction.

Presently some one furnished a piece of cord.

The woman was executed.

It was now the youth's turn.

All was hushed into a silence as deep and impenetrable as the tomb.

The youth caught sight of a form which till then had been hidden under the shadow of the scaffold, and which crept forth in the light like a snake to see him hung.

The form was that of a woman, with a face pale as death, and eyes which shone like living coals.

Those who observed the young man closely saw that his lips quivered for an instant. Conquering this emotion, he made his face appear calm, almost noble, and said, in a firm, musical voice—

"I forgive you!"

The hangman passed a strap round his feet, and secured them with horrible deliberation. He drew a white cap over his eyes and mouth. As he did so, several missiles were hurled at him. The executioner became so nervous that he was hardly able to proceed with his duties. A dog had crept to the foot of the gallows, and uttered a plaintive howl.

In another minute the body of the young man swung round and vibrated in the air.

Then commenced those struggles which, we are informed, are merely muscular and involuntary, but which, nevertheless, are sickening to behold.

But when he loosened his right arm from the rope which had pinioned it, and had thrust his hand into his bosom and tore convulsively at his heart, as if there was the seat of pain, a cry of horror rose from a hundred mouths, and women, who had wished to see death without knowing how terrible it was, shrieked and swooned away.

CHAPTER II.

LIFE.—A LOVELY VISION.

In a street where the sun seldom shone, near to the city prison, there was an old, dilapidated-looking house. On the first floor of this there was a coffin, in which was, to all appearance, the dead body of a man. By the side of this coffin there sat one who had robbed the body of life. He was smoking a short pipe, and occasionally raised to his lips a half-filled glass. This individual was the hangman. In a short time two persons ascended the creaking stairs and entered the room. One of these was an aged ferryman, and the other, his companion, was many years younger. He had red hair, and an ill-favoured countenance enough.

"Your servant, sir," said the elder of the two, as he entered. "I wish you joy of the morning's job."

"Ye doesn't catch me at such another," returned the

executioner, with something like a shudder. "You've come for this, I suppose?"

He pointed significantly to the coffin.

"Exactly. Doctor Heartwell wished us to take it to his dissecting-room as soon as possible. He appears to be in a rare hurry to cut and carve away at it."

"He has his reasons, I dare say," replied the hangman. "They made a great fuss about giving it up, but, howsomever, I worked it to rights after awhile. I expect as how there's some nobs as belongs to this 'ere chap."

He tapped the lid of the coffin as he made this observation; then, rising from his seat, he said—

"Have you brought the brads?"

The old ferryman nodded, and counted out on the coffin-lid several guineas.

"I say, you haven't been much used to London business, have you?" he remarked, as he did so.

"No, never before," returned the executioner.

"How is it Jem didn't do the business?"

"Couldn't—ain't well," returned the other; "besides, it was Jonathan Wild's bridal-day."

"Whew! That's the reason you and the parson wore the white ribbons, then?"

"Yes."

"Who has he married?"

"Mary Duncan, the hempen widow of Scull Duncan, the notorious robber, who was executed at Tyburn."

"It struck me, now," said the ferryman, "that there was something very different in the way them two men were hung. The highwayman dropped with a wild jerk, and broke his own neck in a second; but this 'ere chap seemed only to sink, as though there was a something breaking his fall."

"Shrugged up his shoulders, maybe," said the hangman, "so as to weaken the drop. There's many as does that; but, for my part, I think it's a bad plan: it only makes them linger in their pains."

"You must have had a good deal of experience in your time," said the red-haired man, looking at the withered features of the speaker.

"Pretty well, for that," he remarked, carelessly. "How do you take this—in the coffin, or in a sack?"

"We can't take it in the coffin till night, any way," said the ferryman.

"And you don't want the coffin, I s'pose?"

"No."

"Then I'll give you a sack, and there will be no difficulty upon that head; and so you may be off as soon as you please. How about a conveyance?"

"We've got a cart at the door."

A sack was produced, and the body of the dark young man who had suffered in the morning was placed therein.

"Now, Phil," said the old man, "you are the youngest and strongest: you must shoulder this, and take it down the stairs; for there arn't room for both on us at once; besides, two's company, and three's none."

The fellow laughed at his own pleasantry.

The sack was placed in the cart, and the two men drove off with their burden.

In a short time they arrived in front of a large house in Grosvenor-square. They knocked at the door of this, and were told, by the man-servant who opened it, to go to the rear of the premises, where Doctor Heartwell's dissecting-room was situated.

In less than a quarter of an hour afterwards a strange scene was enacted in this place.

We will take a glance at it.

The doctor's dissecting-room was filled with the mysterious paraphernalia of science. Stretched upon the table was a naked corpse. Two men were bending over it. An oil-lamp, hanging from above, poured a white light upon the scene. One of the two men who gazed so intently at the inanimate figure was the doctor himself. He had grey hair, and a benignant, pleasing countenance. The other was a friend of the doctor's—a young man of about thirty. He was watching the countenance of his companion as much, or even more, than that of the corpse.

"You see," said the doctor reflectively—"this blue and swollen face—these glazed eyes—this flesh which is cold to the touch as frozen clay—and you believe that James Neville is dead?"

"He appears to be so, sir," remarked his younger companion.

"And you?" said the doctor, turning towards the aged ferryman.

"He is dead enough, sir," answered the man.

"Oh, wondrous science!" exclaimed Doctor Heartwell; "thou canst awaken the fire which sleeps and smoulders unseen to common eyes! Thou canst restore life when all symptoms of the vital spark appear to have departed, and brave Death as he sits triumphant on his throne!"

He seized the lower jaw of the dead man, and drew it forcibly downwards.

"Behold! Dost thou not see?" he remarked to those in the room. Then they saw this jaw return slowly to its place like a door closing on its hinges.

The man with red hair, whose name was Bishop, clasped his hands in mute wonderment.

"Take off your coats; I shall need your services," said the doctor.

The old ferryman took off his coat and bared his shrivelled arms. Bishop did the same. Directed by the doctor, he wrapped his hand in wool, and gently rubbed the chest and left side of the body. The doctor's friend warmed some oil over a charcoal stove, and with it rubbed the neck, the veins of which were frightfully distended. This continued for more than a quarter of an hour. No signs of life appeared.

Doctor Heartwell now opened the mouth of the dead man, and took from the throat a small tube. He then went to a mahogany chest; from this he took out some instrument. It was an elastic tube, with a silver mouthpiece at its end, which was hollow and curved, to admit of its passage into the throat.

"Now my poor corpse," said Doctor Heartwell; "even as the aged Samuel restored life to his child by obeying the commands of God, will I, with this feeble breath, fan the fluttering spark of life within thy cold heart."

"He does not give any symptoms of life at present, sir," said the doctor's friend and assistant.

"Wait patiently, and we shall be rewarded for the trouble we are all taking," returned the doctor.

The assistant regarded the speaker with a look of doubt and incredulity.

The doctor forced the instrument he had taken from the case between the teeth of the corpse; and then, applying his mouth to the other end, he breathed his own breath into the lungs of James Neville.

Bishop, at his directions, had gradually increased the friction, and now rubbed with all his strength. He was assisted in the task by the doctor's assistant.

But the flesh was the same ghastly, livid hue, and both began to despair.

The doctor poured some vitriolic acid into a cup, and diluting it with water, made Bishop apply it with his hand. The previous friction having opened the pores of the skin, the powerful acid began to penetrate into the system, and the skin began to glow.

The doctor looked at the assistant in a satisfactory sort of manner. The latter comprehended this look: all was progressing as he desired.

Mr. Heartwell placed his ear to the heart of the prostrate figure.

"His heart beats," he said, calmly.

His assistant uttered a joyful cry.

"Are you sure, sir—are you quite sure?" he inquired hastily, and with evident anxiety.

The doctor nodded. He filled a phial with lukewarm spirits of wine: this he allowed to fall, drop by drop, upon that heart which was fluttering into life.

"Would it not be as well, sir, to give him some brandy?" suggested the assistant.

"Not yet—not at present," answered the doctor. We must wait awhile first. He must not have brandy till he breathes."

A few more minutes passed.

Bishop put his mouth to the blue lips of the patient. "He does not breathe yet, sir," he said, despairingly.

Mr. Heartwell smiled.

"We will see, my friend," he observed, quietly. "Here, take this phial."

Bishop obeyed, and took it from the hands of the doctor, who then unhooked a small mirror from a nail, and held it before the cold lips of the patient. It became immediately stained with moisture.

An exclamation of delight came from the assistant at this discovery.

"Hush! do not let us be too precipitate," observed Mr. Heartwell.

He thereupon inserted a quill between his teeth, and poured a few drops of brandy into his mouth. Bishop was the meanwhile fanning the face and sprinkling it with cold water.

James Neville heaved a long, deep, and painful sigh.

Those in attendance upon him looked at each other with satisfaction.

Doctor Heartwell passed his hands—soft as a woman's—over the body of the prostrate man—diffusing thereby a thrilling warmth through the frame, which gradually became convulsed. A spasmodic movement seemed to pass through the limbs. Presently Neville gave a series of long, quick gasps, and then he moved—he half raised himself up and unclosed his eyes, from which the film of death had scarcely departed.

The doctor's assistant was almost frightened at the sudden change which had taken place.

Presently Neville's eyes were dilated; they became furious and bloodshot; his face, which had been so livid and ghastly turned to red, and from red to purple.

Mr. Heartwell now evinced anxiety for the first time since the commencement of the strange operations.

"Quick—be quick!" he exclaimed. "The mahogany case!"

James Neville raised himself to a sitting posture, and glared round him with frighted eyes. When they fell upon the ferryman they grew large and round, and shone like a cat's.

"Begone, wretch:" he exclaimed. "Hence, begone! thou art the hangman!"

He plunged about, and struck out frantically with his fists, while, at the same time, his features were distorted in a most horrible manner. He shouted and screamed like one who was raving in a violent paroxysm of madness in its worst form.

Bishop now gave Doctor Heartwell the mahogany case.

The latter took therefrom a probe.

"You must hold him down," he observed to his attendants.

This was no easy matter. Bishop and the doctor's assistant forced the patient backwards on the table. Neville struggled like a demon.

"Quick, a rope! this will never do," ejaculated Mr. Heartwell.

A rope was brought, with which they tied him down to the dissecting-table. Bishop applied towels, soaked in vinegar, to his head, and the doctor bled him in the arm.

He soon recovered his senses, and gazed round him with a bewildered and puzzled look. He felt weak—so extremely weak that his brain could not act. He found it utterly impossible to reflect or collect his scattered thoughts. He had a dim remembrance of a terrible and agonising pain; when he endeavoured to recall it more distinctly to his mind, his memory stole from him like a phantom.

There was a thick mist before his eyes, in the centre was a round, luminous globe—it was the lamp in the doctor's surgery. Sometimes he detected the tall shadows floating to and fro—he wondered what these were.

Presently one of them approached him; he saw that it was a man—he glared into his face: it wore a benevolent expression—there was a radiant and pleasing smile upon the lips. Neville tried to smile also; something touched his lips, it was the rim of a glass; he looked at the face through the mist, it was still smiling—he began to understand—it wanted him to drink; he opened his parched lips with difficulty and drank. It was water, and honey-flavoured with aromatic herbs. As he drank, a delicious sensation crept over him—he felt his feet tingle, his eyes sparkle, and the blood grow warm in his veins. It seemed as though he were in some delightful trance which he dreaded to be awakened from—then his fugitive thoughts seemed to ebb off into a delightful vision.

He could not make out where he was—whether in this sinful world or a better; and, indeed, he did not much care to inquire. It was sufficient for him that he was happy and peaceful—all but at rest.

A beautiful mist seemed to envelope him; gradually this began to clear away, and then he saw, standing before him a benignant-looking old man—this was Doctor Heartwell; he gave him one of those paternal smiles, so full of benevolence, which appear only on the lips of the aged.

Neville tried to rise, that he might kiss this smile. The doctor raised his hand deprecatingly; Neville sank back as though under some mesmeric influence which he was bound to obey without a murmur.

The old man appeared to assume a commanding attitude—his height increased, his eyes filled with light and looked at the patient fixedly. Neville could not withdraw his eyes from the doctor, although it weakened them as though he had been looking at the meridian sun. Then the doctor raised his hands, and made mysterious passes.

"Sleep!" he cried, in a deep, sonorous voice.

Neville closed his eyes, trembling.

"Sleep!" said the voice again.

Then his brain—cell by cell, faculty by faculty—dozed into slumber, but he heard, as if in a dream, that voice once more murmur in silver tones—

"Sleep, poor soul, and forget that thou art restored to a wretched and sinful world."

After this Neville's slumbers were deep and profound. Hours passed away.

James Neville slowly unclosed his eyes; he glanced round the room, which was in partial gloom; the lamp had been turned down, and burnt but feebly. Its feeble rays failed to light up, with anything like distinctness, the objects in the apartment. Suddenly the eyes of the prostrate man saw the shadowy form of a young and beauteous female. Her soft tender eyes were fixed upon him. She appeared to be an angel of goodness, who had come to visit him from a far-off world. For a moment he believed her to be a spirit; then, as his senses came to him, he recognised the features of his visitor.

"Miss Darrell!" he exclaimed in a voice of wonderment and deep emotion. "You here!"

"Hush! Do not excite yourself," she answered, "So you know me, then?"

"Yes; and how—what—where am I?"

"With friends. Let that suffice for the present. You live—have been snatched from death by a miracle, and your enemies are cheated."

"Who has done this?" he inquired, hurriedly. "I have been hung—hung before gaping thousands."

"But you have triumphed after all, and now live."

"Aye, live for revenge!" he exclaimed, passionately.

"Hush! Rest in peace for the present."

"How have I been saved—restored? How—tell me how? It is you—you have been the cause of this."

She nodded.

"Heaven reward you for it! Oh, Miss Darrell, had I listened to your counsels—oh, if I had——"

"No more of this," she answered, quickly. "You have had enemies—most bitter enemies."

"And some friends—some good, kind friends," he returned quickly. "Henceforth I shall know how to appreciate them—henceforth I live but for you."

"Silence!" exclaimed Nan Darrell, with something like anger in her tone. "Let there be an end of this, I pray. Live—go forth into the world again, and learn experience. The dead is restored to life, but he may not show himself to those who knew him before—before——"

"Before he was hung!" returned Neville.

"Precisely."

"Neither shall they see Nan Darrell again. I shall go abroad; I shall put the breadth of the ocean between myself and those who have brought me to what I am. You have been my saviour—my good angel. Will you fly with me?"

Nan Darrell turned from the speaker with evident displeasure.

"You do not choose to mate with a criminal," he said sadly.

"What folly is this?" she exclaimed. "How often have I told you not to be so free of speech? You are ready to pay your devotions to any woman, more's the pity."

"I shall be rich—immensely rich."

"What care I for your riches?"

"Oh, my dear benefactress! pardon me. You are too good to look upon the wretched James Neville. Pardon me, I pray!"

"Let there be an end to this," she answered. "I should not have entered the room had I not deemed you were in a sound slumber. I came here to assure myself that you were a healthy man; that done, my task is fulfilled. Farewell!"

"Nay, do not leave me. Let me look at the light which shines from those tender eyes—let me bask in their sunshine."

"Farewell, James Neville," she again repeated, as she made a movement towards the door.

"Your hand! your hand!" he ejaculated.

She walked up to the side of the couch on which he lay, and gave him her hand, which he raised to his lips and covered with kisses. She withdrew it somewhat suddenly, and glided towards the door, through which Doctor Heartwell was about to enter.

"Does he still sleep?" he inquired.

"No, he has awoke. We will leave him now."

The two then passed out of the dissecting-room, and left Neville alone. When they arrived at the doctor's private apartment, Nan Darrell said—

"So I see you have succeeded, Doctor Heartwell. I return you very many thanks."

"Name it not, my dear young lady," said the doctor. "The success of my experiment is in itself a sufficient reward."

"I am desired by those who care for this young man to express their gratitude; and, at the same time, I am anxious to pay you for the trouble you have been at."

The doctor laid his hand upon the shoulder of his young and beauteous visitor, and said—

"No more upon that head, I pray you. There has been sufficient expense incurred already in bribing those who have obtained the body. You must permit me, my dear Miss Darrell, to have my own way in this instance. Nay, do not frown, my pretty lady; I am obstinate."

"I have done," said Nan Darrell, smiling. "I am but an agent for others; and you know best, of course. It is not for me to say more."

The doctor handed her to a seat, and placed wine and biscuits before her.

"We should never have accomplished the business had not this been the marriage day of Mr. Jonathan Wild. The wily thief-taker has been so taken up with the imposing ceremony, that for once he has been caught napping."

"Ugh!" exclaimed Nan Darrell, with a shudder.

"He did all in his power to compass the death of this poor, misguided, and infatuated youth."

"Alas! that is true enough. Misguided and infatuated he has been, and, moreover, spoilt in early culture. Let him go away now, far away from his old associates; for as sure as he remains with them, he will be brought to ruin. Wild has been bribed, without a doubt."

"There can be no question about that. But I have been told that the ordinary and the hangman wore wedding favours at the execution. Is that true?"

"Quite true," returned the doctor. "This marriage of Wild's appears to have created quite a sensation. Rivers of punch and wine have been drained off at the several prisons in the metropolis. The renowned thief-taker seems to have been remarkably liberal."

"He is a vulture—a harpy, who preys upon the weak and unwary."

"And lives like a nobleman upon the produce of his calling," observed the doctor.

In a few minutes after this, Nan Darrell took her departure from Mr. Heartwell's house.

CHAPTER III.

THE HIGHWAYMAN'S FIRST LESSON.

OUR scene shifts to Bagshot. On the road leading to the heath a solitary figure might be seen. He was mounted on a black mare of magnificent proportions, which he rode with the ease and grace of an accomplished horseman. There was not a better in the whole country. Whistling merrily, he walked the animal he bestrode along the high road. Neither horse, carriage, nor vehicle of any description was in sight. The horseman cast a furtive and inquiring glance to the right and left; his eye searched in vain for any other chance traveller beside himself.

"Umph!" he ejaculated. "There does not appear to be much chance for sport to-night, and I am cursed low in the exchequer. 'For God! but a few silver pieces left," he said in continuation, as he pulled out a leathern purse and shook its contents. "This is no time to stand upon trifles; I must shake some *brads* out of somebody, that is quite certain."

He reined up his horse near to a dark clump of trees that stood by the roadside, at the corner of a narrow lane. Some few, fleecy clouds were chasing their way across the moon's disc, ever and anon robbing her silver beams of her borrowed light.

The rider backed his horse into the shadow of the trees, and waited. While he did so, his ears were on the strain to catch the sound of either carriage-wheels or horses' hoofs striking against the hard road. More than a quarter of an hour passed, but no one came in sight.

"Barren as a sandy desert," he ejaculated. "The trade's being overdone; people have become too *peery*. There's such a cursed number of poor gentry that the business will soon come to nothing. Ah!—hark! what was that? Horses' feet, as I live! I must be on to him, whoever he may be. Tom promised to meet me at Smallbury Green; but, as usual, he's after the wenches, I s'pose. Some day or other they'll bring him to his end. Woi, woi, Bess! Steady, lass—steady."

He patted the neck of the beautiful mare he rode—who, in an after day, saved his life by the sacrifice of her own—and fondled her like a pet child. She seemed to understand all he said, for she laid down her ears at the sound of his well-known voice, and then stood as immovable as an animal of either iron or bronze.

The noise of horses' feet became more distinct. The practised ear of the watcher detected that the sounds were produced but by one traveller, who soon appeared in sight, and set all doubts at rest upon this point. As the latter came within a few yards of the dark clump of foliage, the first horseman reined his steed in the middle of the road, and confronted the new-comer.

"Stand!" he exclaimed; "you must pay toll, if you

please. Nay, whether you please or not. So shell out without more ado."

"Wretch! would you turn highwayman?" ejaculated the traveller.

A derisive laugh was the only answer to this query.

"Let me pass before I blow out your brains," said the solitary wayfarer.

Then there was another laugh.

"Turn highwayman, my pretty youth. Ah, ah! you are hot and peppery, my young blade; and, withal, somewhat humoursome. Come, time presses. Your money—out with it."

The young man levelled a pistol at the highwayman and fired. The bullet missed its mark.

In another minute the highwayman was by the side of his assailant, and dealt him a terrific blow with his heavy riding-whip. He was nearly stunned by this; but, nevertheless, had the presence of mind to urge on his horse, in the vain hope that he might get clear off. In a moment afterwards he found himself in the grasp of the highwayman, who dragged him from his seat, and threw him to the ground.

Then, dismounting himself, he wound his hands round his throat, and planted one of his knees on his chest.

"What would'st thou do? Would'st thou murder me?" he inquired, hastily.

"Should it be necessary, I shall not stand very nice about that," was the prompt reply to this query. "Your cash—where is it?" said the highwayman as he proceeded to rifle the pockets of the prostrate man. "By the Lord above, if you give me much more trouble I'll strangle you!"

"I am miserably poor myself. Take your hands from my throat!—for heaven's sake take your hands from my throat! Oh, mercy! any death but this! Shoot me, if you will; but release my throat," exclaimed the young man, in plaintive and piteous accents, while a death-like pallor overspread his features.

"What is this? The marks of a rope, as I live!" ejaculated the highwayman, for he now observed, by the pale light of the moon, a red mark round the throat of his victim.

"I have been hung," said the latter.

The nether lip of the highwayman trembled.

"So young, and tired of life?" he murmured.

"Not so; I was executed a day or two since—executed at Tyburn. My name is James Neville."

"You are a strange customer, and a profitless one. Why, you haven't got enough brads about you to purchase a stoop of liquor. You spent the last, I 'spose, to purchase a rope to hang yourself with?"

"No, no; I was executed at Tyburn."

"None of your d——d gammon with me; who and what are you?"

"I am an outcast—a forger—a convicted criminal, and have suffered death at the hands of the common hangman."

"Cuss me if I know what to make of you! Stand up, man, and let us have a look at you."

As the speaker said this he gave the young man a twist up, which brought him to his feet.

"You are quite a youngster," he said, as he peered into the face of James Neville; "but are a downy one. Now, where have you concealed your money? If you don't tell me, I'll strip everything off you."

"Do as you please; if you pound me in mortar you will get no more than what you have already taken. I was about to seek a friend, to see if I could borrow enough money to leave the country."

"Your name?" inquired the highwayman.

"I have told it you already. It is James Neville—he who was executed for forgery on Jonathan Wild's wedding-day. Now, tell me yours; let there be something like confidence between us."

His companion smiled.

"My name is Dick Turpin," he said, looking hard at the other.

"Dick Turpin! Your hand, my friend; I do not regret meeting you, although I have been put to some pain in consequence. Oh! if you only knew the agony I endured when your hands grasped my throat. When you have been hung you will understand the dreadful sensation."

"Ugh!" ejaculated Turpin, as an expression of horror and dismay passed over his features; "you regularly stagger me," he said, glumpily. "You appear to have began life at the wrong end. What are you going to do now?"

"I care not what, answered his companion. "In me you behold a desperate man. I shall live for vengeance."

"It's a poor thing to live for. You won't get very fat on such fodder."

"No matter; I have been the sport of fate, and I care not what becomes of me."

"You're a fine young fellow: marry a rich heiress. Many worse chaps than you have done so. You are poor, you say?"

"You have taken my all."

"Umph! that's a bright lot to commence the world with. You are not wanting in courage, I should say?"

"I hope not."

"Well, then, turn highwayman. Take your first lesson to-night."

"I have promised to reform."

"Ah, do the honest game. I see, it's slow, and not profitable."

"Will you give me a lesson?"

"In what?"

"In the practice of that calling which has given you such a world-wide celebrity."

Turpin smiled once more.

"World-wide celebrity," he iterated; "that's not exactly the language of our kidney. Maybe you've been to school, and have received the edication of a fine gentleman."

"I have been educated certainly; but of what use has it been to me?"

"Not much, I should fancy."

"Will you take me as a pupil?"

"Well, I tell you what I will do. We will share what we get to-night. I need a pall, and so, for want of a better, I'll take you."

"And I shall have the honour of having been on the road with the celebrated Dick Turpin."

"Yes; and in after years, when I am scragged, and you grow old, you can tell the tale of how you learnt to use your barkers. Come, mount your nag. You are not much hurt, I s'pose?"

"I've got an ugly bump on the head," answered Neville, rubbing his forehead.

"That was your own fault. You had no right to give me so much trouble when you knew there was nothing worth quarrelling for about you."

Neville mounted his steed, while Turpin got across Black Bess.

"Now then for it," he ejaculated, as he rode by the side of his companion. "Are your barkers primed?"

"No."

"See to them at once, then."

Neville at once began to load his pistols.

After this the two rode on together till they came within two or three miles of Bedpont. Turpin and his companion drew up their steeds in a dark, narrow lane.

"We shall have somebody passing presently, I hope," said Turpin. "If not, this will be the sorriest night I've known for a long time."

"I am all anxiety to begin," said his companion. "Mercy on me! what excitement there must be in this sort of life."

Turpin nodded.

"Mind you be guided by me. Don't be in too great a hurry."

"I shall act in obedience to your orders."

"Good; see that you do so. Ah! someone is coming. Now I'll show you a new move. Possibly it may turn

[THE RESUSCITATION OF NEVILLE.]

out more profitable than the usual way. Stay where you are, and do not stir unless I call you; and take charge of Bess."

"Are you going to dismount?"

"Yes."

"What for?"

"You shall see."

Dick Turpin dismounted from his mare. When he had done so, he took off his mask, and pulling a wig from his pocket, he placed it on his head, which so completely metamorphised him, that he could not have been recognised by those who were familiar with his features.

He then walked from the dark lane into the high road. A stout, happy-looking yeoman farmer was coming along this. Turpin now laid himself along the road, with his ear inclined towards the ground. Presently the traveller came up to him, and stared with astonishment to see a man lying down listening at such a time and in such a place. He drew up his horse, and said—

"What's amiss, my man? What do you here?"

Turpin held out his hand to signify his desire that the other should be silent.

"What the plague are you listening like that for?"

"Beautiful! enchanting! Oh, I never heard anything so beautiful!"

"What's beautiful!"

"Oh, I hear such ravishing and melodious harmony—such delightful music—that it is enough to charm me, if that were possible, to sit here till eternity."

"Music! Impossible. I hear none," returned the traveller. "Where can it be?"

"Oh, dear!" exclaimed Turpin, "I've heard a great deal of talk about fairies, but never had any faith in them till now. I used to laugh at the stories which people told of them, but they must be about here somewhere. Oh, those delightful and ravishing sounds. There again!"

"Well, I never heard of such an extraordinary thing. Fairies! and about here. I can't see or hear any."

"Oh, sir," answered the highwayman, "if you only laid down your ear, as I am doing, you would be delighted."

Curiosity, that active principle in the human mind, caused the gentleman to alight.

"Well, it won't be much trouble to see if what you

say be true," observed the traveller. "I never have believed in fairies."

"Oh, but you will now," answered Turpin.

The gentleman began to dismount to hear the enchanting music. Having reached the ground our highwayman said—

"Let me hold your horse, sir."

The owner of the animal handed the bridle to the speaker.

"Now, then, for your music," said the farmer, who proved to be a person of some fourteen or fifteen stone at the very least.

He laid himself down upon the ground.

"Do you hear anything, sir?" inquired his companion.

"Devil a bit!" returned the other. "I can hear nothing but the sound of your voice, the sighing of winds, and the ticking of my own watch."

"Place your other ear to the ground, sir—you will hear then."

The gentleman turned round, with his back towards the highwayman, and listened. This was precisely what Turpin wanted; he vaulted into the saddle of the horse he was holding, and rode off at full speed.

"Hoi! Help! Here, what the devil are you after? you double-dealing rascal!" exclaimed the corpulent gentleman, as he sprang to his feet. "Curse the scoundrel! he has gone off with my gelding. Hoi! Help! Hang it! what a fool I have been."

He made frantic efforts to run, but his weight and age were against him. Neville was at a loss how to act. He did not know where Turpin had gone to, or whether he intended to return at all; but his fears were put at rest when he looked at the sleek-coated and beautiful mare he was left in charge of. However it struck him that it would be as well to make his first essay on the road. He tethered Black Bess to a branch of one of the trees, and when the obese gentleman had got some little distance ahead he rode on. It was not long before he overtook him.

"Hold! Stand! Your money or your life!" exclaimed Neville, using the magic words, which have been handed down by tradition to the present day.

The gentleman saw, to his infinite horror and amazement, the shining barrel of a pistol being presented at him.

"Stand! I can't do anything else," said the traveller, puffing and panting like a grampus. "I'm regularly out of breath."

"Quick! Your money!" said Neville.

"Why, you infernal young scoundrel!" exclaimed the gentleman. "A pretty pack of thieves I have got amongst. Are there any more of ye?"

All this while the fiery eyes of Neville were to be seen through the openings in the mask with which he had been furnished by his companion — they looked along the shining barrel of the pistol.

"Are you mad, that you tempt me thus?" he inquired. "If you delay much longer I will send a bullet dashing through your brain."

He spoke in so serious a tone of voice that the gentleman saw that he meant mischief. He, therefore, pulled out his purse, and handed it to the youthful highwayman.

"You'll be hung one of these days, you young rascal," said the portly traveller. "From your appearance, I should have thought better things of you."

"Your watch, if you please," returned the other.

"Why, confound your impudence, would you take that from me which was my father's, and my grandfather's before him?"

"Can't help that," returned Neville. "You can have it back by paying for it. Send the value, and it shall be returned."

"Where—where am I to send for it?" inquired the gentleman, pulling the watch out of his pocket.

"To Mr. Jonathan Wild's house at the sign of the King Charles the First's Head, in the Old Bailey—send

there any time after to-morrow, and the watch shall be yours upon the payment of its value. We don't rob people of heirlooms, if we can help it."

"You insolent young monkey! to talk to a man old enough to be your father in such a manner as this. A drubbing with a good sound ash would do you good."

"I pardon you," said Neville, in a condescending manner. "I can make allowances for you; it is not pleasant to lose your money, either at cards, on the turf, or on the high road. Yes, I pardon you."

"Is that fellow a companion of yours?" inquired the ill-starred traveller.

"To whom do you allude? I have not, as yet, seen anyone else besides our two selves," answered the young highwayman, with admirable *sang froid*.

"The rascal who has run off with my horse."

"Don't know who you are alluding to. I am not a horse-stealer," said Neville, turning away, saying, as he did so—"Good night, my friend, I cannot afford to waste more time with you. Good night. Remember Jonathan Wild's."

As he uttered these words he moved on his steed, and left the unfortunate traveller to pursue his journey, wherever that might be.

Meanwhile, Dick Turpin had trotted on to Bedfont. Before, however, he arrived at the latter place, he dismounted, and let the horse go by itself, while he followed it at a little distance. He did this, under the belief that the owner of the horse would have some particular inn where he usually put up. Turpin was not mistaken in this. The animal no sooner appeared before the door of a large country inn, when the ostler, who was standing at the door, exclaimed—

"Master — master, here's Mr. Bartlet's horse has come without him."

"Oh, oh!" thought Turpin to himself. "All is as I could have desired. The owner's name is Bartlet, then."

He at once walked boldly up to the bar of the house, and inquired for the landlord, when, upon the latter's making his appearance, Turpin said he had been sent by the gentleman, mentioning the name of the owner of the horse.

"What for?" inquired the landlord. "Does he want me to lend him another horse?"

"No, my friend," replied Turpin. "Not so. He is engaged at play with some gentlemen a few miles down the road, and he desired me to bring you the gelding, and say that he wished you to lend him fifty pounds, which he will return when he fetches the horse."

"Lend him fifty pounds!" returned Boniface. "I would lend him a hundred, if he wished it. He need not have troubled himself to have sent the animal; he knows that very well. I want no security for the money. He's welcome to a thousand or more, if I had it by me. Fifty, you say?"

"Yes, that's what he told me; but, perhaps it would be as well to take sixty or seventy."

"By all means," answered the landlord. "Come inside, and I'll give you the money. Would he like notes or gold?"

"Gold would be best."

"Perhaps I have not so much cash, but I will see."

The landlord could only find fifty pounds in gold, the other twenty he paid in notes.

"All right," ejaculated Turpin. "You must excuse my running away in such a hurry, as he's waiting for me to return."

"Do not stay, my friend. Hasten back as quickly as possible, and make my kind regards to your master."

Turpin did hasten back, but it was by a different road. He deemed it advisable to cut across the fields to avoid meeting with any questioners.

After a smart run and walk, he returned to the dark place where he had left Neville. Upon his arrival there the latter was nowhere visible.

Turpin gave a low whistle, then another. In the

space of two or three minutes after this, James Neville made his appearance with the two horses.

"Bad luck to you!" exclaimed Turpin; "but I began to think the robber was robbed."

"What mean you?"

"Why, that you had mizzled with the finest mare in all England."

"Hang it, man, I'm not so bad as that."

"So it seems. Come—come, Bess."

The noble animal pricked up her ears, and came to her master.

"So, ho, lass! Angry at my absence; is that it?"

The mare pawed the ground with one of her fore feet.

"Gently, girl! gently! You have your temper as well as the rest of your sex. Gently, wench!"

Turpin sprang into the saddle.

"Has she been pretty quiet?" he inquired.

"Yes, tolerably well for that," answered Neville; "but curse me if I know why you made off in so sudden a manner."

"To get these shiners," answered the highwayman, holding up a leathern bag, which was well filled with old spade guineas.

"Found them in a field, I s'pose?"

"No; you are wrong, youngster."

He then explained to Neville the ruse that he had been practising.

"I haven't been idle," said Neville.

"How so. What hast been doing, then?"

"Why, I did not know what your game was. I saw a stout gentleman before me. I dismounted, and followed him. I knew he could not run away from me. When I got up to him, I out with my pistol, and bade him 'stand and deliver!'"

"Ah! ah! Capital. You'll do. Did he shell out?"

"Ay, to be sure; every stiver. Here's his watch, which was his father's and his grandfather's before him. He wants this returned."

"When! Does he?"

"Yes; I told him to send the money to Jonathan Wilds's, and the watch would be there."

"That's right. Why, you're quite a knowing card—you're like a haunch of mutton, all the better for being *hung*, as my old master used to say. Ah! ah!"

And the highwayman laughed at his own wit.

"Where are you off to now?" inquired Neville.

"London," answered Turpin. "Tom King promised to meet me. He's never kept his word, odd rot him for a laggard. I shall see if I can't route him out in some of his haunts."

"We've done business for to-night, I suppose?" said Neville; "so we may as well shut up shop."

He thrust his pistol into his pocket as he made this last observation.

"Oh, I dont know as to that; there may be some more customers," replied Turpin, with a smile.

The highwayman and his pupil then turned their horses' heads towards London, and trotted along the road merrily enough. When they had gone a few miles, they halted to bait their horses. After this they arrived at the great metropolis without any other incident worth recording.

Both of them had removed their masks.

As Turpin caught sight of the mighty city, which was then a dwarf compared to what it is now, he grew little more reflective. There was no wonder at this, or he remembered the number of palls he had missed—palls, or companions, who had been led out from the olls of Newgate to be executed at Tyburn.

A life of crime is always a life of care, for the hearts ofthe wicked tremble for the past, for the present, for the future.

"You've committed forgery, you say?" inquired Turpin.

"Yes," answered his companion.

"What made you do it? You've not been brought up a thief?"

"Ah, my worthy friend and preceptor, that's a long story. Too long to begin now," said Neville.

"You've been extravagant, gambled, or have been fond of women?"

The young man sighed.

"Ah, I am answered," said Turpin. "Now then, we have had a pleasant night together, what do you intend doing? We must square accounts."

"Oh, as to that," returned Neville, "whatever has been earned to-night is fairly yours; but I shall beg something of what I took from——"

"All right; it is all yours. Now, youngster, would you like to come with me, or will you go your own way, and meet me at another time?"

"I'll go where you do, if I am not in the way."

"Good, I'll introduce you into fashionable society, then."

CHAPTER IV.

THE HOME OF THE LAWLESS.

TURPIN and his young companion rode on towards Charing Cross. They went down the Strand, which was still full of noise and light, and through the ponderous arch of Temple Bar into the city—grave, dark, and silent as it is by night.

Then through Leadenhall-street and Aldgate—lighted only by the street-lamps, and here and there by a faint gleam from the window of some cigar-shop or tavern—and they entered a street so broad and bustling that one would have fancied oneself in one of the great thoroughfares of the West-end, were it not for the small size of the houses, and the squalid appearance of the inhabitants.

They had passed the boundary between wealth and poverty—between vice and crime.

They were now in a new world, among a race of men who were governed by different customs—by different fashions, and by different codes of morality, from those of civilised London. They had crossed the frontier of Aldgate pump, and were in the land of costermongers and thieves.

They were in Whitechapel.

It is strange what distinctive features different parts of London have. There is a mixed population in every quarter, to a certain extent, and there are, unfortunately, dishonest people in all quarters; but the unrighteous congregate in certain quarters. At one time Westminster had an unenviable reputation; at another period, Whitefriars.

Dick Turpin walked his horse through the street, which was as broad as Piccadilly. It was Saturday night, and the place presented an extraordinary sight to Neville, who had never been in the locality before. Butchers' stalls extended a considerable distance down the street; the pavement was lined with retailers of fried fish and potatoes, of fruit, of vegetables, and a thousand miscellaneous articles. These were displayed to view by means of stout brown paper candles, which, prepared in some peculiar manner, afforded an excellent light.

"What think you of this neighbourhood?" inquired Turpin, looking at his companion. "It was here that I first started in business."

"Here?"

"Yes. You seem surprised, my friend."

"In what line, if I may make so bold as to inquire?" said Neville.

"In the butchering line," answered his companion, with a smile. "Not butchering my fellow-creatures," he added; "but horned animals and fleecy quadrupeds. Ha, ha! We must now dismount."

"What for?" inquired Neville.

"To put up our horses."

They were in front of a low public-house, with a deeply-pitched roof: so low, indeed, was the house, that visitors had to go down three or four steps to enter the bar. It was evidently very old, from the style in which it had been built.

As Turpin halted, a man made his appearance at the door and took charge of the horses, which he led round the next turning and placed in the stable belonging to the establishment. He did this without asking any questions. He merely looked at Neville's horse, when, upon a word from Turpin, he took them both off.

"You may sleep here to-night, if you like," said Dick to Neville. "They know me, and you'll be all right."

"Are we not going any further, then? Is this the place you were making for?"

"No. Follow me."

Dick suddenly wheeled off to the right, and dived into a labyrinth of dark streets, in which nothing was to be seen except a few shops full of rags and bones, and placards offering a farthing a pound for these commodities. Turpin walked down the street with the assurance of one well acquainted with the locality. He then threaded his way through another street, less inviting than the first.

"Where are you making for?" inquired Neville.

"You will see presently. We are not far off Little Mint-street."

"What a queer neighbourhood! I shall never be able to find my way back."

"Ah, you are used to the swells—you are, my friend. It's as well that you should see something of t'other blokes. Keeping company with the top sawyers always is apt to make a cove proud."

Neville saw him smile, by the light of the oil-lamp, as he made this last observation.

"I am not proud—never was."

"Ah, ah! youngster—can't deceive me. I can see it in your eye."

Neville laughed also at this observation.

They were by this time in a street as dark as a tomb. Its inhabitants seemed to be buried alive, so close and narrow did it appear. The houses on either side projected out at the top and first storey, and, nodding to each other, they appeared to touch at certain parts.

"This is a lively locality," observed Neville. "Where in the world are we?"

"In London," answered his companion, as they both came upon another street.

Dick pointed to this.

"They're a queer lot there, I can tell you," he said, as he took a turning which led him away from the place he had been speaking of.

This odious place was inhabited by nearly three hundred women, the most atrocious and criminal of their sex. There they lived—a republic of demons, admitting only to their homes those men who were allied to them by the bonds of fellowship in theft, in murder, or in lust.

The place was so badly tenanted that Dick Turpin did not care to go down it. He took his companion by the arm, and led him down another street.

Neville felt as though he were approaching the infernal regions.

At the sound of strange steps lights glimmered on all sides, and women poured from every door. It was a loathesome sight. Most of them were clothed in a loose, disreputable manner; their faces were swollen with drink, and many of them covered with bruises and wounds.

They began to surround the young man, as if they would have torn him to pieces, but Dick Turpin interposed his authority, and said a few words in a severe tone, in a language which Neville did not understand.

The rabble parted on one side, angry, but evidently awed.

"Take no notice of them," said Dick. "They think I have brought them a swell with plenty of shiners, but they will not interfere now, after what I have said to them."

"What a horrible place!" answered his companion. I should not like to come here alone."

"They would almost have eaten you up alive if you had ventured by yourself, my friend; but while with me you are quite safe."

"They know you, then?"

"Most of them."

"I wish you joy of your acquaintances."

"I have little or nothing to do with them, and, what is more, don't want. Come along."

The two companions came to a small lane branching off from the street. There were no lights in this lane, and no houses—there was a dead wall on each side.

Dick Turpin drew a dark-lantern from his pocket, and lighted it; he then held this in front of his companion, so that he might see his way as he walked.

Neville proceeded in silence.

"We must be careful here," said Turpin. "I am pretty well known—and feared, for the matter of that—but it is well not to throw a chance away. You follow me."

The lane ended in a yard, and in a tall, dingy house, which appeared as though it had not been inhabited for years.

Here the highwayman came to a halt.

Neville looked inquiringly at him.

"Where are we to go now?" he inquired.

"We have arrived at the end of our journey, for the present, at any rate," was the prompt answer. "Don't you show any fear, or make too many inquiries, and all will be well—only these are a sort of people who are a little shy of strangers. It isn't everyone who is admitted into this select company. Ha, ha!"

And as he made this last observation, he gave a sort of chuckle.

"Hang me if I know what we are coming here for!"

"You're not afraid?"

"Afraid?—no!" exclaimed Neville, indignantly "Afraid? I should hope not."

"You're a plucky card for a young-'un."

"Thank you for the compliment. Praise from Dick Turpin is praise indeed. But what are you doing now?"

"You shall see. We shall not be able to enter here without the usual forms are gone through."

As he said this he picked up a stone from the ground, with which he knocked three times against the door; he then paused for a moment, and gave a single knock.

The door swung open.

"Enter," said Dick.

Neville obeyed, wondering, all the while, what was to be the end of his night's adventure. He observed another door, with a glass window above it.

Neville watched the proceedings of his companion with curiosity.

Turpin wetted his finger, and rubbed it across the window in such a manner that it made a loud screeching noise.

A face appeared at the window, which was protected by huge iron bars.

"Who's there?" said a voice.

"One—or, rather, two who *are on the fly*," answered the highwayman.

"It's Dick's voice, I think?"

"Ah, Dick it is, old shaver, and no mistake."

The door was opened, and they passed through; after this they proceeded down some steps into a large room.

Neville's eyes wandered over this with all the curiosity of a young man who had been unused to such sights. The apartment in which he found himself was thus furnished:—There were two long tables, running from fireplace to fireplace, parallel to each other. They were laid with greasy napkins, iron plates, chipped teacups filled with salt, two small stone jars filled with mustard, and knives and forks chained to the tables. A number of candles in tin shades, nailed to the walls, lighted the room. These, being never snuffed, were appropriately infested with "*thieves*," which streamed in large flakes upon the floor, the seats, and the backs of the guests.

One fireplace was black and empty, but the other flared with an enormous fire—the temple of a blear-eyed, Salamander-looking woman, upon whom were fixed, in one long look of hunger and anxiety, the eyes of twenty men and women, who were seated at the tables, clad in disguises at once loathsome and appalling.

They raised a yell as, a few minutes afterwards, the tables were covered with joints and vegetables, served up on iron dishes, thick with rust.

It was not long before they were all helped; and it was a strange sound to hear the noisy clattering of the knives and forks upon the iron plates, and the tinkling of the chains.

"He's not a bad sort, the man as keeps this 'stablishment," said Turpin, in a whisper, to his companion. "He's one of your rough-and-ready customers, but he's none of your smile-in-your-face-and-cut-your-throat blokes, for all his ugly mug and and swivel eye."

"Where is he?" inquired Neville.

"Ain't here—leastways, not in the room at present."

"Who are these?"

"These? Oh, these are only cadgers," answered the highwayman, with something like contempt in his tone —"only cadgers."

The waitress of the establishment—"Lazy Kate," as she was usually called—now came towards them, flourishing in her hand a brown napkin.

"Well, Kitty, my lass! still as nimble on your pins as ever, eh?" said Dick, with a smile. "What's the news? all quiet?"

"All quiet, and plenty of business, and no inquiries. That's the way to say it, Mr. Richard," said the woman, with another flourish of her napkin.

"You're worth your weight in—in lead," said the highwayman.

As they were conversing with the Hebe of this delectable establishment, those who were at the table, enjoying the delicate viands, turned, ever and anon, an admiring and inquiring glance at the celebrated highwayman, who, however, did not condescend to take any notice of those who were evidently regarding him with eyes of admiration.

"Who do ye want—anyone in particular?" inquired Lazy Kate.

"Has Tom been here?"

"Yes; he came in about an hour ago."

"Did he inquire for me?"

"Yes."

"And is gone, then? or is he upstairs?"

"He went out with the 'Griffin,' but said as how he'd return in less than half an hour."

"Which time has passed, of course. He never keeps his word."

The waitress smiled.

"You are always grumbling at one another, and yet are always together," she said.

"Not always, Kate—not always. Who's up stairs?"

"Why, let's see; there's the Screever—he's up stairs in his room along with the Cracksman and a lot more. They're full o' business they are."

"Ah, these coves drive a roaring trade," said Turpin to his companion.

"Ye've got a swell kid here," observed Kate to Turpin, in a low whisper.

"A swell out of luck, then, if he be one at all," answered the highwayman. "You just mind your own business, Kitty."

"Oh, ye've no call to be huffy, master; I ain't got any curiosity about other blokes' affairs, like most women. I does my business, and lets 'em do theirs. It's see and say nuffin with me."

"Gammon and all," answered Turpin. "Well, Kitty, we'll go up stairs, my lass."

The highwayman caught Neville by the elbow, and conducted him into a room on the first floor. It was small, and almost filled with ragged men and women.

"What are they doing?" inquired Neville.

Turpin gave no immediate answer to this query, whereupon a man, who had heard the question, touched his cap, and said to Neville.

"Maybe, young gentleman, you ain't used to these scenes. They are making a cadger."

"He'll soon get used to them, Mat," said Turpin.

"Is he on *the fly*?"

"Yes; a pupil of mine."

"Can't have a better master."

"And wants to see the various dodges."

"This ain't a bad place to come to for that ere. But I s'pose——"

"Yes; I know what you would say," returned Turpin, sharply. "We shall pass the *wax* round presently. Let's listen to these for the present. Business is on hand, and we won't interrupt them."

At a table, which was a little distance from where Neville and his guide stood, there was seated a man, with a heap of papers before him. He was short and thin, with a crouch in his shoulders, and a villanous cast in his eyes. Close to the table, and rather in front of the assembly, was a tall, pale boy in rags.

"You see that man?" said Turpin.

"Which? He who is seated at the table?"

"Yes."

"I see him sure enough."

"Well, he is known as the Screever."

"As what?"

"As the Screever."

"What does that mean? I never heard of such a word before."

"Very likely not. Your education ain't complete as yet. That man is a writer of begging-letter petitions."

"Oh!" ejaculated Neville.

"Yes, that's his little game; and yonder boy is a cadger, who is about to be initiated into the mysteries of the craft."

Lolling in an arm-chair behind the table, with a huge bit of bread and meat in one hand and a glass of gin and water in the other, and a short black pipe in his mouth, was a burly ruffian with "strength" written in his brawny arms and broad shoulders and prominent heaving chest, with villany in his deep, hollow eyes, his cropped, black whiskers, and his eyebrows, which were half an inch asunder.

Turpin directed the attention of his companion to this man.

"And who is that?" inquired the latter.

"That is the Cracksman, one of the most celebrated burglars of his day—that's who that cove is. He's a pal of the Screever in all lays which the one devises and the other accomplishes."

"He looks a determined sort of customer."

"Hush—listen!" said Dick, placing his hand on the shoulder of Neville to enjoin silence. "Listen, and you will hear what the Screever has to say."

The latter-named personage now began to speak.

"Now, young man," he said, looking up from his papers, "you said you could read, I believe?"

"Yes, sir," answered the boy. "My mot' me go every Tuesday and Thursday to school."

"There, that will do; we don't want to about your mother. This ain't a plac come to—or, indeed, to be talked abo of that. You can read?"

"Yes, sir."

"That is well. Your friends your luck in cadgering in the co as green as their own grass, an

"I should like to try my lu

"Very good. Now, take th the post of every door you according to the character of there. That will act as a cl comes after you, as to wh likely to expect. And when you see any marks, you've only to look at this paper to understand them."

On the paper was written—

⌁ means, "Go on—it's no use."

⌁ means, "Stop and try your luck."

⌁ on a corner house or sign-post, shows which way you have gone.

⌁ on a corner house or sign-post, means, "Go on in that direction."

⊙ means, "Danger."

The boy took the paper, and examined the signs attentively.

"Can you understand it?" inquired the Screever.

"Yes. I don't think there can be any mistake about the matter."

"That's well so far. Now," he said, handing the lad another slip of paper, "this is the recipe for the *scaldrum dodge*."

"The what, sir?"

"The *scaldrum dodge*. It will teach you the art of burning your body with a mixture of acids and gun-powder, so as to suit the terrible accidents you have been in."

"I have not met with any accident," said the lad, with a naïve simplicity which elicited roars of laughter from the assembled company.

"But you must have met with accidents—don't you see that?" said the Screever, petulantly. "You can say you were in a ship that was blown up in a battle, or that you ran into a house on fire to save a child that you heard screaming out of a garret window."

The boy nodded, and the speaker continued, as he handed the lad another paper—

"And here's a recipe for a nice little mixture, which, if you drink in the morning, will make you look pale and green all day. I'll take five shillings for that job; and as you're in a way now to make a fortune for life, you'd better stand a gallon of beer for these gents to christen you."

"Hear, hear! Bravo!" shouted out several voices. "Well said!"

"Ah, Dick!" exclaimed the Screever, who caught sight of the highwayman for the first time since his entrance. "How are you, my friend? Tip us your dandy. Why, who have we here?"

"A friend of mine," said Turpin.

"One of the fancy?"

"He's a fanciful sort of gentleman, I can tell you."

"He's young and green, Turpin. Where did you pick him up?"

"He's young, but by no means green," returned the highwayman; "by no manner of means. He's a won-der—he is. There's not one among us can say what he can; he clips the whole squad of us."

The Cracksman looked hard at the speaker.

"Oh, you may look, Jem. What I say is true enough."

"He's a wonder—he is," said the Cracksman.

"Right you are, old boy. He's been hung at Tyburn, it's more than anyone on us here can say."

declaration on the part of Turpin there was nd sudden consternation amongst the whole

me the cynosure of a hundred pair of

roups of men seemed to hold their whispers of surprise and incredulity om the mouths of several of that

said the cracksman. "This ere it lord, it aint true, it can't be

or not, it's the case, I tell e mark of the rope."

r of Neville, and showed most curious the mark of the nes Neville.

Several of those present shuddered. It is probable they thought of the manner they were likely to end their days.

A tall thick-set man, with a clear eye and short cropped hair, now entered the room. This individual was the landlord of the establishment. He immediately made up to where Turpin stood, and offered his large, brawny hand, and his features, which were ill-favoured enough, relaxed into a grim sort of smile as he caught sight of the highwayman.

Two females had followed the landlord into the room, and came also to pay their respects to Turpin. One of these he introduced to Neville as Wapping Nell, the other he named as Tawny Bess. They were bloated creatures now, but at one time had been possessed of a considerable amount of beauty.

"Mat," said Turpin, addressing the landlord of the chaste establishment, "bring us some lush."

"What's it to be?" inquired the blear-eyed man.

"Some few flagons of ale, and two or three bowls of punch. I shall stand something for my friend."

"No, call for that—not a bit on it," said Mat.

"You go and do as I tell yer."

The landlord disappeared.

"You may have everything in this hotel," said Turpin to Neville—"from small beer to burgundy, from a penny sausage to a brace of Woodcocks—it's all one to Mat."

While the punch was brewing, and Neville and Turpin were conversing to the two delicate damsels who had made their appearance with the landlord, a man came swaggering up to the table at which the Screever sat, and said—

"I've got a job for you, lawyer. How much do you charge for *screeving a brake?*"

"And I say, Screever," cried a woman, shuffling slip-shod to the man's side, and tapping with her sharp boney knuckles on the table. "Have yer any children to let out, and clothes and so on? I'm going on the monkry to-morrer, and I ain't made up my mind whether its to be the *clean family lurk* or the *half shallow*."

"There are my terms," answered the man at the table.

"Let's have a petition, then," said the man, laying down a shilling.

"Without signatures?" inquired the Screever.

"Yes, can't stand more than that. It's more with signatures."

"Of course—it's eighteenpence with signatures, and two-and-sixpence with forged names."

The Screever placed two ink-bottles before him. They were filled with ink of two different shades. Then he spread a bit of paper under his hand and began writing.

"He writes a good hand," said one, looking with admiration at the pen which darted over the paper.

"I wish I could do it," said another.

"If you could you'd d——d soon be lagged or scragged!" chorussed the rest.

The Screever having finished the paper, folded it in true official style, creased it as if it had been long written and often examined, attached the signatures of the ministers and churchwardens, and, dipping his fingers under the fireplace, smeared it with ashes, to the infinite delight of the rest, who swore that there wasn't one in twenty who wouldn't take it for a "rum" concern.

The man having folded his precious document in his *green king's man*, or green silk pocket-handkerchief, and placed it in his hat after the manner of the Per-sians, took his departure. The woman also having made her arrangements and paid the money, left the room.

A little more business was transacted in the same manner.

The Cracksman came up to the table and handed the Screever a jorum of punch. The latter raised it to his lips, and nodding towards Turpin, said—

"Here's your health, Dick, and your young friend's also, whom I hope won't live to be hung again."

"Stow that, Jem—stow that," said the Cracksman; "them 'ere arn't pleasant observations. Lore! vy, they makes a cove think of vat might happen to him. No, stow it, Jem."

"Oh, I've done," returned the Screever.

"I tell yer vat it is, Jem," said the Cracksman: "I 'xpect yer every day to tell me that yer tired of the old trade, and that ye'll stick to screeving for a pack of ragged patterns for the rest of yer life. Yer a-getting witinated, Jem; this half-bull-letter work is corrupting yer mind, old boy."

"I'm not likely to give up trade when there's anything to be got by it," said the Screever. "And I am not afraid of ending my days where you'd have gone long ago if you hadn't had my head to lean upon."

"Ah, ah! Well, don't be huffy, old boy," said the Cracksman, good-humouredly, as he raised his glass on high, and toasted Turpin and Neville. He was about to drain off its contents, when his eye lighted upon the blissful countenances of Wapping Moll and Tawny Bess. He then added to his toast—

"And the ladies, bless 'em."

The Cracksman drank off the contents of the glass he held in his hand.

Wapping Moll and Tawny Bess smiled benignantly on him.

"That man has passed through almost every branch of the trade," said Turpin to Neville, nodding towards the Cracksman. "He began life half shallow in the streets. From a shiverer he became a cadger; from a cadger he became a duffer (pedlar); from a duffer he became an area-sneak, a shop-bouncer, and a foyle-burrer. From a foyle-burrer he became a swell-mobbite, then a rampsman, and lastly, what you see him now, a cracksman. He has ascended from the very foot to the summit of his profession; and, besides, he is up to all the other games that are worth knowing. He has been a 'shoful man,' and 'a smasher,' and a race-course flat-catcher, and was at one time a famous fence."

"Ah," said Tawny Bess, meditatively, "there's no doubt the Cracksman's a great man—a very great man."

While this conversation was taking place, a man of genteel appearance had sauntered leisurely into the room. He was dressed in the height of fashion. His coat was of a dark blue, turned up with yellow, and ornamented here and there with gold lace. Costly lace ornamented his wrists and chest. His features were small and regular, but had a faded and rue appearance.

The new-comer was Tom King, the friend and companion of Dick Turpin. The latter's back was towards him as he had entered that abode of vice. He strolled up to Dick, and placed his hand on his shoulder.

"Tom!" exclaimed Turpin, "you here? It's good for sore eyes to catch sight of you."

King passed his hands through his glossy, flowing ringlets. "Couldn't help it, Dick; 'pon my soul, I couldn't help it. I tried to be with you, old boy, but it wasn't to be done."

"The old story—women!" said Turpin, with a shrug. "They'll be the death of you some of these days."

"Oh, shame on you to say so!" exclaimed Wapping Moll, endeavouring to pout; but her attempt was a signal failure.

Turpin introduced Neville to his companion.

In a few moments afterwards the three men had adjourned to a private room in the establishment. They were accompanied by the two damsels whom we have introduced to the reader's notice as Wapping Moll and Tawny Bess.

Turpin took King apart for a few minutes, and conversed with him in private. The two highwaymen had some professional business to settle. After this had been transacted, they repaired to the table, and proceeded to serve out a hot and steaming bowl of punch.

The two delicate damsels had endeavoured to outvie each other in their attentions to James Neville. The whole of them soon became festive.

Coarse jokes and coarser compliments went round.

Tom King, who, all through his career, had lived in an atmosphere of pleasure, called upon one of the ladies for a song. After some discussion, Tawny Bess sang the following:—

The song I shall sing is about little Dan,
Who vasn't a svell, but a small-coal man.
He says as how, ven he gets control,
He'll make all things dog-cheap—but coal;
And gin shall flow in each man's can,
Says my prime little trump of a small-coal man.
My eyes! vat precious times for ve!
Ve'll sing all day, and live rent-free;
Ve'll make them lords eat husks and bran,
And kiss the great-toe of the small-coal man.

Some don't admire his mug and snout—
Give me the colour vat von't vear out;
A mixture strong of the black and tan
Is the varmint mug of my small-coal man—
My nice little, nasty-faced small-coal man;
The golden flag that decks our van
Is the yellow mug of my small-coal man.

"Bravo! Very beautiful indeed, my charmer! Gad, its brim full of sentiment," said Tom King, as he wound his arm round the singer's waist, and pressed her to his heart with much gallantry.

"Oh! pray, don't do that, sir; I shall be jealous," said Neville, with a smile.

"Sorry to make any man jealous," answered Tom. "Hate jealousy; it's a sauce that don't agree with my stomach. She's yours, sir—yours," he added, as he took the hand of Bess, and led her towards Neville.

"Ah, you two can play well at the spooney game," said Turpin. "This young blade is a good hand at it, I dare be sworn."

"Now, what do you call the spooney game, Master Dick?" inquired Wapping Moll, placing her arms akimbo, and looking like a virago.

"Being cozened, cajoled, or humbugged by a woman," said Turpin, draining off his glass, and bringing it to the table with a loud bang. "That's what I say, and that's what I mean; and so, my fair enslaver, you may take your change out of that."

"Ugh!" exclaimed the damsel; "you are not likely to be humbugged by one of them."

"No, I hope not."

"Come, come, Dick, no wrangling," said King. "Women are angels, every one of them."

"They will be your ruin, Tom."

"They are my blessing."

"Well, you know best, I suppose; but I knock you down for a song. I am charmer here."

"All right," said Tom King; when, after he had cleared his throat, he chanted out the following, much to the amusement of those assembled:—

The name of the song was—

ONE FOOT IN THE STIRRUP; OR, TURPIN'S FIRST FLING: A BALLAD.

"One foot in the stirrup, one hand on the rein,
And the noose be my portion, or my freedom I'll gain:
Oh! give me a seat in my saddle once more,
And these bloodhounds shall find that the chase is not o'er."
Thus muttered Dick Turpin, who found, while he slept,
That the Philistines old on his slumbers had crept—
Had entrapped him, as puss on her form you'd ensnare,
And that gone was his snappers, and gone was his mare.
　　　　　　　　　Hilloah!

How Dick had been captured is easily told:
The pursuit had been hot, though the night had been cold;
So at daybreak, exhausted, he sought brief repose
'Mid the thick of a corn-field, away from his foes.
But in vain was his caution—in vain did his steed,
Ever watchful and wakeful in moments of need,
With lip and with hoof on her master's cheek press—
He slept on, ne'er heeding the warning of Bess.
　　　　　　　　　Hilloah!

"Well, gemmen," said Turpin, "you've found me at last,
And the high-flying highwayman's come to a halt;
You have turned up a trump (for I weigh well my weight),
And the *forty* is *yours*, though the gibbet's *my* fate.
Well, come out what will, you shall own, when all's past,
That Dick Turpin, the dauntless, was game to the last!
But, before we go further, I'll hold you a bet
That one foot in the stirrup you won't let me set."
                                          Hilloah !

" A hundred to one is the odds I will stand—
A hundred to one is the odds you command.
Here's a handful of goldfinches ready to fly;
May I venture a foot in my stirrup to try ?"
As he carelessly spoke, Dick directed a glance
At his courser, and motioned her slyly askanse.
You might tell by the singular toss of her head,
And the prick of her ears, that his meaning she read.
                                          Hilloah !

With derision at first was Dick's wager received,
And his error at starting as yet unretrieved;
But when from his pocket the shiners he drew,
And agreed to make up the hundred to two,
There were *havers* in plenty, and each whispered to each
The same thing, though varied in figure of speech—
" Let the fool have his folly—the stirrup of Bess;
He has put his foot *in it* already, we guess !"
                                          Hilloah !

Bess was brought to her master. Dick steadfastly gazed
At the eye of his mare, then his foot quick upraised.
His toe touched the stirrup, his hand grasped the rein,
He was safe on the back of his courser again !
As the clarion's bray, sounding and shrill, was the neigh
Of Black Bess as she answered the summons, "Away !"
" Beset me, ye bloodhounds! in rear and in van,
My foot's in the stirrup, and catch me who can !"
                                          Hilloah !

There was riding and gibing, much rabble and rout,
And the old woods re-echoed with the Philistines' shout;
There was hurling and whirling o'er brake and o'er briar:
But the course of Dick Turpin was swift as heaven's fire.
Whipping, spurring, and straining could nothing avail—
Dick laughed at their curses, and scoffed at their wail—
" My foot's in the stirrup," thus rang his last cry;
" Bess has answered my call—now her mettle we'll try."
                                          Hilloah !

"Capital !" exclaimed James Neville; " I never heard anything better. Here's a health to Dick's 'Bonny Black Bess.' A finer mare was never crossed by man."

"Ah, ah !" said Dick; "if every woman was as faithful as she is, we shouldn't have much fault to find with them. Here's a bumper to Black Bess !"

The toast was drank with vociferous plaudits.

The noise was at its height, and the convivial party were in a state of uproarious merriment, when a head peered in at the door. It was the landlord, who gave utterance but to one word.

"Ferrets !" he exclaimed, in a low, hissing whisper.

There was a dead pause—a death-like stillness.

A sudden pallor overspread the features of the women, who rose from their seats.

Seth Margut, the landlord, held up his hand to enjoin silence. He blew all the lights out but one; this he concealed in a recess, leaving the room in darkness.

CHAPTER V.

THE ALARM AND SUDDEN FLIGHT.

DICK TURPIN crept softly to where Seth Margut stood.

"What's up ?" he inquired, in a hoarse whisper.

"I can't tell ye who they're arter ; but Wild's chaps are below, and you and yer pals had better mizzle, for it 'ud bring me to an early grave if yer ver taken here —bring me to an early grave, that ed vord."

What he meant by an *early* grave it would be difficult to say, for the speaker was nearly sixty.

"What are they here for ? Who are they in search of ?"

"Tell yer I doesn't know," said Margut ; "they wunt tell me. All I knows is that ye'd better hook it, Dick, you and yer pals. My private 'pinion is that it's Tom they're arter. But be this as it may, ye'd better mizzle. Hark ! they are coming upstairs. Quick ! follow me, all on yer. Ah ! it 'ud bring me to an early grave, that it vord, if any of yer vas taken in this 'ere 'stablishment. Follow !"

Turpin motioned his companions to the spot where he and Margut stood. The former led the way to the top of the house. They all crept softly up, holding their breaths the while.

Lights were flashing below ; these were borne by the peace officers.

"O Lord, Lord ! they'll be upon us," ejaculated Mr. Margut. "They'll be upon us afore we can reach the top."

" I don't hear them," whispered Turpin.

"Doesn't yer? Then I does ; and that's all 'bout it. Yer doesn't hear them, Dick ? Vell, then, ye'd better be operated upon by Doctor Addle, the celebrated oraculist. Doesn't hear 'em ! O Lord, Lord ! but ye must be deaf, to be sure !"

"Where are you leading us to, Seth ?" said Tom King.

" To the top o' the 'ouse : there ain't two ways 'bout it. Yer must get over the roof. Dick 'll show yer how to work it to rights."

"Any port in a storm," said King. " But they've broken up our harmony in a most shameful manner."

" Hark ye. If yer hadn't kicked up such a cussed row, I doesn't know but I'd 'a bin able to 'ave got rid of these ere kiddys, 'cause, yer see, I said there worn't no one upstairs ; but they looked 'spicious like ven they heard yer woices. Oh, cuss 'em ! there they are."

"Where ? where ?" inquired Turpin.

"On the fust landing. Ah ! they're making for the room we've left ; and there's a woman with them."

"What sort of woman ?" inquired Tom King.

" She's young and beautiful," answered Margut. " She's brownish 'air, and a cut on her forehead. I've see'd her afore—I have."

"Curses on her ! Betrayed !" ejaculated King. " I never would have believed it ! Betrayed ! Oh, it's her, sure enough."

He looked over the stairs, and saw the features of the woman who had accompanied the officers. Her face was familiar enough to him. His frame became slightly agitated from excitement.

"It's me they're after !" he exclaimed, placing his hand on Turpin's shoulder. "Your words but just now sounded like an omen. I am betrayed, Dick, and by a woman."

"Good luck to yer !" ejaculated Margut, "but ye must be clean mad to be looking uvver them banisters in that ere manner. Do yer think pipple haven't eyes in their 'eads ? I tell yer ye must be mad to be a-showing yer mug in that ere manner."

The highwayman withdrew his head from the banisters. In a few seconds more they were on the topmost storey of the house.

Seth Margut pointed to a trap-door which led out on to the roof.

"That's the dandy !" he observed, significantly. " Through that ere, and then the devil catch the hindmost."

Turpin, King, and Neville lost no time in unfastening this door ; they then climbed up, and gained the roof of the house. A cry of alarm proceeded from the street, and a pistol-shot came whizzing past those on the roof.

This seemed to arouse those below. The officers rushed upstairs to the top of the house. Seth Margut heard them ascending.

"Close the door, Dick. They are arter yer. Close the trap. Ye'll find a bolt on the other side. Fasten it, or they will be upon yer."

The trap was closed and fastened by those above.

[THE PROPOSAL.]

Seth Margut dived into one of the rooms, and gained another staircase, by which he was enabled to reach the basement storey of his house.

When Wild's men arrived at the upper part of the tenement, they found the trap-door closed and the birds flown.

To make certain of this, they rushed from room to room, and searched in every nook and corner; they then returned to the landing, and began to hammer away at the trap, which, however, resisted their efforts for some time.

Meanwhile the three fugitives had made their way over the roofs of the adjoining houses.

They were, however, not unobserved. There were several officers in the street, who were keeping watch and ward. The silent echoes of the night were awoke by several pistol-shots, fired in rapid succession.

"The rascals haven't hit us at present," said Turpin; "but I don't see any fun in being a mark for them. Let's get out of their sight."

No. 3.

"But how?—how? is the question," inquired King.

"By just taking our way on the other side of the roofs. The thing is simple enough."

"The other side?"

"Yes, surely. Don't you see how exposed we are here?"

"Unfortunately that is but too true."

"Well, then, climb over, man. Follow me, and I'll show you how we shall be able to dodge them. They've not got us yet; neither do I intend they should have us."

The three fugitives now made their way on the other side of the roof; they were then lost to the view of those officers who were stationed in the street.

"The Lord be praised—we shall be a little more peaceable here," observed Turpin.

He had hardly made this observation when, to his infinite dismay, he saw the heads of two persons peering over from a neighbouring chimney.

"Whew!" ejaculated the highwayman, with a pro-logged breath, "the ferrets are in sight. Good luck to you. Tom, hasten forward, or they will be upon us."

He drew from his pocket a pistol, which he cocked, and then stood prepared.

The three fugitives hurried forward, and succeeded in gaining the trap-door of another house.

It now became a question of but a few minutes. By several violent efforts they succeeded in removing the trap, and then all three of them passed through.

Those in pursuit were within a few yards' distance of them when this occurred.

Turpin and his companions rushed down the stair-case of the house into which they had succeeded in gaining an entrance. The passages of this were dark enough—so dark, indeed, that it would, perhaps, have been impossible for the officers who were giving chase to observe their figures, had not the sound of their footsteps betrayed their whereabouts.

As Turpin heard those above leap down from the trap-door, on the landing beneath, he paused in his flight.

"Hold! stay where you are," said Dick.

"Why? What for?" inquired King.

"It will be impossible for us to gain the street before these fellows are upon us; we don't know, the door may be barred and bolted."

"But leap from one of these windows, then."

"Impossible!"

"Why so? We are on the first-floor of the house I should say."

"Without a doubt. But what of that?"

"It may not be pleasant, but we can drop from the window in safety."

"Nonsense, man, and have a dozen pistols fired at us from the street."

"Oh, I never thought of that."

"But I did."

"Oh, you have such a cool head in the case of any emergency. I wish I had."

"So you would if you'd foreswear wine and woman."

"After this I swear to you I will."

"Come in here, they are descending the stairs."

Turpin drew his companion into a room on the first-floor, from whence proceeded the sonorous snoring of some heavy sleeper.

Tom King and Neville entered.

"So that is all right; remain where you are and leave all to me," said Turpin.

"Dick, you have been my saviour on more than one occasion."

"Enough! Peace, man."

The officers were descending in the dark, picking their way along as well as they were able.

"Now, my lovely blokes," muttered Dick to himself, "pride must have a fall, they say. So I learnt, when a good little boy at school. So here goes."

He had by this time slipped the end of a rope, which he had pulled from his pocket, round the last rail of the banisters, about a foot from the stairs. He held the other end of this in his hand, and then concealed himself within the impenetrable darkness of a dark passage which led into the bed-room.

Tramp—tramp the footsteps of the officers came.

Turpin could see the stairs sufficiently clear for his purpose from where he stood.

Wild's men came on. There were but two of them—so the highwaymen judged from their footsteps.

They were right in their conjecture.

They followed one another, for the staircase was a narrow one.

Turpin and his companions remained as silent as the grave. Then, when the first officer reached the last two or three steps of the stairs which led on to the landing in the first-floor, Dick suddenly pulled his rope taut; it caught the man's legs and tripped him up.

He fell forward and struck his head a terrible blow, which rendered him powerless and nearly senseless. His companion tripped also, but did not fall, for he saved himself by catching hold of the banisters. He managed to gain the first-floor landing in a state of bewilderment, from which Dick did not give him time to recover.

He sprang out from his hiding-place, and catching the officer's arms firm he had fairly pinioned him.

The constable began to shout out lustily for his companions.

"By the Lord above if you don't stow that I'll slip my knife across your throat!" said Turpin. "Here, Tom, a rope! Slip it round his arms!"

The officer was bound hand and foot, and a handkerchief was thrust into his mouth.

The other who had been tripped up now began to groan piteously.

"Oh, you're a lovely sort—you are—to come and disturb people in their rest at night," said Turpin. "Come, look sharp, my lads, he'll be waking presently. So, oh, my hearty. Gently, boys, gently."

The other officer was bound.

By this time voices were heard in the bed-room. The first was that of a woman. She spoke in a low voice, but petulantly.

"Whiffin! are you awake? Whiffin! do you hear? There's somebody in the house—there—there—Whiffin! are you going to remain here and be murdered in your bed? Whiffin! do you hear?"

The snoring of the male sleeper ceased for a moment or so. He muttered something in a gutteral tone, and then began once more to compose himself to sleep.

"Whiffin! are you mad! to lay here in this manner? There are thieves, I tell you—twenty or thirty of them, at the very least. I am sure of that, Whiffin. Drat the man! he won't wake up. Do you hear me?"

"What the devil is the matter?" exclaimed Mr. Whiffin, "that you should kick up such a row as this."

"There are thieves in the house—murderers, perhaps. But, law, what matters that to you? You'd let me be murdered before your eyes, I do believe."

"Ah! they won't take the trouble to do that—I am sure they won't," said Mr. Whiffin, who, while he spoke, heard the hurried whispers of the highwaymen.

"D—n it!" exclaimed the woman's husband, "but that is the sound of men's voices, sure enough. Where are my pistols, I wonder?"

Tom King heard the last sentence. He entered the room softly, and said—

"Be not alarmed, my friends. There are no robbers here, believe me—at least, none that intend you any harm. We are officers, and have been in pursuit of a couple of runaways who chose to force an entrance into your house. We have luckily secured them."

"Heaven be praised for that!" exclaimed Mrs. Whiffin.

"Now, Tom, don't be pattering there," said Turpin. "We must be off, or"—he lowered his voice to a whisper—"or some other of the blood-hounds will be on our track."

Without further ado, the three fugitives flew down to the street-door, unfastened it, and gained the street, leaving Wild's men bound fast on the landing of the first-floor. They succeeded in getting clean off—not, however, without difficulty, for those in the street had caught sight of them, and gave chase.

CHAPTER VI.

NAN DARRELL'S HOME.

WE have seen at present but little of her whose name has given the title to our present tale. Let us take a glance at Nan Darrell in her own quiet home. The reader must accompany us for a while to Turnham Green, for it is here that Luke Darrell, Esq., county magistrate, &c., resides. He lives in a large red house, with green plants climbing up its walls and falling down its gable-ends in large festoons. There is a farmyard attached to the house, where there are milch cows, and fowls fluttering, chirping, and feeding together, with some famous black hogs and pigs in their styes. There are also stables and barns, with tiled or slated roofs, and strong oaken doors, through which, as they stand ajar, one can see the flail rising and falling upon the writhing straws. There is an orchard, with a great stone pigeon-house rising from the midst and towering over the trees; a rookery which is silent, for all the birds are feeding in the fields; and a little hamlet seen in the distance here and there between the leaves.

The picture is still unfinished, as every picture is unfinished, without a human figure: it is to colours upon the canvass what the eye is to the face—what the sun is to the sky.

But our picture is not unfinished, for on a roughly-hewn bench before the front door of the magistrate's house sits a beautiful young woman. At her feet crouches a dog, whose wistful glance is ever and anon directed towards her, as though he would fain be the companion and confidant of her reverie; but Nan Darrell is lost in thought. Now and then her glance is directed down the long, white road, which was only lost to view among the dark and silent foliage. After this she would relapse into a state of serious meditation.

She is supremely beautiful. Her eyes of dark hazel are fringed with long silken lashes; her dark chesnut hair is parted over a smooth and polished brow; and there is a decision lurking about her mouth and red lips which declares at once to the gazer that their owner is possessed of an individuality of character which may be for good or for ill as circumstances call it forth. Nan Darrell is in the full flush of maidenly beauty. It is small wonder, therefore, that her grandfather, Luke Darrell, should be proud of his grandchild and adopted daughter.

As Nan glances carelessly down the road she observes a black dot in the distance. In a short time afterwards she discovers this to be a man on horseback, who is galloping towards the house enthroned in a cloud of dust. As he nears the magistrate's residence, Nan sees that he is one with whom she is well acquainted.

The new-comer is well mounted on a high-stepping, flea-bitten horse. He is tall, and of an aristocratic bearing. As he nears the gate of Mr. Darrell's house, he reins up his steed, and takes off his hat gallantly to Miss Darrell, who rises from her seat with a heightened colour in her fresh and beauteous features. She calls out to one of the men who are busily engaged in the barn. The gate is opened and the visitor enters. He then dismounts, and resigns his horse to the care of the servant.

"Now mind you rub him down well, my man," said the visitor. "I had no business to bring him in at such a pelt, for a horse should always go cool in the stable; but the fact is, Miss Darrell, I have been behind-hand to-day with everything, and when I caught sight of your graceful figure beneath the porch of the house, it was enough to make me put my steed out to his best pace."

As he made this observation he sauntered up towards Nan and offered her his hand.

"Is Mr. Darrell within?" was the next inquiry.

Nan answered in the affirmative.

Whereupon the gentleman entered the house.

Mr. Luke Darrell was seated in the old oak dining-room.

The fire was expiring in the grate; the embers began to be coated with a thin grey ash—indeed, to speak the truth, there was no need of a fire, for the weather was warm and genial; but Mrs. Darrell thought it looked cheerful, so she had one.

The magistrate and his wife were seated together in this chamber—he reading the columns of a newspaper, she, with her pale face, watching the sparks as they died out one by one.

Mrs. Darrell was generally sad. Providence had given her but one real blessing—it was a daughter—and for this daughter, who had died in giving birth to Nan, she had never ceased to grieve.

This same daughter—the mother of our heroine—had eloped with a handsome stranger. She had married him, and for some strange reason—some wild infatuation—she had never divulged the name of her husband. The world said—for the world is ever prone to be uncharitable in its conclusions—that the daughter of the magistrate was never married at all. Be this as it may, she kept her secret well enough. She returned home and died.

Mrs. Darrell had been a proud woman, and it was, of course, a sad blow to hear the scandal which had been brought upon her house—a scandal she never could forget.

That is why her face was always pale, and her eyes hollow—that is why she lived but in a reverie. Her thoughts were always in the past; for, with the exception of Nan, she had nothing to care for in the present, and but little to hope for in the future.

The husband and wife were suddenly aroused from their reverie by the entrance of the servant, who said quickly—

"Sir William Blakeley is in the parlour, and wishes to see you, sir."

"Sir William!" ejaculated Mrs. Darrell, in a tone of pleasure, as she glanced at her husband.

The magistrate adjusted his spectacles, and laid down the paper he had been perusing. He then rose from his chair and made his way into the parlour.

A cordial greeting took place between himself and his visitor.

After the usual civilities were over, Nan Darrell took an opportunity of leaving the room, making some trifling excuse for her absence as she did so.

Then Sir William was left to the companionship of the magistrate and his wife.

"Now you have come, Sir William," said Mr. Darrell, "I hope and trust you intend to honour us with your company for some days at the very least."

The baronet smiled one of his most seductive smiles.

"You are very good, Mr. Darrell, and very kind; to say the truth, I never enjoy myself more than when I am at Old Oak Farm."

"You are very flattering to us, I am sure, Sir William," remarked Mrs. Darrell, relaxing from her usual gloomy reverie. "I cannot possibly imagine what charms Old Oak Farm can have for one of Sir William's cultivated taste."

"Nay, you do the place an injustice," returned the baronet. "It is the very picture of comfort—a bower of bliss—a green sequestred nook on life's arid desert, where one may sit down with an esteemed and valued friend, and muse upon the follies and vanities of the world. You will see, Mr. Darrell, that I am getting quite a philosopher."

"You always were, Sir William, you always were," remarked the old magistrate.

"So you see, Mr. Darrell, that young rascal suffered for his crime. It's sad to die so young, but he was a most hardened fellow, and I fear much that it would have been impossible to have reclaimed him."

"I was glancing at the paper containing an account of his death," said the magistrate. "I was reading it when your name was announced. The great man of his time was married on the same day that young Neville was executed."

"What great man?"

"Jonathan Wild."

The baronet laughed.

"He's greater than the prime minister of England, I suppose?" he said, jestingly.

"In his particular line of business he is; and, between ourselves, I think Wild imagines himself far above any officer of the Crown."

"Why, he's a low-bred brute."

"Ah, without a doubt; but he is possessed of a considerable share of intelligence nevertheless. Education is not required in his calling."

"I should imagine not. One thing is quite certain: that James Neville would have escaped and cluded justice had it not been for the said Jonathan Wild."

"Ah, and many others besides him," returned the magistrate. "My dear sir, you know not this man's power."

"Who?"

"Wild's."

"Indeed! Is it so great then?"

"More than you would imagine. He makes thieves; but not only that, he catches them and gets them convicted by his tricks and artifices. The thieves think he can hang or save whom he pleases: it is certain that it is one of his arts to make them believe so. You may imagine, therefore, that Jonathan has no common understanding. To govern a community already fixed and established is more than what may be done by any common capacity; but to form and establish a body of such lawless people into what may be termed a form of Government—to erect a community like that of the bees, in which there should be no drones—in which every member is obliged to go forth and labour, and bring an offering to him—their king—of part of the product of their cunning and dishonesty, is in itself something wonderful."

"It is incomprehensible to me," remarked Sir William.

"Why he lives," continued the magistrate, "he lives, sir, in a kind of credit amongst the people he is robbing every day."

"There can be no question about that."

"And this proves him to be possessed of tact and cunning, and shows moreover that he has been a thorough observer of the humours and weak sides of man."

"Strange, incomprehensible character!" ejaculated Sir William Blakeley.

"He has made himself famous all over London, and he has used several arts to make himself considerable in other parts of the kingdom," said Mr. Darrell. "He is now usually styled 'Thief Taker General of Great Britain.' His house is well furnished, and set out with plate and pictures, &c., and when his wife appears abroad, it is generally with a footman in fine gold-laced livery. He keeps a country house well furnished. He has parks at command well stocked with deer. He dresses well, and when in company he affects the airs and grandeur of a nobleman."

"So I have heard," remarked the baronet.

"You know him I suppose?"

"Yes—oh, yes—I know this celebrity. I have the honor of his acquaintance."

The conversation then turned upon other subjects—the events of the day, the gossip of the town, and a host of other matters.

Sir William Blakeley gave a sketch of fashionable life, and kept up an animated and pleasing discourse till dinner-time.

When this period arrived, the master and mistress of Old Oak Farm repaired to the dining room, where they were joined by Nan Darrell. The baronet was scrupulously polite to our heroine, and payed her marked attention, which she received with a frigidity that appeared to be almost unaccountable in one of her genial temperament.

After the dessert the ladies retired, and left the two gentlemen to enjoy their wine.

In less than half an hour after their departure, Sir William broached a subject which had been all along uppermost in his thoughts. After clearing his throat and swallowing a glass of Burgundy, the baronet said—

"Apart from the pleasure I must ever have in sitting as a guest at your hospitable board, Mr. Darrell, there has been another and more weighty reason which has prompted me to pay you this visit."

The magistrate a-hemmed and looked up, and then over his spectacles at the speaker; the nut he had between the nutcrackers had a respite for a few moments, for Mr. Darrell saw by the face of his guest, as well as from the manner of his speech, that something was coming—something more serious than the usual indifferent topics upon which they had been conversing. Mr. Darrell a-hemmed again, and said something about "His being sure——," of what he did not say—perhaps he did not know. He, however, deemed it advisable to put on a serious countenance, and to assume the attitude of an attentive listener.

"You know, my excellent friend," said the baronet, in continuation—"you know, I dare say, for you are a man of the world and are gifted with an acute perception."

The magistrate a-hemmed and bowed once more. This time it was an a-hem of gratification and a bow of deference.

The speaker continued—

"And such being the case you will have devised by this time that I have looked upon your granddaughter as a young lady whom to see was to admire."

"You are very good, Sir William—very good, I am sure, and flattering. I am glad you have so a good an opinion of our poor Nancy."

"I have, Mr. Darrell; and being a plain-spoken man—not much given to—a-hem!—the *flummery* of fashionable life—if I may make use of so plebian a word—not much given to unnecessary and tedious circumlocution—you will not be surprised, I dare say, if—a-hem!—if I speak at once plainly—if I deal frankly with you——"

"It will be no more than I shall expect from Sir William Blakeley," returned the magistrate, in a hot, flushed, and nervous manner. "Nothing more than I should expect from one who has at all times been so candid."

"I thank you for the compliment."

"It is not a compliment—it is the truth, sir."

The baronet smiled.

"I did not know you were so good a courtier," he answered, jestingly.

"The Darrells were never courtiers, sir—never! not one of the family. No, sir, not for centuries past has there been a courtier in our family."

Whether it was to give force to his words, or whether he felt himself released by this last speech, it would be impossible to say, but at the close of it he cracked the nut which he had been holding all the while unpressed in the crackers.

"I was but jesting, my friend. I don't believe they ever were courtiers. I was but jesting, believe me."

The magistrate gave another bow at the assurance; the baronet went on.

"I was observing," he said, in continuation, "that Miss Nancy was a young lady whom it would be impossible for any one to know as intimately as I have known her without being struck with her grace, beauty, and—a-hem!—amiable disposition."

"You are very complimentary, I am sure. I am delighted to hear these words fall from so complimentary a gentleman as my friend Sir William Blakeley."

"And," continued the baronet, "such being the case it is possible—mind I don't say it is so—but it is possible—that her sweet presence caused me to be a guest at Old Oak Farm more frequently than I should otherwise have been. Now that is not complimentary, Mr. Darrell," said the speaker, as he cut a slice of a pineapple and conveyed it to his mouth.

"Well, a-hem! I hardly know," replied his companion. "I hardly know."

"Well, my friend, open confession is good for all of us. Your granddaughter has made a deep impression on me. I know she is too young for an old, hacknied man of the world like myself—I know that; but then, again, man is a selfish animal, and is but too apt not to give heed to these things. I love your granddaughter—I am devotedly attached to her."

"My dear Sir William!" ejaculated the magistrate—

"my dear Sir William, you positively surprise me. Am I to understand——"

"Precisely; you are to understand, my most worthy friend and adviser in all temporal matters — you are to understand that I am devotedly attached to her; and —and I am here to-day to ask your consent to my becoming a suitor for her hand. I would make her my wife to-morrow, if that were possible."

Mr. Luke Darrell reclined back in his chair. He regarded his visitor over his spectacles, under his spectacles, and through his spectacles. He could make out no lurking, satirical smile upon the face of Sir William Blakeley.

"He must be serious, then," thought the old man; "yet, surely, he never can be serious."

"I would make her my wife to-morrow," iterated the baronet.

"My dear sir!" ejaculated the magistrate.

"Would walk with her before the proudest in the land."

"Gracious goodness!"

"Yes, I love the sweet, entrancing Nancy Darrell."

He cut another slice of pine-apple.

"I am lost in amazement! It never can be true?"

"It is as true as holy writ."

"Wonders will never cease!"

"They have ceased. Men learn to speak as they think, at least, I am doing so now. I love your grand-daughter."

Mr. Darrell rose from his chair and grasped the hand of his companion, which he shook warmly. The magistrate was an old man, his frame oscillated, and his voice became rather tremulous. As he sat down once more in his high-backed, leathern chair, studded all over with nails, like a coffin, for a moment or so he seemed to be gathering himself together, and arranging his ideas, much the same as a lawyer might arrange the papers before him that were connected with an intricate case which was put down for trial.

There was a pause, during which time the pine-apple suffered, for the baronet cut another slice, which he devoured. Then Mr. Darrell found his tongue once more, and proceeded in a more calm manner, much after the style that he was wont to assume when on the bench in his magisterial capacity.

"I cannot conceal from you, Sir William Blakeley, that I am both surprised and flattered at the declaration which you have just thought proper to make. You like candour?"

A nod.

"So do I."

Another nod.

"And I have to thank you for the candour evinced by yourself towards myself in this instance. I say I am flattered. It is natural that I should be so. I am childless, Sir William—childless now."

The speaker's voice faltered.

"Not childless while Nancy Darrell lives."

The old man put up his hand, as though he would fain be heard without interruption.

His companion was silent.

"I say childless; but perhaps I am wrong in saying so. But let that pass. My own Nancy—the mother of the present one of that name—has passed away. Now, my dear Sir William. Eh, dear me! I am not so young as I was; and—and these things upset me——"

"What! I hope——"

Another wave of the hand.

"I say I am not so strong or so young as I used to be; and that, at times—a-hem! I ought to forget the past, and bear my head proudly. But you will wonder what all this means, I dare say? I am wandering from the point. You have indeed done us honour, my dear friend, in thinking of our Nancy. I am afraid she's been a spoiled child; she has had her way in all things, and she comes and goes from Old Oak Farm as she pleases, without any questioning. Alas! her poor mother was spoiled; and was — I ought not to say it

now, perhaps, but she was as self-willed as it is possible to conceive any woman to have been. But——"

The old man paused suddenly.

"But what, my friend — but what?" inquired the baronet.

"Well, you see, Sir William; you like candour—I am sure you do by your conduct towards me. You talk of wedding our Nan; have you considered—have you considered, my friend, that she is an orphan? Have you considered all those antecedent circumstances which, I fear me may, and, indeed, ought to——?"

"To what?"

"Make you pause ere you rush blindly into a match which may prove distasteful to you in years to come."

"For what reason should you suppose such a thing. Oh, no, Mr. Darrell, I am not a man likely to regret having made such an alliance."

There was a hesitating and troubled manner about the old magistrate, as he observed—

"I must take a glance at the past before we come to anything like a conclusion," he said quietly, but with an evident nervousness in his tone.

"You are, perhaps, not aware, Sir William Blakeley, that my late daughter fled from her home with a man who had secretly wooed and won her affections. You are not aware, perhaps, that months passed over before either her mother or myself heard anything of her."

"I have heard some whisperings as to this," returned the baronet.

"It was true enough. Six months passed over. Our only child was lost to us. She was not dead, we knew that from a letter were ceived from her; but, for awhile, she was lost to us. In the letter she had chosen to write, she informed us that she had eloped with her lover, whom she had consented to marry in secret. I suppose that she had some reason for not choosing to return to her home. It might have been shame, perhaps, or it might have been her own wilful nature which prompted her to keep away. There was, and ever has been, a strange mystery about the whole of this dark and melancholy history — a mystery we have in vain endeavoured to penetrate."

The old man sighed, and paused for a minute or so.

"It is hardly worth while, Mr. Darrell, for you to enter into the history of events, the recital of which must necessarily pain you so much," observed Sir William Blakeley.

"I deem it my bounden duty to do so, Sir William," answered the magistrate, "but I will not indulge in tedious detail. It will be enough to declare that neither my wife nor myself saw anything of our daughter for many months. I have already told you this."

"Yes, you did."

"Eventually we heard of her. A message was brought by an old woman — a stranger to us — our daughter Nancy was in London. She was dangerously ill—indeed too ill to be removed. However, at all hazards, we had her brought here to the Old Oak Farm. She was very bad, poor girl—dreadfully bad "—the old gentleman wiped his eyes as he came to this part of his discourse—" so bad, that neither my wife nor myself deemed it advisable to mention anything about her clandestine marriage. If we had done so the probability is that we should not have been able to obtain any information from her, for soon—nay, almost immediately after—her return, her mind wandered—she had grown light-headed. After this, Sir William, she gave birth to a daughter, the present Nancy Darrell, for we named her after her mother—yes, she gave birth to her. My story is almost ended," said the old man, sadly; "there is little more to tell, my friend. The mother died, and the daughter we have here, as you know; and so—so that is the end of this sad history. Of course—of course, I cannot conceal from you, Sir William, that Nancy Darrell, my grand-daughter is—is——"

"What, my friend?"

"Well, she is hardly adapted, from her position in

life, and the circumstances of her birth—she's hardly adapted to become the wife of Sir William Blakeley."

"Mr. Darrell, you must be jesting," answered the baronet. "Not fit to become my wife! And wherefore not, I pray you? What has the accident of her birth to do with me? Nothing at all. It is not the poor girl's fault—she is not to be punished for the imprudence of her mother. How many run-away matches are there every year—nay, every month! My dear sir, you are visiting the sins of the parent on the head of the child. Oh, no, Mr. Darrell, that has nothing to do with the question. I love your daughter's child—I love Nancy Darrell, and, for the rest, why I would wed her."

He again had recourse to the pine-apple.

Mr. Luke Darrell took off his spectacles, and began to carefully wipe the glasses; he then looked at the table-cloth for a minute or so, after which he glanced at Sir William Blakeley.

"Umph! You know your own feelings best," he at length said, slowly. "You ought to know what is likely to conduce to your own happiness."

"Precisely. I hope—nay, I am sure I do. Have I your consent?"

"Consent to become a suitor for my granddaughter?"

"Yes."

"Of course, Sir William, you need hardly ask that; but again I beg of you to pause. Have you—have you made any declaration to Nancy?"

"I do not think I am positively obnoxious to her," said the baronet, with a smile. "Oh, I do not doubt, Mr. Darrell, but I shall receive a favourable answer from her."

"I should hope not. She knows herself too well not to feel honoured by such a preference."

"And, therefore, as far as you are concerned, we may conclude the matter settled?"

"Most decidedly."

The two companions then shook hands once more, and pledged each other in sundry glasses of wine.

CHAPTER VII.

THE BARONET MEETS WITH A CHECK.

Sir William Blakeley had been a frequent visitor at Old Oak Farm. On each occasion that he had chosen to honour it with his presence, Nan Darrell had received from him marked attentions, but, strange to say, she took but little notice of these civilities, and rather seemed to avoid the company of Sir William than court it. He was too acute a man of the world not to be fully aware of this. He was aware, also, that he was distasteful and objectionable to our heroine. Nevertheless, he had made up his mind to have her—that is, if it were possible for him to gain her consent.

In the after part of the day he offered his arm to Nan, and begged him to show her over the farm. Of course, neither Mr. Luke Darrell nor his wife thought proper to accompany them.

The slanting rays of the declining sun lighted up mead, meadow, and hedge-row, as Sir William and his fair companion took their way over the fields at the rear of the farmhouse. It was a lovely evening, and a fair English landscape that the sun shone on. Tourists and Continental pleasure-seekers may say what they will about foreign scenery, but an English landscape possesses charms that are not to be surpassed in more southern climes.

As the baronet and Nan Darrell went through the farmyard, and from thence into the fields beyond, but few words had been exchanged, beyond some passing observations upon the stock and crops of the magistrate.

After awhile the baronet said he was tired, and so he seated himself on a rustic seat, formed out of the remains of a tree which had been sawn down.

Nan sat beside him.

After a few preliminary a-hems, Sir William began.

"My dear Miss Darrell," he said, in his most mellifluous accents, "you may think me a strange creature, but I have been having some conversation with your grandfather respecting yourself."

"Indeed! You might have found some better subject to talk about," said Nan, with a sort of contemptuous smile.

"Impossible—that is quite impossible," returned her companion.

"You ought to be the best judge, I suppose," she answered, carelessly.

"You must know, my dear Nancy—you must allow me to call you so—you must know that you form the chief subject of my thoughts—nay, do not start: upon my soul it is true. I have told Mr. Darrell, this very afternoon, my feelings towards you."

"I do not understand what you mean, Sir William Blakeley. About your feelings towards me?"

"You must, indeed, then, be the very dullest of your sex. I love you, Nancy—devotedly, passionately love you. No man in his Majesty's domains loves with a more deep and absorbing passion than I do. Can I speak plainer?"

"It is plain enough," returned Nancy; "for the matter of that, it is exceedingly plain, and somewhat hackneyed; but I suppose it requires a plain answer?"

There was a degree of coolness and indifference about the manner of Nan Darrell which rather discomposed her ardent admirer.

"Well, a-hem! Yes, of course, it requires a plain answer; but you speak in such a dreadful matter-of-fact manner. Upon my word, Nan, I know not what to make of you."

"I have been frank enough with you at all times," she answered. "Why will you pester me with attentions which are both objectionable and repugnant to me? This is nothing new that you are broaching. I have told you, as I tell you now, that I cannot return your love, as you are pleased to term it."

"Pleased?" he ejaculated.

"Assuredly. I can hardly believe that you can be in love with one who has never given you any encouragement; and, to speak plainly, Sir William Blakely, I think you are too much a man of pleasure and too much a man of the world to lose your heart to such as myself. Be this as it may, I must once more distinctly tell you that I can never consent to look upon you in the light of a lover."

"You are very self-willed and positive. You do not believe in my sincerity?"

"I do not stop to inquire if you are sincere or not. Perhaps you think you are; perhaps you thought so when you wooed your last partner. All this is, however, nothing to the purpose. Perhaps we are not formed for each other, and as to our becoming united—bah! It is out of the question."

"There's Mr. Darrell's consent."

"That is nothing to me. Nan Darrell will choose for herself."

"You amaze me with this obstinacy."

"I tell you, as I have told you before, that I will never consent to become your wife. How many more times will you compel me to say this?"

Sir William Blakeley could ill suppress his rising temper. By a great effort, however, he managed to do so. Then he said more calmly—

"I know not what I have done that you should treat me thus scornfully. Have you a wish to insult me?"

"No; certainly not; but you would not have me play you false by affecting that which I never can feel. I do not love you—I never can, let that suffice."

"But it does not suffice, Miss Darrell. It will **not**

suffice. You must learn to love me. You ought to feel flattered at the offer I am making."

"I do not feel at all flattered."

"By my soul, I never saw such an extraordinary girl. You think I am too old for you, perhaps?"

"No, I do not say you are."

"What is it, then, that makes you so obstinate?"

"Sir William Blakeley," said Nan, in a tone of nervousness, "I think we ought to understand one another a little better than to be thus at issue upon a subject which has been so often discussed. We know each other too well to admit of disguise. It is not for me to censure you with respect to your conduct towards that unfortunate young man who paid the penalty for his crimes at Tyburn Tree. I hope and trust, sir, that you are not as culpable as I have been led to suppose."

"My dear Miss Darrell, you do me wrong. Believe me, you are doing me a serious wrong in supposing, for one moment, that I had any wish for him to be brought to trial. You do me a serious wrong in supposing this; on the contrary, I should have been too glad if he could have made his escape or eluded the officers of justice. In short, I should have been glad if he could have been saved at any cost or by any means."

Nan Darrell gave a smile of incredulity at this observation.

"You do not believe me?" said her companion. "I see from your countenance that you do not believe me."

Nan Darrell made no immediate reply to this.

The question was again repeated.

"I hope and trust you speak the truth," she answered, slowly. "I hope so, for your sake; and, moreover," she added, in a tone of satire, "you are a gentleman, and, as such, should speak the truth. I am also bound to believe you."

This speech did not appear to please the baronet, nor did it re-assure him in any way. He began to be fretful and ill-tempered.

Nan Darrell cared not for this, but continued, as her eyes were bent on the ground—

"I should indeed be sorry if Sir William Blakeley had so serious a charge to make against himself. I hope, for his sake, as well as for the credit of a family of which he is so distinguished a member—I should hope—nay, I trust—that he is guiltless of so foul an accusation as having brought a fellow-creature to so dreadful a doom."

The baronet looked not a little vexed at these observations of his companion, for he was at no loss to divine that they were meant as a sort of playful satire.

"Miss Darrell," he said, after a moment's reflection, "I am afraid that you are pre-disposed to take an unfavourable view of the question. I am aware that the world is but too prone to look on the worst side of things when the character of an individual is concerned; see that you do not follow so unworthy an example. James Neville has expiated his crimes on the scaffold. He was young to meet with so sad a fate; but, believe me, if any act of mine could have saved this unfortunate and misguided young man, I should have been but too glad to have rescued him from the fate which awaited him."

Nan Darrell bowed her acquiescence to this declaration.

"Oh, doubtless, sir—without a doubt," she ejaculated. "I am answered as to this matter—I am answered, sir, believe me."

"Enough," said the baronet—"enough upon a subject which must of necessity be a painful one for either of us to dwell upon. So let that pass. We have another and more important question to answer; at least, you have, my dear young lady. I lay at your feet all my worldly wealth, and offer you an unsullied name. I love you, Miss Nancy. You cannot have been so dull-witted as not to have observed that long since. I love you for yourself alone. You must acknowledge that mine must be a pure, disinterested passion; you must readily acknowledge that. What other actuating principle can there be to prompt me to this declaration, save and except the mighty love I bear towards you?"

"I know not," answered the baronet's fair companion.

"My dear young lady, can there be any other cause?"

"It matters little what is the cause that prompts you to make this offer; that matters little to me. I have given you my answer. Throughout our acquaintance my conduct towards you must have been quite sufficient to declare most unmistakably my sentiments towards you."

"Your conduct! To what do you allude?"

"Sir William Blakeley," returned Nan, "it is useless for you to affect ignorance upon this matter. I have never at any time offered you the slightest encouragement; you know that as well as I do myself. Why, then, pretend ignorance? This is not the first time—no, not the first time by many—that you have broached this question. I tell you frankly that it appears to me to be something like persecution for you to be thus persistent in pressing a suit which is both objectionable and obnoxious to me. I have given you my answer, once for all."

A dark shade of anger passed over the features of the baronet, and he could ill conceal his rage. There was a nervous twitching of the corners of his mouth as he bit his lips with vexation.

"You must be the most ill-advised and capricious of your sex to scorn an offer so honourable to yourself," he exclaimed, sharply. "And, truth to say, I will not—nay, I cannot—believe you are doing so seriously. You, who——"

"Ah, me, who by my birth and parentage is totally unworthy of so honoured a name as the one borne by Sir William Blakeley," returned Nan, quickly.

"Of that I am the best judge," said the baronet. "You must permit me to be the best judge upon that question. I esteem you worthy of me, or I should not make the offer; let that suffice. And for the rest, I declare candidly to you that I will not be trifled with, Miss Darrell. I have made you an honourable proposal, and you must pardon me if I say that you ought to be proud of the preference I have shown you. Believe me that there are many ladies, moving in higher positions in the world than yourself, who would gladly and cheerfully accept my offer."

"I do not doubt it, sir—I do not for one moment doubt this; there are, doubtless, plenty such. 'Twere wiser, therefore, for you to choose from one of these; choose one more worthy than myself."

"I cannot do so. My choice is made; I will have you, or none other. I have had patience enough, you must admit that. Now—mark me well, Miss Darrell—it would be as well for you to pause ere you put this insult on me."

"What insult?" she inquired.

"As great an insult as a woman can give one of the opposite sex—the refusal of his proffered hand. The hand of Sir William Blakeley is rejected with scorn by Miss Nancy Darrell. A fine tale, truly, for the gossips of the town to tell—a fine tale, ending with some half a dozen duels, perhaps."

"But who is there to tell the tale, unless it be yourself?" suggested Nancy. "Who is there that can possibly know of either the proposal or the rejection, besides my grandfather and ourselves?"

"That I am not able to answer at present; but I do not doubt but there will be found some petty, meddling busy-body who will moot the circumstance abroad. I do not doubt that for one moment; but all this is nought to the purpose. You have heard what I have had to say, Nancy. I have declared my sentiments towards you. I have told your grandfather, the good Mr. Darrell, and let me tell you, that it is your bounden duty to obey him in all things. I need not remind you of the trouble brought on your family by your mother's wilfulness. Remember that, Miss

Darrell; and remember, also, that you will be placed in a respectable position by an union with me. I may say, a more respectable position than, perhaps, under the circumstances, you might expect."

Nan Darrell made a face expressive of contempt at the last observation.

"I am sure I am very much obliged to you for this consideration on your part; but, as a respectable position is not what I desire——"

"Not desire it!"

"No, sir, I do not. At any rate, from your hands."

"I tell you what it is, Nancy Darrell," ejaculated the baronet, with considerable warmth. "I tell you what it is; you are a self-willed, obstinate, and, I may say, cold, insulting girl. Thou had'st best not anger me. You will find me no very pleasant fellow to have for an enemy; and enemy I most assuredly shall be if you persist in the course you are at present pursuing. You shall be mine, I tell you that."

"Shall be?"

"Ay, shall be! Mark me well," continued the baronet. "If we are to be enemies, why so be it. In any case you shall be mine. I will find means to reduce you to submission. I have sworn to have you—to have none other but you; and, by all the winds of heaven, I'll keep my word!"

Nan Darrell burst out into a fit of laughter.

"Oh, oh! my brave gentleman, you threaten, do you? —threaten! So be it. I defy you."

"Defy me? Have a care, Miss Darrell—have a care as to what you are saying, or it may be worse for you."

Nan Darrell rose from her seat, and regarded the speaker with a look of ineffable scorn.

"And, so Sir William Blakeley, this is how you would win a young maiden's love—by threats! Shame upon you! I, who never loved you, now both despise and contemn you. I will stay no longer to be subject to insults."

"Insults! What mean you?"

"Ay, to the worst of insults. You threaten to find means to reduce me to submission. By my soul! thou knowest but little of Nan Darrell to talk thus."

"I know mankind, my forward, self-willed lass; and I know, also, something of womankind. I say I will bring you upon your knees to sue to me."

Nan gave a mocking laugh.

"Ah, you are well tuned now," observed the baronet; "but I shall be able to spoil this music, so reflect ere it be too late. Thou had'st best have me for a friend, rather than choose to make me an enemy."

"A friend!" ejaculated Nan, with a sneer. "A friend! A pretty friend, truly."

"I have ever shown a wish to be one."

"To which I have not chosen to respond."

"That is true; but you will have wisdom in the future. You will perhaps learn wisdom when it is too late, like the rest of the world."

"I do not understand your meaning, sir."

"Ah, but you will—you will. Mark you that."

"I have no answer to make to this," exclaimed Nan, casting upon the baronet a malignant look, and taking her way towards the cottage.

She passed on, and left Sir William Blakeley alone.

"So," he ejaculated, "she treats me with sovereign contempt, the self-willed, haughty little jade; and yet she is exquisitely beautiful, and I am more than ever in love with her. She must and shall be mine! I have sworn that already, and I will keep my word in this, however much it may be forfeited in other matters. And now—now, what is to be said to my worthy friend, the magistrate? It will never do to tell him the result of my interview with his capricious granddaughter. Ah, no; it will not be advisable to do that. Has she another lover, I wonder? I never heard of any; but these girls are so cursedly sly in these matters."

The baronet came to a sudden pause in his soliloquy.

"Ah!" he ejaculated, "she knows more of this business — she knows more about the circumstances connected with James Neville than she chooses to declare—there can be but little doubt of that. Or, it may be — ah, it may be — that she has heard some ugly whisperings with regard to my late wife, whose stay was not so protracted as it might have been in this wicked and sinful world. Ugly whisperings! People will talk, and be hanged to them—they will talk."

The baronet rose from his seat and paced up and down the velvety lawn for several minutes. After he had somewhat composed himself he returned to Mr. Darrell's house, which he entered with a smiling, self-satisfied, buoyant countenance.

Mr. Darrell was gracious, and his wife was all amiability. They had already began to look upon him as their future son-in-law. Nan took but little notice of Sir William Blakeley. She remained in the parlour of the house for some little time after the scene between herself and the baronet in the garden; after this she went out upon the plea of visiting some neighbour.

Mr. Luke Darrell and his wife had always allowed her liberty. She had been accustomed to come and go whenever, or in whatever way, she chose. She had an extensive circle of acquaintance, and had all throughout her life been accustomed to spend a day or two, and sometimes many days, with one or the other of these, and no questions were asked. We shall see, as our story progresses, how this unlimited liberty had been used by Nan herself, and what a strange part she was destined to play in life's drama.

CHAPTER VIII.

THE HIGHWAYMAN'S HAUNT.—THE MYSTERIOUS CAVE.

THE reader must be apprised that very many of the incidents which will occur in the course of this narrative are drawn from authentic sources, and have for their foundation something more than the creative power of the romancist. They have for their foundation real facts, which the writer of this tale has had placed in his hands for the purpose of making public. The papers, in which these facts were narrated, were found in a cave. They comprise many startling and strange histories in connection with several celebrated highwaymen, and are the record of those days when the knights of the road were in their full zenith. These were different times to our own, and it is hardly possible for the youths of the present century to satisfactorily account for the daring exploits of highway robbers.

Few of our readers would understand the announcement of the first stage-coach which, God willing, would start from York on a certain day of the year 1750, and which would arrive, under the guidance of providence, some eight or ten days after. This seems, to us of the present day, to be a sort of jest; yet it may serve to give some notion of the infrequency of communication, and this infrequency threw a safety about the highwaymen, which, in this age of electric telegraphs, railways, and fast coaches is no more.

The highwayman who took a purse on the road had then only to ride across the country, and he was, comparatively speaking, as safe from pursuit or recognition as if at the time he had taken himself to some distant land.

The merchant, the lawyer, the farmer, the grazier, the commercial traveller, knew not the safety—or banks the convenience—of paper currency, or the accomodation of a ready or rapid transmission of valuable securities by post.

The grazier who drove up his live stock from the north, returned by easy stages on horseback—in or out of company as he might happen to be prudent or incautious, bold or cowardly—with the proceeds of his sale, in good old-fashionable guineas.

The farmer took his way to market, with leathern or canvass bag, well or scantily furnished, as his worldly means would permit.

[DICK TURPIN AND NAN AT THE COTTAGE.]

The commercial traveller proceeded on his rounds with goods of the more valuable or lighter description, in bulk, on pack-horse, or by broad-wheeled waggon-conveyance — now confined to the lowest and most needy of the populace.

For shorter distances round London and the great towns, there were, it is true, stage-coaches ; but these, from the slowness of their motions, were overtaken or stopped at pleasure, and this offered an easy prey to the knight of the road.

Another cause of impunity, and the contempt with which the laws were. treated by the violaters of them, was the corruption and inefficacy of our police regulations.

A more consummate set of scoundrels—as our criminal annals bear witness—could not be found than our subordinate administrators of justice. Perhaps the most notorious and less principled of these was the celebrated Jonathan Wild, surnamed "The Great." In the course of this narrative we shall have to give a history of this

No. 4.

man's doings, which will also be drawn from authentic sources. So, the reader who may be curious in the analization of crime and erring man, will have abundant materials to ponder over in our story of Nan Darrell.

The lapse of a few years after the period at which our tale opens, shows us seven thief-takers who ended their days at Tyburn Tree for various desperate crimes of which they had been convicted.

Need we wonder, therefore, that brave, daring fellows, such as Dick Turpin or Tom King, should run so striking a career, or that the roads in the neighbourhood of the metropolis should be so infested as to occasion the Duke of Newcastle to declare that, for a man of rank and property to travel fifty miles unmolested was so unusual that it became the exception, not the rule.

The character of Mackheath, in the "Beggars' Opera," is not overdrawn, though some modern critic has declared it to be so.

The scurvy, cogging, petty-larceny. knave of these degenerate-days' thieving can furnish no point of comparison to the dashing, well-dressed, well-mounted man who rode forth with primed pistols and jauntily-cocked hat to take a purse, and in so doing risked his life not so much at the gallows' foot as by the barrel of the man whom he boldly bid to "Stand and deliver."

Numerous are the anecdotes, and many the stories—and popular tradition is not far from the truth in its main features—of the generosity and bravery of those modern knights'-errants, such as Turpin, Du Val, and Tom King.

We must now beg the reader to accompany us to one of those most remarkable haunts—for it was at this place that, years afterwards, the papers were found which has enabled the writer of this work to throw a light on the doings of these celebrated knights of the road.

Just before the traveller arrives at the little village of Ealing, there is a lane on the right hand of the high road leading from London. At the time of which we write it was a deserted, lonely place—and, for the matter of that, it is not much to boast of in the present day —but at an earlier period it was so miserably deserted a locality that few persons would think of venturing down it after dark.

The lane was literally a swamp in some parts, especially in damp weather. Towards its centre—that is, about half-way through—it rose up into a miniature sort of hill, which ran through a dark and uninviting grove of trees. Near to this grove there was a cave, and it was here that, a few years ago, the highwaymen chronicles were found. The reader will not be surprised at this circumstance when he has accompanied us to this lonely and deserted spot, and is made acquainted with its leading features.

How the cave originally came there it would be difficult to say. We must leave antiquarians to speculate as to its origin. Possibly it was the bequest of the ancient Druids. Be this as it may, it afforded a safe retreat to the highwaymen of the day.

It was, in fact, for years their secret haunt.

At the farther end of the cave there was a small opening, which led to the foundation, or vaults, of an ancient edifice, supposed at one time to have been a monastery.

This strange place, with its strange occupants, had remained unknown to any one but these highwaymen. The monastery itself had passed away: the plough of the careful husbandman had tilled the soil upon which it stood; but still, beneath this very soil, there remained the vaults, deep sunk in the earth, where the ascetic monks of old were wont to do penance.

We will now take a glance at the place.

It is night—a dark and starless night. Along the high road leading from Ealing to London a solitary figure is taking her way—for it is that of a woman, or rather that of a girl. This solitary traveller is our heroine, Nan Darrell. She speeds along the road, which is of a pitch-like darkness, there being no lamps to dissipate the gloom. Nevertheless Nan takes her way along without pausing or evincing any fear. She pauses not till she arrives at the corner of the lane we have already described.

Here she halted and looked around. While thus engaged a low whistle is heard.

Nan Darrell waits patiently for a minute or so, and is joined by a man dressed as a countryman.

"This ain't a very lively road, Miss, for so delicate a young lady as yerself, but the cap'n bid me wait for ye, an' I've been here for half an hour, at the very least."

All this was spoken in a respectful and almost friendly manner, although the speaker was as rough a looking specimen of humanity as it was well possible to conceive.

"I should have found but little difficulty in reaching the appointed spot," answered Nan. "Nevertheless, my friend, I am equally obliged to you, and will avail myself of yourself by way of escort. We had better proceed down the lane."

"Yes, Miss, an' ye please—to the cave. There are a number of them in the vaults."

"A number! Eh? I would speak with Turpin. I hope he is there?"

"Aye; he is there, sure enough. Say what they may of Dick, he keeps his word, and ain't one o' yer slippery, uncertain customers like King. We shan't have to lope the dancers (go up stairs); there ain't no call for that—not in the ken we are goin' to."

"The road to your reatreat is none of the choicest," observed Nan.

"Well ye see, Miss, we don't court company. Not but what such a lady as yourself must lend a charm to any place."

"Upon my word you are quite complimentary," said his fair companion with a smile. "How long is it since you have learnt to make pretty speeches?"

The man seemed either unwilling or unable to make a reply.

"Eh! how often? I suspect it is the company you have been keeping. The many gallant gentlemen who honour you with their society has made you quite refined."

"Well, Miss, a cove as waits upon a bridle cull (highwayman) is apt to pick up a bit of their patter. Be keerful, be very keerful in this part of the road. Keep to the right, for the centre of it is under water. Mercy on us, but 'tis a place for a lady like yerself to come down. It is a place. Be keerful."

"Oh, I shall be able to pick my way along, never fear," answered Nan Darrell. "I am used to the country you know."

"Ye trip over the ground like a young fawn," observed the man, who was evidently disposed to be in a complimentary mood.

After a miserable walk through the dark and wretched-looking lane, the two travellers found themselves in front of the cave.

Nan Darrell appeared to know the locality well, for, dark as it was, she entered without hesitation.

When inside the cave she became aware that there were three horses there besides one or two men, who respectfully saluted her entrance.

Her conductor went to the farther end of the place and rolled back a large stone.

An aperture was then discovered, sufficiently large for the passage of one person, who would be able to creep through it by bending either his or her body. Nan did not find much difficulty in passing through this. She then went down a flight of rudely-cut stone steps; then there came another flight; after which she was in the vaults below.

It was indeed a singular-looking place. It was lighted up by three or four candles from carriage lamps. These were placed in cleft sticks. The figures of several men were seated on some barrels which were to be seen at various parts. Some of these men were carousing.

The apartment in which our heroine found herself consisted of an arched vault supported by stout columns.

As Nan entered a man stepped forward from the group of freebooters, and walked up to her side. This personage was none other than Dick Turpin, the celebrated highwayman. Unlike the rest of his companions, his countenance wore a grave aspect. He was, moreover, kind and gentle in his manner towards the beauteous visitant of the highwaymen's haunt.

"You expected me, I suppose," said Nan.

Turpin nodded.

"I could not well leave earlier," she observed, gaily. "But I trust I am not too late."

"No, you are in good time," answered Turpin. "We have business on to-night, but there is a time for all things, Miss Darrell."

Then, as Nan looked inquiringly round, her companion said with a smile—

"Oh, he is not here. Not but he would have been

safe enough; only it is as well for him not to venture out of his present hiding-place. I don't want to see him in *the rumbo* (Newgate), nor in the *spinning ken* (Bridewell) for the matter of that. A *quod cull* ain't a pleasant customer to take charge of a born gentleman."

"I came hither on purpose to see him," said Nan, in a tone of disappointment.

"And so you shall," answered Turpin, "so you shall. I have passed you my word, and you shall not be disappointed. You are in no hurry I suppose?"

Nan hesitated.

"Hurry—no!" she answered, after a pause. "Wherefore do you ask?"

"Because we have a short half-hour's ride or so before us, that is all. Are you willing to accompany me?"

"I have come hither to place myself under your guidance, as I know you are my friend, as well as the friend of one who is, and ought to be to me dear."

"Enough," cried Turpin. "Here, Chitty!"

Nan's conductor to the highwayman's haunt came forward.

"Your servant, captain, your servant," said this worthy.

"Take Bess and the flea-bitten horse to the old oak-tree in the shrubbery," said Dick. "And hark ye, Chitty, see that the girth is all right, for a lady is to ride him."

"One might guess that, master, seeing that the flea-bitten nag has a ladies' saddle on his back," returned Chitty with a laugh.

"Ah, you are a clever fellow," remarked Turpin. "Too sharp by half. I shall never make my money of you that is quite certain."

"Cos vy? I shall be caught up by some one as knows my walue," answered the man.

"There, that will do. Be off and do my bidding. Dost hear?"

Chitty made no further remark, but disappeared at once from the vault.

"Hurrah!" ejaculated a gentleman on one of the tubs, as he held up a glass of sparkling wine. "Hurrah! A toast, comrades—a toast! Health, long life, and happiness to the beauteous Miss Darrell!"

"Health, long life, and happiness to Miss Darrell!" shouted out half a dozen voices.

"Gentlemen, I thank you for your good wishes," answered Nan, quickly.

"Are you going to make this a *boosing ken?*" said Turpin.

"There's not a *bridle cull* in all England who would not lay down his life for Nancy Darrell," said the proposer of the toast, whose voice, by the way, was getting rather thick.

"Go to Mat!" ejaculated Turpin. "I fear me much that thou art more like a *lapping cull* (a drunkard) than 'other thing."

At this speech there was a vociferous roar of merriment, which seemed to rather discompose the gentleman on the barrel, who, however, solaced himself with another glass of wine.

"You know, Mat, you ain't good for anything till you are about half-slewed," said another of the party.

"I know that, my lad—I know that. I drink to live and live to drink," returned the convivial gentleman, who then burst out in a snatch of song—

> "Fill the bottle—pass the glass—
> Hearts beat lighter 'neath its flow;
> Drink to beauty; see! her eye
> Sparkles, brightened with its glow."

"Oh! here's to the bright eyes of lovely woman," said the speaker, as he glanced towards Nan Darrell. "She comes upon us like a glorious rainbow from heaven. Her eye is the loadstone of attraction—her voice is the music of the spheres. Oh, I could discourse for ever on her many charms, and her endless attractions! Oh, woman! lovely woman!"

"There, that will do, Mat," said Turpin, with a smile. "Venus and Bacchus are rare deities in their way, but I suspect you worship the latter more than the former."

"I do not—on my soul, I do not!"

"Oh, hear him—hear this man!" exclaimed several voices. "What will he say next?"

"I love the sex," returned the bacchanalian—"I love the sex. Don't you believe what my companions say, Miss Darrell. There is not a more devoted admirer of the gentler sex than myself."

"Except Tom King," said one of the party.

"Or Claude du Val," ejaculated another.

"Talk of the —— Oh, I beg your pardon, here is Tom."

A man of genteel appearance now entered the vaults. It was, in truth, none other than Tom King.

When he caught sight of Nan Darrell he took off his hat with a grace that would have done credit to a nobleman. Nan held out her hand which he shook warmly, but at the same time he treated her with singular respect.

There was something about the appearance of King —so Nan thought—that seemed to indicate that nature had intended him for better things. His features were decidedly prepossessing. Besides this he had the manner and bearing of a gentleman. His hand was remarkably small, white, and delicate. Indeed, it was as small as many women's.

Neither had he the jaunting, self-satisfied, and in many cases, the audacious bearing of a highwayman; and it would have been difficult for a superficial observer to have even guessed the lawless nature of his occupation, for he was modest and almost retiring in his manner when in the company of virtuous or well-conducted females.

He was a rake, as most of us know, if we are to rely on the history of the times; but he was not a low, sensual rake, or an habitual debauchee. He was, and had been throughout the whole of his short career, the victim of the sex. To the treachery of one of these he owed his death.

Supposing Turpin to be engaged in conversation with Nan Darrell, Tom King strolled up to the group which were a little removed from where our heroine and her companion were standing.

"I do not drive your friend away, I hope," remarked Nan to Turpin. "Possibly he thinks we have some private matters to talk about."

"No," said Turpin, "that is his way. Tom seldom intrudes himself upon others, and, to say the truth, he is generally reserved, save and except at those times, Miss Darrell, when he chooses to unbend in the company of his more intimate associates. Then he can be merry and careless enough."

"And yet it has always struck me that there was a certain degree of melancholy about him, with all his affected merriment."

"There can be no doubt about that. Tom was destined for better things, Miss Darrell. He is an easy, good-natured – fool I was going to say."

"Which you have said," returned Nan, with a smile.

"Yes; but do not misunderstand me. Tom is no fool; on the contrary, he is far ahead of me in many things—and I don't put myself down as a fool yet, either—but he's weak in many things."

"And yet you know him better than most persons, I should say."

"Better than anyone, Miss Darrell—I think I may say that with safety—I should say, better than anyone. He has had many advantages. He has received a good education, which I have not. He came from a first-rate family; and, I think—yes, I think that, at times, the remembrance of his earlier days, and the gentle sisters who are now for ever cut off from him— I think that this renders him sad and melancholy; and so he flys to any excitement to drown reflection."

"Which we are unable to," observed Nan Darrell—"which none of us are able to do successfully."

As our heroine made this observation, her glance was directed towards Tom King, who was engaged in conversation with a small knot of those men who occupied the highwayman's haunt.

His eye met Nan's, whereupon he lowered it, and was about to turn away, when Dick Turpin called to him.

King then came up to the side of Nan and her companion.

"Look here, Tom—we are going to see a certain party to-night; you may guess whom—this lady's father."

"Yes, I understand."

"Would you like to go with us?"

"I will meet you afterwards, where you please."

Turpin smiled.

"Ah, a bird in the hand is worth two in the bush."

"What mean you?"

"Simply what I say, my friend—a bird in the hand is worth two in the bush; and Tom, being by your side, is worth twenty Toms away. That's what I mean."

"Oh, you don't put much trust in my word—that's it, eh?"

"Well, something very much like it."

"I will keep it this time—I will, upon my honour."

"Good. Do so, and I shall think better of you."

Turpin then took his companion on one side, and whispered something in his ear.

King nodded, and, taking his hat once more off, and respectfully saluting Nan, he rejoined his companions.

By this time the man whom we have known as Mat came to the side of our highwayman, and said that the horses were both ready, and waiting at the appointed place.

Dick Turpin and Nan then left the vaults, and proceeded in the direction of the grove of trees where Black Bess and the flea-bitten horse were tethered.

Nan was an accomplished horsewoman, and, after she had mounted her steed, Turpin threw over her graceful figure a cloak of ample dimensions.

In a few minutes or so after this both of them cantered off towards the high road.

CHAPTER IX.

NAN DARRELL'S INTERVIEW WITH HER FATHER.

BUT few words were exchanged between the two during their passage through the wretched lane which led to the highwaymen's haunt. They found it no very easy task to travel along the ill-made road.

Eventually, when they reached the Ealing-road, they seemed to be a little more hopeful, and Nan said to her companion—

"Have we far to go? and what is the reason that my father could not come to yonder place, as he had promised?"

Dick Turpin gave a preliminary "a-hem," and then said—

"Why, you see, miss, gentlemen of our profession can't always do as we could wish. He might have done so, but there would be a great risk. He's under a cloud at present. That old ferret, Wild, wants him—there's no doubt about that; he wants him, and, if possible, he means to have him. My friend, Captain Ragget, don't seem to have been able to square matters with the old thief-taker; and so, you see, there's no help for it, but he must keep out of the way for a time, at any rate."

"Oh," ejaculated Nan Darrell, "what dreadful fatality was it that led my father to——"

She paused suddenly.

"To follow this course of life, you would say," interposed Turpin.

"Yes, precisely."

"Ah, it's too late to talk about that now—too late. When once a man is on the road, he seldom leaves it. There is a charm, my dear Miss Darrell, which you ladies can never understand—a charm even in the very danger attending it. Your father has been a gallant man—has fought for his king and country; and how did they serve him? I need not tell you—with base ingratitude."

"I know. He has often told me that he contracted habits of extravagance when he was better off—habits which he could not give up when circumstances were less prosperous with him."

"Habits which he had no right to give up," said Turpin—"which he had no right. What was the consequence? Had he met with his deserts from the hands of the government, he would not have been what he is now. But its no use our dwelling upon all this You know the greater portion of the history, I dare say."

"Yes, I know a great portion of it; and I know, moreover, that both he and I owe you a deep debt of gratitude, for I know he would have been by this time in prison had it not been for your kindness."

"Oh, don't name that," said Turpin; "don't trouble yourself to thank me. Dick Turpin isn't much used to that sort of thing. Your father, Captain Ragget, and myself were old pals. He's above me, you know, both by birth and education; but still we've always been the best of friends, and I should think it hard if we couldn't serve one another on a pinch. How is Mr. Luke Darrell and his lady?"

"They are well enough," answered Nan, reflectively. "I have been bothered again to-day with Sir William Blakeley."

"Whew!" ejaculated Turpin. "Sir William—eh?"

"Yes."

"And how has he bothered you?"

"The old story—by his attentions."

"Be careful of that man, Miss Darrell—be careful of him. He's cruel and crafty."

"He wants to marry me."

"Marry *you*?"

"Yes."

"By the Lord Harry! I'd see him at the farther end of the world before I consented to that, were I a woman. Marry you, indeed! Ask him how he got rid of his first wife."

"Why, how did he, do you suppose?"

"Can't say; but I can guess."

"Well, how?"

"Not by the fairest means in the world, if report speaks truly. Oh, he's a bad lot, he is."

"Not by the fairest means. Why, he did not surely make away with her? He surely had not the heart to do that?"

"I'm afraid he did, though—that I most certainly am; I'm very much afraid he did. Oh, have nought to do with Sir William Blakeley—have nought to do with him."

"I don't intend; and so I have told him."

"So much the better."

"Ah! it's a sad thing," said Nan, "a very sad thing to be situated as I am, Turpin. My poor grandfather little knows the company I see at times; he little dreams that his grandchild is the daughter of a highwayman."

"And may Mr. Darrell never know it!" ejaculated Dick.

"May he go down to his long last rest without having so bitter a reflection to make his last hours miserable!"

"I say 'Amen' to that prayer, Miss Darrell. Your grandfather is too worthy a man, for all that he is a magistrate and an administrator of the law as it at present stands—he is too worthy a man to be brought to sorrow in his old age."

"He has been indulgent enough to me, and has allowed me latitude enough, for the matter of that, or I could never have done as I have."

"There can be but little doubt of that. He has

allowed you more latitude than any young lady of your age has a right to expect."

"Do you think my father is in danger?" inquired Nan.

"Well, as to that, there can be but little doubt upon the matter. He is in danger, as everyone is who is out of the good graces of Mr. Jonathan Wild."

"Is this man so great, that he should dictate who is to be convicted and who is to escape?"

"Indeed, I fear that such is the case," answered Turpin. "He does a rare business at his house in town. It has been reported that he has his chaplain, groom of the chambers, gentleman of the horse, and others to attend him, and, in fact, that he lives after the manner of the nobility. His table is very splendid, and he seldom dines under five dishes, the reversions whereof are generally charitably bestowed upon the common malefactors."

"Can this be possible?"

"Oh, you cannot guess the influence this man has," answered Dick. "There is a creature of his, by the name of Quilt Arnold, who serves in the quality of clerk on the northern road; there's another, Abraham Mendez, a Jew, who takes charge of the western road. I believe this fellow to be a sober and well-conducted man enough. As soon as anything is missed, the first thing people do is to make for the office of Mr. Wild. If what they want is a trinket, either enamelled or with a painting about it—if it be a particular ring, the gift of a friend, or anything which they esteem above the real value, and offer more for it, they are looked upon as good chaps, and are welcome to redeem it."

"How very kind!" exclaimed Nan.

Turpin continued—

"But if it be plain gold or silver, they will hardly see it again, unless they pay the worth of it."

"And do people often pay for their goods after they have been robbed of them?"

"Very often they do. Some years ago it is true a man might, for half a piece, have fetched back a snuff-box that weighed twenty or thirty shillings, but this was in the infancy of the establishment. Wild has grown wiser, and is enabled to calculate exactly what such a thing will melt down for."

Nan Darrell could not refrain from bursting out in a fit of merriment at the cool manner of her companion.

"If you can hear no signs of your goods," continued Dick, "it is counted as a sign that they are in the hands of irregular practitioners, who steal without permission of the board. In this case it is best to put an advertisement in the public newspapers."

"Then Wild is in league with most of——"

"Of the profession," said Turpin, quickly. Precisely; he is in with all the regular practitioners, and it is supposed that he can save or hang whom he pleases."

Nan Darrell gave a sort of shudder, as she reflected upon the imminent danger of her father, Captain Ragget."

"I can imagine your anxiety," said Turpin, kindly, looking furtively at his companion. "You tremble for the fate of the captain."

"Indeed I do," answered Nan. "If this man's power is so great I tremble for him. What is the reason that my father cannot propitiate this celebrated thief-taker? what can be the reason?"

"Ah, that is more than I can tell," answered Turpin. "Master Wild don't let people know more than is absolutely necessary for his purpose. He has a reason without a doubt, and a good one, too."

"You make me most miserable," ejaculated Nan. Ah, that I were a man to strike down this audacious and vindictive thief-taker."

"My dear young lady he is too desperate a fellow to be dealt with easily, even supposing you were a strong, powerful man. Have you not heard of the recent case?"

"What one?"

"Of the two noblemen who were robbed of several valuables."

"No I have not heard of it, how should I?"

"True, I forgot, I thought I was speaking to one of my own craft. Well then, Lord B——ce and the Earl of H——n were robbed in Richmond Park of a gold watch and a blue sapphire ring of great value, besides a considerable sum in money. Wild was soon on the scent. I know not by what means he managed it; that I will not pretend to determine at present; but he knew the rogues, and being informed of the haunts of one James Wright, formerly a peruke maker on Ludgate-hill, this individual was one of the persons connected with the fact."

"And Wild found him out?"

"Yes, you are right, he did. Having traced him, he apprehended him at the Queen's Head Tavern on Tower-hill. He took him in the kitchen of this establishment before a great number of persons, and after the most obstinate and determined resistance that a robber ever made—for Wright drew his pistols and was well nigh getting the best of the conflict, but Wild being so closely engaged with him he had no time to cock his pistols, and the thief-taker held him fast by the chin with his teeth till he had dropped his fire-arms—he was eventually surrounded and taken to Newgate. He was tried and convicted, and being connected with other robberies in Middlesex, he was executed at Tyburn, being the first malefactor that ever went there in a shroud."

"Poor fellow!" ejaculated Nan Darrell, "poor fellow!"

"You pity him. He was guilty——"

"Well, and what then?"

"Oh!" said Turpin; "true, what then? There are numbers of others equally guilty. I see you have a gentle, sympathising heart, Miss Darrell. Well, this proved a rare good job for Jonathan Wild, who, besides Lord B——'s gold watch which was found in Wright's pocket, had the whole reward as given by act of Parliament for the apprehension and conviction of a highwayman."

"And is it possible that this wretch sells the lives of men in this remorseless manner?" ejaculated Nan. "A time will come when he too shall meet with his deserts."

"Why, my dear Miss Darrell," answered Turpin, "he has but recently laid a paper before the authorities in which he declared that he had been instrumental in apprehending more than a hundred and fifty persons, the greater number of which had been prosecuted according to law, and most of whom had been brought to punishment for their crimes."

"And you, you, dost thou not fear this man?"

"Who?"

"Jonathan Wild."

"I fear no man living when across the back of my bonny Black Bess," answered Dick, patting the neck of the beautiful animal he bestrode. "No, Miss Darrell, I fear no man in his Majesty's dominions while possessed of so faithful a mistress as this same matchless steed, whose feet are fleeter than the wind, and who is as true as the needle to the pole. No, so long as Dick Turpin has Black Bess, he snaps his fingers at fate and at Jonathan Wild, too, for the matter of that. But a time must come—ah! it must come—when these lithe limbs will lose their elasticity—when this bright eye will lose its brightness, and then, ah! then, farewell to the career of Richard Turpin."

"And is your fate so intimately interwoven with the noble animal you place such implicit confidence in?"

"I fear so. May that time be far distant, for she's the only living creature that loves me now," said the highwayman, with a sigh and a strangely altered manner—"the only living thing."

"Nay, not so, Turpin," ejaculated Nan—"not so."

"She's the most faithful, then," returned the highwayman, whose voice had suddenly become plaintive.

Neither of the two travellers seemed disposed to continue the conversation, for there was a silence for some few minutes after this ; at the expiration of which time they came in sight of a low-roofed cottage, which stood in some fields at some quarter of a mile or so from the road.

Dick Turpin pointed to this habitation with his riding-whip. Nan's eyes followed in the direction he was pointing.

"There—there it is," said Dick. "Yonder's the cottage."

"What?—which?"

"The cottage where Captain Rugget lies concealed. It ain't a very lively-looking place."

"Is my poor father in yonder house, then?"

The highwayman nodded an assent to this query.

They turned their horses' heads in the direction, and, in a few minutes more, they were in front of the habitation.

Nan was about to dismount, but her companion desired her not to do so. He then stooped down, and opened a gate at the side of the house. When he had done this, Black Bess, without any guidance from her master, entered the grounds at the side of her own accord.

She was well acquainted with the place.

Nan Darrell followed.

Then Dick Turpin made his way to an outhouse, the door of which he opened with a key he pulled from his pocket. He then dismounted and assisted Nan off her flea-bitten quadruped.

He then took this last-named animal, as well as the matchless mare he had been riding, and led them into the outhouse, which proved to be a rough sort of stable.

When this was done he turned to Nan.

"Now, Miss," said Dick, "I am your humble servant. With your permission we will enter the cottage. It is not my practice, as you will perceive, to take much trouble in having myself announced."

Offering his arm to Nan Darrell, the most celebrated highwayman of his day escorted her into the primitive-looking habitation, the door of which he opened without taking the trouble to knock.

When Nan and her companion entered, the first person they saw was a woman advanced in years, plaiting some rushes, with which she was making a mat. Several newly-made mats were visible in one corner of the room.

She looked up from the work she was engaged on, and adjusted her spectacles.

"All right, mother," said Dick. "Don't flurry yourself, old girl. Has anyone been here?"

"No, Mr. Richard. No; none that you cares about. Only people to see me and the good man."

"Ah, exactly. Where is the good man?"

"Yours, or mine?" inquired the old dame, with a half-comic look.

"Well, yours, I meant; not that I want to see him."

"Oh, he's not far afield. Here, Davy! Davy! Here's Mr. Richard."

At these words an old man, the husband of the woman, came hobbling into the parlour of the cottage.

"Yer servant, sir; and yours, miss," said the newcomer, bowing respectfully to Nan, for, say what you will, beauty will always command a certain amount of adoration from the old as well as the young.

"Well, governor, all's quiet, it seems. No storms ahead, at present?" said Dick, carelessly.

"All has been as quiet as the grave; but, poor, dear gentleman, he do dislike being pent-up in this here sort of fashion; he do dislike it, surely."

"That is not to be wondered at, Davy. We none of us like to be cooped up away from our pals, with the prospect of *rumbo* or *whit* (Newgate) in the distance. It ain't a pleasant prospect, my friend."

Without further ado, Dick Turpin made his way into a washhouse, or what was originally a brewhouse, at the back part of the house. As he did so, he bid Nan follow him. When they had arrived at this place,

Turpin removed a mass of rushes which strewed the floor, and lifted up a trap-door. A series of wooden steps were disclosed.

He signified to his companion that she must descend by these.

Without hesitation she did so. Whereupon Turpin followed, leaving the old man in the brewhouse alone.

Nan then found herself in a place which looked like a cellar : such in reality it was.

There was a table, sofa, and two or three chairs in this place, which was lighted by a solitary candle.

By the side of the table there was seated a man, who rose at the entrance of his two visitors.

It could be then seen that his form was above the middle height, without being actually tall. Although by no means what might be termed a young man, he was yet in the prime of life, and was still remarkably handsome ; but there were traces of care, anxiety, and, alas! dissipation upon his originally fine features.

"Dick, my worthy and most constant friend," said Ragget; "through bad report and good report—through fortune and misfortune, you are still the same—as true as steel, and as constant as the Polar star."

The two highwaymen shook hands warmly.

"Father!" exclaimed Nan Darrell; "dear father!"

Captain Ragget folded his daughter in his arms in one fond, long embrace. Then came one of those scenes between parent and child, to depict which description must necessarily fail.

Turpin paused for a moment at the foot of the ladder by which he had descended. He then said—

"I will leave you for awhile, Captain Ragget, and will return shortly."

The captain nodded, and Dick once more took his way into the brewhouse.

Father and daughter were then left alone. When the first outpourings of affection were over, Captain Ragget handed Nan to a seat. He sat down himself, and contemplated those beauteous features, so full of health, youth, and freshness.

He then sighed deeply, and passed his hand in a troubled manner across his brow.

He seemed to be endeavouring to collect his thoughts and re-compose himself. Presently he rose from his seat and paced up and down the narrow confines of his prison-house.

"Nan," he exclaimed, as he suddenly paused, and brought himself to a halt in a sort of military way, "I have much wished to see you, for many reasons. You know, my girl, that at present I am under a cloud."

Her only reply was a nod. The captain continued—

"And I know not how soon it may discharge itself, and bring me to destruction. But no matter about that, not as yet."

"Oh, father!"

"Nay, do not interrupt me. I am, and have been for years past, prepared for the worst; and, to speak the truth, of late things seem to be coming to the worst. But no matter—no matter. I have something to say to you, my child."

He approached, and, placing his hands upon her marble forehead, caressed her fondly.

"Nan, thou art, as you well know, the daughter of Captain Orlando Ragget, the highwayman, the companion of Turpin and King—of Du Val and Spike. I would not pass away from this world and leave behind me a foul blot upon my child's name. I would not do so if it were possible to avoid such a sad and miserable heritage to one who is to me dearer than my own life—ay, ten times dearer, for that has been forfeited long ago."

"But you do not—you do not leave any stigma upon my name," said Nan, quickly, for she saw her father was deeply moved. "Why trouble yourself about me?"

"My child, it is necessary that I should do so. Now hear me. Thou hast never divulged to any living soul, beyond my companions in—in crime—thou hast never divulged to anyone else the secret of thy birth?"

"Never, never."

"Thou art sure of this?"

"Most certainly I am. Wherefore should you doubt me?"

"I do not doubt you," said Captain Ragget, solemnly, "because I have ever had reason to believe in your truthfulness. No, I do not doubt you; but let me charge you now—let me beg of you as a last request——"

"A last request?"

"Well, no. We will not call it that; but should it prove so, and should circumstances turn out that I do not see you again—we will say for years, perhaps—remember this in all your trials and troubles, for you are young, my child, and must have them—no one passes through the world without them—remember this, as you hope for Heaven's mercy hereafter—that thy father asked but one poor favour of you, not for his own sake so much as for thine. Remember that he begged of you, under no chance or circumstance, to ever divulge the secret of thy birth."

"I will remember."

"Swear it."

"I do swear never to divulge the secret of my birth."

"Good. So far so good. No one suspects at present?"

"No one can do so."

"And the old people—they are kind?"

"Oh dear, yes. It is impossible for them to be more so."

"And you are happy?"

Nan made no immediate reply.

"And you are happy, my child?" again inquired Ragget.

"I should be so, if——"

"Ah, I see, if it were not for my present situation, and, alas! my calling. Enough upon that head. It is too late now for me to be aught else—too late."

He looked proudly at his daughter and reflected for some minutes. He placed his hand on her head, and drew her towards him. Her head reclined upon his chest, while his hand carressed her cheek.

"You will remember what I have been saying, Nan?"

"I shall never forget it."

"How well this secret has been kept. How wonderfully well. A secret that has been in the keeping of one—two women, for you are a woman now."

"Almost," said Nan, with an attempt at a smile. "I shall soon call myself one."

"Thy poor mother died without ever telling the name of her husband. She passed out of this world, and the dread secret was buried with her."

"My mother I never knew."

"No, she died when thou wert an infant, and now—now thou art grown up into a blooming woman, Nan, and still the secret has been kept. Let it be so, for now and hereafter. Thy path in life may be as spotless as mine has been full of crime. Thou mayest yet hold up thine head in the best society, and none will deem that Nan Darrell—the gentle, fair, and accomplished Nan Darrell—is the daughter of Orlando Ragget, the highwayman."

"And did—did Mr. Darrell never know you, then?" inquired Nan.

"No—never. I have seen him, it is true, but I should hardly recognise him. No, my child, we never knew each other. Thy mother was allowed more latitude than was usually permitted to girls of her age. Alas! she made bad use of it in marrying me; but she was true and constant, and we loved each other. She paid a dear penalty for her attachment to me. Heavens! it appears that all I have ever cared about have been sorely chastened by the wrath of Heaven. And, after all, I do not know that this is to be wondered at, seeing the career I have run."

The highwayman heaved a deep sigh.

"Oh, it pains me so much to see you so sorely troubled." exclaimed Nan, winding her arms round her father's neck. "Is there no way of escape?"

"What mean you?"

"No way of escape from Jonathan Wild?"

"Ah, the wretch! I have baulked him for the present, but I know not for how long. Every hour I am in fear of detection."

"What do you purpose doing?"

"I am, as you see, concealed here for the present. Turpin and King are both of them on excellent terms with Wild, and I suppose are likely to continue so, for they appear to have always been in his good graces. Dick has put him on the wrong scent, and it is through him that I am placed here. Nevertheless, Wild is such a cunning rascal that I am, of course, afraid that he will, in the end, prove more than a match for all three of us."

"But is there no way of getting out of this trouble."

"My dear girl, it is not likely that you can understand these things. Alas! you have already been too much called into the association of those who are not fit companions for you."

"I have heard nothing from the lips of either King or Turpin that would cause the most prudent young lady to blush," answered Nan, with sudden warmth. "On the contrary, they have both behaved to me with singular respect and kindness."

"I do not doubt it," answered Captain Ragget—"I do not for a moment doubt it. Whatever they may be, and however they may be connected with lawless characters, they have too much chivalry left in their compositions to say aught that might pollute or offend the ears of a virtuous young lady, more especially when that young lady is known by them to be my daughter."

"Of that I have already sufficient proof."

"But thy walk of life is far removed from such associations. Thou must hold thine head up with the best and noblest in the land. Remember this, Nan, and forget, the while, who—who was thy father; for I would not that my sins should be visited on your head. I am glad thou hast come hither this evening, for many reasons. In the first place, I intend—if it be possible to accomplish it—I intend to leave the country—to go abroad for a time."

"To go abroad?" said Nan Darrell, with some alarm.

"Yes, surely. It is the only course that I can adopt. While here, I am in hourly danger. Turpin knows this as well, or better than I do myself. When once out of the country, it is possible enough that this cloud will blow over; and then, when I am forgotten, I can return, and—and possibly some fresh channel may be opened to me."

"Go abroad! Is there any occasion for such a course?"

"I believe there is, or I should not think of adopting it."

"For how long?"

"That must, of course, depend upon circumstances."

"Is there no other course?"

"Alas! I see no other at present."

"Oh, but this is a sad alternative."

"Why so, my dear girl? It will only be for a time."

"But I do not like to lose you."

"It will only be for a time; and then, again, I shall be out of harm's way, and there will be no risk, as there is at present, by your favouring me with these secret meetings."

"But I have been accustomed to visit you for years past, and no harm has come of it; and I will see my own dear father in any place, and at any time," said Nan Darrell, laying her sweet face on the thick beard of her parent. "I will see him, and no one shall prevent me."

Captain Ragget smiled, half with pleasure, and half sadly.

"Like thy poor mother, Nan—like her, thou art self-willed," he ejaculated.

"And I intend to be self-willed on that point," she answered, quickly.

"Remember what I have told you: never divulge the secret of your birth."

"I will keep my word, depend on it. You need be under no apprehension as to that, my own dear father."

"And so farewell, my child. It will be as well not to prolong this interview. Thou must return to Old Oak Farm as speedily as may be."

"I am in no hurry to return."

"Nay, but Mr. Darrell—the good Mr. Darrell—he will be inquiring for you, perhaps."

Nan gave a toss of her pretty head.

"Let him inquire. What of that?"

"He will think it strange, perhaps, that you should be so long away."

"Dear good kind old soul, he never troubles himself about that. I am accustomed to go from place to place—to stay out—to come and go just as I please, without any inquiries."

"He is a most purblind mortal for a magistrate," said Ragget, with a smile.

"He was always like that, I think."

"He was; but one would have thought that experience might have made him wiser."

"He is so unsuspicious—and—so indulgent."

"I shall ever revere his name for his kindness to you and your mother."

At this moment Dick Turpin appeared at the trap-door.

"Dick, my friend," ejaculated Captain Ragget, "the time is pretty well up, and I am detaining you."

"I *have* an appointment," answered Dick, with a smile. "I have an appointment, so I won't deny it, but it'll keep for an hour or so—therefore don't hurry yourself."

"Nay, I was about to take leave of my daughter a few minutes since. Have you time to see her on the road home?"

Turpin replied in the affirmative. So after an affectionate parting with her father, she ascended the steps, and prepared to accompany her good-natured conductor.

The two were soon again on the backs of their steeds, and cantered on towards Ealing.

When they had arrived within a quarter of a mile of Old Oak Farm, Nan Darrell dismounted, for the purpose of taking her way on foot to the residence of her grandfather.

"I am deeply beholden to you, Mr. Turpin, for all your kindness both to me and my poor father," said Nan, in a sweet voice, made doubly sweeter by the smile she vouchsafed to Richard Turpin.

The highwayman raised his hat respectfully.

Nan held out her hand and once more gave him one of her own sweet saucy smiles. After this she turned towards the house and took her leave.

"Hang it!" ejaculated Dick, "she's an angel; there can be no doubt about that. She's an angel of goodness, and oh! if I were a younger man—odd, rat it! what am I saying? She's not made for the likes of me—she's all too good and gent'e to be in our company at all. The captain's been a fine gallant fellow in his time—so he is now, for the matter of that. But only to think that he should have grabbed hold of a magistrate's daughter, and all so recent, too! Bah! there's a strange mystery about the whole of this affair, and old Jonathan knows more than he chooses to let anyone else know. Wo, wo! Bess—gently, gently, lass. What! are you jealous, wench? 'Fore God, I believe she knows what I've been saying! Never mind, Bess—I'll have no other mistress but thyself. Thou art the most beautiful friend Dick Turpin has ever known, and is ever likely to know, for the matter of that—and so now to meet Tom. Gad, I believe he'll have the pull of me this time, for it's already past the appointed hour."

Turpin trotted slowly down the Ealing-road; and after he had journeyed about half a mile, he was met by the man who had conducted Nan to the highwayman's haunt. He handed the bridle of the flea-bitten horse to this worthy, and bid him take him to the cave.

This done, he turned the head of Bess towards the road which led to Hounslow.

CHAPTER X.

HOUNSLOW HEATH. — THE ADVENTURES OF TWO KNIGHTS OF THE ROAD.

DICK TURPIN trotted on merrily, occasionally indulging in a few snatches of some old song. Although he was a man by no means dispossessed of feeling for his kind, he was of a nature that threw off troubles and gloomy thoughts under the influence of the wild daring life he had led for so many years. Dick was called in the profession a fortunate man. He had hitherto met with fewer mischances than most of his companions. To a great extent this resulted from his squaring matters, as it was termed, with Jonathan Wild. Be this as it may, it is quite certain that he had managed, somehow or other, to steer clear of the meshes of the law, and while many of his companions had had several narrow escapes for their lives, Dick appeared to be the more fortunate man. He implicitly believed that no harm could come to him as long as he had Black Bess in his possession.

And this prediction, if it could be so termed, was verified to the letter. No harm—at least, none to speak of—did befall him till after the death of that magnificent animal.

He trotted on till he came to a small road-side public-house, which stood within about three quarters of a mile of Hounslow. He drew up his mare when he reached the front part of the establishment.

An officious stableman came forward, and evidently recognised him, as he gave Turpin a familiar sort of nod.

"Hay and water, or take her inside?" inquired this worthy.

"You may as well take her in for half an hour or so," answered Dick. "Anybody waiting for me?"

The man gave a nod.

"His horse is in the stable," he observed, confidentially.

"How long has he been here?"

"Can't exactly say, only he's been a fidgetting ever since he has been here. Lord, lord! what a restless piece o' goods that ere pall o' yourn is, I never saw such a chap, he's like a parched-pea in a frying-pan."

"Ha, he don't like to be kept waiting. Is he in the parlour?"

"Blest if I know. I believe he's been in every room in the 'ouse, to say nothing of the grounds, stables, out-houses, and bowling green. What makes him like that? has he got anything alive in his inside?"

"I am sure I can't tell," said Turpin, with a laugh. "I never asked him."

"Well I wish you would, master, "cause it don't appear natural, does it?"

"I'm sure I don't know; there, that will do, lead her into the stable and just give her a rub down."

"Ah, she's a rare sort, she is," observed the ostler, admiring the fine proportions of Bess. She *is* a rare sort, that she is." He went on in this way till he had got her into the stable.

Dick then went into the house, the landlord of which was in the bar; he held out his hand to Dick as he entered, and said—

"Ah, Mr. Staples! How are you?"

"Hearty, thank you."

"And Mrs. Staples?"

"Oh, she's blooming — blooming; and as saucy as ever."

The highwayman turned from the gaze of some rustics in front of the bar, and entered the parlour.

Tom King was seated at one of the tables, playing at cards with some strangers.

"Well, you are a pretty fellow," he ejaculated, when he caught sight of Dick. "You are a pretty fellow;

[THE STOCKBROKER ATTACKS TURPIN.]

"here I've lost hard upon a couple of guineas, and all through you."

"Can't be helped. I am here as soon as I could be. You knew the business I was going on—you knew that well enough, and when a lady's in the case, all things else must give place. Don't you see that, my friend. You are a ladies' man, which I don't profess to be. You are a ladies' man, and ought to appeciate this better than myself."

"Upon my soul! it's bravely spoken. Is it not, gentlemen?" said King, turning to his companions.

"He knows how to make a good excuse," said one of the party present.

"And any excuse is better than none," added another.

"Well, now you have come, you may as well sit down for half an hour or so; the night is yet young."

"It will be only for half an hour, then, at the very furthest," said Turpin.

"Very well; only one of our friends here has volun-
No. 5.

teered a song, and I'm sure you are not one to say nay to a good thing.

"Should be most happy to hear the gentleman sing," said Dick, glancing at a portly, farmer-looking individual, with three double chins and a face the colour of his own mangel-wurtzel.

Many of my readers have, no doubt, at times fallen in with a convivial party of rustics, in some remote country tavern. It is amusing to hear the curious songs some of them sing—songs, indeed, that one would have imagined never had existence.

The song the farmer chose was one set to a quaint and singular air, which had been sung by the peasant girls of merry England for more than a hundred years. The words were as follows:—

As I was a-walking out one day, down by the river side,
A-looking all around me, an Irish girl I spied;
How red and rosy were her cheeks—how coal-black was
    her hair—
How costly were the garments this Irish girl did wear.

Her shoes they were of Spanish black, all spangled o'er with
    dew;
She wrung her hands right piteously.   Alas! it is too true.
"I'm a-goin' home—I'm a-goin home—I'm a-goin home,"
    said she;
"How could you go a rovin' to slight your poor Pollee?"

When last I saw my own true love, he seemed to be in pain;
With sorrow, grief, and anguish his heart was rent in twain;
But there's many a man that's worse than him; so why
    should I complain?
Oh, love! it is a killing thing.   Did you ever feel the pain?

I wish I was a butterfly, I'd fly to my love's breast;
I wish I was a linnet, I'd lull my love to rest;
I wish I was a nightingale, I'd sing to the morning clear—
I'd sit and sing to you, my love, I once did hold so dear.

The songster concluded, Turpin and King had the
greatest difficulty in restraining their laughter, for the
gigantic specimen of Orpheus who had so favoured
them sang the foregoing ditty in a soft, tremulous voice,
and endeavoured to breathe into it a tender expression,
which was such a signal failure, and, withal, so directly
opposed to his appearance, that the effect was, of course,
bordering upon the ridiculous.   However, the two highwaymen complimented him upon his vocal powers,
whereupon King was knocked down for a song.

"And, mark me, gentlemen," said Turpin, "before
my friend begins, I must tell you that this must be the
last, as far as we are concerned; for, however I may
like your company, I must inform you that our time is
up."

"Well, well; if it must be, why, it must," ejaculated one or two of the company; "but we are sorry to
part with you."

Tom King, after he had cleared his throat with a
hearty draught from his cup, sang the following, with
a fine rich voice:—

OUR FATHERS' SWORDS.

Our fathers' swords are on the wall,
    Their blades with rust o'erspread,
And oft those sloth-dimmed brands recall
    The memory of the dead.
For spirits linger round the spot,
    And mourn for ages flown,
When brightly flashed those weapons forth,
    For altar and the throne.

The Grecian's lance triumphant hung
    A trophy in his fane,
And boldest chieftains, bending, sung
    The pæan's grateful strain.
But Him who bids our victory forth,
    A Briton shames to own,
And coldly marks as idle toys
    The altar and the throne.

Time was when, at their sovereign's call,
    A thousand warriors bowed,
And, round their church's head to bleed,
    They hailed the summons proud;
But, now o'er lance, and bow, and sword,
    Some poisonous blast hath blown,
And fainting such the hearts that loved
    The altar and the throne.

The fickle rabble's noisome breath,
    The atheist's laugh of scorn,
The fierce destructive's yell of glee,
    On that foul blast are borne.
'Twixt quick and dead, like Judah's priest,
    Who dares stand forth alone,
And sternly bid the pest-cloud spare
    The altar and the throne?

Who? who?   A faithful few are left,
    The storm who dare defy—
Who've sternly sworn their land to save,
    Or round its bulwarks die.
We wait the foe!   Our fathers' swords!
    Your steel shall yet be shown,
Ere mid the wreck of freedom lie
    The altar and the throne.

We wait the foe!   Proud England's sun!
    Thou hast not, shall not set;
The clouds that dim thy fiery brow
    Shall vanish from thee yet.
In happier days, our fathers' swords!
    Once more shall ye be known,
And halo round, with dazzling blaze,
    The altar and the throne.

"There, gentlemen," ejaculated King, when he had
finished; "it's rather a long one, but from it you may
be able to guess that I am a loyal man.   Ah, ah!"

"It is a beautiful thing," said one of the party.
"Now, gentlemen, I hopes as how you bean't agoin' to
take yourselves off?"

"Indeed but we are, my friends," said Turpin, rising
from his seat, and preparing to take his departure.

Tom King rose also.   The occupants of the parlour
were loth to part with the two highwaymen, who were
either, or both of them, such excellent company.

In a few minutes after this the two highwaymen
were trotting on towards Hounslow.

"Well, Dick, how did you leave the captain?" was
the first inquiry King made after they had mounted
their steeds.   "Down upon his luck, I s'pose?"

"Ah, most cursedly down; and there's not much to
be wondered at in that.   You see, it ain't altogether so
much for himself, for Ragget is a plucky card; but
there's his sweet daughter, whom he loves better than
his own life.   There's that dear girl, you know."

"Oh, she is a dear girl! there can be no doubt of
that," said King, in a suddenly altered tone.   "There
is not the slightest doubt of that.   All too good and
gentle for our company.   Bah! we must think no more
of her, so let that pass."

"I shall begin to think that your soft and susceptible
heart has been stolen from you if you keep sighing in
this sort of fashion," said Turpin, with a smile.

"Dick," said King, in a suddenly altered manner,
"I've a brilliant scheme on to-night.   The Earl of Oxford will pass over the Heath to-night."

"What, Hounslow Heath?"

"Yes."

"Art thou sure of that?"

"Positive, from information I have received from
private sources."

"So much the better.   We all know his lordship by
demanding toll.   Do you know the time he is likely to
make his appearance?"

"I am not quite certain as to that; but I know we
are early enough, or I should not have remained so
quietly with those yokels."

"Our time's our own; we can wait for so distinguished a nobleman.   Hark! what was that?"

"Horses' feet, as I live."

The two highwaymen were now in a lonely part of
the road, and within a quarter of a mile of the Heath.

Turpin and his companion drew up by the side of a
hedge.

"Let us wait here and see who this traveller turns
out to be."

They were, in the position they had taken up, concealed from sight.

In a short time after they had thus ensconced themselves, a solitary horseman made his appearance.   King
was soon enabled to see his features.   He utter an exclamation—

"Old Whitcomb, the stockbroker, as I live!"

"And who may he be?" inquired his companion.

"Who may he be?   Why, the old vagabond prosecuted me once."

"The devil he did?"

"Yes; but I was luckily acquitted.   It was no fault
of his, though.   Now we'll have at him, Dick."

"With all my heart.   But one will be enough for this
business."

"Do you take him in hand, then.   It is possible he
may recognise me by the sound of my voice."

"Here goes, then," said Dick, who drew Bess into the middle of the road.

The stockbroker was within a few paces of him. He checked his horse as he observed the figure of a man confronting him.

"Now, my friend," said Turpin, good-humouredly, "ain't you afraid to travel alone along this wretched road?"

"Why should I be?" inquired the traveller, glancing at the cocked hat and mask of the speaker.

"Oh, I don't know. You have a clear conscience, perhaps?"

"I have; and I fancy that is more than you can say."

"Ah! you are personal, not to say rude. Well, since you have a clear conscience, you had better clear out your pockets; for, you see, I have a heavy conscience, but an empty purse. Come, your money, or——But you know the rest."

"Zounds, man! Dare you to threaten me?"

"I am afraid it would be of no use appealing to your better nature—I am afraid not."

"Wretch! would you rob me?"

"Now, no bad words, Mr. Whitcomb—no bad words, if you please. If you are at all saucy I will blow out your brains without more ado."

As he said this, Turpin levelled the barrel of his pistol.

"Was there ever such a country as this?" ejaculated the traveller. "Mr. Whitcomb, too! The rascal knows me, then. "Hark ye, sirrah!"—this was addressed to Turpin—"hark ye. I am not afraid to travel on this road by myself, for the simple reason that I carry nothing valuable with me."

"Oh, yes you do," answered the highwayman, quietly —"yes, you do. Fork out that bag full of guineas."

"They are not my own."

"No; but they will be mine presently," said Dick, with a smile. "Come, out with them. There, man, don't make so many wry faces, you'll frighten my horse. Your money quickly, or here goes."

"Oh, dear, dear me! to think that I should be caught thus a second time."

"Ah, it's very sad; but the mopusses! Shell out, old cock—shell out, like a man."

"That is every coin I've got in the world," then correcting himself, he added, "leastways, it is every coin I have with me."

"Ah, that's better — much better," said Turpin. "You shouldn't tell stories—it's naughty."

He gave a low chuckle, as he said this, which served to exasperate the stockbroker.

"Is this all you've got?"

"Every penny. You will give me some back, to carry me home?"

"Some back! Well, that's a good joke. Some back! Ha, ha! Why, I want more myself. Have you no South Sea shares? They are looking up, are they not?"

At this query the stockbroker appeared to be perfectly bewildered.

"South Sea shares!" he ejaculated. "Why, you ain't——"

"Oh, no, I am not a stockbroker—I don't dabble on change. You rob in the city by chicanery—I rob on the road, in a straightforward way."

"Well, I declare! Insulted as well as robbed! Upon my soul, your insolence exceeds——"

"My honesty—does it not?"

"In common charity, you will not refuse to give me something to carry me home?" said Mr. Whitcomb. "In that bag you will find forty-eight guineas. Give me the eight, and then I will depart in peace."

"Not a farthing. I have no charity for you stockjobbing fellows, who rise and fall like the ebbing and flowing of the tide—whose paths are as unfathomable as the ocean. The grasshopper in the Royal Exchange is an emblem of your character. What! give you something out of the paltry sum of forty-eight guineas? I won't give you one farthing."

By this time the stockbroker had sidled his horse up to Turpin, who still held the bag of money in his hand. By a sudden movement he struck down the hand of the highwayman that grasped the pistol, and endeavoured to pull him off his horse.

At this juncture King came out from his hiding-place. He caught the stockbroker by the collar of his coat behind with one hand, while with the other he struck him several severe blows in the face with his clenched fist.

"Oh! help! Murder! murder!" screamed out Mr. Whitcomb, now fairly alarmed for his life. "Oh! murder!"

"Silence, you circumventing old rascal!" ejaculated King.

"Oh, let me go, and I'll pray for you hereafter—let me go, dear, good gentlemen."

King released his captive, who at once put spurs to his horse, and endeavoured to get clear off. Tom followed, and kept lashing him with the thong of his riding-whip.

As for Turpin, he could not move for laughing.

In a few minutes after this King returned, hot and flushed with his recent exertion.

"The scrubby old rascal!" he ejaculated. "But he's had it worth his money: my arm is sore with belabouring him."

The two companions laughed again at their adventure.

"Forty-eight guineas!" said Dick, holding up the canvass bag.

"He carried a watch; why did you not take that?" inquired King.

"Oh, let him have it. This is enough for one haul."

They walked their horses leisurely on towards the Heath, after the stockbroker had taken his departure. When they had arrived there, King said—

"I do hope the Earl of Oxford will make his appearance, otherwise I shall be terribly disappointed."

"Why so? His money is no better than anybody else's."

"Ah! it is not altogether that; but I have another motive."

"What may that be, if it's a fair question?"

"Why, I expect a lady will travel with him."

"A lady?"

"Yes, a young and beauteous lady—one of the maids of honour to the Court."

"What matters that to you?"

"I know her."

"And does she know you?"

"Not as Tom King the highwayman."

"Ah! just so; but by some other name?"

"You've just hit it."

"Well, I suppose you are not going to carry off this fair lady."

"Oh, dear, no! exclaimed King, suddenly; "I would not hurt a hair of her head!"

"Whew! that's the way the cat jumps—fine gal. Tom, what a tender-hearted fellow you are where the sex is concerned."

"I cannot help it. They have been my ruin, and they will bring me to my end one of these days; but I cannot help it."

Time has not chilled my heart. It was formed
To love, and (can I hope?) to be beloved;
Sad disappointment to its core has wormed.
Why does it prey on all that ever loved?
But give me love, with all its agonies—
With all its smilings, and with all its sighs—

"Ah! I am not poetical," said Turpin. His companion continued—

For what can fill the void affection leaves,
When the world scares it from its downy rest?

'Tis not the wandering bird alone which grieves
    Its mossy bed : the cell, no longer pressed
By its warm form, nor tended by its care,
    Rots in the sleet or crumbles in the air.

Sigh over the deserted? Who can smile
    Upon the breaking of a faithful heart?
Who does not weep that woman should beguile,
    Since constancy is woman's better part?
Who can put forth the mocking hand in scorn,
    When a disconsolate is left to mourn?

"What is all this about? For mercy's sake, don't get sentimental!" ejaculated Turpin.

"What is it about? That's a pretty question; you've not been listening to the lines I have been repeating, and they are my own composition.'

"Yours?"

"Yes. Part of a poem I have written."

"Ah! I should have been more attentive if I had known that. I beg your pardon for—— Hark! Leave poetry for the present. Methinks I hear a distant rumbling sound. Is it so, or is it not?" The highwayman laid down his head as he said this, while Bess pricked up her ears.

"I think there is a sound of some vehicle. Draw back. They will take this road, I suppose."

"Who?"

"Your friend, the Earl of Oxford."

"Without a doubt. Oh, yes; this is the road he would come."

"Draw back, then, or they will see us, and that may cause some confusion. Will there be any escort with him?"

"I believe not."

"Because, in that case, we should be over-matched, and we had better have brought two or three more with us for so heavy a job."

"But there will be no escort, I tell you. Isn't that enough?"

"Of course it is ; only you said but just now that you thought not. However, we shall see, if this happens to be his carriage. It may be the mail."

"The mail is not due yet for a full hour and a half."

Hounslow Heath looked bleak and cheerless ; and it was a matter of no small wonderment that any one should have been inclined to venture across it on such a dark and uninviting night.

The wheels of some vehicle were heard distinctly by the two highwaymen.

"It will be impossible for us to see if this be the earl's carriage," said King; "quite impossible where we are now. Let us go nearer to the road."

"Do no such thing, I tell you. If we see them they will see us, which is the very thing we don't want. Take them unawares—rush on them all at once. That's my plan. We shall soon know if it be the party we are expecting; and if it is not, what's the odds?"

"I bow to your superior judgment. You are an older hand than myself, and have had more practice. Here, then, we will take up our station."

"So be it."

There was a pause of some minutes' duration after this, during which period both the highwaymen examined the priming of their pistols. Should the approaching vehicle turn out to be the carriage of the Earl of Oxford, they might meet with some resistance; consequently it was necessary to be prepared. A knight of the road did occasionally lose his own life in the practice of his vocation in the days of which we write.

Rumble—rumble—rumble. The carriage approached. There were two bright lights at its sides. These threw a long line of light on either side, piercing the deep gloom of the Heath.

The carriage came within a few feet of Turpin and his companion.

"Now for it, Tom," said the latter.

The two friends then rushed forward, one on each side of the vehicle.

"Stand and deliver!" were the well-known magic words of the craft to which they both belonged, and which they now shouted out in authoritative accents.

An old gentleman was fast asleep in the vehicle.

This was the Earl of Oxford.

He was awoke by the sudden stoppage of the vehicle, together with a faint scream from a young lady who sat opposite to him.

The old gentleman rubbed his eyes, and started up in amazement.

Click! bang!

The footman had fired a pistol at Tom King.

It missed its mark, and in another instant that worthy lay senseless from a blow inflicted by the butt-end of King's weapon.

Dick rode up to the coachman, and, presenting his weapon at that person as though he was picking out a favourite shot in his gold-bedizened waistcoat to bore a hole with the bullet of his pistol.

He was an old man, the earl's jehu. He was very corpulent, and indisposed to move himself, however much he might make his horses move. He felt himself perfectly helpless when he carried his eye to the shining barrel of Dick's pistol. He was as obedient and docile as a very lamb, and would not for worlds have attempted to urge on the noble pair of horses he had consented to drive, as, of course, no other man could drive them.

"You're a better behaved man than yonder fellow," said Turpin, alluding to the servant who had been so punished by King; "a much better behaved man, and, I should say, knew your place."

"I hope I does, sir," answered the coachman.

"Well, then, you won't attempt to move on for the present?"

"No."

"You promise that?"

"Yes."

"Ah ! that is well. Then there is no occasion for me to cover your respectable person with this pistol."

"Oh !" The man gave a sigh of relief.

The Earl of Oxford thrust his head out of the carriage window and endeavoured to make himself acquainted with the cause of the disturbance. He was not kept long in doubt or suspense. Turpin rode up to the side of the carriage, and, presenting his pistol to the nobleman, whose head was visible at the window, he said, in an authoritative tone of voice—

"You will be pleased, my lord, to hand over your purse as speedily as possible, for my friend and myself have but little time to spare."

"Let him get out," said King, who, by this time, had come up to the side of Turpin. "Jump out; we will not detain you long."

"Gracious Heavens! what wouldst thou do? Wouldst thou murder me?" said the Earl, who now began to be seriously alarmed for his own life.

"We never commit any violence unless it be necessary—unless it be absolutely necessary," answered King. "But thou hadst better jump out, for we do not like to be trifled with."

"Oh ! good, kind gentlemen, have mercy on us !" said the young lady, who was the earl's fellow traveller. "Take all we have, but spare—spare our lives."

"You need be under no fear," said Tom, raising his hat to the female speaker. "We would lay down our lives at any time rather than injure a hair of your head."

The young lady gave utterance to a faint scream as the tones of the speaker's voice fell upon her ear. She thrust her head out of the carriage and looked intently at Tom's features, which she seemed to have some faint recollection of, for, as her eye scanned his handsome person, a faint flush crept up into her face.

This did not pass unnoticed by Tom, who turned away his head for a moment, as though he were unable to bear the searching scrutiny to which he was being subjected.

The young lady held out her purse and jewelry towards the highwayman, which Turpin unceremoniously enough transferred to his own pocket.

"There is a ring there that I regret parting with—not so much on account of its intrinsic value, but because it was the gift of one who is now gone, and I may never see more. Perhaps at some future day I may be able to re-purchase it. There is, I think, a place in London where property can be obtained upon the payment of a certain sum. Perhaps you know to whom I am alluding?"

"Your wisdom exceeds your years, madam," answered Turpin. "Doubtless you allude to Mr. Jonathan Wild?"

"I did so."

"Madam," said King, taking off his hat once more, and disclosing his glossy ringlets, "permit me to present you with the trinket in question."

As he said this, he made a motion to Turpin, who handed him the lady's jewelry.

King then presented it to the beautiful young creature in the carriage.

"It affords me infinite pleasure to be able to offer you these trifles back. Accept them from the hands of one who is an admirer of your sex, not the least graceful and fascinating amongst whom is yourself."

As he made this speech, the highwayman handed back the jewelry.

While this was taking place, Dick had pulled out the Earl of Oxford, and began rifling his pockets. The old nobleman offered no resistance.

"I will only take this particular ring," said Constance Armatage—for that was the name of the young female who was travelling with the Earl of Oxford. Then, as she caught sight of her elderly companion in the hands of Turpin, she said, in piteous accents—

"Oh! I pray of you to treat us gently. See your companion," she said, in continuation, addressing herself to King.

"Fear not, madam," exclaimed the latter; "no violence shall be used. I pray of you to take back these trinkets."

"Only this one," said Constance Armatage—"only this one. And if you will let me know where I am to send the sum you may demand for its restoration, I will cheerfully forward it."

"Nay, nay, dear madam, I trust you do not deem me so mercenary as to chaffer with one so fair and gentle as yourself for the price of this trinket. Accept it—accept them all at my hands, and I will thank and bless you."

As Tom King said this, he knelt down on one knee before the Honourable Miss Armatage, one of the most beautiful of her Majesty's maids of honour.

She smiled so sweet and winning a smile that the susceptible and tender heart of Tom began thumping against his ribs in a most unhighwayman-like fashion.

He took a locket from his coat-pocket, and presented it to the fair being before him.

"What is this?" she inquired hastily, and in some surprise.

"Accept it as a gift," returned King.

She handed it back, and gently refused the trinket.

"Nay, Sir Highwayman, thou art somewhat bold, methinks," returned the Honourable Miss Armatage.

"Ladies of her Majesty's Court do not accept gifts from common robbers," said King. "I am answered. Pardon my presumption."

He returned the locket to his coat-pocket, somewhat abashed at his own impertinence.

Meanwhile Dick Turpin had possessed himself of all the valuables on the person of the earl.

One of these was a pocket-book.

"There are a number of papers in that book which are useless to you," said the earl, "but are of the utmost value to me. I pray, therefore, that you take what notes there are, and return me the rest."

Agreeably to this suggestion, Dick opened the book, and handed it to Tom for his inspection. Hastily taking out what he thought of service, he returned the book to its owner.

"Well," said the earl, "thou dost thy business in a courteous manner enough; but a day of reckoning must come. Repent, my good sirs, ere it be too late. Turn from your wicked careers. Take an old man's advice. Depend on it that honesty's the best policy."

"Oh!" ejaculated King, "it is too late for either of us to alter our course of lives; it would be easier for the leopard to change his spots. Adieu, my friend—our time is up."

"Was ever seen such a pair of rascals?" said the earl to his young companion.

In a minute or so after this the two highwaymen clapped spurs to the sides of their horses, and were soon lost to sight.

"Isn't she a lovely creature?" said Tom, when he and his companion had got fairly off.

"A very pleasant damsel, I must admit," returned Turpin. "Who is she?"

"One of her Majesty's maids of honour. The earl is her patron and guardian."

"You seem to be well up in the aristocratic circles, you do," said Dick.

King smiled.

"I intend to have a little further insight into fashionable life," he answered. "What do you think I am in possession of?"

"Well, I don't know."

"Can't you guess?"

"Why, you are such a strange card, that it would be difficult for me to hazard a guess."

"Look here," said King, as he held up a card on which was the royal seal.

"What is that?"

"An invitation from his Majesty."

"Humph! His Majesty, or his Majesty's agent, have an ugly knack of inquiring for gentlemen of our kidney."

"The king holds a levée to-morrow, and this is a passport."

"A what?"

"The bearer of this will be admitted into the palace."

"What good is that to either of us?"

"I shall go," said Tom, seriously.

"You must be mad—clean mad, to think of such a thing."

"Mad or not, I shall go, I tell you."

"Please yourself. You'll have to go alone, as far as I am concerned. Do you think they won't know that your card is the one that was stolen from the pocket-book of the Earl of Oxford?"

"No—not at all likely. At any rate, I shall run the risk."

"You are mad, Tom," said Turpin, in a half contemptuous manner.

The two highwaymen rode on for many miles. They did not deem it worth while to stop anywhere else for that night, so, after they had gone a considerable distance, they took off their masks, and proceeded along like two ordinary individuals.

They eventually put up at a little village inn; there they passed the night.

In the morning they discovered that there was a country fair held within half a mile of the house where they had put up; so, thinking they might have some little amusement, our two highwaymen made up their minds to pay it a visit.

The days of fairs appear to be now passing away, but at the time of which we are writing they were frequent enough in all parts of "Merrie England." Many of my readers will remember the glories of Bartholomew Fair, now a thing of the past.

As Turpin and King strolled through the green lane which led to the spot where the fair was held, they were met and overtaken by a number of rustics, who were, like themselves, bent upon seeing the sights and shows.

One of these—a countryman—entered into conversation with our highwaymen.

"Be'es goin' to the fair, meisters?" said the clodhopper.

"Ay, my friend, we thought of doing so," said Dick. "Are you?"

"Ees, I bees," said the rustic.

"That's right," said Dick, with a sly wink at King. "I suppose there's something worth seeing there?"

"Oh, ees. There bees the pig-faced lady, the smallest man in the world, and the larned goose."

"A learned goose, eh?"

"Ees."

"That must be a wonder. But do you think it's safe to go to this fair?"

"Safe! What do'ee mean?"

"Well, you know, there are generally such a lot of sharpers at these sort of places—pickpockets, and those sort of persons."

"Oh, ah! I'll forgive 'em if they rob me," said the man, with a broad grin; "I'll forgive 'em."

"Will you?" said Turpin, who seemed to think some amusement might be extracted from his newly-found companion. "You'll forgive them, eh? Well, that's kind. I suppose you haven't much to lose? I expect that's about the size of it."

"Ain't I? I've got a goulden guinea."

"What! are you so improvident as to take a real guinea to the fair?"

"Ees, sure; because I bees up to their tricks, I am."

"Humph! you are evidently a sharp fellow," returned Turpin, "that is quite clear you were not born yesterday."

"E-e-ee! Doen't I know that without yer a-telling me?" returned the man.

"I suppose you do. And pray how are you going to take care of your guinea?" inquired Dick.

"I know."

"I suppose you do; but you may as well tell us, because we have several guineas about us. And, after all, I'll bet you an even crown that you lose your guinea before you go home."

"Will yer?"

"Yes, that I will."

"Oh, noa; I ain't to be had. Look here, this is how I shall take care of it."

The countryman then opened his mouth, and pointed to the guinea which he had deposited therein.

"Ah, ah!" laughed Turpin. "Very clever, indeed—wonderfully clever!"

By this time they had arrived at the fair. Grinning from ear to ear, the countryman stood looking at the shows in a state of ecstacy.

"Now we must have the fellow's guinea, if it's only for sport," said Dick.

"Oh, it's never worth while to run any risks on his account," returned his companion.

"Risks be hanged! I'll show you how to work it."

Whereupon Turpin beckoned a boy to his side, who was but a few yards off.

He appeared to be a hopeful youth, to judge from his appearance. Turpin gave him a number of groats and sixpences, with instructions how he was to act. The boy ran after the countryman, while Turpin and King followed at a respectful distance.

The boy, coming up with the countryman, fell before him, as though by accident, and scattered all the pieces Turpin had given him all around; then starting up he raised a most hideous noise, crying out that he was undone, and that he must run away from his apprenticeship—that his master was a most furious man, and that he would certainly be killed.

The countryman and others flocked round, and were evidently anxious to assist the boy in recovering his lost treasure.

The sixpences and groats were picked up one after another, and handed to the lad.

One of the bystanders then said—

"Have you found all?"

"Yes," answered the artful young urchin. "All the silver; but that is of no avail. There is a broad piece of gold, which I was carying to my master, as a token from the country; and unless I take it to him, I certainly shall be killed—oh, oh!"—and here he began to whimper—"Alas! I am undone. What will become of me?"

Turpin and King now advanced among the crowd, and they both appeared to be concerned for the unhappy boy; and seeing the countryman standing by, Dick said that he had seen him put a piece of gold into his mouth.

Upon this there was a yell of execration from the bystanders.

The countryman looked aghast, and did not appear to be able to find words to defend himself. He muttered something, but the rage of those present would not admit of them patiently waiting to hear what he had to say.

"Oh, oh!" sobbed the boy.

"You rascal!" said a farming-looking individual, coming forward and collaring the countryman; "you rascal to rob a poor lad like this!"

"Ye just keep yer hands to yerself," returned the man, who in his trepidation spoke as though he had got something in his mouth.

"Don't leave go on him, maister. If so be as ye want a hand, I'm your man," said a stout-built fellow, who appeared to be a young Hercules in his way.

One or two more stepped forward.

"Open his mouth," suggested Turpin, who could with difficulty preserve his gravity. "Open the fellow's mouth, and see if I'm correct or not. I tell you I saw him put a golden piece into it."

A struggle ensued.

The countryman wrestled with his tormentor; but, although he was a rough sort of customer, he stood but a poor chance against the numbers who were opposed to him.

My reader may readily imagine the noise and disturbance an occurrence of this sort would be likely to create amongst a crowd of persons who were assembled at a country fair. In a few minutes there was a regular uproar.

The countryman was roughly handled; and eventually those who had chosen to become the boy's champions forced open his mouth and drew out the guinea, amidst the groans, hisses, and execration of the assembled multitude.

"I told you how it would be," said Turpin. "Am I not correct?"

"Quite right—quite right—the artful vagabond!" exclaimed several voices. "Take him to the nearest pond, and give him a good ducking!"

Turpin thought the fellow had been punished enough; so, after he had been well kicked and cuffed, he was but too glad to slink off with the loss of his guinea, which was handed to the boy, who was a tramp well known to Turpin.

"I think that little affair has been managed well," said the latter to his companion, King.

"Never saw anything better," returned Tom, who, with his companion, sought a bye-place to indulge in a hearty fit of laughter.

The two friends had made up their minds to enjoy themselves; and, as they had the day before them, they both entered the various booths in the fair.

When they had seen as much of these as they desired, Dick drew his companion away, and they both took a long ramble in the country. After a walk of some miles they arrived at a steep acclivity, which wound round a cliff.

It was a bright, sunshiny day; the air was balmy, and our highwaymen were in excellent spirits. They had been debating with themselves whether they would not pay a visit to a country cattle market which was held at a short distance from the spot they were walking. As they were walking together they observed a man ascending the acclivity. From his appearance they were led to believe the fellow was a foreigner.

They were not wrong in their surmise, as it afterwards turned out. The man was leading a gaily-caparisoned mule, of very handsome proportions. His head was turned away from the animal, and he appeared to be lost in abstraction.

"Dost see yonder blade?" said Turpin.

"Yes, surely. What of him?"

"We'll have a game with him. I like the look of the beast he is leading."

"It's a very handsome animal," returned King.

"And I intend to have it," said Turpin.

"You? How?"

"Follow me."

The two highwaymen walked on, and came within a few paces of the man and mule.

"Now," whispered Turpin to his companion, "the fellow is so lost in thought that he appears to take no notice of anything. All the better for our purpose. You slip the head-gear off the mule, and put the bit into my mouth."

"I don't understand your drift at present, Dick."

"Wait awhile and you will see."

Turpin then went to the side of the mule. As he did this he knelt down and proceeded on all fours like one of the lower animals of the creation.

Tom King slipped off the head-gear of the animal, and put it over the head of Dick, who motioned him to lead away the mule.

This was done, and Turpin trudged after the man, who was a Spaniard, on all fours. They both proceeded quietly enough till they had arrived at the top of the hill.

Then came the discovery.

The Spaniard looked round, and, to his infinite consternation and astonishment, he saw that his favourite mule was transformed into a man.

For a moment or so he stood petrified with alarm, and could not find words to express his surprise.

Turpin regarded him with a look of pity.

"Holy Virgin!" exclaimed the Spaniard, "what is this I see? Where—where is my mule?"

And, as he said this, he looked stupidly at the harness which was round the highwayman's head.

"Do not be alarmed, dear master," said Dick. "Do not trouble yourself at the strange alteration, for, indeed, I was no mule, as you supposed me, but a man of real flesh and blood like yourself."

"You, you—a man—a mule?"

"I was a mule to all appearance, I admit; but am now, as you see me, a man."

"What is the meaning of this?" ejaculated the Spaniard, whose tawny countenance turned a thought paler.

"Listen, and thou shalt learn all," said Dick, in plaintive accents. "Yes, you shall learn all."

The man paused, and listened complacently enough.

"I have said," continued Turpin, "that I was a man, when you purchased me. You must know that I had the misfortune to commit a sin against the Virgin Mary, which she resented so heinously that she transformed me into the likeness of a mule, in which shape I was to remain seven years. That time being expired, I resume my proper shape, and am now at my own disposal. And, oh, my dear master, take warning from all I have suffered—take warning never to be self-willed and obstinate, for, believe me, it is sure to recoil upon yourself sooner or later."

"Is it possible that you have served me as a mule for so long a time?" exclaimed the Spaniard.

"You can best answer how faithfully," replied Turpin. "And allow me to take this opportunity to return you, sir, my most sincere thanks for all your goodness towards me, for since I have been in your service you have put me to no excessive labour — none more than what you or I, or any other mule, might be able to bear. I have to thank you for all the considera-

tion you have shown me. You used to give me nice warm mashes when I was poorly, or had caught cold; and, indeed, you always showed every consideration for me. I might have fallen into much worse hands. Accept my thanks for all this."

"Oh, dear, dear! and you was such a beautiful mule. I was taking you to market to see if I could buy another to run in double harness with you."

"I am sure I'm very sorry," said Dick, who saw he had got hold of a customer who believed every word he had been saying—"very sorry I am. But, you see, as I am now restored to my original shape, why, I must remove this."

He then threw aside the gear that was around his head, and made a graceful obeisance to his late master.

They repaired to a neighbouring house, and Dick stood some ale to the Spaniard. After this he returned to where Tom King was, with the real mule by his side. Turpin briefly explained the particulars of his interview with the Spaniard, at which both the highwaymen laughed most heartily.

"And did the fellow believe you?" inquired Tom.

"He took it all in as natural as you please. He is a Spaniard—so he gave me to understand; and being a stanch Catholic, my tale sounded like truth."

"What shall we do with the mule?"

"He's a beauty," said Dick; "but he's of no use to us. Suppose we send the boy with him on to the market, and let him sell the animal for whatever it will fetch?"

"Agreed; that would be by far the best course. But where is the boy?"

"I told him to come to the house where we put up, and no doubt he will be there before this."

The highwaymen now retraced their steps, and in a short time were at the public-house.

The boy was waiting for Turpin, and had been at the appointed place for more than an hour.

The mule was given into his charge. He was told to take it on to the market, which was at about three miles distance.

Turpin bought a bridle for the animal, and the boy, mounting it, proceeded on his mission.

The two highwaymen followed in about half an hour afterwards.

It appeared that the man who had lost the mule went into the market to purchase another. The first one he met with was his own. He looked hard at the boy who was in charge of it, and then, stepping up quietly to the side of the animal, he said—

"Ah, I see you have committed another sin against the Virgin Mary; but I shall be careful how I buy you again."

And with these words he turned upon his heel, and left in search of another mule.

Turpin and King arrived soon after this, whereupon the boy, who was one of the Screever's pupils—and a bright one too—made them acquainted with the particulars of the man's visit.

Ultimately the animal was sold; it fetched a good price, and the two highwaymen walked off with the proceeds.

"Now," said Dick, "we'll have one more shy at something, and then return to town."

"With all my heart," said King. "I feel in such excellent spirits, that I am game for anything. But I must not forget to-morrow."

"What's up then?"

"The king's levée."

Dick gave an impatient shrug, but refrained from making any observation. He gave instructions to the boy to meet him at Seth Margut's, and in a few minutes after this, the two highwaymen were on their travels.

After proceeding for some miles without any particular incident occurring, they arrived in sight of a commodious roadside inn.

Turpin pointed to this, and said to his companion—

"The fellow who keeps that place is a scaly rascal, and we will serve him out."

"How? In what way?"

"You shall see. I will go in and call for a cup of his best ale: he always sends this in a silver goblet to his best customers."

"Well, what of that?"

"I'll show you how to mace him out of one of his goblets."

King laughed, but he did not clearly understand his companion's drift.

"Listen," said Turpin. "I will go into the house; you may walk your horse leisurely down any of these lanes. When you see me leave the house——"

"Well, but I shan't see you if I'm going down these lanes."

"No matter. Give me half an hour or so, then you stop at the house. Let your horse have a little hay and water, and you walk into the parlour—that one you see yonder, with a bay-window in front."

"And what then?"

"Call for a cup of ale, a glass of wine, or whatever else you may think proper to take. But, mind, don't appear to know me, if we should cross each other."

"Good; I will follow your instructions."

"When you are in the parlour, feel under the tables, and you will find under one of them a silver goblet. You may put this in your pocket, and leave the house at your earliest convenience. You understand?"

"Most clearly."

"Remember my instructions. We will meet down the road. I shall take my way leisurely on to London."

With these words, Dick left his companion and entered the roadside inn.

Dismounting from his horse, he entered the parlour, which was without any other visitor besides himself.

He called for a cup of ale, which was brought, as he expected, in a silver tankard.

When this was placed before him, he ordered a plate of cold meat.

Having finished this and the ale, he strolled to the bar, and chatted familiarly with the landlady. It so chanced that one or two other customers entered the parlour while Dick was at the bar. They did not, however, stay long, for in a few minutes after their entrance Turpin saw them take their departure.

Soon after this, he desired to know what he had to pay.

The waiter came to the bar and whispered to the landlord, who was in his own private room behind the bar. The latter then came forward, and looked suspiciously at Turpin.

Then there were some more whisperings between the landlord, his wife, and the waiter.

"Now then, missus, look sharp. What is the reckoning?" said our highwayman.

The landlord came forward.

"Reckoning, indeed!" quoth the publican, opening the flap of his counter, and coming in front of his own bar. "You're not going off in this fashion; no, no, don't you think it. You give me the silver goblet you have pocketed."

"What does the man mean?" said Turpin, turning towards the landlady.

"Oh, I dare say you don't know what I mean—of course not. It's no use you Lunnon sharpers trying it on at the 'Warbling Waggoner'—so I tell you."

"Upon my soul, I do not know what you mean."

"Well, it's just this," reiterated the landlord; "you had a cup of ale brought you in a silver goblet, and you've drank the ale, but no goblet can we see."

"I left it in the parlour," said Dick; "I'll swear I left it in the parlour. Why, man alive, I've not stirred outside the threshold of your house since I first entered it!"

"I know that," returned Boniface; "and I don't intend that you should stir till you have given me my property; so mind you that. Come, give it up at once."

And, as the speaker said this, he placed his hand on the shoulder of his customer, and would have shook him, only he saw mischief in his eye.

"Now, look here," said Turpin, playing carelessly with his riding-whip, "let us understand each other. My fingers are itching to give you a good horsewhipping for your insolence. What do you take me for, you bloated old grampus—eh? What do you take me for?"

"I thought you were an honest man."

"You thought!"

"Yes."

"By the Lord above! I did not know that you could think."

"You give me my silver cup."

"I left it in the parlour, I tell you."

"It ain't there, sir," said the waiter.

Turpin, the landlord, and the waiter now entered the room. A search was made in vain for the cup, which was nowhere to be found.

By this time a constable made his appearance.

The landlord of the "Warbling Waggoner" had sent off a stable-boy for this worthy when he first learned of the missing property.

An angry altercation ensued. Turpin insisted upon being searched.

This was done, but no cup was found.

"Is it not monstrous, that I am to be insulted in this manner," said Dick, turning to the officer, "when I have never moved from the house since my first entrance? I shall enter an action against this man for making a false charge. Other persons have been in and out of the room. Why should I be made accountable for the lost property?"

The constable admitted that the landlord was in the wrong.

Eventually Turpin paid his reckoning, and was suffered to depart in peace. Before he did so, however, he gave his name and address, both of which, it is needless to say, were fictitious.

Mounting his horse, the highwayman left the "Warbling Waggoner," apparently in high dudgeon, although all the while he was laughing in his sleeve at the success of his ruse.

In a short time after his departure, Tom King made his appearance at the inn.

The landlord, who was chafing and fretting at his loss, made Tom acquainted with all the particulars. The latter smiled to himself, and said that he would prefer having his ale brought in a less costly vessel. He then went into the parlour.

Refreshments were brought him. When he was left alone to discuss these, he felt under the table for the cup in question. True enough, it was there.

Turpin had stuck it to the bottom of the table with a piece of cobbler's wax.

King let it remain in its position for some little time.

He commiserated with the waiter and landlord upon the loss. When he was ready to take his departure, he removed the goblet and put it in his pocket. He then mounted his horse and rode off, well pleased with the success of his adventure.

He overtook his companion at about three miles' distance from the "Warbling Waggoner."

Dick laughed heartily when King showed him the silver goblet which he had walked off with so easily.

The two highwaymen then took their way to London.

CHAPTER XI.

THE ROYAL LEVEE.—TOM KING'S ADVENTURES.

TOM KING had determined upon being present at the *levée* which was to be held at the old Palace of St. James's. If that building could speak—if the bricks of which it is composed were sentient—what a tale these could tell, or rather, what a multiplicity of tales could they whisper to the ears of the curious.

King, as we have already stated, was a gentlemanly, and, indeed, at times he might be deemed an aristocratic personage. I should find it difficult, perhaps, if I were to endeavour to describe what an aristocratic-looking individual is like; so must content myself by asserting, without fear of contradiction, that when he was made up and on his best behaviour, away from his companions, King would find but little difficulty in passing himself off as a gentleman, even among the upper ten thousand, many of whom, by the way, are more easily deceived than you are yourself, my unwashed artizan.

Tom had determined, if possible, to be present at the king's *levée*. It would be difficult to give a reason for his strange determination. It resulted more from whim or caprice, perhaps, than from any other cause. Be this as it may, he seemed bent upon carrying out his project. Turpin in vain reasoned with him upon the folly of his making such a dangerous attempt.

"All right, old boy," answered King, "I will run all risks."

"But you know, as well as myself, that the palace is not without the ferrets. There are detective officers about the State apartments, and in every part of the place."

"No matter. I shall be disguised, and they will not interfere with me—there is no fear of that."

"You are obstinate, Tom—as obstinate as a mule, and I suppose you will have your own way in this as in other things. If you get yourself into trouble, you will know who you have to blame."

"Not you, at any rate," returned King, "certainly not you. I shall have no one to blame but myself."

Wishing his friend farewell, Tom King took his way towards a set of chambers he rented at the West End of the town.

It was there that he purposed dressing in the Court-suit with which he had provided himself.

Now, although King had in his possession the card which he had taken from the portmanteau of Lord Oxford, it would be impossible for him to enter the sacred precincts of the palace unless he personated some well-known person. It would, of course, never do to present himself as Tom King, the highwayman.

He was prepared for this.

It so happened that Tom bore a great resemblance to a young baronet of the period. This gentleman's name was Sir Piers Shafton. He seldom made his appearance in the select London circles, as he generally confined himself to his own country seat.

Tom knew the whole particulars of Sir Piers' habits and history, and he could at any time make up—to use a theatrical phrase—for the young baronet; he determined, therefore, to enter the palace as Sir Piers.

My readers must not think this an extraordinary occurrence.

It has been said that truth is stranger than fiction, and we often find this to be really the case. Many of our readers will doubtless remember the circumstance of a ticket-of-leave man being presented at Court only a few months ago. It is, therefore, no matter of surprise that a handsome, dashing, gentlemanly-looking young man should be able to obtain an entrance into the palace in the reign of the first George.

King and Sir Piers were about the same age and the same height. Added to this, the highwayman was acquainted with one or two of the baronet's servants, so that he knew something of the movements of the gentleman he was going to represent.

Tom made his way to his chambers. The boy he generally left in charge of these came down the stone stairs, and informed his master that a magnificent Court-suit had arrived on the previous day.

Tom knew this as well as the lad.

He said but little, and ascended the stairs and sought his own rooms.

Now, the suit, which had been sent home by a fashionable tailor, was an exact counterpart of one worn by Sir Piers himself. There were also the same sort of mountings to the sword-hilt, the same description of embroidery on the vestments, and the same kind of buckles to the shoes.

Altogether the make-up was excellent.

Tom King eyed his garments, which were spread out on several chairs, with evident satisfaction. He proceeded at once to encase himself in the gay vestments; but when he had put the last garment on, it occurred to him that he had forgotten to have his head operated on by a first-class hair-dresser.

Hastily denuding himself of his fashionable apparel, he sent the boy for a barber.

In a few minutes after this the lad returned with a proficient in the tonsor's art.

King's head was operated upon in a satisfactory manner by this worthy. When he had taken his departure, the highwayman once more encased himself in his Court-suit.

He then sent out his boy for a chair. Upon this arriving, King entered it with all the grace of a man of fashion.

The chair proceeded with its precious burden towards St. James's Palace.

The streets were crowded with vehicles of every description, the pathways were lined with pedestrians, and the windows and balconies of the houses were filled with spectators.

The avenues leading from the palace presented a gay appearance enough. Ladies of all ages and sizes were visible from the windows of their carriages. Many of these were loaded with jewelry—the elderly ones especially—and plumes of feathers nodded from their heads.

Most eminent persons of the day were presented at the king's *levée*.

There were Sir William Windham and Sir Robert Walpole—the author of celebrated popular works, many of which are read in our own time; there were also Francis Atterbury, Bishop of Rochester, William Pulteney, and John, Lord Hervey.

Each and all of these personages were notabilities at the time of which we are writing.

Most of my readers have read in the papers accounts of the conflicts—for they can be termed little else—that took place in the staircase and passages leading to the throne-room of St. James's Palace. Of course these conflicts only took place on those particular days when it pleased the reigning sovereign to give a drawing-room, as it is termed, or hold a *levée*.

Tom King was conveyed in his chair to the entrance of the palace. He alighted, and presented himself at the door. He presented his card of admission, and, at the same time, begged that the attendants would announce him as Sir Piers Shafton. He passed into the passage, and from thence into the crush room, which was so densely packed with distinguished personages that our highwayman found himself so pushed, shouldered, and hustled, that he began to vote the aristocratic persons a set of boors, so little care did they seem to evince for the genteel observances of society.

After waiting like the rest for a considerable period of time, Tom eventually succeeded in ascending the grand staircase by slow degrees, and finally reached one of the ante-rooms. Here he paused for breath, and began to look around him with some degree of curiosity.

A galaxy of beauty stood around. Fair creatures, made doubly fair by the aid of art; dowager duchesses, who were there for the purpose of bringing out some pet who was perhaps destined to become the belle of the season.

There were a vast number of nobodies—that is, nobodies as far as intellect was concerned; but they were, nevertheless, scions of some noble house, and this gave them a pretext for appearing in the presence of Royalty. There were also ambassadors and attachés from foreign Courts—schemers, politicians, diplomatists; a few—a very few, men of science; and a host of nondescripts, who had, by some means or other, managed to attach some notoriety to their names.

As King was looking about, examining the countenances of those assembled in the ante room in which he now found himself, he was addressed by a pale-faced young man whom he had noticed more than once in the crush-room below.

"You do not honour these rooms much with your presence, sir," said the individual in question.

"Not much, it must be confessed," said Tom, in an easy, careless, drawling manner, which he copied from some exquisites whom he had heard talking in the crush-room. "To speak the truth, I do not care a great deal about paying so dear a penalty for the honour of serving his Majesty. I know not how the ladies can bear all this heat and crowding, but for my own part, I have once or twice wished myself in my own cool, quiet retreat in the country."

"It *is* a crush," said King's companion; "there can be no doubt about that. It *is* a crush."

"Fearful."

"But then, you see, what will not a woman do to be presented at Court, and be elbowed by a prime minister? Anything, sir—anything in the world."

"I suppose so," returned King. "The place is very full, and you are better acquainted than myself with most of those present, I dare say."

"No, no. I recognise a great number here, as a matter of course; and so do you, I should suppose."

"Oh—ahem—yes."

"I am addressing Sir Piers Shafton, I think?"

Tom King gave a bow of assent to this query.

"Oh, I have heard of you often enough, although I have not had the pleasure of meeting you before. I have heard of you from my friend Toulmin. You and he graduated at Oxford together."

"Yes," answered King, who did not know what else to say. "How is he, and when did you see him last?"

"When did I see him? Why, my dear Sir Piers, how could I see him unless I choose to sail for the Indies?"

"Ah, true," said Tom, with a laugh.

"He chose to leave the land which gave him birth," said the highwayman's companion; "he would go to that clime which is the grave of so many Europeans. And so it's a chance if we either of us ever see him again."

"Quite a chance."

"But I must do him the justice to say that he always spoke in the highest terms of you. Indeed, I never heard any man speak better of another than he did of his friend, Sir Piers Shafton."

"I believe I was a favourite with him," said King, who began to feel very uncomfortable at the turn the conversation was taking. "By the way," he added, quickly, "who is that elderly gentleman?"

"Which—which do you mean?"

"He who is the centre of the group yonder."

"Well, that is a gentleman by the name of Gordon. He was supposed to be mixed up with the South Sea Bubble, but he managed, somehow or other, to clear himself of the charges made against him, and is, as you see, received at court."

"And who is yonder gentleman?" inquired King.

"That one to the left of the group?"

"Yes."

"Why, surely you know him? That's the celebrated Mr. Addison—you certainly know him?" said his companion, with surprise.

"Ahem! My sight is defective, and I cannot recognise persons at a distance. Oh, yes; I see it is Mr. Addison, sure enough. What mistakes one is led into by being near-sighted."

"I am near enough to you, but I suppose you do not recognise me?" returned the other.

"Well, no. Your features appear to be familiar to me, but I cannot remember your name—that is, assuming I ever knew it."

"I don't think we have ever met before. My name is Smithers—the Honorable Charles Smithers, at your service."

King bowed low; his companion did the same.

Mr. Smithers turned out to be a very pleasant fellow. He continued to converse with his newly-made friend, and the two seemed to be well pleased with each other's company.

The former introduced the highwayman to a number of persons, whose names the latter would have some difficulty in recollecting; for there was so much bustle and confusion that there was but little time allowed for calm reflection.

At length they reached the throne-room, and both passed before his Majesty, who bowed courteously to each, and then, after an observation or two, they passed on.

All had, up to this time, passed on pleasantly enough, and if Tom had made his way out of the palace, like a prudent man, he would not have been put to the shifts he was obliged to resort to.

While he was standing at the further end of the room he heard a few hurried whispers, and he soon became aware that a number of eyes were directed towards him.

Then there was some more whispering.

Tom King began to feel particularly uncomfortable, for, up to this time, he appeared to have passed without any notice from the assembled guests, except the Hon. Mr. Smithers, who had treated him with the utmost courtesy and kindness. That individual was engaged in conversation with a bevy of fashionable beauties. King thought that even he began to regard him with mistrust.

What could be the meaning of this strange alteration?

King was not long left in doubt as to its cause; for, to his infinite horror, Sir Piers Shafton himself entered the throne-room. There was, therefore, not much to be surprised at in those present regarding the baronet's double with looks of wonderment.

The resemblance between the two persons was re-markable. The Honorable Mr. Smithers, was puzzled to know which was the real personage, and which was the impostor. He was almost inclined to believe in King being the real Simon Pure.

There was a sort of confused murmur. Sir Piers upon his entrance into the throne room, regarded King with a look of contempt and disgust.

The highwayman now began to see that matters assumed a very serious aspect. He made his way to the door of the throne-room, and gained the passage.

Here he was addressed by one of the attendants of the palace. This person looked hard at him, and said—

"There is evidently some mistake, sir, and a very serious mistake. Pray who have I the honour of addressing?"

"Sir Piers Shafton," said the highwayman, with the utmost *sang froid*.

"You cannot leave the palace, sir, for the present," answered the official, in a polite, but nevertheless firm manner.

"Cannot leave?" said King. "I do not understand you, sir. Cannot leave! And wherefore not, I pray you?"

"There are very good reasons why you should remain."

"I do not understand the meaning of these observations. Have a care, sir, as to what you are saying. Is it customary for gentlemen to be put under arrest, or have their liberty interfered with, in the precincts of his Majesty's palace?"

"Pray may I inquire how you obtained admittance?"

"How? Why in the usual way, of course. I handed my card to one of those who are in the vestibule."

"There cannot be two Sir Piers Shafton here to-day; and yet——"

"And yet what?"

"There are two gentlemen who lay claim to that title."

"Ridiculous!" ejaculated King. "Let me pass, for I am in a hurry to return—let me pass, I say."

"I have orders not to let either yourself or the other gentleman leave the palace till this unpleasant affair has been inquired into."

"I never heard of such an indignity being offered to any gentleman. However, as you appear to be obstinate, I will remain; but why I am compelled to do so, I have yet to learn."

"We are informed," said the man, "that some one has obtained admission into the palace by means which it is not possible to say now with anything like certainty; but some one has assumed the name and dress of Sir Piers."

"Do you know the baronet?" inquired King.

"I have seen him at a distance; but——"

"Well, if you have seen me, you ought to know my features again. Do you mean to say that I am an impostor? or what do you mean?"

This was spoken in such a tone of confidence that the man was staggered. He began to doubt whether he was not mistaken.

"You will be pleased to answer my question," continued King. "There is something exquisitely ridiculous in a man endeavouring to argue me out of my own identity. Do you, or do you not, know me to be Sir Piers Shafton?"

"Well, if I were to be asked the question——"

"If you were to be asked! Why, you are. Your answer."

"I should be inclined to say that you were Sir Piers; but, then, you know——"

"What?"

"That my word is one thing, Sir Piers."

"And, I should hope, a word that could be relied on."

"I hope so—I hope so, Sir—Piers."

"There appears to me to be some strange mystery in all this," said King—"A mystery which I am quite at a loss to comprehend. I don't suppose either yourself or any of the other officials connected with the palace would willingly or purposely insult me; nevertheless, this conduct is strange, to say the very least of it—strange and incomprehensible."

"You will oblige me by remaining here," said the man, who was by this time convinced that King was really what he represented himself to be. "I should be sorry to cause any unpleasentness, but we have all of us a duty to perform."

"Unquestionably."

"And I am sure you will excuse me if I endeavour to do mine with as much consideration for the feelings of others as circumstances will admit."

"That is right enough."

"And I will put it to yourself, Sir Piers. There is another person who has entered here, who affects to bear that name and title besides yourself."

"I cannot help that. It is no fault of mine."

"Certainly not; only, for your own sake, I should suppose you would wish him to undergo an examination, and be called to account for the unwarrantable liberty he has taken with an honoured name."

"Yes, that may be, and indeed is, true enough; but you see, my friend, I have important business on hand—an appointment, in fact, to see a gentleman, who will be on the sea before morning; and, if I miss this appointment, I shall miss seeing one of my oldest friends, who is about to leave this country for years. I quite agree with you that this matter should be subject to the most rigid inquiry; and, had I time, I would remain here till midnight rather than the question should be evaded; but I have not time."

The official of the palace hesitated.

King's manner was so like an innocent man that it carried conviction with it; and, had there not have been strict orders given for the detention of both gentlemen—the real and fictitious Piers Shafton—it is more than probable that our highwayman would have been allowed to depart in peace.

"So you see how the case stands," said King, after a pause.

"Oh, yes, sir, I see that plain enough; but our orders are imperative. You really must excuse me if I am compelled to carry them out."

"That is enough. I have done," said Tom King. "Where — where is this gentleman who has assumed my name and costume?"

"In the throne-room."

"Well, the matter can be soon settled. I will await your return. Go, therefore, and bring him hither. Oh, dear me, the matter can be soon settled."

"Will you wait here?"

"Of course I will."

The man took his way into the throne-room.

"Now, what is to be done?" said King to himself. "Make a rush for it at the door? Oh, no; that would never do. I could not get through the streets in this costume, even supposing I were able to get through the doorway. Alas! Dick was right enough. And yet, to stay here and argue with Sir Piers—to try and persuade him that he was mistaken as to his own identity, would be the act of a madman. Where can I go? Mercy on me! if there isn't one of Wild's men in the passage. Ah, it's all up with me."

Tom King cast his eyes around. His danger now rendered him desperate. To wait where he was would be an act of madness, and yet he durst not venture below. He went along the passage which led to the throne-room, unobserved by those below, for a party of persons who were ascending the stairs concealed him from sight.

At the end of the passage he came to another flight of stairs.

He ascended these, and gained the apartments above. They appeared to be entirely deserted.

He went from room to room, in the hope of finding some place where he might conceal himself.

In one of these rooms was a small ebony cabinet. He tried the doors of this, but they were locked.

A sudden thought struck him.

The cabinet was in a corner of the room which was so dark that it seemed to be admirably adapted for concealment.

Upon his examining the cabinet still closer, he found that if he could get on the top of it he might lay concealed; for there was a large piece of ornamentation in front of it, which would effectually hide his body when in a recumbent position.

Being an expert climber, he managed to succeed in gaining the top of this piece of furniture, which was massive and cumbersome.

He stretched himself full length on its summit, and felt that there were three chances to one of his being detected.

This done, he awaited the result with a throbbing heart.

Everything seemed to be as quiet as the very grave in these heavy, but costly-furnished apartments.

Tom King felt that a desperate case required a desperate remedy, and it was more than probable that Wild's men were on his track. Even if such were the case, he felt sure that they would not be permitted to enter the private apartments of the palace.

So far he felt himself safe.

We must now return to the throne-room.

The gentleman usher proceeded thither, and in a few minutes succeeded in finding Sir Piers Shafton.

He informed the baronet that a gentleman awaited his appearance in the corridor.

Sir Piers at once turned from those with whom he was conversing, and followed the official to the spot where King had been seen last.

He was nowhere to be found.

Then came expressions of surprise, and inquiries as to the missing man.

Those who were in charge of the various avenues leading to the interior of the palace were questioned closely. Of course no one knew anything of the fugitive, but they each and all declared that he had not passed through any of the entrances.

The natural surmise was that he had concealed himself in the crowd of persons, either in the throne-room or one of the apartments contiguous to it.

All these underwent a strict search, but no Tom King could be found.

A person with a white wand came forward, and said that there must have been some negligence on the part of the officials in charge of the various entrances, as without a doubt he had passed through one of them.

A general panic seemed to seize those in charge of the entrances, and each man endeavoured to justify himself.

"It was impossible for the fugitive to have escaped," so they all of them declared.

"Where is he, then?" inquired the gentleman with the white wand.

This was a question easier asked than answered.

No one could tell.

Presently some person, more imaginative than the rest, said that possibly he had dropped from one of the windows into the gardens at the rear of the palace.

Upon this a party was sent to make a strict search in them.

It is needless to say that they did not meet with any success. Disconsolate and crestfallen, they returned to the gentleman with the white wand, and informed him of the failure of their expedition.

Sir Piers Shafton, who was a quiet, gentlemanly man enough, himself began to view the matter as something less serious than those who were connected with the palace. He could hardly refrain from laughing outright when he looked at the disconsolate countenances of the palace officials. He turned to the gentleman with the silver stick, and said—

"Well, after all, if it be true, as you suppose—if it be true that this gentleman has escaped through any of the doors, what then? I don't see that it is a matter of such great moment. I am the party who ought to feel the most aggrieved. And I frankly confess that, at first, I did feel very much annoyed at such a circumstance; but now that it's all over, I can afford to laugh at it."

The gentleman with the silver stick was not paid for laughing: he held his appointment to look serious and uphold the dignity of the Court. Oh, dear, no!—laugh, indeed! He was paid a princely sum for doing little enough, so he had no time to laugh—and he had not the disposition to do so, even if he had time. He stood grave and erect, and cast a look of anger at those underlings who were nearest to him.

Then there was a pause.

The hounds were at fault.

The fox had doubled on them, and the scent was lost. Sir Piers Shafton again spoke.

"I do not see that this is so serious an affair as you seem to think it," he said, quietly; "for, after all, it may prove to be a joke on the part of some half-witted youngster, who has thought himself very clever in personating me."

"He was not half-witted," said the official who had conversed with King; "he was anything but half-witted, Sir Piers. The fellow was too clever by half—in fact, so clever that he fully persuaded me that he was really what he represented himself to be."

"He had audacity enough, at any rate," replied the baronet, "to send for me to be confronted with him, although it would appear that he had not the temerity to wait till I made my appearance. Let him go his ways. For my part, I should hardly think it worth while to take any further trouble in the matter."

"But, Sir Piers," remonstrated the gentleman with the silver stick, "this is no light matter. There must be some gross neglect somewhere, or this person could never have made his escape."

"We don't know as yet that he has made his escape," said one of Mr. Wild's followers, in a voice half oleagenous and half husky. "For my part, I have very great doubts about his having got clear off."

Silver stick gentleman turned sharply round upon the thief-taker gentleman.

Silver stick was no match for thief-taker in either sharpness or power of perception; and silver stick knew this, although he affected to be oblivious to the galling fact.

"What do you mean?" he inquired of the speaker.

"Why simply this—that the gentleman may, after all, be concealed somewhere."

"But we have searched," said silver-stick.

"Where?"

"Everywhere."

"No—begging your pardon—not everywhere. There are other apartments in the palace besides those you have been in."

These words fell upon the ear of silver stick like a peal of thunder.

Was it possible—could it be possible, he asked himself, that anyone would have the temerity to enter the king's private apartments?

He forgot, poor man, that the timid hare, when hunted, would rush into the presence of royalty itself, or anywhere else where it could get shelter.

"The other rooms in the palace!" he iterated. "No, we have not deemed it necessary to enter those."

"It would be as well to do so," suggested Mr. Wild's man. "You know, I've had to do with a lot o' slippery customers."

"Humph! oh, yes," returned silver stick, who felt his dignity compromised by being in converse with a low thief-taker. "I dare say, my man, there may be some truth in what you say. We will have the other rooms run through."

"Shall I go with you?" inquired Mr. Wild's representative.

"You! Oh, dear, no," returned the other, in an injured tone, "certainly not."

He gave a haughty wave of his hand as he said this, and gathering together a knot of officials, he proceeded at the head of these into the various rooms of the palace.

Now, we have had, in our own day, numerous instances of persons being concealed in the royal palace. Many of our readers may remember the boy Jones, who managed to secrete himself successfully on so many occasions in Buckingham Palace. The account which this lad gave of his adventures would appear to be almost incredible did we not know that the statement was a true one.

It is not wonderful, therefore, that Tom King was able to secrete himself, more especially when we bear in mind that to search every nook and corner of St. James's Palace would be a much longer task than anyone might at first suppose—indeed, it was almost impossible to do so with anything like satisfaction by making a cursory survey.

There were so many hiding-places in the palace—such a number of nooks and curves in the various apartments, which were of such an irregular form; there were, moreover, so many passages winding about in all parts of the building, that unless the concealed person happened to fall in with one or the other of the various domestics, there would be every chance for him remain *perdu* for a considerable period of time.

The party of officials went from room to room, and instituted what they supposed to be a rigid search. At length they arrived at the apartment where Tom King lay concealed. The latter heard the sound of approaching footsteps, and durst scarcely draw his breath.

Now came the question whether he was to be ignominiously handed over to the constabulary force, or whether he was to be allowed a little respite.

He lay at full length on the top of the ebony cabinet. Curiosity would have prompted him to give one glance out of his hiding-place, but prudence forbid such an act. He lay like a rat in its hole, and listened to the few words which fell from those who were in search of him. Presently he heard their footsteps in the room which he had chosen for his hiding-place.

Then the murmur of voices was more distinctly audible. King heard the footsteps of the men going from place to place — from one piece of furniture to another.

Cupboards were opened, and closed again.

The hangings of the bedstead were drawn on one side. Curious eyes peered beneath them, and grunts of dissatisfaction were given as no trace could be found of the fugitive.

Soon after this the party came in front of the cabinet where Tom lay concealed.

The gentleman with the silver stick pulled out of his pocket a large bunch of keys, and opened the doors of the cabinet. As he did this, Tom King was in a state of desperation. What if they should search the top? All would then be over. There was, however, but one alternative. This was to quietly await the result with calmness and resignation.

The doors of the cabinet were slammed to, and relocked. Then the party paused.

To King, the pause seemed to last an age.

"As I suspected," said silver stick. "As I said from the first, he has made his escape by one of the entrances. I knew that."

Sir Piers Shafton now made his appearance.

"Any success?" he said.

"None, Sir Piers—none. There can be but one conclusion to arrive at."

"What is that?"

"He has got clear off."

"Well, you ought to know best," returned the baronet. "For mine own part I think there has been already too much trouble spent over this ridiculous business. After all, no very great harm has been done, and I am disposed to look upon the whole affair as a very good joke. I would, as far as I am myself concerned, much rather the matter was let alone. Say no more about it, and few persons will be any the wiser.

By making a fuss about it, what will be the natural consequence? we shall only attract attention to a circumstance which certainly will not redown to the credit of——"

"Certainly not to the credit of the palace officials."

"I do not see that they are to blame. It is easy for a single individual to slip out when the place is so densely crowded. No, no; after all there is little blame attached to anyone, and so I beg of you to let the matter rest where it is. Say no more about it, and I promise you that neither you nor anyone else shall hear anything more about it from me."

He was a good-natured, easy-going man, was Sir Piers Shafton, and never had, at any time of his life, courted publicity.

"Oh," ejaculated the gentleman with the silver wand, "you promise that you will not make any inquiries, Sir Piers?"

"Certainly not. I do not wish to get anyone into trouble. Of course, I do not restrict myself in my own private circle of acquaintance. I shall see if I can find out who has played me this trick. It is possible that I may be able to learn; but, then, no one will know besides myself. You have nought to fear.

"That will suffice," said the silver stick, waving his men away, who were but too glad to obey. They left the room immediately.

"I'm sure, Sir Piers Shafton, I have to thank you for the courtesy and kindness you have evinced throughout this unpleasant business," said the silver stick gentleman.

"Not at all; pray don't trouble yourself to thank me. I was vexed at first, I frankly confess; but now I am enabled to view the matter in a different light, and the last feeling I should have connected with it would be anger."

"You are a good sort," murmured King, who was cramped by remaining in one position. "You are a good sort; but you would be a deal better if you would take yourself off."

"I hope and trust his Majesty does not know that an impostor has been here," said the palace official.

"No, I think not; and, indeed, to say the truth, I should hope that his Majesty has something better to engage his attention than any such ridiculous circumstance as the one in question."

"I do hope his Majesty is not aware of it," murmured the man once more.

"Oh, dear no! make your mind quite easy upon that head. When I found that some one had been representing me, I deemed it advisable not to present myself to my sovereign."

The two personages then left the room.

Tom King breathed more freely, he was now the sole occupant.

CHAPTER XII.

TOM'S ADVENTURES.—STRANGE DISCOVERIES.—THE MAIDS OF HONOUR.

It would be no easy task to describe the sense of sudden relief which the highwayman felt when the officials of the palace had taken their departure. It was as though a heavy stone, which had almost suffocated him, had been removed from his chest. It was impossible to tell what other dangers he had to pass through before he could succeed in regaining his liberty; but the worst was over for the present. It was not at all likely that there would be any re-examination of the room—at any rate, the fugitive felt himself safe for a few hours.

He must trust to fortune and his own good luck to help him through the difficulties which his own imprudence had caused him to be placed in.

He remained in his place of concealment hour after hour.

As he was not acquainted with the interior of the palace, he durst not move lest he should stumble upon some one or other of the domestics. In such a case there would be no escape, so King deemed it best to remain and await the issue.

The apartment in which he had ensconced himself was, luckily for him, one that was not occupied at the time he took possession of it; neither was it likely to have a tenant, for the person who usually made it his resting-place was away, and would not return for some days.

Tom King was not aware of this; nevertheless he found it empty, and, from the appearance of the room, he was in hopes that it would remain so.

In this he was not mistaken.

Hour after hour passed. The shades of night crept on, and in a short time the fugitive found himself almost in utter darkness. It is true that a faint streak of light crept into the room through the windows. This proceeded from the oil lamps in the street.

King began to feel lonesome and melancholy—his spirits began to be depressed.

It was slow work for one of his lively nature and active temperament.

He began to think that the inmates of the palace did not pass so happy a life as those outside its walls.

Perhaps he was right in this surmise also.

After all, happiness is pretty equally distributed, and it does not always consist in costly furniture, unbounded wealth, and high-sounding titles.

It wanted about an hour to midnight when our highwayman, worn out by excitement, fell into a deep sleep.

How long he had been slumbering he could not tell, but he awoke with stiffened limbs, resulting from his constrained position, and the hard substance on which he had been lying.

He felt chilled, too, and the current of his blood seemed to have stagnated.

He could bear the confinement no longer, so without further hesitation, he descended from his resting-place, with as little noise as possible.

He gained the floor, which was covered with a thick carpet that deadened the sound of his feet as he took his way along.

All was as silent as the grave.

Tom walked across the room, and made towards the windows; he looked through one of these, and saw the court-yard beneath.

A sentry was pacing this with measured tread.

As he neared the window King drew back and let him pass.

He had not the most remote idea as to what part of the palace he was in.

It was enough for him to know that he was there, and the next question was how he could get clear away.

At first he had thought of opening the window, and dropping into the yard beneath.

After a moment's reflection, he came to the conclusion that this would be impossible, for even supposing he succeeded in gaining the court-yard in safety—which was a matter of doubt—he would be sure to attract the notice of one of the sentries, then he would either be shot at once or else captured. His ultimate fate, after this, there was not much doubt about. So he dismissed this thought from his mind, being fully convinced that such a course would be impracticable.

He now crept softly to the further end of the room, and discovered a door which led to another apartment. As the door was partially open, Tom peeped into the adjoining apartment.

From some cause or other, this was much lighter than the one he had occupied.

He went through the doorway and looked about him. Not a soul was visible.

The room in which he found himself was tenantless, like his own.

When he made this discovery he began to regain his

courage. Possibly he might light upon some means of effecting his escape.

The thought gave him new courage, and he walked boldly across the room, at the end of which there was a long, winding passage.

Tom proceeded along this, and then arrived at a long gallery.

He was not at all aware that he was nearing that part of the Royal palace devoted to the use of her Majesty's maids of honour.

Nothing daunted, he went along the gallery, and then arrived at the bottom of a little staircase.

He crept softly up this, and when at the top he found himself by the side of a small apartment, if it could be so termed. It was, in reality, little larger than a good-sized closet.

King entered this, and then paused to recover his breath.

He was quite charmed with his position.

The place seemed admirably adapted for concealment. It was, in fact, a niche, or nook, which had been cut out of the solid masonry of the building.

He was not aware that it communicated with the king's study by a secret flight of stairs.

Perhaps, if he had known this, his confidence would have deserted him.

Wondering what it had been intended for, Tom looked about with inquiring eyes.

He observed some loopholes or niches in the wall. They were high up, near to the ceiling of the room.

A soft, mellow light shone through them.

King could not comprehend where this came from. Anxious to ascertain as much as possible, he wheeled a table to the side of the wall, and mounted it. He was then enabled to look through one of the loopholes.

He stood spellbound at the picture that was presented to his gaze.

Tom King had a full view of the apartment occupied by the maids of honour.

Nothing could be more enchanting than the appearance of the luxurious dormitory of these persons, with its six small bedsteads, each with hangings of light grey-coloured damask, bordered with scarlet fringe. A soft and velvet-like Turkey carpet covered the floor, and the walls were hidden entirely by tapestry, the subject of which was some charming idyl of an early English poet.

Shepherds habited in satin, and shepherdesses in tight boddices trimmed with flowing ribbons, having led their fleecy herds to the borders of a limpid stream, were whispering fondly together beneath the shady beech-tree branches, whilst amorous fawns, entirely concealed by the green rushes, watched their graceful motions.

The mellow and subdued light of an embossed silver chandelier, with globes of pale-blue stained glass, threw a soft shadow on the graceful forms of these shepherdesses, who almost seemed to breathe, and to realise the enchanting dream of I know not what golden age, at once poetical, fabulous, impossible, and illusive.

At the end of this room there were two grated windows, which opened on to the gardens of the palace.

On the opposite end might be seen a Venetian mirror, set in a dark tortoise-shell frame, with a rim of gilded brass.

But this mirror, instead of being suspended according to the reigning fashion, was closely fixed at a considerable height into a niche in the wall, whilst the dark hue of the tortoise-shell from a thousand golden arabesques stood out in strong relief, presenting two or three loopholes most ingeniously hidden in the wall.

It was through one of these that our highwayman was taking a survey of that sacred apartment, which was devoted to the use of the maids of honour.

He thought, as he gazed on the enchanting scene which lay before him, that he was compensated for all the day's troubles.

Perhaps many of our readers might have thought the same.

It was a gorgeous sight.

From the apertures in the wall everything passing in this room might be seen and heard—from the dark little hiding-place which had been cut in the thickest part of the wall.

It was from this spot that King was enabled to have so fine a view of the sleeping chamber of the beauteous nymphs upon whose lovely forms his eyes were so intently fixed. All his troubles were for a time forgotten; he lived only for the present hour.

Before him lay beauty in various attitudes of soft and languid repose.

To a man of his impressionable nature what more could be desired?

He felt as though he were gazing upon some forbidden Paphian bower—some delightful Garden of Eden, where sin and sorrow never entered.

It was four o'clock in the morning when our tender-hearted highwayman ensconced himself in that retreat, which had been designed for royalty alone.

The windows of the sleeping-apartments of the maids of honour were open, for the perfume from the huge nosegays of roses and violets which were placed there in huge china vases would have been otherwise too oppressive.

Darkness still reigned around, and a thousand stars gilded the horizon; the perfumed breeze from the gardens of the palace wafted in at every breath the odour of flowers.

We have already stated that it was four o'clock in the morning, and in the apartments devoted to the maids of honour five young persons were sleeping.

Whoever has observed another in a state of repose may often draw from it some striking analogy to their waking character, from the unconscious, unstudied, and almost involuntary attitudes which this state exhibits.

Observe, therefore, these young girls' repose—what a contrast, full of meaning, their different attitudes express.

One girl slept a quiet sleep: her gentle and regular breathing heaved but slightly her tranquil breast, over which her arms, white as marble, were modestly crossed.

Did not this form reveal that the youthful and polished brow had never known one shade of care—never been ruffled by one sad emotion? And did it not also reveal the indolent and unexcitable nature of its possessor?

And, in truth, this one of the maids of honour was calm and impassable: her neck, white as alabaster, could scarcely be distinguished from the sheets of her couch, white as the driven snow.

The highwayman regarded each of the sleeping beauties with eyes of admiration. They had each of them a style of beauty which was peculiarly their own.

He glanced at a neighbouring couch.

On this there is a young girl of twenty years of age, with her queen-like figure, her masculine and regular features, and her proud head—placed high upon her pillow, and resting on her bended arm; her hair of raven black is long and thick, and floats over her magnificent though dusky shoulders in dishevelled masses; her eyebrows of a deep jet are represented by a scarcely perceptible line, and, although wrapped in slumber, her cheeks are partially tinged with red; her marked nostrils are slightly dilated, and her upper lip, red as coral, is covered with a soft down, and curled with a scornful smile.

What a remarkable expression is depicted in that fearless attitude—in that bold form! especially when you contrast its decision with the calm features of that timid and half fearful young girl whose soft face has a startled expression, and who, sleeping in the arms of an amazon, seems to nestle there for safety.

And in this case appearances are not deceitful, for the brown Theresa Valpy is self-willed, passionate, and proud; and no nature can be more yielding and gentle than that of the fair and charming Constance Armatage, who has, however, transgressed the commands of her governess by leaving her couch to share that of her friend, and to talk with her those airy nothings, those undefined projects, and those nameless hopes — the golden dreams of life's nursery.

What an admirable contrast they present! How admirably those charms enhance each other!—the one delicate and fragile, the other bold and masculine—the one of a complexion so glowing and vermillion-hued that it almost seemed dyed by the burning sun of Asia, the other of so ethereal and pure a complexion that she seemed to have caught the mellowed and chastened rays of the moon.

As Tom King caught sight of the fair and gentle Constance Arnatage, his heart beat audibly.

He remembered well enough her kind bearing when he and Turpin had stopped the carriage of her guardian, the Earl of Oxford.

He remembered this well enough, but he had little dreamed that in a night or two afterwards he would be looking into the bed-chamber of so fair a creature.

Had she been present at the king's *levée?* was the first question he asked of himself.

And had she recognised him in his disguise? was the next question.

He had supposed her to be far away from London.

In this he was evidently mistaken.

How young, how fresh, gentle, and beautiful she looked!

All goodness, and all tenderness!

He would gladly—cheerfully have laid down his life then and there to have had one tender embrace from her. But then he sighed to think how far—how very far she was removed from him.

She was, in truth, a divinity far beyond his reach.

Of what use, therefore, was it for him to look upon a sun which only blinded him with its radiance.

He turned to the next bed, and, as his eye suddenly rested on it, his cheek suddenly blanched, for the features of the sleeper who rested on the couch were more familiar to him than those of the Honorable Miss Armitage.

They were those of our heroine—Nan Darrell.

"Miss Darrell here!" murmured King. "Here, in the royal palace, and in the apartment occupied by her Majesty's maids of honour? She must be here only as a visitor. Surely she has not been presented at Court under a feigned name, like myself. Ah, no; she is not likely to do that."

Again he turned his face towards her couch.

Nan, in many respects, presented a singular contrast to her companions. She appeared to have sunk to sleep after much reflection and weeping, for her cheeks bore the marks of freshly-shed tears. The cause of this, King was, of course, perfectly at a loss to account for, unless it was occasioned by the position of her father.

Her head still seemed to rest in deep thought, on a hand of so rare a beauty that the taper fingers recalled the pure and exquisite pencil of Raphael.

Her face, in the attitude of repose which she had taken, possessed an indescribable charm, owing to its peculiar and varied expression of firmness and resolution. Her forehead was high and polished, and her dark eyebrows were beautifully arched and well-defined, while the silken lashes that shaded those closed lids were so uncommonly lovely that they seemed to surround them with a halo of glory.

But — a rarer beauty still — each separate feature of this expressive face. was so interesting that, once seen, our heroine—Nan Darrell—could not easily be forgotten. Her complexion of clear brown harmonised well with the intense black of her eyes, which, when open, were singularly expressive; and, then, her hair, extremely fine, but almost straight, fell in long, flowing waves, like a black veil, over her shoulders and bosom, which the constant agitation of her troubled sleep had partially disclosed.

But, painful and restless, this repose was broken by sudden starts, which betrayed either some deep emotion or, it might be, some sudden thought which passed through the brain of the sleeper.

The highwayman was spell-bound to the spot. He did not feel disposed to move from his hiding-place. An hour passed away. After this, Tom felt still fascinated by the sight which lay before him. Nevertheless, after awhile, he descended from the table upon which he had been standing, and sat himself down in a carved, high-backed chair.

He then began to reflect more calmly upon his position.

It was quite certain that he could not expect to be an inhabitant of the palace for any length of time without being discovered.

His Majesty was not bound to provide him with board and lodging for the remainder of his life.

How to escape was the most important question.

It was clear enough that Nan Darrell was on good terms with the maids of honour, or she would not have been permitted an entrée into their sleeping apartment.

If he could only manage to attract her attention, and have a few words with her, she might possibly devise some means or hit upon some plan to release him from his present position.

But how was this to be effected? was the next question he asked himself.

This was not an easy one to answer.

The minutes flew by. Another hour passed.

Tom once more mounted the table, which he had drawn up to the side of the wall where the loop-holes were.

The maids of honour still slept. The ground-glass lamp paled before the effulgence of the god of day.

The sun had arisen.

The silence which had reigned throughout the apartment was soon to be over.

The golden rays of the sun kept creeping into the dormitory of the maids of honour, and, even as its rising splendour awakes the birds nestling beneath the leaves of the trees, so, indeed, would it soon unclose the beauteous eyelids of those young girls, which were just before heaving with sleep.

Then would they greet with indifference, or with joy, or with melancholy, the opening day. Then, perhaps, they would close them again directly, dazzled with the refulgence of the rising sun, because the dawn of wakefulness has its presentiments as well as the dawn of sleep.

And so with these young girls. One would smile at the hopes of a new day before her, another would regret bitterly the solitude and silence of night, whilst others saw with indifference another day added to its predecessors.

The first who awoke was Theresa Valpy.

Probably she did not wish to enjoy unshared the gladdening sight of a fine morning; for scarcely had she opened her large, brilliant eyes before, in silvery tones, she called the other maids of honour.

"Come, come, you idle girls! You have slept long enough, my friends. Awake. See, a more auspicious sunrise never gave promise of a finer day; and is it not a shame to be slumbering thus? Awake!"

The soft tones of the melodious voice soon aroused the sleepers, who replied, each in their own manner, to the fair Theresa's jesting.

King thought their glances were directed towards the aperture through which he was, like another Peeping Tom, taking a survey.

Whether it was this or from motives of delicacy, we will not attempt to determine, but, at any rate, the highwayman descended from his perch, and once more betook himself to his carved chair.

Soon after this the maids of honour were up and dressed, and were gathered together in a graceful group around an ormulu-table which was placed near to the window which overlooked the gardens in the rear of the palace.

Again the eye of King was fixed to the loophole in the wall.

"Well," exclaimed Theresa Valpy, "the crushing and crowding is over. Heaven be praised that his Majesty does not hold a *levée* every day in the week!"

"Human nature could not stand that," said another of the maids of honour, stretching out her pretty arms and indulging in a long yawn.

"Oh, fie!" exclaimed Miss Valpy. "What! not yet awake."

"Oh, I am awake enough," answered the young girl; "but you will permit me, my dear Theresa, to expand my chest and inflate my lungs with the fresh morning air."

"It is a beautiful morning," observed the Honorable Miss Armatage. "It makes one long to be away from smoky London—far away in the country."

"Oh, oh! and to be stopped by some handsome highwayman—eh, Constance?" said several voices.

No. 7.

King thought he observed a heightened colour suffuse the face of Miss Armatage at this speech.

"It would be hardly worth while, for the purpose of being robbed," answered Constance. "What say you, Miss Darrell?"

"Oh, I—I have never experienced the sensation," answered Nan, "and so am unable to say whether it is a pleasant one or otherwise."

"You may be sure it is pleasant," said Theresa Valpy—"that is when your knight of the road is a gentlemanly and courteous individual, which, sooth to say, many are."

"By the way," said another of the maids of honour, "what a strange circumstance that was with respect to Sir Piers Shafton."

"What was that?" inquired Theresa, languidly.

"Why, there were two Sir Piers Shaftons at the king's *levée* yesterday."

"Two?"

"Yes, two, my dears. Some one chose to represent

Sir Piers; and when he was discovered—or, rather, when the real baronet made his appearance—the fictitious gentleman suddenly disappeared. Whether he vanished into air, or up one of the chimneys, or how he managed to take himself off, will be a matter for future historians to discuss. He went his way somewhere, and was no longer visible to mortal eyes."

"A wise man for so doing, I should say," observed Theresa Valpy—"a very wise man. When the real gentleman made his appearance, it was discreet of the other to retire from the stage."

"It is something marvellous, though, how such a circumstance should have occurred," observed Nan's companion and bedfellow.

"My dear," said Theresa, "you may depend upon it that there is some deep-laid plot in all this. My own opinion is that the person who represented Sir Piers Shafton was a foreign spy."

"You don't mean that!" exclaimed Theresa's companions.

"Oh, but I do, my dears—I make no doubt of it."

"Much more likely that he was brought hither, and assumed the disguise, in consequence of some affair of the heart," observed Nan Darrell.

The young girls clapped their hands with delight. This supposition was received most favourably.

"Miss Darrell has more acuteness and perception than any of us," said Miss Armatage, with a quiet smile.

"Oh, dear, yes," answered the maids of honour; "she is not so closely shut out from the external world. Besides, her grandfather is a magistrate."

Nan Darrell smiled as she said—

"And what has that to do with me? I do not sit in judgment on offending persons."

"No, but you learn something from your relative," answered Theresa.

"Well!" exclaimed King, "I have come into the palace for something—so it would seem. Why, these said maids of honour seem to know all the proceedings of one's friends."

In a short time after this, three young girls left the apartment.

Constance Armatage and Nan Darrell were left to themselves.

Tom King was glad of this, as possibly it might afford him an opportunity of exchanging a few words with Nan.

It was impossible for him to attract her attention, from the position he had taken up, but he might be able to waylay her in one of the passages of the palace.

He determined, therefore, to keep watch over the movements of the two friends—for in a short time he learned from their conversation that they were intimate friends.

He was not a little astonished when he made this discovery.

He soon learned that the two young females had been school-fellows, and were still on the most intimate terms of friendship together.

"Do you know, my dear Nan," said Miss Armatage, "that the observations which Theresa has made have awakened in my mind a train of reflections—indeed, a very long train of reflections?"

"Indeed, dear! How so? and to what do these all tend?"

"Well, you must know, in the first place," said Miss Armatage, "that my companions have often rallied me about my predilection for lawless characters. You smile, as well you may. But hear me to the end."

"I have not sought to interrupt you, dearest."

"No, no—you are too well-bred to do that. Well, as I was saying, they have often rallied me, and wherefore, think you? Simply because I have chosen at times to defend them. It sounds supremely ridiculous for a young lady of quality to take upon herself to defend the most lawless persons; but I am just going to tell you something."

"Yes—I am all attention."

"Well, you must know that, very many years ago—before either of us were born, perhaps—there lived and moved in respectable society a very handsome and gentlemanly man, who has often been an attendant at this very palace when it pleased royalty to hold a drawing-room. This gentleman whom I am speaking of was an intimate friend of my poor dear father's; and I have often heard him speak of the gallant, handsome, and courtly Captain Orlando Ragget."

At this part of her companion's discourse the countenance of Nan Darrell became suddenly pallid, and a perceptible tremor shook her frame.

Miss Armatage did not observe the effect her words had upon Nan, but continued with her description of our heroine's father.

"Well, you must know, dear," said Miss Armatage, "that the said captain was badly used—most scandalously used by the government. I am sure I cannot tell you all the particulars of their conduct towards him; but I remember, when I was quite a child, that my poor father used to take his part, and go on rarely against the government for their behaviour towards him. I think—but I won't be certain of this—I think that the captain, disgusted with the powers which had treated him so shamefully, espoused the cause of the Pretender. Now, you know, we must not talk treason within the walls of the palace."

"I should hope not," returned Nan Darrell.

"But I think that he did espouse the cause of the Pretender. If such were the case, it is not to be wondered at that there should be so large a price set on his head."

"A large price set on his head! What do you mean?" inquired Nan, with such quickness, and in so anxious a manner, that her tones startled her companion.

"My dear Nan," said Miss Armatage, "one would suppose that my tale interests you more than it does myself."

"Well, yes, it does—I am interested, I confess. A price set on his head! Is—is the captain still alive, then?"

"Alas! yes. Now, you must hear me to the end, dearest—you must hear me to the end."

"I am all attention. Pray proceed."

"I must go back to the place I left off at, as we used to say when at school. I was saying that the captain had been hardly dealt by."

"Yes, I remember."

"So, from being a respectable gentleman, honoured by his king and country, he became—what, think you?"

"Nay, I know not."

"He became a highwayman!" exclaimed Constance Armatage; "a highwayman, dear. What think you of that? He was a personal—nay, almost intimate friend of my poor father's. Driven to desperation, I suppose, and being too proud to ask favours of his friends or the government who had so ill-used him, Captain Orlando Ragget became a highwayman, and associated with the notorious Dick Turpin and the not less infamous Tom King."

At these words Tom withdrew his head from the aperture. He felt disposed to leave the spot at all hazards; but yet there was a sort of fascination which kept him from moving till he had heard the fair speaker out.

"Yes, for years he has followed this lawless occupation—so I have been informed. Of course, I do not choose to say to any of my friends that the prescribed Captain Ragget was ever received in our family."

"Oh, no, of course not," said Nan; "it would not be prudent to do so. But pray proceed."

"His career will soon be brought to a close," said Constance Armatage. "This wretched person——"

"Who?" inquired Nan Darrell.

"Captain Ragget."

"Oh, yes—of course—I forgot."

"This wretched person is at present hiding from the officers of justice. He is concealed in some lonely cottage; I don't know where this cottage is, but it is somewhere in the suburbs of London."

"Indeed!"

"Yes, it is somewhere not very far off; and he has been hiding at the place for weeks; they say he intended to get clear off and make for the Continent, but, poor man, he will never be able to do so now. I wish he could."

"Bless you for saying so!" ejaculated Nan Darrell.

"Eh? What?" returned Miss Armatage, who was again surprised at the tones of her companion's voice.

"Because you have such a good heart, and this proves it more than ever. You ever evince consideration for this lawless man—you who are nobly born and tenderly nurtured."

"And is that any reason why we should not feel for the oppressed or downtrodden?" said Constance.

"No, no, of course not; only many in your station of life would turn away in disgust at the very name of so lawless a character."

"More shame for them," answered Miss Armatage. "He was an honourable gentleman at one time was Captain Orlando Ragget; and we none of us know what led him into so sad a career which he has chosen to follow. He might have been sorely tempted."

"She is an angel of goodness," ejaculated Tom King, as he heard the last words fall from the lips of the fair speaker; "she is an angel of goodness, that she is."

"But," said Nan, "you have not concluded. You were saying that the career of this unfortunate gentleman was about to come to an end."

"So it is. He has been a lawless man—he has committed a number of robberies—has been running a sad career for very many years past. This is all bad enough, but there is something worse than all this: he is obnoxious to the government — obnoxious on account of his political, or supposed political, principles. Possibly he may, after all, only be sacrificed to others; be this as it may, he will be sacrificed, and will die on the scaffold. Why, dear, how pale you look!"

"I do feel rather faint," said Nan; "but it is nothing. I shall be better presently."

"Does my tale so move you, then?"

"Oh, dear no. It is not that."

"What is it, dearest? I will say no more if the subject be a painful one."

"Oh, pray proceed. I am better now, indeed I am. Proceed. You do not think, then, that it is possible for the captain to escape?"

"Quite impossible."

"Why so?"

"For a very excellent reason. Jonathan Wild—you have heard of him, I suppose?"

"Oh, yes. I have often listened to my grandfather give an account of him."

"Jonathan Wild has sworn to take Captain Orlando Ragget either dead or alive, and, depend upon it, the old thief-taker will keep his word."

"But if he does not know where the captain is, how then?"

"Ah, my dear, but he does know. He has only learnt, so I am given to understand—he has only learnt this a few hours ago."

"Are you sure of that?"

"Quite certain; for, you must know, that I heard the whole history of this yesterday. One of Wild's men was in conversation with a gentleman whose name I am not at liberty to divulge, and, by the merest chance in the world, I overheard their conversation. I should not have listened to it, but I could not do otherwise, for there was no escape from the situation in which I was placed, and thus it is that I have been able to furnish you with that part of the history of Captain Ragget which will be a portion of the concluding chapter of his life. But, law, my dear!

I know not why I should trouble you about such stuff. You don't know Captain Ragget, and, of course, cannot even have the remote interest in him than I have myself."

"I am truly sorry for him," said Nan, sadly; and at the same time she found some difficulty in repressing her tears.

"And now, my dear, let us change the theme which has become a thought too sad," said Miss Armatage; "let us change the theme. You saw Sir William Blakeley in the State apartments?"

"Yes."

"And he saw you?"

"I dare say he did. What of that?"

"What of that, you cunning little trickster—what of it? Why, the eyes of the baronet were engaged in contemplating the beauties of my friend. He could not —maybe, would not spare even a cursory glance for anyone else. Now, don't blush, dear."

"Blush, indeed!" said Nan. "I care nought about Sir William Blakeley, and never shall."

"Why, my dear, the baronet doats upon you."

"How do you know that, Constance? By my faith! but you seem to know everybody's business."

"How do I know it? Well, that is a good joke. Why, almost everybody knows it. Why is it that he is so continually down at Old Oak Farm? Not to discuss potatoes with the good Mr. Luke Darrell, nor to frame laws with the worthy magistrate. The reason is obvious enough. It is yourself, my dear—your own sweet self, that attracts him."

The news which Nan had received respecting her father most completely disturbed her spirits, and she could not find it in her heart to put on a cheerful countenance.

She longed to get away, so that she might give her father notice of the danger and risk he ran by staying at his present quarters; and yet she dared not tell her friend or appear to be over-anxious.

Nan had promised to stay a day or two in St. James's Palace. She was the guest of the Honorable Miss Armatage, who had always treated her more like a sister than aught else.

Constance Armatage was an orphan, and upon her father's decease had been placed under the guardianship of the Earl of Oxford, whose carriage had been so unceremoniously brought to a standstill by Dick Turpin and Tom King.

Now, Nan was most anxious to leave the palace; and all the while her friend was rattling on with a lively discourse, Nan was thinking what excuse she could make for her immediate departure.

There could be but little doubt as to the credibility of the information she had received from Miss Armatage.

Her father's career was about to be brought to a close.

This was the first time Nan had heard that Captain Ragget had been an intimate acquaintance of the Armatages.

This information but added poignancy to her sorrow.

"And so you do not care about Sir William Blakeley —eh?" said Constance Armatage, after a pause. "Well, for my part, I think him gentlemanly enough; but then perhaps, after all, he may be thought too old for you."

"It is not that only," answered Nan.

"Oh, you object to him for other reasons."

"Yes—most decidedly, I object to him."

"Well, my dear, he is not a repulsive person. Any woman might look upon him with something like respect, if not with love.

"Respect!" returned Nan, quickly.

"Yes, dear. Wherefore not?"

"I do not respect him."

"Why, positively, Nan, you surprise me—not respect Sir William Blakeley!"

"Certainly not. I will tell you frankly, my dear Constance, I have but a very poor opinion of Sir William."

"But why? Has he done anything to forfeit your good opinion?"

"He has done nothing as far as I am concerned; but there have been strange stories bruited about, which I hope—which I sincerely hope, for his own sake, are not true."

"How so? What were these? Come, tell me, Nan. We were always such excellent friends, and never used to have any secrets from one another. Why should we now?"

"Why, indeed? Well, then, in the first place, there have not been wanting persons who have asserted that he treated his wife with unkindness. Nay, more: it has been asserted——But I feel that I have no right to enter on this painful subject."

"Oh, yes. It will go no further—you are quite sure of that."

"Well, then, it has been asserted that his wife was brought to an early grave by his means."

"Oh, it is not—it cannot be true. I never will believe that."

"Nor would I willingly."

"My dear Nan..you are really prejudicial, I fear."

"I hope not. But you have heard of a young man by the name of James Neville."

"Neville—Neville? I remember something about such a name. Pray, tell me, what of him?"

"He ran a sad career, and ended his days upon the scaffold."

"Well, what has that to do with Sir William Blakeley?"

"Oh, I cannot tell you the whole of the history, as I am acquainted with but part of it myself. Neville was patronised at one time by Sir William, who led him into all sorts of extravagances far beyond his means; and eventually the misguided youth—for he was little else—was induced to commit forgery. I do not know for a certainty, but I believe that Sir William was but too glad to have him out of the way—he cared not by what means."

"What for?"

"Neville asserted that he had been cheated out of all his property by the baronet."

"And do you believe such a statement?"

"I can hardly answer that question. One thing is quite certain."

"What is that?"

"Why, that Sir William Blakeley was in constant communication with Jonathan Wild just before Neville's capture; and another thing is equally certain, and that is this, Sir William was but too glad to find that the miserable young man was doomed to suffer death. But there is a long family history connected with this James Neville. Understand me, I am not for one moment disposed to defend Neville—that is, as far as his guilt is concerned. Neither have I, or rather had I, any very exalted opinion of his character; but he was badly used by Sir William. He was acquainted with some of his secrets, and, therefore, the baronet was but too glad to see him brought to his end.

"Upon my word, Nan, you are terribly prejudiced, I must confess," said Constance Armatage, with a smile.

"It may be so; but I don't like Sir William Blakeley, and will never consent to be his wife. No, never!"

"And have you told him so?"

"Most certainly I have. It is not at all likely I should deceive him or anyone else upon that point."

"I know you were always a self-willed little thing, Nan," observed Miss Armatage, with a smile. "And so, my dear friend, if such are your feelings towards the baronet, why think no more of him."

"He won't let me think no more of him," said Nan Darrell. "Notwithstanding all I have said to him, he still persists in pressing his suit."

"Ah, it is evident that the man must be madly in love. Poor fellow! I pity him."

————

CHAPTER XIII.

TOM KING MEETS WITH FRIENDS. — HIS ESCAPE FROM THE PALACE.

CONSTANCE ARMATAGE rose from her seat, and passed out of the room, soon after the above conversation had taken place. She told Nan Darrell, as she left, that she would be with her again in the course of a few minutes.

Tom King heard her footsteps in one of the corridors not far from the snug nook in which he had been so fortunate as to conceal himself.

He listened attentively.

The footsteps were evidently nearer.

He descended from his table, and emerged from the small apartment which had afforded him a temporary shelter.

In a minute or so he saw Miss Armatage approaching. What was to be done? Should he draw back into the dark recess? or should he at once put a bold face on the matter, and trust to her mercy?

He chose the latter alternative.

He went out into the passage, and presented himself to the fair maid of honour.

The Honorable Miss Armatage drew back in evident surprise as she observed the figure of a strange man.

In a minute or so more, she recognised him as the same individual who had assumed the name and habiliments of Sir Piers Shafton.

Perhaps most young women, under the circumstances, would have screamed at the sight of so strange a personage near to the sleeping-chamber of the maids of honour.

Miss Armatage, however, retained her self-possession. She stood for a moment or so without uttering a word.

"My dear madam," said Tom King, "When was ever man in distress without enlisting the sympathy of the kinder and gentler sex. Your pardon—your pardon, I pray you."

"Pardon for what?" inquired Miss Armatage, quite naturally.

"You behold before you an unfortunate person whose own imprudence has brought him into a labyrinth of troubles. May I ask your aid——"

"In what way, sir? I do not understand you."

"Madam, I am most anxious to escape unobserved from this palace."

"I am thinking, sir, that it would have been better for your own character if you had never entered it."

"Without a doubt. But, oh, my dear lady, have pity on me! Is there no way of escape?"

"Every passage is guarded."

"Are there no private entrances through which I may make my exit?"

"None. How long have you been here?"

"Since yesterday."

"My duty would dictate that I should make one of the palace officials acquainted with the fact that an intruder is within the walls of the palace. That ought to be my course of action; but, although such might be my duty, I would much rather some other person performed so unpleasant a task."

"Oh, for the love of grace, do not!—I conjure you not to adopt such a course!" said King, in moving accents, as he dropped on one knee before the beautiful young female. "Have mercy—have pity on me! Pray show me some way by which I may escape from my enemies."

"I am not aware, sir, that anyone is his Majesty's palace is an enemy of yours."

"No, no—I do not mean that," returned King. "Pardon me—I hardly know what I am saying. I am driven to such a state of distraction by the terrible situation in which I find myself, that I lose all my presence of mind."

The Honorable Miss Armatage hesitated.

Now, King knew enough of the sex to be aware that

when a woman hesitates there is hope. He again besought her to take pity on him.

"I wish you had met with anyone else rather than myself, for it constrains me to do something which must of necessity be painful to me, or else to forget the duty I owe to my sovereign. Assuredly you have no right within the walls of the palace."

"I admit it."

"You had no right to assume the name of an honourable gentleman."

"That I also admit."

"Neither have I any right to connive at your escape, were that possible."

"Oh, say not so, madam—I pray of you not to say so! Cold duty might prompt you to hand over an unfortunate, although not a criminal man, to the proper authorities, but your gentle nature would revolt at such an act—I am sure it would. I will not do you so great an injustice as to believe otherwise."

"You will be doing me an injustice, sir, by supposing that I should so far forget the duty I owe to my sovereign as to connive at the escape of one who has obtained an entrance into the palace by means which, to say the least, do not appear to be either creditable or honorable," said the Honorable Miss Armatage.

"Madam, your own gentle nature would prompt you to aid an unfortunate man," answered King.

"I have yet to learn that you are unfortunate. You are a perfect stranger to me, and therefore I am equally at a loss to account for your singular conduct and your still more singular appearance in a part of the palace which is seldom visited by strangers. Unfortunate you may be, for aught I know; but if you are offering this as an excuse for the assumption of a title and name which you had no right to assume, it seems to me that your plea would be but a poor one."

"I am not offering any excuse," answered King. "At some future day I do hope that I shall be able to justify myself. Till that time I must be content that I should fall under the censure of the Honorable Miss Armatage."

"You know me, then?" said the lady, in some surprise, while at the same time she stared at the speaker —"you know me?"

"Yes, madam, I know you," answered King, hanging down his head, and heaving a deep sigh.

"I remember—that is, your voice sounds familiar to me. Where have we met before?—or have we ever met? Your name?"

"At present I am under a cloud," said King. "You must pardon me, therefore, if I endeavour to preserve a strict *incognito* even from the fair Miss Armatage, whose very name awakens in my breast chords of the most tender sympathy. Madam, for the sake of those few who esteem and love me, I implore of you to show me some way of escape."

"You are asking that of me which I shall find impossible, however much I might feel disposed to do so. It is utterly impossible."

"Is there no way of escape?"

"None that I know of."

"By disguising myself—by changing my costume, I might be able to pass the entrance without notice," suggested King.

"I do not think it likely; but even if it were, I do not see very clearly how you would be able to alter your appearance sufficiently without being recognised. If you think so, you had better adopt that course, as it will, perhaps, relieve me from my present embarrassed position. If I could aid you without compromising myself, sir, I would most willingly—most cheerfully do so."

"I believe it, madam. Accept my most sincere and heartfelt thanks."

"Hush, hush! there are footsteps. Some one approaches. Withdraw to your hiding-place. Stay—it is the king's guard. Follow!"

The Honorable Miss Armatage caught the highwayman by the arm, and drew him along a winding in the passage. She pulled from her pocket a bunch of keys, and then unlocked a dark cupboard in a corner of the passage. She threw open the doors of this, and bade Tom King enter.

There was not much difficulty in his doing so, as the doors of the cupboard went down to the ground.

Without a moment's hesitation, King ensconsed himself in this retreat.

Miss Armatage closed the doors of the cupboard, and locked them.

In a minute or so after this a troop of the king's guards passed along the passage.

Tom King heard the heavy and measured tramp of their feet, and congratulated himself on being in a place of concealment.

The guards disappeared.

Miss Armatage had taken her way back to the sleeping-chamber of the maids of honour.

Nan Darrell was seated at the ormulu table, near the window.

She had been weeping since her last conversation with her friend, but had dried her tears, and endeavoured to put on as cheerful a countenance as possible.

"My dear," said Constance Armatage, " I have a strange story to relate."

"More stories," said Nan, sadly.

"Nay not a story; but I have met with an incident —a most remarkable incident.

She then related to Nan Darrell all the particulars of her interview with Tom King, with which the reader is already acquainted.

Nan rose from her seat, and looked inquiringly at her friend.

"What do you purpose doing, then?" she inquired, quickly.

"Upon my word, dearest, I hardly know. I thought it best to come hither and consult you."

"Consult me?"

"Yes, you are quicker witted than myself, and are better able to advise me how to act."

"We must determine pretty quickly or we shall have some one or the other of our companions returning."

"No fear of that; Theresa and her two friends have other matters to discuss, and will not trouble us for the present, I dare say. Now, say dearest, what is to be done?"

"You wish to befriend the young gallant, I suppose?" said Nan Darrell, with a smile.

"Well, yes. I do not like to see him in such trouble; and, at the same time, should be sorry to hand him over to the authorities, although I know it would be my duty to do so."

"But it would not be mine," suggested Nan.

"Certainly not. Were I in your situation, there would be no occasion to hesitate in the matter."

"I am not a maid of honour," said Nan; "and, consequently, am free to act as I please. What say you, then, to my showing him the way out?"

"Can you?"

"I can, if you will tell me where he may pass out from the palace with safety."

"I hardly know how to advise you in the matter. It would never do for this erratic gentleman to attempt to pass through any of the doorways, he would be sure to attract the notice of the officials."

"What course do you think had better be adopted?"

"I am sorely puzzled."

"He is locked up in a closet, you say?"

"Yes; a closet in the corner of the passage, which is devoted to the use of myself and Theresa Valpy."

"Upon my word, if he were found there, you would be sadly compromised."

"I should so, without a doubt; but it is too late to talk about that now."

"I tell you what," said Nan, quickly, as a sudden thought seemed to pass through her brain. "Suppose you let me see this extraordinary gentleman, and have a few minutes' conversation with him. By the time I return you may have succeeded in lighting upon some plan by which he may be saved.

"Good! so be it. Here are the keys, my dear. Take them. This is the key that fits the lock of the closet in question. Go and see this mysterious cavalier, and tell me what you think of him. Whether you deem him honest or dishonest?—worthy or unworthy."

"How can I tell that?"

"Oh, by his looks."

"What! judge a man in a dark closet by his looks?"

"You will hear his voice."

"I dare say I shall."

"That may serve as some guide. There is sometimes more in a voice than in aught else. Go, dear—go."

Nan Darrell took the bunch of keys from her young and beauteous friend, and proceeded with them to the closet where Tom King was concealed.

She unlocked the door, having first ascertained that no one was in sight.

When she opened them, an exclamation of surprise escaped her. She saw at once that the fugitive was no other than Tom King himself.

Nan Darrell had no difficulty in recognising him, even disguised as he was in his Court-suit.

"You here?" she ejaculated, in some surprise.

"Yes, me—even me, Miss Darrell."

"Thou must have been mad to have been so rash and inconsiderate, you who are——"

"Surrounded with dangers enough without seeking fresh ones. You are right, Miss Darrell—quite right."

"And you are bringing others into difficulties as well as yourself."

"I never dreamed of seeing you in the old palace of St. James."

"Hush! Do not speak so loud—there may be some eavesdroppers. What do you purpose doing now?"

"Anything you may suggest. I would fain escape from my present difficulties. In you I feel that I have a friend."

"Oh, my poor father!" ejaculated Nan. "Even now, while we are conversing, I fear that he may be captured. If I find the means of getting you clear off, will you promise me one thing?"

"Name it, and you may command Tom King while he has life. He is your devoted slave."

"A truce to this; but listen. My father's place of concealment is known to Jonathan Wild. Can you—will you take horse at once, when outside these walls, and gallop off to the cottage where he is concealed, and warn him of his danger?"

"I pledge you my most solemn word to do so without a moment's delay."

"You must change your attire," said Nan.

"Of course. That will be but the work of a few moments, for I have chambers within half a mile of the palace."

"Good. Now—mark me, King—I trust in you. I shall find it difficult to leave the palace immediately—I shall find this difficult, if not impossible."

"And even if you were to do so, you could not reach the cottage near so quickly as I can myself."

"No; then I shall rely upon you. Now, as to the means of escape?"

"That you must determine."

"I will consult with Miss Armatage."

"She's an angel—an angel of goodness!" exclaimed King, passionately.

"Oh, women are all angels with you," returned Nan, with a smile. "Drop all your amatory speeches for the present; there is some important business on hand. Remain where you are till my return."

With these words, Nan Darrell closed the doors of the closet, and having turned the lock, she retraced her steps to the apartment where she had left the Honorable Miss Armatage.

"Well, what think you of this remarkable individual?" said Constance Armatage, when her friend presented herself in the apartment where we first saw the maids of honour.

"Poor gentleman! Some means must be devised for him to make his escape."

"You think so?"

"Yes."

"And would advise me to connive at it?"

"I should, were I in your situation."

"Well, since that is settled, the next question comes as to the how."

"Is there no window through which he could make his exit? Better men than he have had to adopt a similar course."

"Without a doubt. There is this window, for instance."

"Which is so closely barred that there is not a passage left for an insignificant little urchin."

"I have it!" said Constance Armatage, clapping her hands with joy at her own discovery—"I have it! There is a small window which looks over the ornamental gardens of the palace; it is not barred like the rest. What say you to conducting him to this?"

"Nothing could be better. Let us hasten at once and put your suggestion in practice."

"But then the window is too high from the ground for anyone to alight with anything like safety. Oh, no, my dear; upon second thoughts I fear much that this scheme would be impracticable."

"Let us try—let us see this window you are speaking of."

"I should be sorry if the poor gentleman were to lose his life—I should be indeed very sorry."

"Come, let us see the window. Take me to it, and then we can determine."

Nan Darrell put her arm round the waist of her friend, and the two proceeded along a gallery to the back part of St. James's Palace.

The window was high, without a doubt; but it was in so dull and deserted a part of the building, that it appeared to Nan to be admirably adapted for the purpose. She therefore, without hesitation, declared it to be her opinion that it would be best to lead the fugitive to the window in question.

"As you please," said Miss Armatage. "I must frankly confess that I am not at all pleased with the part I am playing in this transaction; but having gone thus far, why, I suppose there is no help for it. How this gallant is to alight on the ground below with anything like safety to his own life and limbs, must remain a mystery—for the present, at least."

"We will see about that," answered Nan, who then led the way back to the place where the highwayman was concealed.

As she proceeded hither, she said, to Miss Armatage—

"You know, dear, I should be sorry to see you get yourself into any trouble for a stranger, and now I know where the place is, perhaps you had better return to the apartments of the maids of honour, and leave me to take charge of this misguided and very silly young gentleman."

"Nay, I would not have it so," answered Miss Armatage. "I do not see that it would be at all fair to shrink out of the question, and leave you to bear the brunt of this business. No, no, Nan; we will stand or fall together."

"But consider, my dear, your fall would be a much more serious one than mine."

"Possibly so; but what of that? It is but fair that I should take my share of the risk. I was the first whom this young gentleman addressed; and, moreover, he affects to know me."

"To know you?"

"Yes—me. Is there anything so surprising in that?"

"No, I don't know that there is. And pray, my dear, can you return him the compliment? Do you know him?"

"I think I have seen him before; and I am sure

the tones of his voice have fallen on my ears on more than one occasion."

"Do you know his name?"

"Haven't the slightest idea of it."

Nan Darrell breathed again.

"And, what is more," continued her companion, he refused to give me his name."

"You asked him, then?"

"Yes. He addressed me by mine, and so I was curious to ascertain where we had met before, so. in return, I inquired of him who I had the honour of addressing. He told me he must preserve strict *incognito* for the present, and so, of course, I did not seek to penetrate his disguise."

"It's a most mysterious business, it must be confessed; however, poor fellow, he seems to be in some trouble, and it would, therefore, be a matter of charity to get him out of his present difficulties."

The two young ladies now arrived at Tom King's place of concealment.

The door was opened, and the highwayman stepped forth.

Nan Darrell bid him follow, which he did, in silence.

Several passages were passed through, when ultimately the three persons arrived at the window, which was in a part of the palace seldom troubled with any intruders.

It was, therefore, all the better adapted for their purpose.

"Now," said Nan, "this will be your best, if not your only chance of escape. If you drop on the grass-plot beneath this, and manage to alight in safety, I think you may manage to gain the park without attracting the notice of any one."

"But the sentinel?—how about the sentinel?" said King.

"There is no sentinel in this immediate locality," answered the Honorable Miss Armatage. "When you reach the ground, wait in the corner of the two walls, and should there be anyone about you can betake yourself to yonder building, which is used as a sort of seed-house and receptacle for garden implements; you will be able to conceal yourself there without much difficulty, that is, assuming you reach the ground in safety."

"And the sentinel?"

"There is one who paces backwards and forwards by the side of those palings; you can easily watch him till he gets out of sight, and then——"

"I can make for the park with all the haste possible," replied King.

"Precisely. Now you know what to do, the next question is, how you are to reach the ground in safety."

Nan Darrell took a scarf from off her shoulders, and handed it to Tom King.

The latter immediately understood the purpose she handed it to him for. He began to roll it round and round until he had made it into the form of a thick rope.

Nan smiled to see the facility with which he adjusted it.

"What is that for?" inquired Miss Armatage, in some surprise.

"You will see, my dear madam, in a minute more," answered King, who soon began to fasten one end of the scarf to the frame-work of the window.

When this had been done he looked out.

All was quiet; not a soul was visible.

"Now for it. Escape or capture! which is it to be?" As the highwayman said this he mounted on the sill of the window. "How shall I ever sufficiently thank you for all your kindness?" he said, turning towards Miss Armatage.

"Lose no time in unnecessary words," answered the maid of honour. "Time presses, and the best thanks you can give to me, is to make good your escape as speedily as possible."

"I am ever bound to you," returned King.

"Hush! Not many words," murmured Nan Darrell. "We may be overheard."

"I thank you for the reproof."

"You will not forget your mission?" whispered Nan, to the highwayman. Remember, life or death depends upon the issue. You will not forget the charge I have given you?"

"Were my life to be forfeited by keeping faith with you, it should be done," answered Tom. "Fear not, Miss Darrell. I shall to horse at once—that is, assuming I manage to get clear off. If not——"

"Oh, do not anticipate any mischance."

"Let us hope for the best. In any case you may rely upon me."

This conversation had taken place in whispers, which were inaudible to the Honorable Miss Armatage.

Tom King balanced himself on the sill of the window; he looked out of this.

From the position in which he found himself, he was enabled to see far over the grounds of the palace. No one appeared in sight.

It was yet early, and many of the inmates of the royal residence had not emerged from their respective dormitories.

Consequently there was a better chance for him to make his escape.

He now caught hold of the scarf, and threw his feet off the window-sill. In another second or so he was dangling in the air.

He slid down the scarf, and, when at the end of this, he dropped to the ground with the lightness of a cat.

Both his female preservers were watching his proceedings from the window above.

When the highwayman reached the ground, he pointed to the scarf.

Nan Darrell understood his meaning. She drew it up, and then untied the end of it, which had been fastened around the wood-work of the window. In a minute more she began to unfold it, and return it to its original form.

Another wave of the hand from Tom King was understood as meaning that his two preservers should leave the window.

They took the precaution to close it before they did so.

This done, they returned to the apartments of the maids of honour.

"I wonder whether he will succeed in getting clear off," said Miss Armatage.

"I hope so," answered Nan Darrell.

"He's a gentlemanly young man."

"Very much so."

"I wonder who he can be. Have you any idea?"

"Me? Well, that's a good joke. You have had a much longer conversation with him than myself, and certainly ought to have elicited from him something," said Nan.

"Not a scrap of information have I been able to obtain. However, I dare say we have not seen the last of him."

"Oh, I should say not. He will be sure to send us a letter of thanks—that is, assuming he gets clear off."

"I should say so. I think he has been brought up a gentleman; and yet——"

"Yet what?"

"Why, something struck me that his voice sounded like—like one of the masked highwaymen's who stopped the Earl of Oxford's carriage."

"What an idea!" said Nan Darrell, in some confusion.

"Well, it did strike me so at one time; but, of course, I must be mistaken. Many voices are alike, or nearly so."

"Upon my word, Constance, your friends may well rally you."

"What for?"

"For your predilection for highwaymen. Your mind seems to be always running on them."

"It was a foolish thought, I must confess, and, to say the truth, one to which I should not choose to give expression to anyone but yourself; so there's an end of it. You know I was frequently chided for being so ready to speak my mind on all subjects, and it's a habit I don't seem to have been able to get rid of."

We must now return to Tom King.

He was glad to find that Nan Darrell understood the signals he had made, for although none of the occupants of the palace had seen him drop from the window, there were persons in St. James's Park whose notice might very naturally be attracted by the scarf. He was glad, therefore, when he observed his two friends disappear with the garment in question.

Tom looked around him, and made a careful inspection of the place.

To his left, outside some iron railings, a sentry "walked his lonely round."

To his right there was a long, low building.

This was the one Miss Armatage had spoken of as a place likely to afford him shelter.

Tom felt that the worst part of the affair was this: he was dressed in full Court costume, and it was not usual for gentlemen to walk the streets of London, in broad daylight, habited as he was.

Where to hide his diminshed head, was the question.

While Tom was debating within himself, he heard, much to his horror and dismay, the sound of voices.

They seemed to proceed from persons in close conversation.

He looked to the right and left, and then observed two individuals taking their way along the centre gravel-walk.

Tom was at no loss to comprehend that one of these personages was none other than his Majesty himself. The other gentleman he did not know.

Had their eyes been glancing in the direction where he was, they could not have failed to see him.

Luckily their eyes were bent on the ground.

Still, their presence was most embarrassing to our highwayman, who began to think he should never be able to leave the palace.

His Majesty and the gentleman with whom he was conversing were, in all probability, conversing about State affairs. So Tom King thought. At any rate, they were bent upon walking up and down the gravel-walk. Should they do so for any length of time, it was quite certain that they would eventually discover the intruder—that is, assuming he continued to remain in his position.

This, Tom did not think at all advisable.

But he was unable to gain the door of the green-house, or place for the reception of garden utensils, because he would have to pass within sight of his most gracious Majesty, who would not be particularly gracious to our highwayman if he happened to discover him.

Under these distressing circumstances, Tom King was forced to hide himself behind some laurels till his Majesty and his companion passed. After this, he managed to gain the house for the reception of garden utensils, seeds, &c.

He opened the door, and rushed in.

Judge his horror when he discovered a man there.

King hesitated for a moment, and deliberated with himself if he had not better at once attack and overpower the person; but, upon second consideration, he thought it advisable to propitiate him as best he could.

The fellow stared, as well he might, at the appearance of a stranger in such a place.

King thought it best to assume a confidential tone.

"Well, my friend," he said, in a familiar tone of voice. "His Majesty is stirring early this morning."

"Ye—es," said the man, who was one of the under-gardeners.

"I saw him pass," said King, "so I crept in here to be out of the way."

The gardener made no reply to this, but made towards the door.

"You had better not go out at present," said King.

"Why not?" inquired the man.

"Because I do not desire it. That is why."

"You?"

"Yes, me. Does that astonish you?"

"Well, for the matter of that, I shall be glad to learn who you are."

"Hark ye, my excellent friend, let you and I understand one another. I can see that you are not to be gammoned. You think I am an intruder here. Now you look here. Listen to me for a moment. I want to take my departure in peace, and if you endeavour to prevent me, by the Lord above! as sure as you are a living man now, I will stretch you lifeless even where you stand!"

As Tom King said this, he drew the sword which depended from his hip, and pointed it towards the man who had evidently, upon his first entrance, suspected something was amiss."

The gardener was an arrant coward. He turned pale at the sight of King's shining weapon.

"Oh, oh! pray don't—pray don't. What have I done that you should draw upon me?"

"You have not done much at present; but I suspect you—I suspect you from your manner. So mark me. I intend to keep my word. Are we to be friends or not?"

"Oh, dear me; friends, I hope, sir.

"That is well. Now give me the key of this door. You have it with you, I suppose?"

The man replied in the affirmative.

"Then hand it over at once."

"Yes, sir."

The key was handed to Tom King, who then walked up to the door of the house, and locked it.

"Safe bound safe found!" said the highwayman. "There's two, and all told. Now, my man, you will be pleased to sit down, either on that barrow or on the basket next to it, which ever suits your fancy best."

The gardener seated himself.

"That's right, make your life as comfortable as possible. Now, I dare say you may be able to give me some little information. By the way, this door can be locked from the outside, I think?"

"Yes, it can."

"You are sure of that?"

"Quite sure."

"So much the better. Well, now, in the first place, can you inform me how long it is likely his Majesty will be in the grounds?"

"I am sure I don't know; but I should say not more than half an hour at the longest."

"Good! Well, now, you must understand that it is my object to get away from these 'halls of dazzling light' as soon as possible. You see yonder palings, those at the end of the gardens?"

"Yes, I see them. Those behind the hedge?"

"Precisely. Well, now, suppose a man — myself for instance — managed to scale them, what would be the consequence? Is there a sentry beyond them?"

"There is a sentry, certainly; but he might not see you."

"You think I could get clear off?"

"Yes, I think you could; but it's more than my place is worth to be talking with you thus."

"And it's more than your life is worth not to do so," said King, half drawing his sword from its scabbard. "Which is the most valuable—your life, or your place?"

"Oh, don't, sir!"

"You have not answered me."

"My life is the most valuable. Oh, consider, sir, that I have a wife and three small children depending upon me for support."

"I will consider this. Now, look here. Do you see? I will give you these five gold pieces if you promise to aid me in my escape."

"What do you want me to do?"

"Nothing."

THE STRUGGLE IN THE VAULT.

"That is easily done," returned the man, with a smile.

"It is not what I want you to do, which is, as I have already told you, simply nothing; but it is what I want you not to do. Now, do you comprehend?"

"Not exactly."

"Let me make my meaning more plain. When I leave this place I shall lock you in. You will not be able to follow me; I shall take care of that."

"I have no wish to do so."

"That matters little; I will take care you do not. But what I want is this. You must not make a noise, or raise an alarm, for, if you do, as sure as you are a living man, I will have my revenge."

"Oh, don't talk in that way! Pray don't, sir. I can't stand it—indeed, I can't!"

"When I leave here, I want you to be as silent as the grave—only for about a quarter of an hour; that will suffice. If you do this, these gold pieces shall be yours. If you do not do this, I shall be compelled to run you through the body."

No. 8.

"I would much rather have the gold pieces——"

"Than the cold steel. Precisely. You are a sensible man. What say you, will you keep your word?"

"As to what?"

"To remain quietly here when I take my departure."

"You are going to lock me in, you say?"

"Of course, I am; but you have a tongue, and may use it. I am debating with myself whether it will be advisable to silence that for ever."

"Oh, mercy! mercy, sir! I pray of you not to talk in that sort of manner. I swear to you that I will be as silent as the grave."

"Good! Then we understand each other; and the gold pieces shall be yours."

"Thank ye, sir."

A quarter of an hour passed away. At the expiration of which period the king had returned to the palace.

Tom unlocked the door of the green-house.

He was anxious to be off on account of the mission that he had promised Nan Darrell to perform.

He could not see anyone in the ornamental grounds of the palace.

All seemed to be quiet.

He began to think it was time for him to make a rush for it. He gave an eye to the gardener, who was still seated on the barrow.

"I shall place these gold pieces under the third garden-pot outside. Do you understand?" he said to his companion.

"Yes sir."

"When I am clear off, you will be able to get out of this place, for I shall leave the key outside the door. Some one will be by, and unlock the door for you."

"Very well, sir."

"And if you behave yourself as you ought to do, why you know the rest — when you get out you will know where to look for the gold pieces."

"I promise to obey you. I call heaven to witness that I will not raise any alarm till you are clear of the palace grounds."

"Good. I shall remember you hereafter," said King, as he shut the door of the green-house, and locked it."

He then, agreeable to the promise he had made to the gardener, placed the gold pieces beneath one of the flower-pots outside the green-house.

He pointed to this, and called the man's attention to it as he did so. After this he made towards the iron railings which skirted the end of the ornamental gardens, and divided therefrom St. James's-park.

He gained these without any interruption, and at once proceeded to scale them.

This was but the work of a few minutes, and our highwayman eventually, after all his trials and troubles, had the satisfaction of alighting, safe and sound, in the park.

He felt very uncomfortable in his court costume, as he was naturally fearful that it would attract attention. So he hastened on, and succeeded in finding a chair.

He entered this, and bid the bearers of the same proceed forthwith to his chambers.

In less than half an hour he alighted at the door of his apartments, and rushed up stairs, but too thankful to be again free.

He at once began to change his attire, and, in the course of another half hour, he was trotting past Tyburn tree, on the road to Acton.

Tom did not let the grass grow under his feet—to make use of a somewhat hackneyed phrase.

He put his horse into a sharp trot, being well aware that time was of the utmost importance.

He had promised Nan Darrell to hasten at once to her unfortunate parent, and make him acquainted with the dangerous position in which he was in.

By the time Tom had arrived at the cottage where Captain Ragget was concealed, his horse was covered with foam—for its rider had put him out to his best speed. He guessed, shrewdly enough, that the probability was that he was riding for life or death, and careless man as Tom King was in many things, he was not unmindful or neglectful of any pal who was in misfortune.

Captain Ragget had always been a great favourite both with Tom, Dick Turpin, and, indeed, most of the highwaymen of the day. There was no time for hesitation, had there been he would most likely have sought out his friend Dick, and taken his advice how to act; but the importance of his mission would not admit of that, so he had chosen to hasten off at once to the captain, without more ado or further parley. It was lucky he took the resolution to do so.

Had he been an hour or two later, his journey would have been a fruitless one.

When he arrived in front of the lonely cottage, he dismounted, and entered without further ceremony.

The old woman was plaiting rushes as industriously as she had been when Turpin and our heroine had paid her a visit.

King appeared to be in breathless haste. His first question was—

"Am I in time?"

The old woman looked at him in some surprise, and did not make any immediate reply.

"You are in a hurry, my young master," she at length observed.

"Hours, it may be minutes are of importance," answered King, quickly. "Am I in time? Where—where is Captain Ragget? Has any one been here? Is he safe"?

"I can't answer all these questions at once," said the woman. "Deary me, why what a heat and fluster the man is in to be sure."

"Is Captain Ragget below?"

"Ay, sure he is."

"That is well, heaven be praised."

"And likely to be there for the present."

"Not so; he must leave at once—on the instant, or—"

"Or what?"

"Why some one will take him away, that's all."

"You don't mean that," said the old woman in some surprise, as she rose from her seat, then she added—

"What's up, then?"

"Why mischief's in the wind, that's what's up. If old Wild hasn't been here as yet, depend upon it, not many hours will pass over our heads before he honours you with a visit; so mind you that."

"Does he know—?"

"Ay, he knows that our friend has made this his hiding-place, he knows that perfectly well."

"Impossible."

There, don't be after contradicting me in that sort of manner. I give you notice, luckily, in time, Captain Ragget must away with me. For the rest, you will know best how to receive him or his followers."

"I doesn't want to receive him at all and be hanged to him," exclaimed the woman.

"The captain, I want the captain," said King, taking his way to the back of the house and searching for the trap-door. He was not so well acquainted with the place as his friend and companion, Dick Turpin, so he was not able to alight upon the entrance into the cellar below. The old woman, who had followed him, pointed this out, and in another minute Tom descended the steps and found himself in the presence of Captain Orlando Ragget.

"I am glad enough to see you, cap'en, I can tell you," said King, cheerfully, "because it gives me hope."

"Hope! What is there to hope?" inquired Ragget. "Very little for me, I fear."

"My good friend," said Tom, "not an hour is to be lost. You must leave this place; Wild knows you are here."

"Ah! is this so? Then there must have been some treachery."

"None that I know of. I have ridden hard all the way from London to warn you of your danger. I'll tell you all about the affair, how it was discovered, as we go along. We must to horse, and away at once. There is no time for hesitation."

"Away—away! What, leave here?"

"Most assuredly. To stay would be certain destruction."

"But where—where would you have me to go?"

"I am rather puzzled to answer that question satisfactorily. For the present you had better go to Seth Margut's."

"Ugh! I like not the place."

"Nor I; but we are in no position to pick and choose. We must away, I tell you. Why do you hesitate? Even while we are talking, we may be both captured. You don't know the necessity—the fatal, positive necessity there is to obey me."

"Who sent you hither? Dick?"

"No; your daughter."

At these words, the countenance of the imprisoned man turned suddenly pale; nevertheless, he murmured a blessing on the head of his daughter.

"She sent you hither? Nan sent you? Where——"

"Oh!—ah!—exactly. Where did I see her? Precisely. Where do you think?"

"At the farm?"

"No; at St. James's Palace. But we mustn't lose time by idle discourse. Arouse yourself, cap'en—shake yourself together, and put your best leg foremost. We'll do the cursed old thief-taker, after all. Ah, ah! we'll trick him."

Captain Ragget hastily attired himself, and then gathered up those few spare articles of clothing which were scattered about the cellar.

The head of the old woman appeared at the trap.

"Hark ye, missus," said King. "You had best burn every paper, or whatever else the cap'en leaves behind him. You had best burn the whole lot, so that there will be no trace left. And mind you stick out back and edge that you never saw such a person as the cap'en—never knew such a person—and never heard tell o' such a person."

"Ay, ay; trust me for that. It's little enough they'll get out o' me," said the woman—"precious little, I can tell ye. I'll burn everything."

"Do so; and the sooner the better, for there's no knowing how soon the ferrets may be here. My word! the ferrets here, with no rats to hunt—ah, ah! Come along, cap'en."

Tom and Ragget ascended the flight of steps, and then the former proceeded towards the stable which lay at the back of the cottage. He had handed his own horse to a boy when he first entered the little wicket-gate.

He had given instructions to this lad to get the captain's horse ready for starting at a moment's notice.

The boy had obeyed the orders which our highwayman had given. Both horses were ready.

Tom King returned to the cottage, and informed Captain Ragget that all was prepared; whereupon he and his companion mounted their steeds; and, after leaving a handsome sum of money with the old woman, they galloped off towards London.

When they had travelled some little distance, King said—

"It will never do to take the direct road, my friend, or we may possibly meet with those whom, of all other persons in the world, we wish to avoid."

"I leave the arrangements to you," returned Ragget.

"I am as little anxious as yourself to make the acquaintance of these worthies, so we'll e'en take a circuitous route to the great metropolis."

"As you please."

"I would make for the cave, but, you see——"

"What? Should I not be more secure there?"

"Well, you might be, and you might not. You know, I suppose, that a large price is put upon your head?"

"Without a doubt."

"And although Dick and myself can trust most of the chaps who go to the cave, still there may be some danger. Money is tempting, although it be blood money—about the worst that is paid; and you are not so well known to all there as myself and Turpin. They think you above them."

"Above them! And wherefore should they think that?"

"Well, you are a gentleman," returned King, with a smile.

"I was one," said Ragget, bitterly. "So were you, at one time. So, indeed, are you now, for the matter of that."

"A very sorry one, I'm thinking."

"Well, we will not trust these fellows. You know them best."

"We had better do as I propose, and hasten at once to Seth Margut's; that is by far the wisest course. We will consult with Dick after this, and arrange our future

plan of action. You are in the black books of Jonathan Wild, cap'en, there is but little doubt of that—you are in his black books."

"Curse him! Yes, I know it."

"And Margut is as true as steel."

"You think so?"

"I know it, and that is better. *Experiencia docet.* You see, I've not forgotten all my Latin."

"How came you to learn about this business? You promised to tell me as we proceeded on our journey."

Tom King then entered into the full particulars of all that had befallen him in St. James's Palace. He gave his companion a history of his strange adventures, and wound up by relating to him the brief conversation he had had with Nan Darrell. When he had concluded, Captain Ragget said, with considerable feeling—

"I am sure, King, I am deeply indebted to you for your kindness, and do hope and trust that a time may come when I may be able to repay you and Turpin for this and other acts of consideration. Alas! I have but few friends now."

"You were intimate with the Armatages at one time, I think?"

"Yes. How did you know that?"

"I heard it from the lips of the Honorable Miss Armatage herself. She is a friend of Miss Darrell's."

"Is Nan acquainted with *her?*"

"Yes; she was the maid of honour of whom I have been speaking."

"Oh, yes! I forgot—of course. Yes, I was, indeed at one time an honoured guest of the Armatages; but now—now——Well, no matter. It will not do to dwell upon these things now. When I think of the past, as most of us are apt to do—at times when I think of this, it seems to drive me mad—what I am, and what I might have been."

"You must cheer up, cap'en, and not dwell upon painful subjects now. You want all your pluck to pull through this business."

"Indeed I do."

"Once clear off to the Continent, you will be out of harm's way."

"Ah—once clear off. That is easier said than done."

"There is but little to prevent you doing so—very little."

"Well, we shall see. For the present——"

"You had best take up your quarters at Seth Margut's."

The two companions trotted on at a brisk pace.

King endeavoured to keep up the spirits of the captain, who was evidently thinking of brighter days. Poor fellow! he had been at one time a gallant officer and an honourable gentleman, but he had sadly fallen from his high estate, and had become what we have seen him upon our first atquaintance — a proscribed man—a highwayman, with the terror of the gallows before his eyes.

He rode on in company with his friend and companion, who led him by a circuitous route to London. Eventually they arrived at the street we have already described, where Dick Turpin had taken James Neville upon the night of the latter's first initiation in the life of a highwayman.

King was, of course, as well acquainted with the locality as was his friend and ally, Dick.

After going through the usual formalities, he obtained an entrance into the inner penetralia of the place.

Taking but little notice of the groups of men and boys who were assembled in the large room, Tom made his way to that part of the premises where he had been informed by Lazy Kate her master would be found.

Master Seth Margut was in one of the up-stairs rooms.

"Now," said King, when he arrived in sight of Margut, "I've a whisper for you."

"Strike me silly if it ain't Tom!" ejaculated Margut.

"Tom it is."

"And t'other gentleman?"

"In trouble—up a tree—under a cloud," said King, significantly.

"Oh, that's it, eh?"

"That's it, and nought else ; so mind you keep him as dark as a nigger while he's with you."

"Oh, he's to stay here, then?—but in course he is. All people who are under a cloud like to come to old Seth Margut's. 'Cos vy? 'Cos he never splits upon a pal—that's vy."

"And a good reason too, Seth—a very excellent reason," remarked King. "There's nothing much to be wondered at in that. Ain't you as true as steel, old boy? and as sharp—as sharp as a needle?"

"Come, come, don't pitch us any o' yer gammon, 'cos I can't stand it, Tom—no, indeed, I can't."

"Well, you must understand that this gentleman must be stowed away somewhere out of sight. You'll be paid handsomely for the accommodation."

"Oh, there ain't no call to say aught about that 'ere," observed Mr. Margut—"no manner o' call to say that. What I does I does, and what I can't do—vy, I can't, and so that's all 'bout it."

"Nothing can be clearer," answered King, with a smile, turning towards his companion. "By the way, I have not introduced you to my friend."

"Yer might ha' done that when ye first come in."

"True ; it was very remiss. Well, this is Captain Ragget, once an officer in the Guards, but now, alas ! obliged to be be on guard himself."

"Your sarvant, sir," said Margut, making a sort of obeisance. "I hope as how we shall be able to queer the knowing ones, arter all. It shan't be no fault o' mine if we don't."

"I am much obliged to you for that declaration," observed Ragget. "I have been swimming in troubled waters for a long time past."

"Now, where are you going to put my friend?" inquired King.

Mr. Margut looked, for a moment or so, at the speaker, and then, without more ado, went to a side cupboard in his room, and took therefrom an old battered lantern ; the candle of this he lighted, and then motioned for his two visitors to follow him."

They did so in silence.

They went down flight after flight of creaky stairs, and eventually arrived at the basement story of the house ; this consisted of several large kitchens.

"Now," said Margut, "I'll show you as nice a little hiding-hole as ever man desired to see. Oh, it's a purty place—a very purty place it is, and no mistake—leastways, it ain't purty to look at, perhaps ; but that goes for nuffin. Handsome is as handsome does. It's safe —or ought to be."

"Where would you lead us?" said King.

"Ye shall see, my brave swells—ye shall see. "Follow."

Seth Margut then led the way into a dark room at the rear of the house. It would have been no very easy matter to guess what this had been used for. It might be a cellar, or it might be a kitchen. At all events, it looked uninviting enough.

"Is this the crib?" inquired King.

"No. Yer hasn't come to it just at present. Wait awhile, and ye shall see what ye shall see, as the conjurer says."

He then removed a stone from the ground, whereupon an opening was disclosed, through which a flight of stone steps could be seen.

"Now, then, gentlemen, follow me," said the landlord of the place.

Captain Ragget and King followed Seth Margut down the stone steps, and soon found themselves in a sort of vault, which had an earthy, unpleasant smell. It was a wretched-looking place, and the only light which found its way into it came from a small grating at the further end.

"Is this where you are going to lodge the captain?" inquired King.

Seth Margut nodded.

"It's a most miserable hole," observed the highwayman.

"Jest you look here, Tom."

"Well, I am looking."

"Vell, then, he wants to be out o' harm's way—don't he?"

"Yes."

"In course he does. Vell, can there be any more secure place than this, eh?—I should like to know that. It ain't at all likely anyone will come here to seek him."

"Perhaps not."

"Oh, vell, if yer don't like this, vell and good. I thought as how yer friend had got the ferrets arter him."

"So he has."

"Vell, then, he mustn't be too particular 'bout the comfort o' the place he has to live in," said Margut.

"This will do exceedingly well, my friend," observed Captain Ragget ; "nothing could be better for the purpose."

"Good, cap'en. Then here ve'll make you as comfortable as possible. Ye'll be a goodish bit alone, but we can't help that. Ye'll be vell cared for. It 'ud bring me to an early grave—that it vould—if any o' my true and 'ticular friends were to be nabbed out o' this 'ere crib ; it 'ud bring me to an early grave—that it vould."

Captain Ragget could not refrain from smiling at the *naive* manner of the speaker.

"And so here you must take up your quarters," said King, as he walked about and made a closer inspection of the place. "Any rats here, Seth?"

"Vell, there may be a few," answered the landlord. "But, lord love you ! they're all respectable, well-behaved animals, and vouldn't hurt a hair o' anybody's head."

"Wondrous kind creatures they must be !"

"As tame as a kitten, and as harmless as a dove."

"Well, what shall we do now?"

"Vot do you mean?"

"Shall I leave you to his 'charge'?" said King, addressing Ragget.

"Yes. I feel that I am in good hands, and am well content to take my chance here."

"Good. Then I shall say farewell, cap'en."

"Shall you see Nan?"

"Yes."

"Tell her that I am in a place of safety ; you need not say where for the present."

"No. I will see you again, and we can arrange about that hereafter."

"Yes. And so, my good friend—my excellent and well-beloved friend, farewell !"

"Farewell, cap'en. Keep up your spirits, and look on the bright side of things. We shall be able to put the double shuffle on old Wild after all. Keep up your spirits."

And, with these words, Tom King ascended the stone steps, and took his departure.

Seth Margut then proceeded to make the wretched place as comfortable as circumstances would admit.

He caused some furniture to be brought down from one of the rooms above, and after putting the apartment into something like " ship-shape," he, too, took his departure, and left the miserable man alone with his own gloomy thoughts—alone with all his bitter memories.

CHAPTER XIV.

THE CAPTURE OF CAPTAIN RAGGET.

SOME three or four days had passed over since the incidents described in our last chapter, and but little had occurred to break the intolerable monotony of the prisoner's life.

Seth Margut had shown every attention to him, and all the delicacies the house could furnish were at his service. Still, Captain Ragget found himself miserable enough. There was little to be wondered at in this. Every hour he dreaded the appearance of the renowned thief-taker or his myrmidons. There was no telling when Wild might choose to swoop down upon his prey; and there was no telling, moreover, what mysterious means he had of learning where those "who were wanted" lay concealed.

Still, under all circumstances, Captain Ragget felt that he was, perhaps, in the most secure place it was well possible for him to pick out.

All sorts of characters visited Seth Margut's establishment; and as a large reward had been offered for the capture of Ragget, it was more than probable that some one of the frequenters might have been tempted to "split" upon the captain—that is, assuming they knew him to be concealed below; but Seth Margut kept this a profound secret from his customers—at any rate, as much of a secret as it was possible for him to do under the circumstances.

As a matter of course, there were treacherous people even in so respectable an establishment as Mr. Margut's. The last-named individual was well aware of this himself; and it was his custom, as he truly expressed it, not to let his right hand know what his left was doing—a very admirable plan, it must be confessed, considering the characters he had to deal with.

Tom King was right when he said that Seth was as true as steel. He was, and always had been, true enough in most of his dealings; and it is but justice to his memory to inform the reader that, ignorant man as he was, and so closely connected as he was from his avocation with all sorts of thieves and lawless characters of every description, he never sold one in the whole course of his life. And he might, many a time and oft, have had bags full of golden guineas for doing so, or even dropping a hint of the whereabouts of gentlemen who were wanted.

I am not writing this much, my friends, for the purpose of investing lawless and wicked men with imaginary virtues, and I am not about to inform you that Seth Margut was a whit more honourable than his fellows. He had his motives for pursuing the course of conduct he had adopted. But, then, his betters had theirs also; and therefore they were even with him, as far as that was concerned.

Seth declared that it would bring him to an early grave if anyone was captured at his house.

It is quite certain that such an occurrence was not at all likely to bring him to an early grave, if it brought him to his grave at all; but it is equally certain that it would have troubled and harassed him most terribly, and would, no doubt, have occasioned him much unhappiness.

He took every precaution it was possible to protect Captain Ragget. He waited upon him when he had time; and when he had not, he sent the most trusty of his followers to serve the captain. But, with all these precautions, a train was fired, and an explosion took place.

I will endeavour to describe to you how this occurred —or, rather, how it was at first manifested to Mr. Margut.

It appeared that Captain Ragget had become nervous and fidgetty. He told Seth that the eyes of some one had peered through the grating of his prison-house. Margut laughed at this, and said it was impossible; nevertheless, he made some inquiries. He examined the rear of his own premises, and found that it was impossible for anyone to get near the railing in question.

Then he sought the captain once more, and informed him of this.

Still the captain persisted in his statement.

Seth Margut went away, and sought his trusty man— the one that usually waited upon the captain in the absence of the master. He said to this worthy—

"Have you noticed anything 'ticular about the chap below?"

"Devil a bit! He seems lonesome like, and off his feet."

"Off his feet be blowed! He's off his head, I'm afeard."

"Law! No—never!" ejaculated Margut's serving-man.

"Well, he's precious queer and fanciful."

"What about?"

"Thinks as how he'll be nabbed."

"Oh, that be hanged for a tale! There ain't any chance o' that where he is—not the slightest chance of it."

"I hope not?"

"I'm sure not."

With all this Margut himself began to be uncomfortable and fidgetty. He could not tell why any more than this, that the captain still persisted in his story of the curious eyes peering in at his grating.

Another day or so passed over.

Mr. Margut was in the large room, which I described in an earlier chapter. An heterogeneous throng of individuals were assembled in this room.

All of a sudden Mr. Margut observed a general movement. They crept into corners, they slunk off into various parts of the house, and crept away so quickly, that anyone who had seen them and the sudden stop there was to the uproarious conversation and occasional burst of merriment, would have come to the conclusion that they were suddenly transformed into so many spectres.

"Vell, I'm blessed!" exclaimed Mr. Margut, who was before the large kitchen fire, attending to the culinary operations of the establishment; "vell, I'm blessed! Vat's up now? Are they all mad that they should cut off in this 'ere sort of manner—vell, I'm blessed!"

Mr. Margut was wrong—he was not blessed.

Mischief was in the wind.

He turned round to see what was the matter.

He was not kept long in suspense.

Mr. Jonathan Wild, with three of his followers, stood before him.

Seth Margut could hardly breathe. An ashy paleness was observable on his features. The great thief-taker was before him.

"Muster Wild, as I'm a sinner!" exclaimed Margut, as though he were addressing some imaginary person.

"The same, at your service," answered Jonathan.

"Ah?" exclaimed Seth, who now began to recover his courage, and endeavoured, by a great effort, to muster an air of intrepidity to his brow. "You're arter some one, I guess?"

"Yes, some one who is concealed here," said Jonathan, looking hard at Margut.

"Oh, indeed—here!"

"Somewhere in these premises. You had better lead me to him at once."

"Me?"

"Yes, you. There's nothing surprising in the request, is there?"

"Vell, I doesn't understand your drift, Mr. Wild, at present—upon my soul, I doesn't understand it—no, indeed, I do not."

"Look here, man," said Jonathan, laying his hand upon the other's shoulder. "It will be quite as well for yourself, Mr. Margut, if you do understand me. Let me speak as plain as I can. You have a party concealed here; his name is Orlando Ragget, and he must be forthcoming, or——"

"Or what?"

"Or we'll fetch him out or take you in his stead."

"Oh take me and welcome. Take me as soon as you please," said Margut, laying down the knife and fork which he had in his hand. "You may take me in welcome, if that'll do any good, I shall make no resistance."

"Now you just shut your potatoe-trap, and hold your jaw," said Jonathan. "You ain't Orlando Ragget, and I mean to have him before another half hour is over either of our heads."

"I hope you may," said Margut, who now felt that he had a great part to play, and made up his mind to go in for first class acting. "You know I couldn't refuse you anything, Mr. Wild," he said, in his most wheedling accents. "If Mr. Ragget was only here——"

"If!" returned Jonathan, sharply. "Stow all that gammon, and don't keep palavering there like an old fool as you are. If! indeed. The captain is here, and so you had best bring him forth at once."

"He is not here—leastways, not to my knowledge," said Margut, with an an undaunted bearing and a bold countenance.

"You lie!" said Jonathan—"you lie, you old rascal! By the lord I've a great mind to shake the life out of you."

And suiting the action to the word Wild caught Seth Margut by the throat and shook him savagely.

"You ought to be ashamed of yourself, to lay your hands upon a man who is almost old enough to be your father," said Margut. "Shame on you, Mr. Wild, I thought better on you."

"Now don't go for to aggravate me, Margut," said Jonathan, "for I tell you I shan't be at all nasty particular, and so I give you fair warning. Bring out this man without further ado!"

As he said this he gave a violent stamp on the floor with his foot.

"I tell ye I doesn't know nuffin' about the chap," said Margut.

"I tell you not to aggravate me, or may be I shall forget that you are old enough to be my father. We know this chap is here, and more than this, he has been here for some days past. We knew that also."

"You are misinformed."

"Get out with you," returned Jonathan. "When am I misinformed? He is here, so out with him."

"Vell, ye won't believe me, I s'pose, and so ye must do as ye please. I doesn't know sich a person as Orlando Ragget."

"You're a lying old vagabond, that's what you are!" said Jonathan Wild, contemptuously. "Search the place." This latter observation was addressed to his followers. "And as for you——"

"Well, what of me?" inquired Margut.

"Why we shan't trust you out of our sight, that's what's about you."

"Oh, thank you for nuffin'," said Margut.

"And so you'll be pleased to follow us."

As the thief-taker said this he laid his hand on the shoulder of his companion and caught him by the collar of his coat.

Mr. Margut offered no opposition, but walked on by the side of Jonathan, whose men were by this time peering into every nook and corner.

"We must go to the basement story of the house, it's there that we shall light upon my gentleman."

As he said this he watched the countenance of Seth Margut narrowly.

"Eh, Mr. Margut," said Wild.

"I beg yer pardon—vat were ye saying?"

"The basement story of the house — that's where this pretty bird is caged. Eh, Mr. Margut?"

"Oh, sir, I have no answer to make. In course you know best, or ought to do, which I s'pose is much the same thing. As long as you are satisfied I shan't complain."

"Oh, a very patient and sensible man, and a wise man, too—more than I had given him credit for," resumed Jonathan, in a half-sportive and a half-sneering tone.

They proceeded to the basement of the building, and soon gained the kitchen. Then Mr. Wild opened his

eyes to their full extent, and began, for the first time since his entrance into Mr. Margut's house, to peer curiously about.

"Now, you may as well save us unnecessary trouble. You may as well do the agreeable, Seth Margut, and turn out the rats for my dogs to chase. Dost hear?"

"I hear," returned Margut.

"But don't seem to heed much, if we are to judge from your appearance. Where have you concealed this fellow?—eh?"

"I shall not make any reply. I've already given my answer. I tell ye I doesn't know sich a person."

"Yes, gammon and all," remarked Wild.

Seth Margut had the greatest difficulty to preserve his undaunted bearing. The thief-takers were now in such close proximity to the place where Captain Ragget was concealed that he felt a sickness come over him as he observed their eyes wander about from place to place and from corner to corner.

"You know, Margut, this is all humbug. You might try it on with some persons, but you know it won't wash with me; and you ought to know better than to attempt to come the old soldier over me, whom you must know is up to every shift and move. You must be a fool as well as an arrant knave to try and dodge me."

"I dare say I am."

"I am sure you are, and that is more."

"I know my business, and I s'pose as how you know yourn, so let there be an end as far as that ere is concerned. I ain't a-goin' to try and play the old sodger, nor nuffin' o' the sort."

"You'll find it won't wash at this establishment," observed Wild. "We put our washing out, we do."

"Does yer, though. Ah, I s'pose yer oblegated to get other people to do yer dirty work sometimes."

"Just so. That's why we have such clean hands ourselves."

"Ah, you are a beauty, you are."

"Always was, and always intend to be."

"Did yer mother ever have any more o' yer sort."

"No; couldn't be expected. By-the-bye, have you got a lantern, Margut, that you could oblige us with."

"A what?"

"A lantern. I know you would do anything to serve an old friend."

"Ah, yes, anything in the world."

"Well, you see this place is rather dark."

"It is so. It always was dark?"

"And so."

"Well, what?"

"You must find us a light."

"With all the pleasure in life," said Mr. Margut, who was but too glad to get an excuse to run up stairs. "I'll go and fetch yer a light."

"No yer don't," said Wild. "None of that. You don't leave this place."

"What would you have me do, then? I can't make ye a lantern, an' I can't whistle for it; leastways, if I do it won't come."

"S'pose not."

"What would you have me do, then?"

"Call at the bottom of the stairs to one of your people to bring a light. That's what yer can do."

"Ah!" sighed Margut, who saw there was no chance for him to get out of the sight of the wily thief-taker. "Call to them, there is no one who will hear me."

"Oh, yes there is."

One of Wild's men now came forward, and informed his master that he had a lantern, and consequently there would be no necessity to call in the aid of Mr. Margut.

That worthy turned pale as he observed Jonathan Wild in a most deliberate and business like manner begin first to light the lantern, and when that had been effected, to hold it down towards the ground, and examine the flag-stones with considerable interest.

"Well I never!" ejaculated Mr. Margut.

"Hilloa! What's that?" exclaimed Wild.

"Oh nuffin'."

"Some one spoke!"

"Ah, did they?"

"Yes; you know they did."

"I never heard anyone but myself, and I'm sure I ain't afraid of my own woice."

"Ah, I dare say now you fancy yourself a mighty clever fellow, but you know, Margut, you've got your match."

"A deuced sight more than my match when I come along side o' you."

"Humph! You're complimentary, you are, and yet you were not particularly glad to see me. Now, Margut, stow all this; where is our man?" said Wild, turning sharply round upon his companion. "It's of no use your trying to throw dust in my eyes, you've got the bloke here safe enough."

"Here?"

"Yes; somewhere about here."

Wild looked suspiciously about. After awhile he took the lantern from the hands of one of his men, and holding it down towards the ground he made a close and careful inspection of the stones.

The front apartment on the base of Seth Margut's residence was subjected to a rigid scrutiny.

Then a like course was adopted with the rest.

At length the thief-taker and his followers came to the last of the three cellars.

Seth Margut felt his knees knock under him, his teeth chattered as though he were in the frigid zone. He saw no escape. Discovery was now certain.

Jonathan Wild examined stone after stone. At length his quick eye lighted upon the loose flag.

He turned sharply round upon Margut.

"You keep your prisoners, Mister Margut," said Wild, "almost as safely as we do in the stone-jug. By my soul, but this does yer credit—infinite credit. So, oh! we shall soon be able to unearth the fox. Perhaps you will just show us a light, Mister Margut," said Wild, in continuation, handing the lantern to the party he was addressing.

There was no help for it; Mr. Margut was compelled to lay hold of the lantern and assist the thief-taker in his search.

Wild withdrew the flag-stone from its resting place, and then gave utterance to a grunt of satisfaction.

A gleam of light found its way into the vault where Ragget was confined.

The thief-taker drew a pistol and was about to descend when Captain Orlando Ragget, who believed himself to be betrayed, gave a wild cry of rage and despair and rushed up the stone steps. Finding that his hiding-place was discovered, Captain Ragget made up his mind to make a rush for it.

He nearly upset Jonathan Wild by the impetuosity of his assault. The latter, however, soon recovered himself and grappled with the highwayman. A desperate struggle ensued, Ragget endeavoured to release himself from the grasp of Wild, who, however, held on like a bull-dog.

"The game's up, Captain Ragget," said Wild; "you may as well go quietly. You've gone to the length of your tether, and so be a wise man, and——"

"Wretches!" exclaimed Ragget, "I'll die first. Unhand me!"

As he said this, the captain flung Wild back, and pinned him against the wall. He then pressed his knuckles against the throat of his adversary. In a few seconds Wild felt all the horrors of strangulation.

His face had become of a deep crimson and was fast assuming a still darker hue.

Wild struggled in vain to release himself, but he was had at an advantage, and was almost powerless.

Seeing how he was situated, one of his men pressed forward to render him assistance.

"Fair play's a jewel," observed Mr. Margut. "A bright jewel it is, and two upon one ain't at all the thing. Let 'em fight it out."

The thief-taker's man uttered an expletive which would not sound well or decorous in genteel society, and began at once to assist his master.

Winding his arms round the body of Ragget he succeeded in pinioning him.

"Now then, Parkins, a rope," said Wild's man to one of his companions, who was standing a few paces off with a rope in his hand.

This was slipped round the arms of Ragget, and wound round his body.

He was now at the mercy of his captors, and Wild was, luckily, soon enabled to recover his equilibrium.

Crest-fallen and dejected, Captain Orlando Ragget glanced from one to the other.

His brow darkened as his eye lighted upon the countenance of Seth Margut.

"Oh, oh," sighed Margut, who, shivering and shaking like a willow in the wind, had some difficulty in restraining his tears. "Oh, don't look at me in that 'ere manner," said Margut; "pray don't—'cause why, I can't bear it. No, indeed I can't. Don't go to think that I had any hand in this 'ere business, cap'en, for I am as innocent as the blessed babe wot's unborn."

"Peace!" said Ragget, "I don't want to hear any of your protestations. I am captured—sold! and there's an end on't."

"Not sold—not sold by me, as heaven is my judge! I wish I——"

He was about to take some impious oath, but Captain Ragget restrained him.

"There is no necessity for you to call anyone to witness your innocence," he said, holding up his hand deprecatingly.

"Vot! yer doesn't believe me!" said Margut—"yer doesn't believe vot I've been a-saying, eh? Tell me that, and Seth—old Seth hasn't many hours to live. Strike me silly, if I have sold you!"

"As far as that is concerned, Master Ragget, said Wild; "I think I can answer for his standing your friend through thick and thin. Howsomever, the chances of war are against you, and so——"

"But don't blame innocent people—don't do that; 'cos it ain't the cheese. No, I'm blest if it is the cheese; and so that's all 'bout it," interrupted Margut, who was well nigh half beside himself at the turn affairs had taken.

"And now, hark ye, master," said Wild, addressing the landlord, "your's is a rosy game, I dare say; but you'll find some thorns among the roses some day or other if you don't keep your weather eye open. So, mark ye that."

"I doesn't understand vat ye mean," returned Margut.

"Well, it's just this," returned the thief-taker; "you've been harbouring persons who have offended the laws of their country, and it's a nice pretty waggon-load of lies you've been telling me, haven't you?"

"I doesn't understand."

"Oh, of course not. It isn't convenient to understand; but you just look here, Master Margut. Take the advice of a fool for once. Don't you come any more of these hanky panky tricks. I tell you for your own good, mind—for nothing more than that. I tell you that you'll find your own head in a hempen noose one of these days."

"Oh, thank ye for nuffin', Master Wild," said Seth Margut. "I'm sure I'm much obleeged to you, I am—very much obleeged to you. You knows yer business, and I knows mine, I s'pose."

Captain Ragget listened to the conversation between the two, from the tenor of which he was led to the conclusion that Margut was blameless, as far as regards any betrayal of himself.

The highwayman glanced at the last-named personage, and said—

"I have done you an injustice—a great injustice.

Let me at once hasten to repair the evil. You have not betrayed me."

"As there is a judge above us all, I have not !" returned Margut. "And hark ye, Cap'n Ragget, I would ha' given this right hand—ay, and the arm to boot, rather than ye should ha' been taken out of Seth Margut's house, bound and a prisoner."

"I believe that," returned Wild, who, after the trouble he had had to find out Ragget, was now very well pleased that he had so far succeeded. "I believe old Margut is as sorry——"

"As you are glad," observed the latter.

"Yes; you take the words out of my mouth."

"I wish I could take your prisoner out of your hands—that's what I wish ; and now, since ye ha' got him, just tell us who did split upon a cove ; just tell us, Master Wild."

"Ah, you're clever, Margut, but ye see there never was a sharp blade but what ye might find a sharper. Make your mind easy on that score ; no one has split upon you—not a living soul."

"Gammon and all."

"No ; as I'm a sinner, I speak the truth."

"Vell, then, how—how did ye know o' this ?"

"Oh ! where he was concealed ?"

"Ay."

"Well, you see, the next time you put a cove in a vault, just take my advice—don't put him in one that has a grating in it ; leastways, not when the grating can be looked through by other eyes than your own."

"Curse it ! It was true about them eyes, then ?" ejaculated Seth Margot.

"Didn't I tell you so ?" inquired Ragget.

"Vell, in course you did ; and I didn't believe you—no, that I didn't."

"I saw two eyes peer into my cell through the grating."

Jonathan Wild smiled.

"There's not much to be wondered at in that," said the old thief-taker. "It's like enough that a pair of eyes may have peered in—not only likely, but certain that they did."

"How could that be possible ?" inquired Margut.

"Well, you see," observed Wild, "I told you that you were a clever fellow ; there can't be any doubt of that. But did it never occur to you that people go up the sewers in London—that there are a large class of men who, armed with a shovel and a lantern, go groping about the sewers. You've got an extensive acquaintance, Margut, and I should have thought you might have known some of that kidney."

"S'pose I have, what o' that ?" returned Margut.

"Oh, nothing — nothing in particular. Only they might have told you that the grating that was in the gentleman's cell could be reached by no other means except by going up one of the sewers."

"And that's how you found him out—eh ?" said Seth Margut, with a sigh of relief. "That was it. Oh, fool that I was not to have thought o' that !"

Jonathan Wild chuckled at the rueful visage of Margut ; but as he had already wasted more time in idle conversation than was usual with him, he marched off his prisoner without further ado.

CHAPTER XXV.

THE HIGHWAYMAN IN NEWGATE.—ATTEMPTED ESCAPE.

CAPTAIN ORLANDO RAGGET had been handcuffed before he left the house of Mr. Seth Margut. At first he had been under the impression that he had been betrayed by the latter individual ; he had, however, dismissed this unworthy thought from his mind after hearing the conversation of the thief-taker and Margut.

Ragget was taken by Wild and his followers to a narrow street, at the corner of which there was a tax-cart. In this there was seated a rough, ill-favoured looking man, who was bound and handcuffed.

"A cracksman," said Wild, nodding significantly towards this individual. "Two's company when three's none."

"And is he to accompany us ?" inquired Ragget.

"Yes. He's a bird fresh caught—about a couple of hours or so before yourself. He's been a fool, that's what he's been."

"And a rogue as well, I suppose ?"

"Well, he was always that, and he's not likely to alter now ; he has always been that, ever since he was weaned, I believe."

Ragget mounted the cart without any more observations. Wild and his men followed ; and in a minute or so after this, the vehicle was on its road towards Newgate.

Upon their arrival at the prison, they were taken through the lodge. They went up a flight of stone steps, and one of the turnkeys, who had joined them, tapped at a thick oaken door, which was studded with iron nails and secured with a gigantic lock.

The cracksman and Ragget were immediately admitted into a little room, which was almost entirely filled by a clerk's desk and stool.

Upon this stool was seated an old man, with a pair of iron-rimmed spectacles on his nose, making entries in an account-book.

The turnkey who had opened the door to them now closed it with an ominous sound. The key clanked loudly in the lock.

Ragget shuddered. He was in prison.

The turnkey unlocked another door, and then disappeared. In a few minutes he returned, and ordered the prisoners to follow him. They entered a snow-white arched corridor, which was lined with iron doors. Here they were separated, and taken into different reception-rooms.

Captain Ragget remained for some time in the cell where he had been conducted, in the company of a single turnkey, who stood by him rigid and voiceless as a statue, watchful as a lynx. This Ragget perceived, in those keen, suspicious eyes which, restless as the body was immovable, seemed to be searching into his very heart.

So he assumed an air of dejection, and kept his eyes always fixed on the ground.

Presently the cell-door opened, and a gentleman in plain clothes came in ; he had a ruddy complexion, with a brown moustache and beard. Ragget recognised him immediately, not that he had ever seen the individual before, but from descriptions he had heard he conceived him to be the governor of the city prison.

He was not mistaken in this supposition.

"So, Captain Ragget," observed the governor, "you have come here at last, eh ?"

From the tone and manner of the speaker, the prisoner concluded that he was known to the governor.

"Did you expect me, sir ?" inquired Ragget, not knowing what else to say.

"Most certainly I did, and have been expecting to see you for a long time past—a very long time, eh, Mr. Wild ?" said the governor, turning to the thief-taker, who had followed close on the heels of the former personage.

Wild chuckled, but made no reply.

"Our friend has kept his word," said the governor, in continuation, now once more addressing himself to the prisoner. "At present you are not convicted of any crime, but there are a number of charges against you."

"I suppose so, sir."

"Still, Captain Ragget, you shall be treated with kindness and forbearance by myself, I promise you that, and, indeed, I may add that it has usually been my practice to treat all those persons who are under my charge with as much consideration as is possible. You shall not be an exception to my usual rule."

"I am much obliged to you, sir," answered Ragget.

"You've been in the army ?"

THE ESCAPE DEFEATED.

"Yes."

"Ah, I have heard of your name, years and years ago, and so, Captain Ragget, out of respect to the name you once bore—you will pardon my being so plainspoken—I shall feel much pleasure in showing you every attention it may be possible for a man in my position to do towards one who is placed under my charge."

Orlando Ragget bowed low at this speech, and once more murmured—

"I thank you, sir."

The governor proceeded—

"You must be aware, prisoner, that there are certain rules and regulations in this prison which must be enforced."

"I suppose, sir, it is my business to act in obedience to the rules?"

"No doubt. And therefore, in the first place, we must go through the forms prescribed by the authorities, and put you through the ordeal of a warm bath."

No. 9.

Captain Ragget had been so intent on displaying an absence of curiosity in the presence of the turnkey, that he had not observed a bath in the corner of the cell.

"Turn on the tap, Barker," said the governer.

And in a few moments the bath was filled with hot water.

Having unbound his hands, they both stood by him as he undressed, and while one searched every article of clothing as he threw it on the floor, the other watched him narrowly, to see that he secreted no forbidden implements.

The contents of his pockets were handed to the governer, who explained to him that, although the prisoners were not permitted to retain money in their possession, they could direct it to be spent in any way they desired, supposing that it was in a way the governor approved of.

"Have you searched all the linings, Barker?" said Jonathan Wild.

"Yes, sir; and there wasn't so much as a needle amongst them," answered Mr. Barker, in a confident tone of voice.

Captain Raggett, who was just at that moment stepping into his bath, gave a sigh of relief when he heard that nothing was found.

"Ah, you are sure?" said Wild, once more scrutinizing the man with one of his most searching glances. "You are quite sure?"

"I shouldn't have said so, Master Wild, unless I felt confident," answered the man, rather petulently.

"Oh, ah! Of course not."

"I don't think anything has escaped my search," said Barker.

"Humph! I know your usual care," returned Wild. "I am sure I should be the last man in the world to imagine for one moment that you would neglect your duty, Barker. You have made a rigid search; that is enough."

Ragget, all the while, was watching the countenances of those present. In spite of himself, he looked anxiously at them. This glance was not lost upon Wild, who, quick as lightening, seemed to suspect something. What, he was unable to clearly comprehend.

The governor looked at the fine form of Captain Ragget. His long, black locks fell over his shoulders; as yet they were not sprinkled with grey. He had been, and, indeed, still was, a remarkably fine man. His countenance was indicative of high intelligence, and his frame, without being as athletic as the cracksman's who had been taken to Newgate with him, was well knit and symetrical.

The governor of the prison looked admiringly at Ragget, although the post he occupied was one which usually hardens and brutalises the mind to human suffering and human crime. But he had three children, and these softened his heart in his few hours of freedom, and, while teaching him that he was a father, taught him also that he was a man.

"Poor fellow!" he murmured, "he's been a gentleman at one time—a fine dashing gentleman, and now—now he has to submit to all these indignities, and is as sure of the gallows as the brute Wild brought with him. I wonder if he has any wife—any children, who care about him, and who will mourn his untimely end. Poor fellow!"

He gave a sign to the turnkey, and was about to turn away.

Captain Ragget was half lying and half sitting in his bath, luxuriating in the soft warmth which so refreshed his sore and wearied limbs. He started. A rough hand seized him by the hair, and four fingers played at hide-and-seek among his flowing tresses till they met a hard substance lying *perdu* in the midst. Round this scissors played, with short, quick clips.

A handful of dark hair fell circling in the bath, and the turnkey, with a growl of satisfaction, displayed a small file and picklock, of exquisitely-tempered steel.

Ragget burned with rage and spite.

The file and picklock had been given him by Tom King, who advised him to conceal them in his hair, in case he should need them at some future time.

The prisoner turned sick at heart when he found a malicious grin pass over the features of Jonathan Wild.

The governor of the prison paced the corridor for the next ten minutes or so, under the pretence of superintending the arrangement of the prisoner's rations, which ascended from the kitchen in a great tray; he did so that he might not witness the first indications of bitter disappointment which passed over the features of Captain Orlando Ragget.

Wild all this while regarded his victim with the eye of a lynx.

On the return of the governor, he called another turnkey, and ordered him to have the prisoner's clothes brushed and cleaned.

Without making any remark on the discovery of the file and picklock, the governor said to Ragget—

"You have got plenty of money, and your clothes are good; we shall, therefore, allow you to wear your own clothes, and to procure your meals from an eating-house, if you prefer it. You will see, by the printed copy of the rules which is hung up in every cell, that you are not allowed to have more than one pint of wine or one quart of malt liquor daily, and that if you undertake to board yourself, you must do so altogether. Besides this, you will be allowed books to read, paper to write upon, and other little comforts under my supervision."

The prisoner bowed at the observations.

The governor continued—

"We have no desire to behave harshly to you during the time you will have to spend with us before your trial; and I hope you will have the good sense not to compel us to be more severe by any refractory behaviour or attempts to escape."

He emphasised these last words most particularly; and Mr. Wild gave a grunt of satisfaction, and said—

"Because, you know, that game would be quite hopeless."

"Ahem! Precisely," returned the governor. "And now, Orlando Ragget, I trust you may not have any reason to complain of my conduct towards you; and, at the same time, permit me to express a hope that you will, at least, return good for good, and that I shall have no reason to complain of your conduct while you are under my charge. As to your future fate, that must be left to the jury, and the discretion of the judge whose duty it will be to try you."

Captain Ragget made no reply to this speech; and, when the governor and Wild had left the cell, the turnkeys returned with his clothes, and, standing by him till he had dressed, they conducted him to a cell, which was numbered 3.

Upon their arrival here, they showed him how to ring his bell, how to pull back the slide from the grating when he wanted fresh air, and how to manage the water-taps and bed-furniture.

They also informed him that, when he wanted anything from the town, there was a prison servant attached to the establishment, whose office it was to run errands for the prisoners waiting for trial, for first-class misdemeanants, and for the officials.

The turnkeys made all these explanations with a courteous accent, for turnkeys have a sort of veneration for great criminals.

They also went out of the cell backwards, as if they were retiring from the royal presence, and locked the door with an ostentatious noise, that they might thereby strike a wholesome awe into the mind of Captain Ragget.

The wretched prisoner was melancholy enough when he found himself left alone, a prey to his own gloomy and distracting thoughts. He sat for nearly two hours on the wooden stool in his cell without moving, and swallowed up in one bitter, savage, burning thought. A great poet has said, that "Bitter is the grief that's devoured alone;" and, without a doubt, Captain Orlando Ragget found this to be the case. At the end of the second hour of his incarceration, he sprang from his seat, and, uttering curses, he ran frantically round his narrow cell.

He wanted to get out. For what?

That he might take one more look at his daughter. That he might clasp in his arms once more, with fatherly embrace, the beauteous and loving Nan Darrell.

As this thought crossed his mind, he yelled with agony.

One of the turnkeys opened the door, and told him that he must make less noise. There was a punishment for making a noise, and he pointed to one of the printed rules.

Captain Ragget gave a hollow laugh, and squatted dejectedly on the stone floor of the cell.

The turnkey, who was used to all sorts of tantrums in fresh prisoners, could therefore make allowances, and so, after repeating his warning, he shut the door.

Once more Ragget was left alone.

An idea of escape crossed his mind.

"Could it be possible for him to once gain the outside of the cruel stone walls?"

This was a question he repeatedly asked himself.

"Such things had been done."

He bit his nails to the quick as he reflected on all these things. His own past life, now so vainly deplored; the love of his own, gentle Nan — how happy was he that she did not bear his name. There was some comfort in that: he might die on the public scaffold, and the secret of her birth might die with him; but then—ah, then, he could not see her. He dared not let her come to Newgate, or their relationship might be suspected—nay, it might be discovered thereby.

At length, worn out, Captain Ragget sunk off into a fitful and uneasy slumber.

He awoke on the following morning unrefreshed, feverish, and nervous.

His morning meal was brought him, which he had some difficulty in eating. Ragget saw but little of either of the turnkeys, for his breakfast had been brought in by the prison-servant, who appeared to be like the rest—a cool man enough.

The prisoner paced up and down his cell, thinking of escape all the while; and so the time passed till dinner hour. When this had arrived, the servant brought a wooden tray in. There were two dishes, each surmounted by a wooden cover. One contained three slices of roast mutton, and the other five potatoes.

"Governor thought you'd like a little dinner," said the man, kindly; and he propped up a slab which was hanging from the wall, placed the tray on it, reached down a salt-dish from a shelf in the corner, where it had grown dusty, in company with a Bible and two hymn-books.

"Will you take any beer or wine?" asked the man.

"I should like some wine," said Ragget.

"Oh, I dare say. I suppose you've been accustomed to take your wine?" remarked the man.

"What makes you think that, my friend?"

"Oh, I don't know; but I should say you had been born a gentleman, and had kept topping society in your day."

"You seem to be a man of penetration," said the prisoner, with something like a laugh. "But I suspect you have heard some observations fall from the governor?"

"You are right," returned the man. "The governor said that you were a real, downright gentleman at one time."

"I'm much obliged to him for the compliment; but those days are long since passed, my friend."

"Well, I hope you will live to see better days."

"There's but little chance of that; but thank you for the wish all the same."

"But wait awhile, and I'll fetch you some wine. What shall it be—port or sherry?"

"Sherry, if you please."

"All right," said the man, who then disappeared.

In a few minutes he returned with a pint of sherry.

"It's against the rules to have more than this," he observed, in a confidential tone.

"That will suffice," answered Ragget.

He drank some of the eating-house sherry, which, bad as it was, encouraged him to eat a few mouthfuls of the mutton which had been brought him. This awoke him from the stupor into which he had fallen, and which had been almost madness.

His thoughts were still the same; but now they formed themselves into but one word. That was *freedom*, which he whispered to himself repeatedly, and which he endeavoured to form into schemes.

It might be a month, or even five or six weeks, before his trial came on; but even supposing it were but one month.

It would not be less than that. In a month there were thirty days.

In these thirty days there were seven hundred and twenty hours.

A third of these would be devoted to sleep, to meals, and to times when it would be dangerous, if not impossible, to work.

That would leave him four hundred and eighty hours, or nearly twenty-nine thousand minutes, to escape in.

After his trial, they would be sure to confine him in a stronger cell, and, perhaps, iron him hand and foot.

Ragget determined at first to allay suspicion, and to make everyone believe that he was resigned to his fate. This would throw his keepers off their guard.

Accordingly, when the man came in to take away the tray, he sent a message to the governor, requesting to see him.

The latter came almost immediately, and looked keenly at the prisoner.

"Do you wish for anything?" he said, slowly. "Is there anything that can be done to make your lonely hours less miserable than I know they must of necessity be?"

"I have to thank you, sir, for your good intentions," said Ragget. "You were kind enough to say that I might have books and papers."

"Most certainly. There can be no objection to that."

"I will avail myself of the privilege, then."

"Very well. Here are paper and pencil; write down what you want, and the messenger shall fetch them for you from the circulating library."

Captain Ragget wrote down the titles of several works.

"I shall read a great many books, sir," he said, smiling. "To sit here without occupation would drive me mad."

"I can readily understand that. Have what you require. We put no limit to the number of volumes; have as many as you like."

"Thank you, sir."

"Besides, they will keep you out of mischief: idle people are always mischievous."

Ragget did not much like this last observation.

"Out of mischief!" he iterated.

"Yes. You know the old adage—'Idleness is the root of all evil?'"

"Oh, as for the matter of that, it's but little mischief that I can do here," observed Ragget, with an innocent air; "but yet I might possibly take it in my head to scrawl upon these white walls, or tear the prison-rules. That would be mischievous enough in its way."

The governor made no reply to this, but contented himself with observing that he should have his books in less than an hour's time.

But, on leaving the cell, he called all the turnkeys before him, and ordered them to watch No. 3 night and day, as he was convinced that he would endeavour to make his escape.

It was Wild who had first put this idea into the governor's head, which had been, perhaps, strengthened by the prisoner's manner.

The turnkeys looked astonished, but, of course, promised to obey the injunctions of their superior.

At four o'clock No. 3 was summoned to chapel, and was ushered into a long line of fellow-prisoners, some of whom were clad in the uniform of convicted criminals.

All the officers accompanied the prisoners into the chapel, and stood in the gallery above the seats of the prisoners, every movement of whom they commanded with their eyes.

It seemed, however, to Ragget that he himself was the focus of attention—the cynosure of numerous pairs of eyes; for, glancing carelessly round the building—as is usual for people to do on first entering a place of worship—he observed that several pairs of eyes accompanied his own in whatever direction he turned them, and also that several more were fixed upon his individual self.

This glance, cursory as it had been, had shown him that the chapel-windows were only protected with one bar, which fell down the centre, and which left an opening on each side, sufficiently small to prevent a sudden escape, and sufficiently large to admit of a slim man squeezing through, with time and trouble.

His heart beat quickly, and he clenched his teeth.

He stiffened himself, to prevent his emotion being perceived by the eyes in the gallery.

To deceive them, he did not look round any more, and, giving his attention, not to the chaplain—for that would have been a transparent act of hypocrisy, and sufficient in itself to have excited suspicion—but to the title-page of the prayer-book, and to other indifferent little matters, as anyone else who had been sent to church by compulsion might have done.

He was trying to guess, all the while—

First, what the chapel-windows opened out upon.

Secondly, whether the chapel-door was locked at night.

An answer to the first question was soon given by the rattle of carriage-wheels, which he could hear plainly; and sometimes he fancied that he could catch the fainter hum of voices and footsteps.

This proved that the chapel was close to the street. If he could only get there, he could easily escape! How the thought seemed to wind round his heart, and to trickle into his brain!

It seemed to endow him with fresh life.

But, then, he had seen that there was a lock on the door—a massive lock.

This might occupy him some hours to pick with such rude instruments as alone he could possibly obtain. He sighed for those which Tom King had given him.

Happening to look down upon the floor, he could scarcely believe his eyes when he observed a needle there.

It had probably been dropped by one of the female prisoners, who, at the regular chapel-hour, sat together in a large pew surrounded by a red curtain, but who occupied the seats of the male prisoners when attending the school-class, which was held in the chapel once a-day.

It has been said often enough that drowning men will snatch at a straw. The needle in question was an apt symbol of this, for Ragget's eyes were ever and anon directed towards it.

In a few minutes after he had first discerned it, he managed to drop his hymn-book; he picked it up directly, and with it the needle, which he secreted in his shirt-sleeve.

As he returned the hymn-book to the ledge of the pew, he managed to display the palms of both his hands, so that no one might suppose that they contained anything besides the book.

As they were being marshalled out of the chapel, he blundered against the door, so that it almost shut.

He took hold of the lock to swing it open again, and, in so doing, slipped the needle into the key-hole.

He could examine it the next day, when he went out, and if the needle was still there, it would be a proof that the door had not been locked.

He opened his books, dog-eared them, wrote notes on the margins, and littered them together, as if he had been diligently employed with them.

But he was too excited to read.

He could not even sit: he paced to and fro, thinking and muttering to himself.

At dusk a turnkey came in, and lighted his lamp.

As soon as he heard the key in the lock, he sprang to his stool, and was poring over his books before the door was opened.

He chuckled to himself as he reflec t ed that he would be able to assume anything, or pretend to be occupied about anything, while the ponderous lock was being turned.

This was some security, for he felt assured that they could not suddenly, or without notice, come into his cell, and take him unawares.

"Indeed, it is fortunate that these gaol-hounds bark so loud," he ejaculated to himself; "the more so as the poor wretch they have to watch courts obscurity. I shall thus be enabled to have timely notice of their entrance."

He was pleased as he reflected on this.

He spent the whole of that night and the next day in deep thought.

It seemed almost like wasting the most precious hours for him to do so; but, as yet, he had not matured his schemes—not shaped his course of action.

Precious as every hour—nay, every minute was, he felt the necessity—the vital necessity there was for him to act with caution, and not to attempt putting into practice any crude or ill-digested plan of escape.

For the question of escape occupied the whole of his thoughts. He knew the price which had been set upon his head, and he was well aware, also, that the governor, however friendly or good-intentioned he might be, had a peculiar interest in taking care of one who had been, and still was, deemed so great a criminal.

The half-hour of evening prayers seemed insupportably long. He quivered all over with impatience and anxiety.

As he passed out, he thrust his finger in the key-hole.

His heart bounded. The needle was still there.

He had now only to work through his cell door into the corridor, from which the chapel was entered.

He could easily turn his bed-clothes into a rope, by which he could let himself down from the chapel window.

As soon as he returned to his cell, he stooped down, and examined the lock attentively. He was occupied some time at this.

After a long inspection, he came to the conclusion that it would be easier for him to dig a hole in the wall close to the lock, far easier than endeavouring to pick the lock itself, which he felt would be an impossibility without the necessary implements. It would have baffled the skill of the most experienced housebreaker, and Captain Ragget, although a determined and desperate man, had never been much used to picking locks, and in this respect would most likely have proved but a poor hand compared to the cracksman who had been brought with him to the city prison. He then decided that his best plan would be to make a hole close to the lock, wrench the staple away, and then force back the bolt, as if it was being unlocked by a key.

But as the captain was rising from his knees, he discovered something in the centre of the door, which, strangely enough, had entirely escaped his attention before.

This was a small round grating, a little larger than a man's eye, with a flap hanging before it, on the other side.

While Captain Ragget was staring at it, and fingering it with considerable curiosity, he heard a soft step, so soft, indeed, that he did not think it was close to him.

At the same time the flap was gently raised, and its place was taken by a large, brown eye, which sternly surveyed the interior of cell No. 3, and the astonished countenance of its inmate.

Then, as if satisfied with the impression it had made, the eye disappeared, and the iron flap descended as noiselessly as it had been raised.

Captain Ragget sat on his stool, and bit his nails, with vexation. The discovery he had made did not in any way tend to render him comfortable. He was watched, that was quite certain.

"Ah, ah!" ejaculated Ragget, "this is a hound that does not bark, and there is more mischief in him. I see I must be careful of his fangs."

He resolved to begin work as soon as it was dark, and watched the shadows, as one by one they fell, through the little window, upon the floor of his cell. He waited till the turnkeys who brought the prisoners their suppers of bread and gruel, and lighted their lamps, had gone their rounds; he then wrenched off one of the hooks upon which his bed was suspended at night, and crept cautiously towards the door.

It was about ten o'clock when he had done this. He could hear voices, and was afraid to begin; so he sighed heavily, and once more sat himself down upon his wooden stool.

He thought of three companions who had been so staunch and true to him in the hour of his misfortune —of Dick Turpin, Tom King, and even old Seth Margut, in whose sincerity he now fully believed; then the current of his thoughts wandered off to the earlier and less sinful days of his life; and then came upon his memory the tones of a young, sweet voice, and, as they broke upon his ear, there stole a bright light into his eyes. And yet, how he had wronged the woman who first taught his heart to love—even to adoration. How dearly she had paid for her attachment to himself. And now, her daughter—the innocent and loving Nan —she might have to eat the bitter fruits of his wickedness.

Captain Ragget rose from his seat, and began once more to pace the narrow limits of his prison-house with restless and uneasy strides.

He stared vacantly at the red flame from his oil-lamp, which flickered and flared, casting strange, fantastic shadows on the walls of his prison. As he was thus occupied, he was calculating what he should do when he had once fairly escaped.

When he heard a clock strike eleven, he sprang from his seat, and, still grasping the hook with which he was to catch freedom, he again knelt down before the door.

All was silent. He chuckled gravely, and struck the hook into the stone.

A cloud of white dust flew from it.

He raised his weapon again, when he fancied he heard a step.

He listened.

There could be no mistake. It was a slow, regular step, like that of a sentry on guard.

He waited till the sound had passed — till it had grown faint—till it had become inaudible.

He remained on his knees listening.

He heard it again — again it approached — again it became inaudible.

His hopes were suddenly dashed at this discovery.

He felt as if he were about to swoon.

There was a mist before his eyes, and horrible lights flickering. and strange noises murmuring.

Something seemed to be swinging too and fro inside his head, like the pendulum of a clock.

It was but too evident that the corridor was watched both by night and by day.

It was impossible to force the door without being heard.

It was impossible to enter the chapel without being seen.

He felt his way back to his seat.

He sat there till the grey light of morning shed its cold, wan rays into his cell.

This light, ghastly as it was, appeared to inspire him with strength and hope; for he now rose, drove the hook back into the wall, removed the white dust which was scattered on the floor, and suspended his bed to the hooks on each side of the cell, like a hammock, flung himself upon it, and fell into a sound sleep.

The turnkeys who watched No. 3 observed nothing remarkable in his demeanour during the next four days, except that he seemed to be always at his books, and he was so busy with these that he scarcely raised his head when they came in.

The prison-servant complained that he was perpetually being sent into the town on errands.

"He takes such odd fancies into his head," said this man. "Sometimes it's books, sometimes it's pens and ink; the last thing he must have is pencils and injee-rubber, and big sheets of white card-paper, because he's going to do a turn at drawing. He is a restless, fanciful fellow, and no mistake."

"But he don't have anything from the eating-house now," answered one of the turnkeys. "He says prison fare is good enough for a nobleman, and never wishes to board better than he does at the City Hotel. So he goes in for the regular thing now—pint of gruel and six ounces of bread for breakfast; meat, or a basin of soup, and eight ounces of bread for dinner; and the breakfast allowance for supper."

"Well, he is an odd card," observed the deputy-governor; "there's no mistake about he's being a queer one. But he's more knave than fool; so keep your eyes open and your mouths shut."

"He's been a gentleman at one time, so the guv'nor says," remarked one of the turnkeys.

"Oh, of course! they are all gentlemen when they come here—gentlemen who live by their wits. And a dueced good living it is at times."

On the sixth day after the date of his captivity, Captain Ragget was still in his bed, although it was ten o'clock in the morning.

He was aroused by the unlocking and opening of his door.

The governor, three turnkeys, and Jonathan Wild entered his cell.

The governor was dressed in his military uniform; and while he caressed his imposing moustache, he cast a suspicious glance around.

"What, prisoner! are you still in bed?" he said, with a martial frown. "You must be aware that this is contrary to the prison regulations?"

"Ahem! Yes, sir, I know it is; but, alas! sluggishness in the morning was always one of my foibles."

"Humph! Strange, that, for a military man."

"I acknowledge it to be one of my faults."

"It's time you broke yourself of such a bad habit."

"I was not aware that it was considered so grave an offence in a place where a man has nothing to do to beguile the tedium and irksomeness of imprisonment."

"Nothing to do!" exclaimed the governor. "My men inform me that your time has been pretty well occupied with your books and—ahem—and your drawings. I hope, Captain Ragget, you are not endeavouring to make a plan of the building?"

"Lord, sir! what possible use could that be to me? I should not be able to take it with me to the other world."

"No, perhaps not; yet still it would be more seemly for you to rise a little earlier. But, perhaps, you have your reasons."

And as the governor made this last observation, he waved his hand towards the bed.

He exchanged a significant look with Jonathan Wild.

The three turnkeys approached the bed, and requested the prisoner to get out.

When he had done so, they searched the bedclothes with great care, as also his own clothes, before allowing him to put them on.

"There is nothing here, sir," they said, with an evident air of disappointment and surprise; "and we don't miss anything from the cell."

Jonathan Wild, who had been standing by with his arms folded across his breast, had not removed his eyes once from Ragget's face.

The old thief-taker had succeeded in intercepting one furtive glance.

"I don't see any hasp to the window," said Jonathan, calmly. "How is that? It is concealed somewhere in the cell, sir."

This last observation was addressed to the governor, who said sharply—

"What have you done with it, prisoner?"

Captain Ragget protested that he had not seen it, and

that it must have been removed before he came into the cell.

They then made another search, which was ineffectual as the previous one.

The hounds were evidantly at fault.

Wild said—

"Stop a minute."

"What for?" inquired the governor.

"One of you had better climb up to the window," observed Wild, who seemed to have been struck by some sudden thought.

The panes of this were made of fluted glass, which was very difficult to see through. In addition to this, a louvre-light—or *lobber-light*, as the prisoners were wont to call them—was hung before the window. It was a great shade, made of sheet-iron, or sometimes painted tin, which prevented the prisoner from seeing anything else, even when the window was opened.

This, the reader must be informed, was never allowed. There was an express rule and punishment for climbing up to the window, and prisoners had to content themselves with a mouthful of fresh air per day, which came through the grating.

One of the men climbed up to the window.

Jonathan Wild and the governor conversed in whispers.

The poor prisoner felt his last chance was about to fade from him.

Presently Wild detached himself from the side of the governor, and once more addressed himself to the turnkeys.

"Search the louvre-light," he said. as he looked maliciously at the countenance of the prisoner.

Then there came a dread suspense which was awful to the prisoner, who, by a gigantic effort, endeavoured to muster an air of intrepidity to his brow.

The hasp was produced, chipped at the end and covered with dirt.

An exclamation of surprise escaped the governor.

Wild was immoveable, but there was an expression of satisfaction displayed in the corners of his hideous mouth.

The hasp had evidently been used on the prison-stones.

"Now you see, sir," said Wild; "and seeing's believing, I s'pose?"

"Quite right, Mr. Wild. Your sagacity is undoubted, as also is your penetration. You were quite right in your suspicions, and you have been exactly right in your suggestions. I have to return you my thanks."

Wild bowed. He walked to the side of one of the walls, and tapped this with his stick for awhile; he repeated this process at various parts, till at length he found a place that yielded to his stick.

He directed the attention of the turnkeys to this.

They pounced upon it, and grubbed at it with their hands.

This disclosed an opening in the wall, almost large enough to admit a man.

A still greater and more violent expression of surprise escaped from the governor.

The hole had been pasted over with sheets of white drawing-paper smeared with prison-gruel, which made admirable glue or paste.

After this had been done, it had been powdered over with the white dust of the stone, till it had become, not an imitation, but a fac-simile.

The governor could not help admiring this masterpiece of industry and art; and even Wild appeared to tacitly acknowledge that it was creditable.

But this tribute to his skill was but a poor consolation to Captain Ragget, who was sadly crestfallen.

After all the pains that he had been at, he found himself even worse off than when he first entered his prison-house.

A shade of anger had crossed the brow of the governor. He was vexed at the discovery—the more so as Jonathan Wild had been the chief cause of it.

"Orlando Ragget," said the governor, in a severe tone, "I have treated you well; and how have you repaid me?"

The prisoner made no reply, but hung down his head.

"By ingratitude," said the governor—"by base ingratitude. I have tried to make you as comfortable and happy as circumstances would permit, and you have tried to disgrace me. I shall henceforth confine you in a stronger and less commodious cell. Dogs that bite us when we fondle them must go to dirty kennels and rusty chains. Barker, you have your orders."

Barker touched his cap.

The governor, with a flourish of his cane, was about to depart, when Wild whispered something in his ear. The two then went out together.

The turnkey, after this, said to Ragget—

"Come with us. You are to be removed. You have heard what has been said."

This fresh disappointment had so stupefied the the prisoner, that he appeared to be unable to realise the depth of his humiliation. He had seen the governor's lips move, but he had not heard him speak.

Neither did he hear the turnkeys.

So they shook him roughly by the shoulders, when he rose and followed them mechanically.

They took him down a flight of steps, and through a yard. In this yard was a small covered building, fitted up with little cells, each of which contained a prisoner.

They retained him there for a few minutes, and then conducted him to a corner of the yard, in which were two iron doors.

One of these was unlocked, and he was thrust into a low, small cell, the walls of which were covered with damp, and which emitted a cold earthy smell, as if it now tasted the sun and the fresh air for the first time.

He sat down upon the rough stones with his elbows on his knees—with his face burried in his hands.

He had been within a few hours of his liberty—he had been robbed of his life when he had almost grasped it in his hands.

Besides this, he had seen some of his fellow-prisoners at work—he had seen how they obeyed the orders of men who spoke to them, not with words, but with gestures and bells.

Their infamous dress; their miserable white faces; their servile compliance, had filled him with terror and dismay.

He looked up at the window, which was little less than one great iron bar.

He sounded the walls, so thick and so strong.

He breathed the air of his new cell, and it chilled him to the very marrow.

He thought of all he had gone through.

Who had he to blame for this discovery?

None other than his sworn—his bitter, vindictive enemy, Jonathan Wild.

Even as the thought crossed him, the door of his cell was opened, and the thief-taker made his appearance.

At a sign from him, the man handed the keys to Jonathan, who closed the door without a word.

He then stood looking at his victim with a look of strange satisfaction.

Ragget was trembling all over, and his eyes shone with a fierce light.

"So," said Wild, "you would be free—free, eh?"

"Wretch!" exclaimed Captain Ragget; "atrocious wretch! without one touch of compassion in your callous heart. Hast thou come here to torture and torment me?"

"You're a troublesome customer, Captain Ragget," said Wild. "A very troublesome customer; but you are overmatched, and I may as well tell you, once and for all, that you might as well think of carrying this building on your back as to endeavour to escape from it. So rest content with that piece of information; but——"

"But what?" inquired Ragget.

"Why, you ought to have come to me in the first instance, that's what you ought to have done, instead of giving me all the trouble you have done. Do you think it's likely we are going to lose you after all the bother we've been at? Bah! man, not for ten times your worth."

"I'll have nought to say to you. Leave me," exclaimed Ragget. "I would rather see the common hangman than you."

"Oh, you'll have that pleasure, I dare say, some time or other; and I fancy the time is not far distant," returned Jonathan, with a mischievous chuckle.

"I will send for the governor, if you don't leave me to myself," answered Ragget.

"Nonsense, man. It is not for you to threaten or command. Conduct yourself with a little more patience. You have had lenity enough shown you, and don't seem to appreciate it. Our governor thought well of you."

"Until you, with your malicious, slandering tongue, made him think otherwise. If it had not have been for you, I should have been, by this time, outside these accursed walls."

"Very likely," returned Wild. "Indeed, more than likely, for I must do you the justice to say that your escape was well planned, and that it does you infinite credit. No doubt you would have been soon outside these walls; but you see that there was an eye watching over you, and, for the rest, you find yourself in a worst position than heretofore."

"Worse! Well what of that? My case is hopeless, Mr. Wild, and you know it. All the eloquence that the most skilled counsel could use would not weigh as a straw in the scale. I must be found guilty, and—and the rest is easily told."

"Oh, you make a good guess, Master Ragget; I believe your case is hopeless."

"You know it is."

"Nay, I don't know, but I believe—I think," returned Wild. "We have all of us our thoughts on most subjects. Now, you see, I have mine with regard to yourself, and if you like to turn king's evidence against—against one or two whom I shall name, why——"

"Wretch!" exclaimed Captain Ragget, rising up to his full length, and assuming a threatening attitude—"Wretch! dost thou dare to make such a suggestion to me? And is it for this that you have sought me here?—that you have thwarted me in my attempt to escape?"

"I should have done that, whether or not," answered Wild, with the utmost coolness; "but, at the same time, that is the reason why I have sought you here. Are we to be friends or enemies?"

Captain Ragget regarded Jonathan with a look of ineffable scorn and contempt, but made no reply.

"You had better consider seriously of what I have been saying," observed the thief-taker. "You had much better do that ere it is too late."

"Have I lived to be insulted thus?" exclaimed Ragget. "Is it possible that I have sunk so low as to have such a proposition coolly made to me? Turn king's evidence against my best friends! Not if it were to save my worthless life twenty times over, if that were possible."

"It will be your only chance to save it," returned Jonathan. "I can tell you that, without fear of contradiction—it will be your only chance. And if you value your life, which most men do—humph! which most men do—why, you're a green 'un if you don't act according to my instructions. That's all I have to say."

"I do not fear death," answered Ragget.

"Fear!" exclaimed Jonathan, in a husky voice. "What wretch is there condemned to death who does not quake at the sound of his own voice—who does not shudder at his own thoughts? When people are with

you, though they be your gaolers—when the sun shines upon you, though it be only with a pale ray, you feel——"

"Sun! What sun?" inquired Ragget. "There's none here, in this wretched place."

"No, I forgot they have removed you from your old quarters. Well, no matter for that. When you are alone and in darkness, you think of things, I'll be bound, which make your heart sick."

"I do so; what of it? Are you come here to gloat over my agonies?"

"You might be free. Are we to be friends or enemies?"

"Away! I will have nought to say to thee."

"I have done," returned Wild, turning away and opening the door of the cell with the ponderous key—"I have done, and you are a fool for your pains."

He paused for a moment on the threshold.

"You are a fool for your pains, Captain Ragget."

"Away, wretch! Begone!"

Jonathan Wild disappeared. He thrust his head in again, however, and, with a hideous grin, said—

"I shall not see you again till the morning you are to be hanged."

He then slammed the door to and disappeared.

When Wild had taken his departure, Captain Ragget sank into a state of utter prostration and despair. He crouched in the furthest corner of his cell, gnawing his hands and uttering deep groans.

CHAPTER XVI.

THE FORTUNES OF THE PRETENDER.—NAN'S INTERVIEW WITH HER FATHER.—ANOTHER PLAN OF ESCAPE.

CAPTAIN RAGGET remained for a long time in a state of deep dejection. The words that had fallen from Jonathan Wild were in themselves significant enough. Indeed, the wretched prisoner felt that there was but little hope for him.

None, unless he could escape; and then, when once free, he would make for the Continent.

The suggestion which Wild had made was not a new one to the captain, who at any time might have gained a free pardon by betraying his associates.

But Captain Ragget had chivalrous notions of honour; and, hunted as he had been for so many months, the last thought that ever crossed his mind was to turn approver, or king's evidence, against those who had been his intimate friends and associates.

He had been mixed up with many persons who espoused the cause of Charles Edward—the Pretender, as he was called.

There could be but little doubt but Captain Ragget was acquainted with much valuable information respecting those persons who had been partisans of Charles Edward, and this information the governing powers were anxious to obtain; and hence it was that Jonathan Wild had received instructions to take into custody the celebrated highwayman, Captain Orlando Ragget—and hence it was that the persecution of the last-named individual was more than an ordinary persecution.

It will be as well for the information of those readers who may not be acquainted with the history of the Pretender, to give a brief description of those events which occurred in England a few years before the capture of Captain Orlando Ragget.

It was at this period that the son of the old Pretender resolved to make an effort for gaining the British Crown.

Charles Edward, the adventurer in question, had been bred in a luxurious court, without partaking of its effeminacy.

He was enterprising and ambitious; but either from inexperience or natural inability, utterly unequal to the undertaking.

He was long flattered by the rash, the superstitious, and the needy; he was taught to believe that the kingdom was ripe for a revolt, and it could no longer bear the immense load of taxes with which it was burdened.

Being at this time furnished with some money, and with still larger promises from France, which fanned his ambition, he landed in Scotland on board a small frigate, accompanied by the Marquis of Jullibardine, Sir Thomas Sheridan, and a few other desperate adventurers.

Thus, for the conquest of the whole British Empire, he only brought with him seven officers, and arms for two thousand men.

The boldness of this enterprise astounded all Europe.

It awakened the fears of the pusillanimous, the ardour of the brave, and the pity of the wise. But by this time the young adventurer arrived at Perth, where the unnecessary ceremony was performed of proclaiming his father king of Great Britain.

From thence, descending with his forces from the mountains, they seemed to gather as they went forward, and advancing to Edinburgh, they entered the city without opposition.

There, again, the pageantry of proclamation was performed, and there he promised to dissolve the Union, which was considered one of the grievances of the country.

However, the castle of that city still held out, and he was unprovided with cannon to besiege it.

In the meantime, Sir John Cope, who had pursued the rebels through the Highlands, but had declined meeting them in their descent, being now reinforced by two regiments of dragoons, resolved to march towards Edinburgh, and give the enemy battle.

The young adventurer, whose forces were rather superior, though undisciplined, attacked him at Preston Pans, about twelve miles from the capital, and in a few minutes put him and his troops to flight.

This victory, by which the king lost five hundred men, gave the rebels greater influence; and had the Pretender taken advantage of the general consternation, and marched directly to England, the consequences might have been fatal to freedom.

But he was deterred by the promise of succour which never came, and thus induced to remain at Edinburgh, to enjoy the triumphs of an important victory, and to be treated as a monarch.

While the Pretender was thus trifling away his time at Edinburgh (for in dangerous enterprises delay is defeat), the ministry of Great Britain took every precaution to oppose him with success.

Six thousand Dutch troops that had come over to the assistance of the crown were despatched northward, under the command of General Wade.

The Duke of Cumberland soon after arrived from Flanders, and was followed by another detachment of dragoons and infantry, well disciplined and inured to action.

Besides these, volunteers appeared in every part of the kingdom, and every county exerted a vigorous spirit of indignation against the ambition, the religion, and the allies of the young Pretender.

However, he had been bred in a school that taught him maxims very different from those that then prevailed in England.

Though he might have brought civil war, and all the calamities attending it, with him into the kingdom, he had been taught that the assertion of his right was a duty incumbent upon him, and the altering of the constitution, and perhaps the religion of his country, an object of laudable ambition.

Thus convinced, he went forward with vigour; and having, upon frequent consultations with his officers, come to the resolution of making an irruption in England, he entered the country by the western border, and invested Carlisle, which surrendered in less than three days.

He there found a considerable quantity of arms; and there, too, he caused his father to be proclaimed king.

General Wade, being apprised of his progress, advanced across the country from the opposite shore; but receiving intelligence that the enemy was two days' march before him, he returned to his former station.

The young Pretender, thus unopposed, resolved to penetrate farther into the kingdom, having received assurances from France that a considerable body of troops would be landed on the southern coast to make a diversion in his favour.

He was flattered, also, with the hopes of being joined by a considerable number of malcontents as he passed forward, and believed that his army would increase on his march.

Accordingly, leaving a small garrison in Carlisle, which he should have left defenceless, he advanced to Penrith, marching on foot, in a Highland dress, and continued his irruption till he came to Manchester, where he established his head-quarters.

He was there joined by about two hundred English, who were formed into a regiment under the command of Colonel Townley.

Captain Ragget was amongst these, holding the rank of major.

Ragget had been disgracefully treated by the Government before he joined the forces of the Pretender, and, doubtless, it was for this reason that he had been induced to do so.

It would appear that his whole life had been one grand mistake, otherwise he never would have sunk down so low as to have been what we have found him in the opening of our tale.

After the Pretender had been joined by Townley's regiment, he marched on to Derby, intending to go by the way of Chester into Wales, where he hoped to be joined by a great number of followers; but the disputes between his own chiefs prevented him proceeding to that part of the kingdom.

He was, by this time, advanced within a hundred and twenty-six miles of the capital, which was filled with perplexity and consternation. Had he have proceeded on his career with that expedition which he had hitherto used, he might have made himself master of the metropolis, where he would certainly have been joined by a considerable number of his well-wishers, who waited impatiently for his approach.

In the meantime, the king resolved to take the field in person; but he found safety from the discontents which now began to prevail in the Pretender's army.

In fact, he was but the nominal leader of his forces, as his generals, the chiefs of the Highland clans, were, from their education, ignorant and averse to subordination.

They had, from the beginning, begun to embrace opposite systems of operation, and to contend with each other for pre-eminence; but they seemed now unanimous in returning to their country once more.

The rebels accordingly effected their retreat to Carlisle without any loss, and from thence crossed the rivers Eden and Solway into Scotland.

In these marches, however, they preserved all the rules of war. They abstained, in a great measure from plunder; they levied contributions on the towns as they passed along, and, with unaccountable precaution, left a garrison at Carlisle, which, shortly after, was obliged to surrender at discretion to the Duke of Cumberland, to the number of four hundred men.

The Pretender having returned to Scotland, proceeded to Glasgow, from which city he exacted severe contributions.

He advanced from thence to Stirling, where he was joined by Lord Lewis Gordon, at the head of some forces which had assembled in his absence.

Other clans, to the number of about two thousand, came in likewise; and from supplies of money which he received from Spain and from some skirmishes in which he was successful against the Royalists, his affairs began to wear a more promising aspect.

Being joined by Lord Drummond, he invested the castle of Stirling, commanded by General Blankeney;

[THE INTERVIEW.]

but the rebel forces, being unused to sieges, consumed much time to no purpose. It was during this attempt that General Hawley, who commanded a considerable body of the forces near Edinburgh, undertook to raise the siege, and advanced towards the rebel army as far as Falkirk.

After two days spent in mutually examining each other's strength, the rebels, being ardent to engage, were led on in full spirits to attack the king's army.

The Pretender, who was in the front line, gave the signal to engage; and the first fire put Hawley's forces into confusion.

The horse troops retreated with the utmost precipitation, and fell upon their infantry; while the rebels followed up the blow, and the greater part of the royal army fled in the utmost confusion. They retired to Edinburgh, leaving their conquerors in possession of their tents, their artillery, and the field of battle.

Thus far, the affairs of the rebel army seemed not unprosperous; but here was an end of all their triumphs. The Duke of Cumberland, at that time the favourite of the English army, had been recalled from Flanders, and had put himself at the head of the troops at Edinburgh, which consisted of about fourteen thousand men.

With these he advanced to Aberdeen, where he was

No. 10.

joined by several of the Scotch nobility attached to the House of Hanover; and, having revived the drooping spirit of the army, he resolved to find out the enemy, who retreated at his approach.

After having refreshed his troops at Aberdeen for some time, he renewed his march, and in twelve days he came up to the deep and rapid river Spey. This was the place where the rebels might have disputed his passage; but they lost every advantage in quarrelling with each other.

They seemed now totally void of all counsel and subordination, without conduct, and, what was worse, without unanimity.

Nothing but discord reigned in their camp. No attention was paid to the orders of their leaders, which, upon every opportunity, they treated with disdain. Unity was the bond that ought to have bound them together; but, in the place of it, we had "a house divided against itself," and we all know the result—it must fall.

Such a state of affairs could not last long, notwithstanding the well-meant endeavours of some of the rebels.

After a variety of contests with one another, they resolved to await their pursuers upon the plains of Cul-

PUBLISHER'S NOTE

pp.75-80 are missing.

loden, a place about nine miles distant from Inverness, embosomed in hills, except on that side which is open to the sea.

There they drew up in order of battle, to the number of eight thousand men, in three divisions, supplied with some pieces of artillery, ill-manned and ill-served.

The battle began about one o'clock in the afternoon, and the cannon of the king's army did dreadful execution among the rebels, while theirs was totally unserviceable.

One of the great errors in all the Pretender's warlike measures was his subjecting wild and undisciplined troops to the forms of artful war, and thus repressing their native ardour, from which alone he could hope for success.

After they had kept in the ranks, and withstood the English fire for some time, they at length became impatient for closer engagement, and about five hundred of them made an irruption upon the left wing of the enemy with their accustomed ferocity.

The first line being disordered by this onset, two battalions advanced to support it, and galled the enemy with a terrible close discharge. At the same time the dragoons under Hawley, and the Argyleshire militia, pulling down a park wall, feebly defended, fell upon them sword in hand, and committed terrible slaughter.

In less than thirty minutes they were totally routed, and the field covered with their wounded and slain to the number of three thousand men.

The French troops, on the left, did not fire a shot; but stood inactive during the engagement, and afterwards surrendered themselves prisoners of war.

An entire body of the clans marched off the field in order, while the rest were routed with great slaughter, and their leaders obliged, with reluctance, to retire.

Civil war is indeed terrible; but much more so when heightened by unnecessary cruelty.

How guilty soever an enemy may be, it is the duty of a brave soldier to remember that he is only to fight an opposer, and not a supplicant.

The victory was in every respect a decisive one, and humanity to the conquered would have made it glorious.

But little mercy was shown on this occasion. The conquerors were seen to refuse mercy or quarter to the vanquished—to the unarmed and defenceless. Some were slain who were only excited by curiosity to become spectators of the conflict, and soldiers were seen to anticipate the base employment of the public executioner.

The duke, immediately after the action, ordered six and thirty deserters to be executed. The conquerors spread terror wherever they came, and, after a short space, the whole country round was one dreadful scene of plunder, slaughter, and desolation; justice was forgotten, and vengeance assumed its name.

In this manner were blasted all the hopes and all the ambition of the young adventurer, one short hour depriving him of imaginary thrones and sceptres, and reduced him from a nominal king to a distressed, forlorn outcast, shunned by all mankind, except those who sought his destruction.

To the good and brave, subsequent distress often atones for former guilt; and while reason would speak for punishment, our hearts plead for mercy.

Immediately after the engagement, he fled away with a captain of Fitzjames's cavalry. This individual was none other than the wretched man, Orlando Ragget, whom we have seen a fettered prisoner in the cells of Newgate.

When the horses of these two fugitives were fatigued, they alighted, and separately fought for safety.

For some days Charles Edward wandered in this country, naturally wild, but now rendered formidable by war, a wretched spectator of all those horrors which were the result of his ill-grounded ambition.

There is a striking similitude between his adventures and those of Charles the Second, upon his escape from Worces·

He sometimes found refuge in caves and cottages, without attendants, and depended on the wretched natives, who could pity, but were unable to relieve him. Sometimes he lay in forests, with one or two companions of his distress, continually pursued by the troops of the conqueror, as there was a reward of thirty thousand pounds for taking him, dead or alive.

Sheridan, an Irish adventurer, was the person who kept most faithfully to him, and inspired him with courage to support such incredible hardships. He had occasion, in the course of his concealment, to trust his life to the fidelity of above fifty individuals, whose veneration for his family prevailed above their avarice.

One day, having walked from morning till night, he ventured to enter a house, the owner of which, he well knew, was attached to the opposite party. As he entered, he addressed the master of the house in the following manner:—

"The son of your king comes to beg a little bread and a few clothes. I know your present attachment to my adversaries, but I believe you have sufficient honour not to abuse my confidence or to take advantage of my distressed situation. Take these rags, that have been for some time past my only covering. You may probably restore them to me some day, when I am seated on the throne of Great Britain."

The master of the house was touched with pity at his distress, and assisted him as far as he was able, never divulging his secret.

There were few of those who wished for his destruction that would choose to be the immediate actors in it, as it would have subjected them to the resentment of a numerous party.

In this manner he continued to wander among the frightful wilds of Glengary for nearly six months, often hemmed round by his pursuers, but still rescued from impending danger by some lucky accident.

At length a privateer of St. Malo, hired by his adherents, arrived in Lochnanach, into which he embarked, in the most wretched attire.

He was clad in a short coat of black frieze, almost threadbare, over which was a common Highland plaid, girt round by a belt, from which was suspended a pistol and a dagger. He had not been shifted for many weeks. His eyes were hollow and his visage long, and his constitution greatly impaired by famine and fatigue.

He was accompanied by Sullivan and Sheridan, two Irish adherents, who had shared all his calamities, together with Cameron of Lochiel and his brother, and a few exiles.

They set sail for France, and, after having been chased by two English men-of-war, they arrived in safety at a place called Roseau, near Morlaix, in Bretagne.

Perhaps he would have found it more difficult to escape had not the vigilance of his pursuers been relaxed by a report that he was already slain.

In the meantime, while the Pretender was thus pursued, the scaffolds and gibbets were preparing for his adherents. Seventeen officers of the rebel army were hung, drawn, and quartered on Kennington-common, in the neighbourhood of London. Their constancy in death gained more proselytes to their cause than even, perhaps, their victories would have obtained.

Nine were executed in the same manner at Carlisle, and eleven at York.

A few obtained pardon, and a considerable number were transported to the plantations in North America.

The Earls Kilmarnock and Cromartrie and Lord Balmerino were tried by their peers, and found guilty.

Cromartrie was pardoned, but the rest were beheaded on Tower hill.

In this manner victory, defeat, negociations, treachery, and rebellion succeeded each other rapidly over some years, till all sides began to feel themselves growing more feeble, and gaining no solid advantage.

Government mistrusted numbers of persons whose positions in society ought to have been a guarantee for their integrity; and we have entered into this brief

[HARRIET HAWKER.]

"Good. Then be ready to meet me to-night at the corner of Acton-lane."

"Right you are!" ejaculated the Puddler.

"We must go separate at first, my lads," said Brady, *alias* Neville, "and be all of us in disguise. Harry here will find us whatever we want. If either of us should get boxed up in the jug, the others must help the canary-bird out of his cage, and cheat the beaks again. I will write down some notions I have on this point, and you shall decide upon them afterwards. Bring me some pens and ink."

While Matchet was eating and Brady was writing, the Screever whistled a popular thieves' air in an undertone, and Harriet Hawker remained apparently in deep thought, sometimes glancing furtively at her handsome *vis-à-vis*.

He handed the paper to his confederates. The Puddler frowned over it, not because he disapproved of the ideas, but because he found it difficult to decipher the words in which they were conveyed.

Honest English was as unintelligible to him as the hieroglyphics would be to us.

No. 11.

Having mastered the preliminary obstacles, however he testified his delight by knocking down a chair on each side of him with his fists, and handed it to the Screever, who, on reading it, appeared no less charmed with its contents.

Then they drew close together, and conversed for some time in a low and earnest voice.

An hour afterwards, the two men passed out. This time, they carried large parcels under their arms, and each, with a nod, went his way.

The dark-eyed young man was still seated in the parlour, inhaling the fragrance of a genuine trebucha.

Harriet Hawker entered the room. She now wore a blush silk dress, which displayed to advantage her hands and neck, which were white as Parian marble. She was very beautiful, but round her eyes and mouth there were lines and wrinkles, unnaturally deepened by the life of anxiety she had led.

A life of crime is always a life of care, for the hearts of the wicked tremble for the past, for the present, and the future.

"James," she said, coming towards him.

"Excuse me, my sweetest pet," answered the young man, in tones which were half sneering; "excuse me, but I am no longer James Neville. That respectable individual was executed at Tyburn. I am Mr. Thomas Brady."

"I know. To the world you are, but I called you by your real name."

"My dear girl," answered her companion, "there is nothing real in the existence of a thief—it is as ephemeral as butterflies and other poetical insects. I have changed my name as I have changed my language, my associations, my habits, and my honesty."

Mr. Thomas Brady took three or four long puffs from his cigar, which had been trying to go out under cover of his eloquence.

"I will call you what you wish," she answered, gently, "if you will listen to what I am going to say."

"Well, go on; but mind, if it's too long a story you've got to tell, I don't promise to listen," said her companion, carelessly.

She buried her face in her hands. Brady took the cigar out of his mouth to smile.

"You spoke of changing, James—for I shall cling to the name by which I have known you so long—and that very word has strengthened me in my determination. I have been a thief ever since I can remember; and, oh! how bitterly I repent the crimes which others taught me to commit—how sincerely I desire to atone for them by a life of virtue and repentance!"

She buried her face in her hands once more; then, after a pause, she proceeded—

"Would you like to hear my history?" she said; and she raised her beautiful eyes, which were now floating in tears. "It will, perhaps, make you pity me. It was my own mother who taught me to steal, James—who beat me when I returned without any money—who trained me to look upon the gallows without fear or horror, as other children are taught to look upon a happy death-bed and peaceful grave. I was very quick and nimble, and soon made myself proficient in picking pockets and counter-snatching. As soon as I found that I could steal for a living, I ran away from that which I had called a home, and went into the service of an old woman, who dressed me in fine clothes and sent me to churches and theatres, where my lady-like looks enabled me to mingle with rich people without their suspecting that I was a thief, and to steal such numbers of watches and bracelets that before I was seventeen I was as celebrated as Moll Cutpurse of old.

"By escaping from the clutches of the old Jewess, who thought she had me as her slave for life, and by diligently saving my money, I was enabled, after a time, to rent this house, and set up in business as a receiver of stolen goods. I also used to ply my trade of shoplifting in the fashionable quarters, parading as my duenna Mrs. Durant, whom you remember, and whom I discovered in a Mint lodging-house, playing at hide-and-seek with the police, about an attempted infanticide, or something of that kind. I do not know where she is now."

"Oh," said Brady, drily.

"Thus, you see that few have had more experience in theft than myself, and few have had such success.

"I have never been in prison; I am rich; I have had nothing to discourage me. If it were possible for a thief to be happy, I should be so. But I am not—I am most miserable."

"I am sorry to learn that," said Brady.

"It is true, James; I am, indeed, miserable."

"Oh, I, on the other hand, am a thief pursued by justice, who, fortunately for me, is blind in fact as well as in fable, and you see I am happy enough."

"You are happy now, because you are tasting triumph for the first time, perhaps; but it will soon turn bitter in your mouth. You are happy now, because you have earned the respect of villains; but the time will come when you will sigh for the goodwill of honest men. Oh, James, let us turn before it is too late. We are well off; we have not the excuse of necessity for crime. Think, oh, think before you endanger your life and liberty in this world, and your eternal happiness in the next."

"What do you propose, then?" inquired her companion.

She placed her white hands upon his shoulders, and her lips upon his cheeks.

"Might we not marry, dear James? I should be so happy if you would make me your wife! Sometimes we would travel to France or Germany, and see all the grand sights of the world; and sometimes," she added, in a voice hushed as a sigh, and melodious as a song, "we would return to some secluded spot, and there dwell in delicious solitude."

Her gliding step—her glittering eyes—her fragrant but fiery breath, as she approached, made her resemble a serpent which uncoils itself to spring.

He shuddered, in spite of himself; then he rose, and exclaimed, in a voice of thunder—

"Marriage! and can you say that word?".

"Oh!" she cried.

And she clenched her hands and recoiled back a few steps.

"You have told me your history," he said, recovering his sang froid, and lighting a fresh cigar at the dying ashes of his first; "permit me to relate to you the history of another young lady. You will find it very interesting indeed: so romantic, that it almost borders upon the incredible; so instructive, that it becomes an actual warning to all who might, by chance, become acquainted with its heroine. Her name was Jane Williamson."

The woman uttered a horrible cry.

Brady closed his eyes, and allowed the smoke to curl voluptuously from between his lips.

"Her name was Jane Williamson. She was the daughter of a farmer. A gentleman from London saw her, and was struck with her beauty. He feared to marry her, for he was old, while she was very young. But she told him, with embraces which were meretricious as those of a courtesan, that she loved him. He married her, and before two months were over he found that she had a lover. He forgave her as they say God forgives the sinner who prays to Him for mercy. In return, this angelic creature robbed him of every farthing he possessed, and eloped with her lover."

"I was his tool—I was at his mercy; he made me do it!" exclaimed the woman, in passionate accents.

"Liar and murderess!" shouted out Tom Brady. "That man—your partner in vice—your accomplice in crime—was discovered lying on the high road, his face covered with dreadful spots, and all the signs of death by poisoning within his frame. Therefore, my dear Harry, since I have no ambition to play Duncan to your Lady Macbeth, or to have my tea sugared with arsenic any morning that you happen to sit down to breakfast in a bad humour, I most politely decline your offer!"

She looked at him calmly, gave a low moan, and fell like a corpse to the floor.

He surveyed her with the inquisitive look of a prize-fighter who wishes to see what effect his "punishment" has had upon his adversary—a look in which sympathy is the least ingredient.

"Well," he said, slowly, "it appears genuine, and I suppose, must be attended to."

He knelt down by her, and, forcing the mouth of the gin-bottle between her teeth, made her swallow a few drops. This seemed to revive her.

I write seemed, for Harriet Hawker had only pretended to faint, in order to gain time to think. She had been studying a part while lying prostrate on the ground; now she began to play it."

She raised herself feebly, and gave him her hand.

"You have found me out, Neville," she said, slowly; "yes, you have found me out, and so further deception would be useless. To carry out my ambitious projects,

I wished to try a new field of action abroad, and to have with me a husband of gentlemanly appearance and great ability; but I find that it is not so easy to dupe you as it was some time ago. There is no occasion for us to quarrel. Let us both forget this interview, and let only the relation of thief and thief exist between us."

He looked at her eyes: they met his calmly and unflinchingly.

"Bah!" said he, taking her hand. "You are, after all, a sensible woman, Harriet. As you suggest, we will drop matrimony for the present, and—ahem—stick to business."

"It shall be the business of my life to destroy you," she murmured to herself.

And when she was alone, she took a terrible oath.

CHAPTER XVIII.

A BEAUTIFUL FIEND.

I NOW enter upon a fearful study. It is that of a heart which, though young, is severed, withered, depraved, and which can no longer throb for aught but gold or blood. It is that of a mind which is strong to resolve, patient to wait, relentless to execute. It is that of a woman who possesses the face of an angel and the passions of a demon of hell.

Harriet Hawker had once in her life become human: she had loved. She had offered a man this love, which was as fiery as her rage. He had refused it; and, in refusing it, he had told her the terrible secret of her life. By some means or other, he had discovered the crimes of her girlhood—adultery, theft, and murder. For this she hated him, and with no common hate—for this she determined to be avenged, and with no common vengeance.

Retiring into the depths of her black heart, she concocted a plot which will make you shudder as it unfolds its poisoned folds.

First, she knew that it would be necessary to blind the eyes of her victim before she raised the knife to strike.

And as victims destined for the sacrificial altar were, in times of yore, decked with beautiful flowers, and marched to death to strains of martial music, so Harriet Hawker, summoning all her glorious beauties, all her fiendish arts to her aid, attempted to blind this young man with her kisses, to crown him with garlands of illicit love, and lead him towards the precipice while her voice murmured music in his ear.

Thus she gained an influence over Tom Brady which, forearmed as he had been by the knowledge of her crimes, he would at one time have deemed impossible.

All was prepared for the first act of the drama of death; but now she required a tool. She sought among the streets, and examined faces as they passed. She required, as her dupe, a young man of susceptible affections and a ductile mind.

She found him at last, and it is thus that she laid her snares.

At the time of which I am writing, the Ex ter Change was frequented by half the lounging world of the metropolis. Here wild animals were to be seen. It was a great market for the sale of ornaments, and pretty girls, modestly dressed, were to be seen parading about.

One afternoon, when the lounge was at its zenith, a young man, fashionably dressed, entered. A moment afterwards a woman, thickly veiled, was to be seen immediately behind him. When she saw that he was there, her eyes gleamed through the veil. Raising it, she disclosed a face which was pale, chaste, and beautiful as a Madona.

Presently he passed her, and she fixed her eyes on him. As he felt those eyes, so full of languour and love, upon him, he started and blushed.

She did not blush, but she looked upon the ground, and turned modestly away.

He followed her.

She left the Change. She had no need to look round: with the ears of a hare, she heard the steps behind her.

He passed her, and glanced at her over his shoulder. She gave him another look. He walked slowly, that she might overtake him. Then he passed again, and spoke to her.

She answered him in a confused tone.

He asked her, stammering, if he might escort her.

"But I do not know you, sir," she said, gently.

"That is true," he answered, with a sigh.

She placed her hand on his arm.

"I will trust myself with you," she said, with a frankness that pleased him, and with a smile that enraptured him.

Before half an hour had passed away, they were acquainted with the secrets of each other's lives. She was a dressmaker. Her father and mother were both dead; they had apprenticed her to Madame Hue, and in her fine school of needlework she had become a first-rate workwoman.

Madame Hue had wished to keep her, and had even offered her a place as "first hand." with its salary of a hundred a-year, but she was tired of the late hours and the large work-room, and its eternal hum of voices and crackling of needles.

She wished for independence, and had taken a first-floor to herself, near Golden-square. As she was clever in her business, she earned enough, by working hard, to support herself, and even contrived to send a present sometimes to a bedridden aunt, who was dependent upon charity for those little luxuries which are the same as necessities to sick people.

His name was William Hargrave. He was the son of a baronet, who was rich and liberal. He told her that he had every enjoyment he could wish for, but that he was not happy. He said he had no one to love him: his mother had died when he was young; he had no sisters.

He had sickened of those pleasures of the town for which so many young men but too often ruin themselves; he never entered his club: he did not care for the society of men; he felt himself alone in the world.

The young dressmaker gave a smile. It was evident that he was romantic.

She retained a kind of reserve during this interview, but consented to meet him the next day, at the corner of Charing-cross.

"I have no work to do just now," she said; "but when fresh orders come in, I shall have to stay at home and be very industrious."

He met her several times in this manner. When he invited her to accompany him to places of amusement, she always refused.

"We cannot talk to each other there," she would say, and then she would caress his arm with her soft, white hand.

His cheeks would flush as he received these caresses. She always watched him, and would smile to herself when she saw how powerless he was when he was with her.

One day she said—

"I cannot meet you to-morrow. A lady has given me an order for a dress; she wants it immediately, and I must not stir from home until it is finished."

"I should like to ask a favour of you," he said.

"What is it?"

"But I am afraid you will not grant it."

"You do not know until you tell me what it is."

"No, because I am afraid to."

"Am I so terrible, then?"

"I should hope not. Oh, dear, no; it is not that exactly."

"What is it, then; are you afraid of me?"

"Yes, I am."

"That is strange. I must be terrible, then."

"No, I am afraid of you because—because you are so lovely."

"Oh!"

"And because you are so good—so virtuous."

She pressed his hand.

"You are a noble fellow, William—very different to other men. Tell me what it is that you want."

It was the first time she had called him by his Christian name.

He stammered, blushed, and said—

"I should like—I should like to come and see you."

"What! in my own room," she exclaimed, with a start. "It would not be proper, would it?"

"Oh, dear, yes, I think so; and, ah, me! I should so like to come."

"But you, who are accustomed to so much luxury, would be disgusted with my poor abode."

"Bah!" he ejaculated; "you do not know me yet, to talk in that way."

"But——"

"What, dearest?"

"You are the son of a baronet, and are so much above a poor dressmaker."

"If that be your only objection, I will insist upon coming."

"Oh! you insist. You suddenly alter your tone."

"If you please," said the young man, humbly.

"Well, but understand I shall not leave off work for you."

"I should be sorry if you did; on the contrary, I will try and help you."

She laughed outright at this declaration.

"And a great deal of use you'll be, I dare say," she observed, playfully. "But now I must go and buy the material for the dress."

They shook hands. Then Hargrave took the hand which she had ungloved, and placed it between his. He looked at her, and was ravished with her beauty. How pure and white her forehead was! and her cheeks were tinged with a delicate colour; her lips red and pouting; and her eyes so sweet, so pure, so limpid that he could read, or fancy he could read, all the secrets of her heart therein!

Poor dreamer!

"But you have not told me your address," he murmured.

She nestled her bare hand a little closer between his, and whispered softly her name and address. Then they parted.

CHAPTER XIX.

WOMAN'S ARTS.

A CLEAN maid-servant showed William Hargrave up to Harriet Hawker's work-room. It was a small, bare room, with printed patterns pinned against the wall, and a large deal table in the centre, strewn with needles, stilettoes, piercers, bodkins, scissors, and other implements of the craft. She was sitting in a wooden chair, and held before her a square deal board.

She rose when he entered, and took his hat and gloves from him, and seated him in a chair close to her.

"Now, mind what I told you," she said, smiling; "I must go on working."

"May I talk to you?" he inquired.

"Oh, dear, yes; you may talk as much as you please —that will not interrupt me."

"Well, I shall ask for explanations of your millinery proceedings."

She burst out in a fit of laughter, at which he looked rather disconcerted.

"Do you think that I am a milliner, then?" she inquired. "Milliners only make bonnets and caps."

"And which is the most difficult, then—millinery or dressmaking?"

"It requires taste to be a milliner," she said, "and art to be a dressmaker."

In the meantime, she had pinned a piece of white calico upon the board, and upon that had placed a paper pattern, which, she informed her visitor, was a bod,dice or corset-pattern.

Having pinned the pattern to the lining, she pierced holes along the lines that were inked upon the pattern. Removing this, she seized a pair of formidable scissors, and proceeded to cut out the lining into shape, the pierced holes acting as her guide.

"We experimentalise upon calico," she said. "It would not do to make any mistakes with the material."

She took a piece of grey silk from a large deal table, spread it upon the board, placed the lining over it, and cut out the material from the lining, as she had previously cut out the lining from the paper pattern, with this difference—that she divided the solid piece into five or six smaller pieces; for the body of the dress, which appears an uniform whole to masculine eyes, is, in reality, composed of distinct and several members. Each of these pieces she *basted* (sewed slightly) to the lining, and finally stitched them together.

William Hargrave watched with wonder her little hand, which moved with such rapidity, and her needle, which twinkled like a gleam of light.

He watched her thus for three hours. Then she held up to him the body of the dress, with an air of pride.

"Is it complete?" he inquired.

"No. I am going to trim it now."

"You must not work any more; I am sure you have done enough."

"Oh! no, indeed—I have not. We must not dawdle much over our work; ladies are always so impatient to have their new dresses."

She took up a piece of ribbon-velvet, and placed it on the body in squares, graduating it from the top downwards; after which she stitched some velvet buttons down the front, leaving a space of an inch and a half between each. Finally, she took a strip of whalebone, and, cutting it into pieces, placed one in each seam of the body.

"That is to make the dress set right," she said. "And now my labours are finished, as far as the body is concerned."

"But what is this for?" he said, laying his hand upon a packet of wadding.

At this moment the servant came in, and handed her a letter. She read it, and immediately burst out crying.

He knelt down before her, and, taking her hands in his, implored her to tell him the cause of her unhappiness.

"Oh, my poor aunt!" she murmured—"my poor aunt!"

And she told him, between her sobs, that the only son of her bedridden aunt was a cabinet-maker—that he had been unfortunate in business, and had become a bankrupt—and that in three days he would be in prison.

"You gentlemen," she said, "who jest with each other about the Insolvency Court and Whitecross-street Prison, cannot, perhaps, understand the horror the poor have of being sent to prison. To be imprisoned for debt is almost the same as being sent to gaol for theft. We have always been very poor, sir; but there has never been the least blot against our good name before. We are as proud of that good name as a lord of his title or a king of his crown. Oh! if he were sent to prison, it would kill my poor aunt—I know it would. It would kill her—it would kill her!"

"But listen to me," said William Hargrave, clasping her hands impetuously—"listen to me. You say that in three days he will be sent to prison?"

"Three days will soon pass," she said, mournfully.

"What is the amount of his debts?"

"It does not say, sir. But read the letter yourself."

She showed him the letter. It was written in a cramped hand. He read it. When he had done so, he said—

"Do they live near each other?"

"Yes, close. He lives in the village, and aunt lives about a mile from it."

"The bank will be shut up now," he said, looking at

his gold watch; "but to-morrow I will go there, at ten o'clock, and take all the money I have. I dare say I shall have enough to settle matters with the bailiffs."

"What?" she cried, starting to her feet.

"I say I shall go to the village with you to-morrow, and get your cousin out of trouble."

Harriet Hawker turned from him, and covered her face with her handkerchief. Then she relaxed the muscles of her face, and a black tide of passion surged across it, while her eyes shone like those of a wild beast.

Revenge was at hand.

"You are a generous man!" she exclaimed, turning to him with the utmost composure. "You are an angel of mercy, who will save a woman from death, a man from misery, and a family from shame."

Then her voice became inexpressibly soft and sweet.

"William, I love you! From this hour, I am yours. I will lay down my life for you—I will be your slave."

He was kneeling before her. She took his hand between hers, caressed it, and cradled it on her bosom. He became almost delirious: he was in heaven. He believed, poor man, that he was loved, and loved for the first time. Blind, infatuated fool!

"We are lovers now," he murmured.

"Yes; and like true lovers, we will wander to-morrow in the woods, and gather the last flowers of autumn. We will plight our troth to one another, and carve each other's name on some old beechen tree."

"To-morrow!" he ejaculated. "Oh! that it were to-morrow. I shall not sleep to-night; the hours will pass like days."

"You must sleep," she said, caressing him, "and then, perhaps, you will dream of me, "Oh, it is so delightful to dream of those we love! For three nights, William, I have dreamt of you. Those nights were not long and weary, for you were always with me."

"And you love me?" he murmured.

"I love you with all my heart, with all my soul, with my life."

He closed his eyes, and fell into a celestial trance.

Her hair had become unloosed, and swept over his face; her hands fondled him. Sometimes she stooped, and kissed his forehead.

There was a low knock at the door, so low that it was a mere sound—a whisper of the hand.

She started like a guilty thing.

It was followed by two more.

She bent her lips to his ear, and said—

"William, dearest, you must leave me now."

"Leave you?" he murmured.

"Yes; the people of the house will think it strange if you stay here so long. To-morrow, dearest, I shall expect you."

"To-morrow?" he repeated, almost mechanically.

"Yes, to-morrow."

She led him to the door of the room. They embraced each other on the threshold. His embraces were warm and passionate, as those of a young girl who burns with virgin love. Hers were cold and false, as those of a courtesan who sells her kisses for daily bread.

When the servant had let him out, she returned to her mistress.

"Well?" said the latter.

"He's returned, and is in the parlour," answered the girl.

"Come back already?"

"Yes; something wrong, I think. When I let him in, he was looking as black as a thunder-cloud, and called me all the names he could lay his tongue to, when he heard you had some one with you."

"I will go to him directly, and you can pack up these things and put them away in the lumber-room—I shall not want to use them any more."

"The trick's done, is it, then?" said the girl.

"It will be to-morrow," and with these words, Harriet Hawker went down into the parlour.

"Where have you been?" said Brady, savagely.

"On a good lay," answered Harriet, calmly. "And you have just bungled one, I suppose, with your theatrical airs, and your coat buttoned up to your throat like an officer."

"There's been no bungling of mine. The Screever's nabbed, if you want to know what's up."

"The Screever nabbed?"

"Nabbed for that little job in the country, by a woman who knew him. The devil's in the women, I do believe."

"Ah, it was no wise thing to go to that fair; but you will have it that the yokels don't know great A from a bull's foot, when they are as peery as you are, sometimes."

"It's no use talking about it now," said Brady, sulkily. "I shall have to run my neck into a noose to prove an *alibi*, if that be possible. That's what we agreed upon beforehand, and I suppose I ought to stick to it. But let that pass. What is this lay you were talking about?"

"A young gentleman will escort me into the country to-morrow."

"Will he?"

"I have made him suppose that I am a dress maker, and that I have a relative who is going to be sent to gaol for debt. This debt he means to pay."

"You made it a high figure, of course?"

"I did not name the figure, so he will bring all the spare blunt he has."

"Where do you mean to take him to?"

"Woodford."

"The dark road?"

"Yes."

"By the withered oak?"

"That is the spot I have chosen."

"Ah! ah! indeed! I don't know how it is, but I have mislaid my pistol somewhere."

She gave a laugh, and said—

"Do you want to shoot him, then?"

"Shoot him!" said Brady; "oh, no, I must be driven hard before I kill a man for a bit of dirty money when there's plenty to be got without. But if you shove a pistol into a man's face, his hand finds its way to his pocket twice as quick as it does for a knife or a neddy (life-preserver)."

After conversing for half an hour upon other matters, Tom Brady rose.

"Where are you going now?" she inquired.

"To the ken," he answered. "There's a chapel there to-night."

"Well, what am I to understand? Is it quite settled about to-morrow?"

"Yes. To-morrow, about noon, in the dark wood, by the withered oak-tree."

"Yes; and to-morrow," muttered Harriet Hawker, to herself, "you will place a cord round your own neck which will strangle you again whenever I raise my hand."

And the woman, as she made this observation, gave a hideous and horrible laugh.

CHAPTER XX.

THE DEATH STRUGGLE.

WILLIAM HARGRAVE was awakened by the bright sun, which, streaming upon his face, reminded him how he was to spend the day which so smiled upon him. He rose and dressed himself quickly, with a sparkle in his eyes and a smile upon his lips.

He was at the bank-door before it opened, and marched to and fro before it with impatient strides.

When he asked for the whole of the balance due to him, the clerks raised their eyebrows, and the veteran cashier, looking gravely at him through his spectacles, handed him a heap of bank-notes with a sigh.

Hargrave laughed.

"He thinks I want it for debt at play," he said, to himself.

He made for the livery-stables, and gave his orders, and in ten minutes a thoroughbred was harnessed to a handsome two-wheeled vehicle.

He sprang into the seat, and the ostler, running, led the horse out of the yard, and, taking off the horse-cloth with a graceful flourish, saluted him as he passed.

It was half an hour before the appointed time, but Miss Hawker was ready, dressed in a black silk dress.

"Is it not a delightful day?" he said, as he handed her into the vehicle.

"Yes," she answered; "it is one of the last smiles of the year. Heaven would not frown upon the kind deed that you will do this day."

"Do not speak of that. I shall be fully rewarded by the pleasure of spending a holiday with you."

"Will that be such a pleasure, then?" she inquired.

"Oh, yes. I have not forgotten what you have said—that we should plight our troths to one another, and carve each other's name upon some old beechen tree."

They were now in the Oxford-road.

"Stay," she said. "We must not forget to buy the sacred knife."

"That's true. I had quite forgotten it."

In a short time they came in sight of a cutler's shop. He reined-in his horse. An urchin, standing on tip-toe, took its head.

They both alighted, and went into the shop.

"Now, you must let me choose for you," she said, in a coaxing manner.

They were shown several knives. She found them all too small.

At last the shopman opened a packet which he brought from another room.

"These are the famous Spanish knives," he said; "they would do for anything."

"Buy one of these, William," said Harriet Hawker.

He bought one, and placed it in his breast.

A smile crept over her thin lips: the plot prospered.

The horse, delighted at regaining his liberty, pranced, reared, and finally dashed off at a gallop. William glanced admiringly at his companion.

"Any other woman would have screamed," he remarked.

"I am not easily frightened," she replied.

In two hours they were at Woodford. William Hargrave, burning to console the sufferings of her poor aunt, proposed that they should visit her immediately.

"Very well," she said; "as you please. I will show you the way, for it is a pretty walk."

They entered a wood of oak and fir-trees, whose dark green branches flung sombre shadows on the earth. They walked together for some time in silence—Harriet Hawker engrossed by the thoughts of her daring scheme; William Hargrave depressed, in spite of himself, by the noon-day twilight of the place, and by its deep, mysterious, and almost impenetrable silence.

After a while he spoke.

"This is by no means a pretty walk," he said. "It is so very dark, and, see, the ground is literally covered with thorns."

"We are in the forest."

"What forest?"

"Epping."

"Oh! of course, I know that. I do not visit this part of the country often."

"Have you ever been here before?"

"No, never. How narrow the path is, dear. Your dress will be torn to shreds. You must have mistaken the way."

"No; I have not done that."

There was something strange in the tone of her voice. He looked at her for a moment. Her eyes were cold and glazed. There were drops of perspiration on her brow. He touched her hand—it was trembling.

"There is something the matter, dearest. You have lost your way in this terrible forest. You are alarmed at something. What is it?"

"No," she said; "indeed, I am not frightened. How should I be when you are by my side?"

All traces of a path had now disappeared. They were in the very midst of the thickest part of the forest. They could no longer see the sun.

"Why do you not speak to me," he cried. "You promised that we should gather flowers together. But it appears that you have brought me into a wilderness. There are no flowers here; there are nought but thorns."

As he spoke, a noise like the stifled laughter of some madman sounded above their heads. It was followed by a rustling of branches. Harriet lost her self-command and screamed.

It was only a large white owl, which had been disturbed from its perch, and which almost immediately disappeared.

"We are nearly out of the forest, now," said Harriet. "I see a circle of light above the trees."

A few steps more, and they entered a perfect little oasis of verdure and flowers, with a huge withered oak standing in the midst.

"Ah!" he cried, "this is the surprise you have been preparing for me. Well, then, I will reward you."

He rapidly plucked a bouquet of wild flowers and placed them in her hands.

She did not move; her eyes were wandering. He kissed her on the forehead, on the eyes, on the lips. She did not move. This only impassioned him the more. As he attempted to crown her with flowers, his hands became entangled in her long and silky hair.

"I love you with my soul," he cried, and he poured on her kisses that were as hot as fire.

"He will not come," she murmured to herself.

He observed her coldness and became suddenly calm.

"You are afraid because you are with me in this lonely place. But do not fear, dearest. I love you too much to insult you with so much as a bad word or even an imprudent look. I love you as a woman, but I worship you as a saint."

"I do not fear you," she answered, quickly, as she caressed his face with her treacherous hand.

"Let us kneel among these flowers," he said, "and plight our troths to one another. Dearest," continued the young man, in a solemn voice, "we now kneel in the temple of God, of which the green earth is the floor and yonder blue vault the glorious dome, this spot, strewn with flowers, the altar, and, hark, there are sweet birds singing our marriage hymn. Do you love me, Harriet?"

"I love you, mine own, I love you," she answered.

"Will you swear to be mine before God—the high priest who unites all loving hearts?—that you will be true to me?—that you will never injure or desert me?"

"I will swear it."

He raised his hands with hers towards heaven, and made her repeat the oath.

As she repeated the words, she concealed her head in his bosom that he might not see her smile. He kissed her hair, and wound his manly arms round her form.

"If he does not come I am lost," she said to herself; "but I must keep this dreamer here. Yes, I must keep him."

She raised her head, and pouted her lips towards him. When those lips touched his they intoxicated him. He closed his eyes, while a thousand voluptuous sensations darted through his frame.

Sometimes he stopped to sip a kiss from that delicious mouth—sometimes to pour words impassioned, rapturous, inarticulate, into her ear.

Suddenly her eyes gleamed. She tore herself from him, and ran to a little distance.

He also rose wondering.

She heard the branches crashing, and footsteps rapidly approaching.

A man, bareheaded, and with a naked knife in his hand, sprang into the open space, and cried out, in a loud voice—

"Your money or your life!"

William Hargrave was for a moment completely staggered, but that was all. He drew the knife he had bought, and said, quietly—

"I have been in Spain, and know how to fight with knives; and, mark me, if you attack me I will kill you."

He took of his coat as he spoke, and wrapped it round his left arm.

This was what Harriet Hawker anticipated when she made him buy the knife. Brady would be compelled to commit murder or to die. If he conquered he would be henceforth in her power. If he was killed she would be revenged.

Brady bared both his arms, and approached him like a cat.

Hargrave shuddered at the sight of those dark eyes which were so malicious—so determined. He glanced at Harriet Hawker. She gave him a look. To gain such another he would have willingly died.

Then the duel commenced.

Brady sprang past him, striking at him, and wounding him slightly in the shoulder.

The wound, which would have chilled a coward, only served to fire William Hargrave.

Turning round, he faced his adversary, and rushed swiftly on him, with dilating eyes. Brady struck at his heart. He received the knife in the folds of his coat.

Brady could not extricate it, and abandoned it with a curse. Then seizing Hargrave's armed hand by the wrist, he turned his leg round his, and forced him to the ground.

But Hargrave, muscular as Hercules, struggled to his knees, bringing the other with him.

Brady seized his throat with both hands.

Hargrave stabbed him repeatedly in the sides, and in the back; but, from his cramped position, could not wound him dangerously.

Then they rested; and, with their faces but a few inches apart, glared savagely in the whites of each others eyes.

Without moving his eyes, which would have warned his opponent of what he was going to do, Hargrave made an incredible effort, and forced the robber to the ground.

He raised his knife.

But Harriet Hawker did not yet wish to be revenged.

"Oh, William," she cried, "do not—oh, do not kill him!"

At the sound of that voice, which the poor young man loved so well, his eyes wandered, and his grasp insensibly relaxed.

Quick as fancy, Brady bounded to his feet, tore the knife from his hand, and buried it up to the hilt in his breast.

His face became livid, his eyes rolled in frightful agony, and the blood bubbled from his mouth.

Brady, beholding death before him, was horror-struck. He knelt down by the side of his victim, as if to implore his forgiveness.

The murdered man tried to speak, but the life-blood rushing from his heart prevented him. At last he murmured one word, in a voice which was half stifled.

That word was "Harriet."

He thought of her when he was dying.

His murderer had his hand between his hands, and groaned aloud.

"Harriet! Harriet!" cried the poor, dying voice.

"Yes," she said, and she bent over him.

His eyes dilated with horror. Her face was cold and impassible as that of a marble statue.

He tried to take her hand—it cost him such pain that he almost expired. It was some minutes before he could speak again.

"Harriet, do not look like that. Tell me that you love me."

She gave a hideous laugh, and pulled the watch from his breast.

"Yes," she said; "I love you for this."

He uttered a horrible cry.

She drew the notes from his pocket.

"And for this," she murmured.

Tom Brady grew pale.

The dying man looked at him.

"Raise me," he said, in plaintive accents.

Brady passed his arms round his waist, and raised him, almost tenderly.

The blood, which streamed from three wounds, began to mingle.

He could only speak in a hoarse whisper, which was interrupted by spasms of pain.

"I pardon you," he said. "You have killed me, but you have not deceived me."

He turned towards her, and the flame of life expiring with him burst into strength for one brief moment ere it for ever died. He struggled to his feet, and extended his pale hand towards her.

"Assassin!" he cried, in a terrible voice, "I leave you in the hands of God!"

His eyes turned glassy; he gave a deep sigh, and fell back dead.

Brady covered his face with his guilty hand. He was now a murderer.

Harriet Hawker began to deliberately count the bank-notes.

Brady was too much occupied in contemplating the prostrate form of him whom he had deprived of life. He took but little notice of the woman whose machinations had brought about the tragedy.

While she was counting the notes, another figure came upon the scene. It was that of a low, ruffianly-looking man.

He cast a greedy look upon the notes, and, stooping over her, snatched them out of her hand.

Harriet Hawker screamed.

The man ran off into the thick part of the wood.

Harriet rose to her feet and madly followed him, shrieking out as she did so.

She was fleeter of foot than the man, and soon overtook him.

"Wretch! give me back my notes," she exclaimed, as she wound her arms round him.

"Your notes," he ejaculated, with a brutal laugh; "your notes, murderess!"

She started back for an instant, but soon recovered herself.

"Give them back to me? What, oh; oh!—help—Tom—help," she screamed out at the highest pitch of her voice.

"Silence, you she-devil," exclaimed the man, as he struck her in the face with his clenched hand, and endeavoured to shake her off.

"You shall not go; I will not leave you," she ejaculated. "No, not if you kill me."

A struggle ensued. Harriet clutched at the notes.

The man held them above her head, out of her reach.

She fought with him like a tigress; she screamed out and bit him.

There was a rustling of the branches of the foliage heard at no great distance.

"Leave go, I say," exclaimed the ruffian. "Leave go, or I shall cut your throat."

He was evidently alarmed.

She still clung to him. The sounds increased. The man became wild with fury.

Harriet Hawker seemed desperate; she clung to the ruffian most perseveringly.

He drew a knife from his pocket, unclasped it with his teeth, and plunged the blade of it into her throat. A jet of blood spirited out from the wound.

The hands of the woman relaxed, and, with a savage yell, he unclasped them, and threw her to the earth; he then ran off at headlong speed.

She endeavoured to rise, but found herself too weak and faint to do so. The life-blood was ebbing fast. Retribution had come quickly upon her.

She groaned in anguish. She was alone, too far removed from Tom Brady for him to be aware of her situation.

She endeavoured to call out, but the effort was a vain one; she started at the hollowness of her own voice.

The wound was a mortal one. The weapon of her assailant had severed the jugular vein, and she had not many minutes to live. She felt herself to be fast sinking, and would have given all she possessed in the world to have some one by her side; but she lay upon the moss-covered earth, with the current of her life ebbing fast.

She closed her eyes in horror. In a few minutes more she was senseless; she had swooned from loss of blood. From this swoon she never awakened.

Harriet Hargrave had paid the penalty of her great crimes. She was dead.

The ruffian who had attacked her was not mistaken when he supposed some one was at hand.

A lady and gentlemen were taking their way through the forest. They were both mounted on horseback.

As they passed the spot where the dead body of William Hargrave lay, sounds of voices met their ears. They approached the open glade, and the prostrate figure of Tom Brady was the first thing that attracted their attention.

The two travellers reined up their steeds. The gentleman dismounted, and catching hold of the arm of Brady, he helped him to his feet. The latter was weak from loss of blood, but, nevertheless, thanked the cavalier who had proffered his assistance.

When he had risen, the cavalier looked for a moment inquiringly at him, as though he were anxious for some explanation, as to the cause of his accident.

At length his eyes lighted upon the dead body of the unfortunate young man.

Uttering an exclamation of surprise, he said:

"What's this? Two men in this lonely part of the forest; one wounded and the other dead, perhaps."

"We have fought and—and he has fallen," returned Brady.

"A duel," said the other.

"Something like a combat, about—about a woman."

"And were there no witnesses to this deed of blood?"

"None, save her who was the cause of our quarrel."

"Where is she now, then Mercy on us, but there is something truly horrible in all this. Two men fighting to the death, with the bright sun of heaven looking down upon their wicked deeds. Who and what is this gentleman?" said the cavalier as he went to the side of William Hargrave and stooped down and looked into his face. "Mercy! mercy on us! this young man is our friend, our dear and valued friend William."

"Who?" inquired the young lady.

"William—William Hargrave!" ejaculated the cavalier. "There has been some treachery, some foul work done here."

At this speech Brady was about to make off, but he was seized upon and forcibly detained by the cavalier.

"Thou shalt not go till thou hast given an account of this to the proper authorities," ejaculated the young man. "My friend Hargrave was not a man to quarrel with any one for any trival cause. Thou shalt not go; I consider you now my prisoner. See, here is a spare horse—my servant's. You will be pleased to mount this, and we will away to the nearest magistrates."

"Is the poor gentleman dead?" inquired the young lady, across whose features a death-like pallor had spread.

"Alas, yes, I fear so," answered her companion, who looking again at the features of Hargrave became assured of the fact.

"Yes, he has passed away. There can be no mistake, there are the lineaments of death, once seen never to be forgotten."

The young lady pressed her hand to her side.

"Oh, that we should meet with so terrible and dreadful an incident as this!" she exclaimed, in piteous accents. "What wilt thou do, Herbert?"

"We must away at once to the magistrates," he answered, then turning to Brady, he said, "Mount, sir, mount at once. You are not to weak to ride gently through the forest."

"I feel very weak," said Brady.

"Possibly so; but no assistance can be rendered to you here. When once out of the forest you can go to the nearest surgeons and have your wounds dressed. Mount, I beseech you. If you are an innocent man you will be able to prove it, if not, it will be my duty to hand you over to the proper authorities. Where is the woman you were speaking of? The one whom you said witnessed the fatal encounter."

"Alas! I know not."

"You do not know. Methinks that seems strange. She cannot be far hence I should suppose."

"She fled after a ruffian who endeavoured to rob her."

"Upon my soul this is altogether a strange business. There is an air of mystery about the whole affair that perfectly bewilders me. I hope and trust that you are speaking the truth, for—for to judge from your appearance, you are not a common robber I should suppose."

"I have told you the solemn truth, answered Brady.

"Humph! Well, I hope so. Now mount, and we will away."

Brady, or Neville—for it was by that name we first knew him—mounted on the back of the spare horse, and in a minute or so after this the three individuals were threading their way through the forest. When they got towards the outskirts of this, Brady cast a furtive look around. This look was not lost upon his male companion, who at once caught hold of the bridle of the guilty man.

"You are my prisoner," observed the cavalier; "and I feel it a duty incumbent on me to see that you do not escape. Mind, I am not for one moment assuming that you are a murderer, on the contrary. If you are innocent, you will be but too glad to have an opportunity afforded you of proving yourself so. First, we had better proceed to the nearest surgeon, where you can have your wounds dressed and attended to; after that, we will go to the magistrate's."

"I am in your hands, sir," answered Brady, "and will do as you think best."

After his wounds had been strapped up, he was taken before a magistrate, who committed him to prison till the coroner's jury had sat upon the body of the murdered man.

The sequel is easily told. Tom Brady, *alias* James Neville, swallowed poison in the absence of his gaoler, by whom he was found dead in his cell. Thus ended the last act of this sanguinary drama. The man who had stabbed Harriet Hawker was never discovered.

CHAPTER XXI.

JONATHAN WILD AND THE BARONET.—THE RIVALS.

WE have already described how Captain Orlando Ragget succeeded in making his escape from Newgate.

In less than half an hour after the discovery, Jonathan Wild was made acquainted with the fact.

When the old theif-taker was informed of it, he was perfectly furious, for he was to have received a large sum of money upon the death of Ragget. He was not, therefore, a little chagrined when he learned that, with all his cunning, he had been tricked. His first act was to send out his emissaries in all quarters, to endeavour to capture Ragget.

This time, however, Wild and his assistants were not successful. The captain managed to elude them, and got clear off, and was stowed away in the hold of a vessel which was about to set sail for India.

No one suspected his hiding place. The captain of the ship had espoused the cause of the Pretender, and

[THE LOVERS.]

had known Ragget when Charles Edward landed in England, consequently there was a strong feeling of friendship existing between the two.

Ragget succeeded in reaching Calcutta in safety.

Here he was far removed from his enemies, but, before leaving, he had not been able to take farewell of his beloved daughter.

He wrote to her, however, and gave the letter in charge of Dick Turpin.

It is needless to say that Dick duly delivered it to the party it was intended for.

All the vindictive feelings were aroused in the breast of Wild when he learnt that he had been cheated of his prey. Like a hungry and savage beast, he was ready to snap at anyone or anything.

He had agents in every quarter, and soon after Ragget's escape he learnt a secret which he thought he might turn to excellent account.

This secret was the parentage of our heroine, Nan Darrell.

He found out that she was veritably the daughter of Captain Ragget. When the old thief-taker learnt

this, he chuckled to himself; he might transfer his vengeance to the captain's child Anyhow, he might make some profit by the information.

Wild was in his house in the Old Bailey when one of his men informed him that Sir William Blakeley wished to see him.

Of course Sir William was at once shown up into the favourite apartment of Jonathan Wild.

Sir William did not appear to be in a particularly good humour, for a frown was on his countenance, across which a dark shade of displeasure had passed.

"So," ejaculated the baronet, "this fellow has escaped, it appears—this traitor to his sovereign—this wholesale robber. Very pretty, truly, that stone walls, bolts, and bars cannot be made strong enough to cage such fellows as Ragget.

"Humph! yes, it is a pity," said Wild, in his usual brusque manner, "but they ain't, you see."

"No. No news of him, I suppose?"

"Got clear off. Given us the slip. Got clear away."

"Well, it's a pretty story to tell a few, that's all. A very pretty story."

No. 12.

"These things can't be helped, Sir William. It's no use repining at them. I am quite as much vexed, if not more so, as yourself, or anyone else; but I keep a quiet tongue in my head, and submit to my fate with the best grace I may. It's no use repining."

"I have not come here to complain or find fault with anyone. Ragget's gone; he's saved his neck from the halter, and so let there be an end to that matter. I have come here upon a different business to-day."

"Ah! what may it be? Anything that I can do for you?"

"Well, I don't know. Listen. I have made an offer to a capricious little jade who treats me with scorn and —a-hem!—contempt."

"Whew!" said Wild. "I don't see very clearly how I can help you in that business—leastways, not at present."

"Possibly not; but hear me to the end, if you please."

"I am all attention. Be seated, Sir William—be seated, I pray."

Wild handed his visitor a chair.

"You must understand," observed Sir William Blakeley, "that there is a reason, perhaps, for this girl's conduct, as, indeed, there is a reason for every one's for the matter of that. She has an idea that I have been the cause of that unfortunate young man's being brought to justice. Perhaps, you may make a shrewd guess as to whom I am alluding. I mean James Neville."

"Precisely," said Jonathan, sententiously. "The fellow has just committed suicide."

"Suicide!" exclaimed the baronet. "Why, he was executed at Tyburn. Surely you must remember that?"

Wild gave a sort of chuckle.

"That is true enough," he replied; "but the fellow managed to come to life again, and lived to commit a murder. He was captured, and swallowed poison when in prison; and so there is an end of him. But proceed with your story, I pray. Do not let a little affair of this sort discompose you."

"Well, as I was observing," continued the baronet, "there is a prejudice in consequence of my being mixed up with Neville's affairs."

"What is the name of the lady?" said Wild, with a grin, who knew, however, as well as Sir William did himself.

"Miss Darrell," answered his companion.

"Humph! She need not be so wondrous particular. Howsomever, that's neither here nor there; and, of course, it's no business of mine. What is it you want of me? Something, I suppose, or else——"

"I should not have been here. Precisely. You are right. Well, then, I am not a man to be easily baulked, and, what is more, I won't be."

"No, of course not; fool if you were. 'Faint heart never won fair lady,' as the old saying is."

"And what I propose is this."

"Well, what?"

"I propose to carry her off by—by force."

"Nothing could be better devised."

"And it is for this purpose that I have waited upon you. I want your assistance."

"Oh!" ejaculated the thief-taker. "The scheme is a good one, and you want my assistance." He threw himself back in his chair, and appeared to be reflecting for a minute or so. "My assistance? Yes, that you can have."

"I can?"

"Of course; there can be but little doubt of that. You can have it for the usual consideration."

"Certainly; I do not expect any man to work for me without being paid for it. Name your terms."

"Yes. I dare say we shan't disagree; but, you see, there is something else in the market, which, possibly, may fetch a larger sum."

"What! has anyone else been? Surely, you do not mean to say that there is another suitor?"

"Oh, no, I do not say that; only—well, Sir William I will endeavour to deal candidly with you. It has ever been my practice since my first entering upon business. I think there is a mystery about the birth of Miss Darrell."

"There is? How know you this?"

"We know everything," returned Wild, with a smile.

"Humph! Well, you are right enough; there is a mystery connected with her birth. I do not deny that. But what has that to do with you?"

"Well, something, seeing that I know who her parents were."

"Her mother was the daughter of Justice Darrell; but her father—I believe no one knows who he was."

"Yes," chuckled the old thief-taker, "some one does. I do."

"You will be conferring an inestimable service upon me if you say who he was, or who he is, if he be still alive."

"Oh, he is alive and well; but as to the service——"

"Ah, I understand: you don't render any but for a consideration?"

"Exactly—that's it."

"Well, you have never found me illiberal. Name your terms, and I will give it my consideration—that is, supposing the information is of any service to me."

"Oh, as to that, I shall leave the payment to yourself, Sir William. But I can tell you that my information is rather important; and I suppose you, of all men in the world, must, of necessity, be the most interested. Who do you think is the father of Nan Darrell? But, lor'! you would never guess. None other than Captain Orlando Ragget!"

The baronet started from his seat in undisguised surprise.

"Impossible! It cannot be! Nan the daughter of a highwayman! You must be mistaken, Wild."

"Oh, dear, no. My information can be relied on. I tell you that she is the daughter of Ragget; I have the whole history by heart."

"How long have you known this?"

"But a few days since."

"It never can be!"

"I tell you that I know it for a certainty; and, of course, you can make what use you like of it."

Sir William Blakeley took out his purse, and laid before the old thief-taker a huge heap of bank-notes.

"These are all yours if you can but prove your assertion."

"I shall have but little difficulty in doing that: I have the proofs in the house."

"Give me them, and the notes are yours."

"Thank you. This is what I call business. I had always a good opinion of Sir William Blakeley," said Wild, as he took his way towards a desk which stood on a side-table in the room.

He opened this, and carefully selecting therefrom a bundle of papers, he placed them before Sir William.

"You will find enough evidence there to prove the parentage of Miss Nancy Darrell. Read them at your leisure. Should anything more be needed, come to me again, and I dare say I shall be able to produce witnesses to complete the case, as we say in the legal profession. In the meantime I——"

"Yes, yes—the notes are yours."

"And should you need me again——"

"I will call. This has somewhat altered my arrangements for the present."

The baronet rose, and seemed about to take his departure.

"There is nothing more, for the present, I suppose?" said Wild. "And therefore, as I have a number of persons below, waiting to see me——"

"Yes, I understand. I will not trespass further upon your valuable time."

Upon this, Sir William left the house of the thief-taker, taking with him the papers.

He went to his town house, and took a hasty glance

at these papers. There could be but little doubt as to their authenticity. Without entering into a full description of their contents, it will suffice for our purpose to state that they afforded sufficient evidence to any reasonable person of the parentage of Nan Darrell.

Sir William Blakeley, when he had possessed himself of the contents of the papers, at once proceeded towards Old Oak Farm.

He felt that he now had Nan Darrell, to a certain extent, in his power: he had gained possession of her secret. Armed with this, he made up his mind to subdue the scornful yet beauteous young maiden. He loved Nan in his own peculiar way, which, to say the truth, was selfish enough.

He liked her none the less when he learnt that she was the daughter of a highwayman.

When Sir William arrived at Old Oak Farm, he found Mr. Luke Darrell was away from home, fulfilling his magisterial duties.

Sir William Blakeley inquired for Miss Darrell.

She was in the garden attached to her grandfather's house.

The baronet sought her; he wandered about for some time, and eventually found Nan in the shrubbery. She was conversing with a young man, in a familiar, or, it might be, in a loving manner.

The demon of jealously rose up in the breast of the baronet; he, however, endeavoured to put a good face on the matter, and offered his hand to Nan with his accustomed courtesy.

When the first salutations were over, Nan Darrell introduced her friend: it was Sir Piers Shafton—the same individual whom Tom King had personated at the king's *levée*.

He bowed politely enough to Sir William, and soon afterwards made some excuse to enter the magistrate's house.

When he had gone, there was an awkward pause. Sir William did not know very well how to open the proceedings; after awhile, however, he said, carelessly—

"Sir Piers Shafton here, eh? Have you known him long, then?"

"Oh, dear, yes, for some time," returned Nan. "I can't call him a particularly *old* friend, but he is a much-esteemed one."

"Oh, indeed! I am glad to find you in such good company, Miss Darrell, in the absence of your relative, the good Mr. Darrell."

"The good Mr. Darrell is engaged fulfilling his magisterial duties," returned Nan.

"So I should suppose. You were surprised to see me, I presume?"

"Not at all. Sir William Blakeley is too constant a visitor at Old Oak Farm for me to be in any way surprised at his appearance."

She was about to turn away, when her companion said, somewhat sharply—

"Do not leave, I pray you. I have something to say, and am desirous of having a few words with you in private. We can talk here without any interruption."

Nan signified her assent to this proposition simply by a nod.

"Good, then; hear me, if you please."

"I am all attention."

"Miss Darrell, I have come once more to renew the offer I have made to you. I hope that you have had time enough to consider over all that I have said; that you will think proper to treat an honourable offer with some little better grace than you chosed to do on the occasion of my last visit."

"I am still in the same mind that I was then, Sir William Blakeley," answered Nan, "and I must, therefore, perforce, give you the same answer."

"Insolence!" ejaculated the baronet, not being able to smother his rising passion. "I presume, madam— if I am to judge from appearance—I presume——"

"Well, what, sir?"

"That in Sir Peirs Shafton I behold a rival!"

"I am not aware that I am in any way accountable to you for my actions, or who I may choose to consider my friends."

"Is it or is it not so? Answer me that!" ejaculated the baronet.

"I have always liked candour," answered his companion, "and since you press the question, I may as well tell you at once that I am engaged to Sir Peirs Shafton."

"Engaged—engaged to Sir Peirs!" yelled out the baronet, now fairly beside himself with rage. "And do you dare—have you the audacity to tell me this to my very face?"

"Audacity! If there be any in the case it belongs to Sir William Blakeley," returned Nan, bridling up.

"Now, mark me!" said her companion, almost choking with rage. "I have warned you before this time—I warn you not to raise the devil that is within me! I swear by all that I hold sacred—I swear that you shall never have Sir Peirs!"

"Indeed! And pray who is to prevent it?"

"I will!"

"You?"

"Yes, me, and none other; I will prevent it. I will bring shame upon you. I will, if needs be, bring your legal relative with sorrow to the grave, for I hold in my possession a secret—a dread secret, Miss Darrell, scornful and insolent as you have been to me. I hold a secret in my possession that can crush and annihilate you!"

Nan Darrell turned pale. She thought of that secret which had been kept so long and so well, and she trembled.

"You hear me!" said the irritated speaker—"you hear me!"

"Yes, I do, but cannot comprehend your meaning."

"It will soon be plain enough. I know the secret of your birth!"

As he said this he regarded her with a look of savage triumph, for he saw the effect that his words had upon her.

"The secret of my birth!" she uttered, slowly.

"Yes, madame, of your birth. How like you that?"

"You might have employed your time better I should have thought, than interfering in that which does not concern you!"

"But it does concern me, and most naturally concerns me. I seek to make you my future wife."

"I will thank you to drop that question for the present, at all events. I can never be your wife!"

"Aye, but you must, you shall! I am not to be made a fool of, to be hoodwinked or cozened! You shall, Nan—you must! One word from me would put an insurmountable barrier between yourself and Sir Peirs Shafton. But one word, and then farewell to all your hopes with him—he is too proud a man to wed one whose name will bring upon him the scorn of the world."

"I know not why I should remain here to be insulted in this manner," said Nan, in moving accents; "and I know not why anyone, professing to be a gentleman, should so far forget himself as to insult one of the opposite sex who is not able to defend herself. It says little for your good taste or feeling."

"You have had but little care for my feelings," returned her companion, quickly; "it would appear that you never have had any. And, as far as insults are concerned, I must frankly admit that I have had my share of them. But a truce to these taunts; let us recur to the business on hand. I know the secret of your birth, and you force me to speak plainly. It is not likely that Sir Piers, or any other gentleman besides myself, will think of espousing you, when it is known that you are the daughter of a traitor and a highwayman!"

Nan Darrell uttered a scream at this declaration. Her worst fears were realised: Sir William Blakeley did know her secret. His last speech gave unmistakeable evidence of that.

"You are not so dull withal as not to fully comprehend this fact," said Sir William, in continuation. "But I—I, who have loved you, and who still do so, am ready to make you my wife; and, of course, we can keep the secret to ourselves. Is this nothing? Do you not think that I must esteem you more than anyone else in the world to let this weigh as nothing in the scale. Many men would have turned from you when they knew this; but I, on the contrary, am here to renew my offer, which you cannot—nay, you dare not, but choose to accept."

"You surprise me, Sir William Blakeley—you surprise me in many ways," returned Nan Darrell.

"Have I been telling any falsehoods?"

"That is best known to yourself. I have not, as yet, accused you of having done so."

"You know, I suppose, as well as myself, that Captain Orlando Ragget—he who, but a few days since, escaped from the condemned cells of Newgate—is your father?"

"I deny it."

"You do? Well, that will avail you nothing. I may as well tell you that I hold in my possession papers which prove the fact beyond a question. More than this, I shall be able to produce witnesses whose collateral testimony will put the matter beyond the shadow of a doubt. It is no use, Nan, for you to endeavour to brave the question out. I told you before that it would be better for your own sake that we should be friends than enemies, and I now again repeat that declaration. Con it over; remember that I hold a power over you for good or for ill. As the wife of Sir William Blakeley, the noisy tongues of the evil-disposed will be silent; but, mark me, if you endeavour to thwart me—if you dare to think further of yonder fellow, as there is a Judge above, I shall visit your wilfulness with a signal—a terrible vengeance. His wife you never shall be, I promise you that. No, never! I have said it, and I intend to keep my word."

"I should like to see the proofs you speak of."

"You can do so at any time you please. But I suspect, Miss Darrell, that you yourself have known all along who your father was. Not so Mr. Luke Darrell or his aged partner; they are neither of them aware of the fact, and I know it would be a terrible blow to them both if they were apprised of it."

"Oh!" ejaculated Nan, piteously, "you never would be so cruel—so wicked, as to tell that to my poor dear grandfather. That would stoop his head with shame, and bring him, in all probability, to his grave. You never would do that?"

"Not unless I were driven to it by the obstinacy of their grand-daughter. The whole affair is in your own hands. Accept me, and a bright and beaming future dawns before you; reject me, and there is little else but despair."

"But I have plighted my troth. I am pledged to become the wife of Sir Piers Shafton."

"Does your grandfather know this?"

"Yes, and approves of the match."

"Methinks he has acted strange to me, then, seeing that I have a prior claim. He passed his word that all should be done to further my suit. By my faith, but I have as good reason to complain of his conduct as I have of your own."

"Understand me, Sir William Blakeley. In justice to my grandfather, I must inform you that it was not until I had distinctly informed him that I would never consent to become your wife that he agreed to look upon Sir Piers Shafton as a suitor for my hand."

"You told him that, did you?"

"Of course I did, and I told him the truth. I informed him, moreover, that I had given you a decisive answer. Then, and not till then, did he countenance the visits of Sir Piers."

"Very pretty, truly—a very pretty piece of business altogether, I must declare. I am much obliged to you for your candour," said the baronet, with an ill-disguised sneer. "But you will have to alter your tune now, my lady, or it will be worse for you. Mark that—you must alter your tune. No more Sir Piers Shaftons at Old Oak Farm."

"That is my business, not yours."

"I say it is mine."

"And I say it is mine; and so there we are at issue."

"Remember what I have told you."

"Oh, sir, you can threaten."

"And keep my word, if needs be."

"This is a strange way to win a young maiden's love. I defy you!"

"Defy me?" said the baronet, with a laugh.

"Yes," replied Nan, although her heart failed as she said so.

"Very well; you know the consequences of your obstinacy. If we are to be enemies, so be it."

"Give me a little grace—time to think all this over," she said, hurriedly. "See, here comes Sir Piers."

Sir Piers Shafton presented himself, and taking precedure of the other baronet, he offered his arm to his betrothed, and walked triumphantly with her towards the house, chatting familiarly and pleasantly with her as he did so.

The rival baronet followed at a respectful distance.

The pangs of jealousy were raging in his breast, and, master as he was, of diplomacy or *finesse*, he could with difficulty conceal his chagrin.

All this while his rival was quite unaware of the state of his feelings towards the fair creature on his arm.

They entered the house.

Old Mrs. Darrell—undemonstrative Mrs. Darrell, with a deep grief lying at the bottom of her heart, which she had fed and nutured for I know not how many years—received them and apologised for the absence of her husband.

It is possible that the old dame suspected that there was something the matter, for her manner was rather flurried, if such a term can with propriety be used, as applied to one of her phlegmatic nature.

The two baronets were handed to seats, or rather seats were handed to them.

Sir Piers, who had seen his rival for the first time, was particularly affable, and began an animated conversation—that is, animated as far as he was concerned.

"As to Sir William," he replied to the discourse in little else but monosyllables.

The old lady sat in the chimney corner with her hands crossed over her, thinking of those by-gone days which would never come again to her, nor to you, or me, dear reader, nor to any of us. Nan was, of course, dashed in spirits in consequence of the painful interview she had had with Sir William Blakeley.

Sir Piers Shafton, who was quite unconscious of either the jealous feelings of Blakeley or the conflicting emotions which arose in the breast of Nan, rattled on in an animated style of conversation.

After some time had passed, Mr. Luke Darrell returned, and was much surprised to see the two baronets at Old Oak Farm. His manner was a little hesitating, to Sir William more especially.

It was, therefore, rather an awkward family-party assembled round the old magistrate's table.

At length Sir Piers Shafton made a motion to go. His carriage was ordered, and, after some little private conversation with Nan at the outer gate, the worthy baronet's carriage whirled off with its owner inside.

Sir William Blakeley was driven to a state of desperation when he observed Nan accompany his rival to the outer gate of Old Oak Farm. He took an opportunity of taking her on one side, and as he caught her violently by the wrist, he said, in a voice of ill-suppressed rage:—

"So, you are going to play me false. Have a care—

have a care. I caution you for the last time—the last time, remember. As there is a heaven above, I will take signal vengeance on you if I find you see that man any more."

"Not see him?" ejaculated Nan Darrell.

"No; not see him, upon any pretext."

"I am not going to be dictated to or commanded by you."

"I shall give you eight-and-forty hours to make your election," said the baronet; "that will be plenty of time, at the expiration of which you will be able to determine what course you intend to adopt. Remember, you cannot—nay, you shall not be the wife of Sir Piers Shafton. I will take good care of that; and so it is only aggravating me and deceiving him by your encouraging his visits here, and once more I bid you be careful of aggravating me, for it will go hard with you if you once turn the great love I bear towards you into bitter and vindictive hate."

"Hate, Sir William?"

"Aye, hate, Miss Darrell. There is no hate so intense as that which a man feels for a woman who has deceived and betrayed him."

"I have never done either. From first to last I have frankly avowed my feelings towards yourself. I have never, for one moment, endeavoured to deceive you; and as to betray——"

"Ah! you can talk bravely, madam. You can smile, but play false all the while."

"This is not true," said Nan Darrell, indignantly, "and you ought to know yourself better than to thus insult one whom you profess to love so fondly."

"Profess? whom I do love."

"Well, we will not quarrel about terms. Whom you do love, if that pleasures you."

"I give you eight-and-forty hours to think over my proposition. Is that long enough? or do you desire any extension of the time?"

"That will suffice."

"Good. Then so be it. At the expiration of that time, I will be here again to receive your answer—yea or nay. Remember, Nancy Darrell, this is the turning point of your life. Should'st thou choose to make an enemy of me—as assuredly thou wilt if thou dost not consent to become my wife—should'st thou do this, there will be nothing but a dreary, dark, and desolate future for you. So mark you that—a dreary, dark, and wretched future. Thy father has got clear off. I will not disguise that from you, for it is like enough that thou knowest this as well as myself. He has sailed for the Indies, and, in a brief space of time, 'tis like enough that he may reach that far-distant shore in safety, but I tell you this plainly, that even there he is not safe. I have the means—mind, I have the means to bring him to justice, even at that remote part of the globe. I hold the master-key of your fate and of his. So beware how you trifle with me. I will be here the day after to-morrow to receive your answer, which must be a final one. See that you are ready to give it. Save yourself—save your own good name in the eyes of the world. Save thy father, and spare the good Mr. Darrell the deep humiliation which must fall upon him when he learns that his grand-daughter has a highwayman for her father. Farewell, till the day after to-morrow."

"Farewell!" said Nan Darrell, sadly, while her eyes were bent upon the ground; "farewell, Sir William Blakeley!"

"And remember," murmured the baronet, as he mounted his horse preparatory to going, "remember all I have said."

"I am not likely to forget," ejaculated Nan. "I will remember."

Sir William Blakeley took his departure; the noise of his horse's hoofs were heard on the high-road.

Nan Darrell listened untill the sounds of these grew indistinct, and at length inaudible. Then she turned sadly away, and entered the home of her grandfather, to drain the cup of sorrow alone and in silence.

CHAPTER XXII.

THE BARONET GROWS DESPERATE.

SIR WILLIAM BLAKELEY returned to his house in town. Perhaps he had never, in the whole course of his life, been so determined to gain possession of a woman as he was to obtain the beauteous Nan Darrell; and yet he had had amours enough in his time. It is something remarkable that he should have still been so enamoured of our heroine after he discovered her parentage, but, to say the truth, there was a great deal more of the evil than the good in Sir William's composition. He did not despise the gallant and courageous Captain Ragget, for he knew perfectly well that he was not a wit more honest—nay, nothing nearly so honest if the truth were told—than was the dashing, reckless captain himself. Ragget's dishonesty had been, in a measure, compulsory; he had been compelled to yield to the force of circumstances. Blakeley, on the contrary, had been a villain at heart, and had gained his wealth and position by unscrupulous conduct as regards to the means.

Since he had seen Sir Piers Shafton at Old Oak Farm, he was more than ever bent upon gaining possession of Nan.

Jealous feelings made him pass a restless night, and he counted the hours till the time he was again to present himself at the magistrate's house.

When it did arrive, he was there at the appointed period.

Nan's answer was brief enough. She distinctly declined having him as her husband.

Threats and entreaties were alike useless—Nan was inexorable.

Sir William declared that he would go at once to Mr. Luke Darrell and tell him all.

Nan bid him do so, as she was prepared for the worst.

A violent altercation ensued, but it was all in vain.

The baronet, strange, savage lover as he was, could not prevail upon our heroine to alter her resolve.

He left the magistrate's house in a violent rage. So violent, indeed, was this, that he did not even enter the habitation, to pay his respects to Mr. and Mrs. Darrell.

He rode back furiously to town, and at once hastened to Jonathan Wild's, and made him acquainted with the state of affairs.

"Well," said Jonathan, "Luke Darrell, Esq., is a most worthy gentleman, and much respected by all who know him."

"What has that to do with the matter?" returned the baronet. "It is not in his power to alter the resolve of a self-willed, obstinate little minx, although she may happen to be his granddaughter."

"Oh, I ain't speaking of that," said Wild. "Only, you see, if you want the girl carried off, I can't have any hand in it."

"You can't?"

"No, not directly; but I'll tell you what I can do."

"What is that?"

"I can recommend you to some one who may do the job for you. Carry her off, Sir William; get her in your power, and then work upon her feelings."

After some further conversation, the two separated, and on the following day a mysterious individual presented himself at the baronet's house. This personage was admitted at once, for Sir William had left word with his servants that whoever called and inquired for him should be shown into his library.

The preliminaries were arranged.

The man departed.

That same evening, as Nan was taking her accustomed evening ride on her broad-set, shaggy little pony, she was suddenly confronted, in a bye-lane, by two ruffianly-looking fellows, who were mounted on two powerful horses.

They regarded Nan with looks of malevolence. They both wore masks ; and, from the position they had chosen to take, it was next to impossible for our heroine to pass ; she, therefore, pulled the check-rein of her little pony, and waited the result with some misgivings.

One of the men urged forward his horse, and came to the side of Nan, who then found herself suddenly lifted off the back of her pony ; and before she had time to utter even a cry, her assailant threw her across the withers of his own horse, and said to his companion—

"Come along, Jem. It's all right."

Upon this, Nan Darrell uttered a piercing shriek.

The ruffian stifled her cry by putting his hand across her mouth.

She struggled desperately with him, but found herself no match for her athletic assailant, who said—

"Thou hadst best be quiet. No harm is intended you, only come peaceably and you shall be placed with friends."

"Who and what are you? and what means this strange outrage?" inquired Nan.

"That you shall learn shortly. You must accompany us. If you endeavour to raise an alarm or seek to escape——"

He said no more but drew a clasp knife.

Nan Darrell shuddered. She was in a lonely part of the country far away from any human habitation, and the shades of night had wrapped the landscape in gloom.

She felt, therefore, that she was completely in the power of the two ruffians, and therefore submitted with the best grace she could.

They moved their horses forward, which were soon urged on to a trot. In a short time they neared the end of the lane.

"Better blindfold her," said he who was behind.

"Oh! no, no. I will go quietly, but do not blindfold me," said Nan, beseechingly.

There was a momentary pause. The two fellows whispered together, then one of them drew a handkerchief from his pocket and handed it to his companion, who forthwith tied it round the brows of our heroine.

They then once more put their steeds in motion.

Nan judged that they had got to the end of the lane and were in the high road. She came to this conclusion from the hard nature of the ground, which rang beneath the horse's feet.

She made no observation but quietly awaited the result of the proceedings, which she was quite at a loss to account for in any satisfactory way.

They had not gone very far when she found that they suddenly urged on their steeds into a gallop. Then the sounds of other horses' feet were heard in the rear.

It appeared as though some one was giving chase, for, after awhile, Nan heard one or two shouts as though they proceeded from persons behind.

She sincerely hoped that there might be a chance of a rescue, and yet she hardly dared think such was likely.

At length the horse she was across was urged on into a furious gallop.

She debated with herself respecting the propriety of calling out for assistance, but upon second thoughts she did not deem this advisable.

If any one was giving chase it was certain that they must be aware of her situation, and she remembered at the same time the threat which the ruffian used when he desired her to submit in peace to her fate. Under all these circumstances she determined to remain passive and await the result.

She became more and more convinced every moment that some one was following far behind.

She was assured of this when she heard one of her companions say in a hurried whisper—

"Put him along, Jem, good luck to yer—put him along ; they are gaining upon us, and have got at the top of the hill."

Upon this the two horsemen managed to increase their speed.

Nan Darrell inwardly prayed that succour would arrive.

Minutes seemed hours in such a case.

She now felt that they were taking their way over some rough ground. This was apparent by the motion of the horse, whose feet no longer made a loud ringing sound.

At length the horses came to a halt. Nan was carried into a cottage. The bandage was removed from her eyes, and she was informed by her captors that she must consider herself prisoner. In a minute or so after this, Sir William Blakeley presented himself.

"Wretch!" exclaimed Nan ; "so you have been the cause of the malignity which has been offered me !"

"You are in my power," said Sir William, "so have a care as to how you behave yourself. I have sworn that you shall never be the wife of Sir Piers Shafton, and I intend to keep my oath. You must and shall be mine !"

"Never !" exclaimed a strange voice, as the window of the room was thrown open, and the figure of a man was seen to jump into the apartment. He was masked, and immediately after him there came another.

Sir William Blakeley drew his sword, and shouted out.

The two men who had brought Nan to the cottage made their appearance immediately.

"Remove her," said the baronet.

"Remove yourselves, scoundrels, or it will be worse for you !" said Dick Turpin, for the two personages who had come to the rescue were none other than Turpin and King.

The former presented a pistol at the head of Sir William Blakeley. Blind with rage, the baronet drew his sword and made a lunge at Turpin.

Dick skipped adroitly on one side, and then fired his pistol, shattering the right arm of the baronet, who, with a howl of rage and pain, tottered back a few paces, and leaned against the wall for support.

A combat ensued, in which Turpin and King came off victorious. The two creatures of Sir William were wounded, and sought safety in flight, and our two highwaymen bore Nan off in triumph and restored her to her grandfather.

But little now remains to be told.

Sir Piers Shafton, when he learnt of his rival's conduct, challenged Sir William Blakeley. This challenge was accepted, when it was agreed that they should stand back to back, walk about a dozen paces, and then turn round and fire. Sir William walked about half the distance, and then, suddenly halting and presenting his pistol, he fired and shot his antagonist in the back.

Believing himself to be mortally wounded, Sir Piers Shafton took deliberate aim, and fired at the man who was little less than a murderer.

The ball passed through the heart : Sir William leaped up, and then fell to the earth a corpse.

Sir Piers, although very seriously wounded, eventually recovered, and married our heroine, Nan Darrell, with great pomp and ceremony.

Nan would not consent to become his till she had made him acquainted with the fact of Captain Orlando Ragget being her parent. Sir Piers, with a generosity which formed part of his character, waived all considerations, and made Nan his wife.

Captain Ragget amassed a large fortune in India, and, through the instrumentality of Sir Piers Shafton, his Majesty was prevailed upon to grant him a free pardon ; he then returned to England.

As to Turpin and King, most of our readers know the end of them. The latter fell by the hand of Dick, who shot him by an accident when he was struggling with the Bow-street officer who was capturing him.

FINIS.